Mark A Wilson

To Joelle Elmhorst

NIGHT JUSTICE

WRATH OF THE VIGILANTE

Mark A. Wilson

MARK A. WILSON

PublishAmerica
Baltimore

© 2012 by Mark A. Wilson.
All rights reserved. No part of this book may be reproduced, stored in a retrieval system or transmitted in any form or by any means without the prior written permission of the publishers, except by a reviewer who may quote brief passages in a review to be printed in a newspaper, magazine or journal.

First printing

All characters in this book are fictitious, and any resemblance to real persons, living or dead, is coincidental.

PublishAmerica has allowed this work to remain exactly as the author intended, verbatim, without editorial input.

Hardcover 9781462664696
PUBLISHED BY PUBLISHAMERICA, LLLP
www.publishamerica.com
Baltimore

Printed in the United States of America

Dedication—
To My Fourth Granddaughter

Mallory Elizabeth Wilson

A special acknledgement to my wife Brenda Kay (ou are the air that I breathe, the warmth that surrounds me and the love in my heart)

Waking up with a pounding headache, Jason Karsten knows it is going to be another bad day. Throwing the covers off and rolling out of bed, he shuffles his feet as he makes his way into the bathroom. After taking a long look at himself in the mirror, and mumbling out loud that it is going to be a bad day he quickly swallows several aspirins. He is having so many of these bad days that it is growing more difficult for him to control the anger and frustration that he is feeling.

The news that was on the TV, and the internet from the night before are still fresh on his mind. As much as he tries he cannot rid his subconscious of the terrible images that he saw and which are now are running through his head. Something deep inside of him is slowly taking over his physic, and he can feel its anger grow more each day. The news each day is always the same, more murders, another rape, and several senseless muggings.

The crime rate in his city is the highest it's ever been, and the brutality of the crimes is getting worse.

It frustrates him that the police can't do enough to control this chaos and disorder that is so disrupting to everyday life.

Living in the city of Landore in the state of Wissota it is a small city compared to the larger metropolitan Cites. With a population of just over 200,000 it has up until a few years ago avoided the violence and corruption that plagues so many other cities its size. Once quiet and orderly, the citizens of Landore took great pride in all that their city had to offer. The parks and recreation areas were always kept neat and attractive. The down town businesses often had their merchandise right out on the sidewalks for the shoppers to look at as they leisurely strolled about.

Unemployment was very low which kept the crime down, which in turn gave the cities residence a happy outlook and attitude. But like a disease with no cure the exploding drug trade quickly transformed their peaceful city into a nightmare.

Not since the days of the mafia have the citizens of Landore seen such violence and corruption.

In the 1950's the mob ruled the city with an iron fist, they controlled the alcohol and tobacco sales.

Gambling, racketeering and extortion was another means of making money for the mob. For years the police did little to stop them, many in city hall were on the mobs payroll.

After several brutal murders that went unsolved, the people of Landore finally had enough and with the help of federal agents like Elliot Ness, famous for his arrest of the Chicago mob boss Al Capone, they got their city back.

That of course was before Jason's time, but he has read all the old newspaper articles about those days. How groups of gangsters would pull up in front of a store and begin shooting out all the windows. This was a warning to the store owner that he had better pay up the protection money demanded by the mob or else things will get much worse.

There was a lot of killings back in the 1950's and even into the 1960's, until the federal government stepped in and arrested most of the mob bosses. Things in Landore quieted down after that, and in the years that followed the city had a reputation as a clean and friendly place to live.

Now with the new crime wave taking over the city it seems like Landore has gone back in time. The streets are once again haven for murders and criminals of all types. City hall has done little to nothing to stem the tide of this growing problem. It is widely believed by the citizens that certain people inside the court house are taking bribes from the drug dealers, and in return these officials are looking the other way when crimes are committed.

To Jason, it seems that society is in a downward spiral, its once moral and ethical dignities are eroding like the ice on a warm spring day. At one time in the distant past, regular citizens were not afraid to stand up against lawbreakers. These common everyday people watched their neighborhoods closely, and called each other when someone suspicious was roaming in the area.

How when one home was broken into they all felt violated, they rallied the police department to step up patrols in their neighborhood.

Those were the days Jason remembers, the days of his youth. He can remember walking down the nearly deserted streets late at night to the nearest gas station to buy a can of pop. He had no worries or concerns. Those he did meet on the street would smile or say hello as they passed by.

Most of the streets at the time when Jason was growing up didn't even have streets lights. No one had ever gotten shot or even mugged in his neighborhood. It was peaceful and quiet late at night. The thought that something bad might happen on one of his late night forays never entered his mind.

The thought of those days brings a half smile to his face. Yes, he would very much like to go back to that time period again. Life then seemed worlds apart from the scene just outside his apartment window. The police sirens constantly echo up and down the streets at all hours of the night. Gun shots can be heard along with the squealing of car tires indicating that another crime has been committed.

But with a heavy heart, he knows that is impossible to go back in time. However, he still has the memories, and in his heart he believes that someday this city could again return to what it once was. The proud people of Landore will once again walk the streets with their chins up and smile at those they pass by.

Now days there are no more neighborhood watch groups, no one is speaking out in disgust when a crime is committed. Their calls to the police are now falling on deaf ears, fear and disconcert has begun to grip the city.

In just a few short years the city's image of a good and decent place to live and work had plummeted. Home owners have now put steel bars on their windows and doors, and a fence surrounds every yard.

The peaceful tranquil of everyday life, and the smile on everyone's face is gone. This is replaced with quick stares, and rude gestures. The people now hurry about their business, not wanting to stay on the street any longer than they have to.

With gun shots and screams heard every day it is a constant reminder of who is in charge, and Jason can't blame these citizens for the way they feel. He too has become accustomed to the violence and carnage that is wide spread and only seems to be getting worse. He often will fantasize that a day will come when some super hero will descend upon this city and wipeout all the criminals.

This mysterious crusader will also go on to clean up city hall, and restore the people's faith in the police department. It will be a God send and the people will idolize and admire what this nameless hero/vigilante is doing. After this super hero has rid the city of all its lawbreakers, he will just disappear into the night. Gone before anyone can find out who he really is, or where he had come from. A nameless champion of justice that will quickly turn into an urban legend, his mystic and imaginary will grow with each passing year.

But Jason knows such a thing happening is only in his dreams; the world has no more heroes.

The men and women that lead this country through the great depression and then went on to save the world during World War Two are all gone. Those that are still alive reside in nursing homes and are old and frail.

The guardians of the constitution, the protectors of freedom and the supporters of moral integrity have all passed into history.

This generation that has arisen since that time has no foundation, no solid footing. They have neither struggled nor sacrificed, and they have not been witness to the world on the brink of collapse.

Jason knows that our greatest generation is gone and with it went everything that is good and pure and decent in this country.

His grandfather fought in the Second World War, but he spoke very little about what he did or saw. He would tell Jason, "Wars are terrible, and so many good men did not come home. No one should have to experience the horror of battle. Those memories are best kept in the past, as they can do us no good now."

It seemed to Jason that for a generation that saved the world that they would be more inclined to boast about their heroics and accomplishments.

But that generation was not brought up that way, they were taught that when they had a job to do that you did it right. There was no need to brag, no desire to sensationalize their accomplishments.

The world was saved and now they went back to rebuilding the country. These heroes and saviors just wanted to get back to a normal life and forget what they had experienced.

Jason traces the root cause of this degradation in his city now to when the courts began handing down very lenient prison sentences.

After committing a crime the criminals these days have no fear of getting caught and arrested. None of these convicted felons are being sentenced to long prison terms, not even for serious violent offences. Overcrowding in the jails and prisons is a major reason for this reduction in prison sentences.

A few years earlier the high courts had stopped all overcrowding of these federal and state prisons. New State and Federal guidelines mandated a max number of prisoners a facility could house. Now criminals looked forward to being incarcerated, and their short time behind bars was a way to get free medical care. While incarcerated the state pays for any medications they may need, along with any counseling for drug or alcohol addiction.

The time off the streets is also a way for these criminals to recruit new members into their gangs. They will convince the young prisoners about the money they can make working for the different street gangs. The bright lights, money and excitement lured countless young men and women into a life of crime.

Little did they know that they were the foot soldiers, the ones that did the dirty work for these gangs and criminal organizations. These new recruits are usually initiated into a gang by first receiving a severe beating. Next they had to prove their worth, which meant they must kill a rival gang member. This almost always resulted in them getting arrested and sent back to prison. Here in prison their job was to recruit new members, it is a vicious cycle.

The time these criminals spend behind bars also afforded them access to prisoners that came from different parts of the country. Prisoners exchanged ideas, formed new alliances, the prisons are a learning center for would be criminals. Many gangs and organized crime operations are actually run from inside these prisons. With the help of the guards, who are bribed by either money or drugs, information is passed from prisoners to their gang members on the streets.

Only those at the very top of these gangs and criminal organizations are out of the reach of the law. It is these drug kingpins and crime bosses that control large parts of the city. With the drug trade being very lucrative, this meant they could bribe the police, judges and district attorney's.

With the laws protecting the criminals more than their victims, it seems that society was going backwards to a more lawless existence. Good decent people were abused by crooked judges and district attorney's.

Greed is everywhere, as chaos runs rampant through city hall and the police station.

It has only been a month since Jason had sat on a jury that sent a major crime figure to jail. One rotten apple off the streets didn't even make a dent in the crime spree which is moving like an epidemic across the city. He did feel a measure of pride that he did his civic duty, and because of that we have one less crime boss in the city.

Retributions by the gangs against anyone testifying against certain criminals are often severe, and sometimes results in death. People on juries feared for the safety of their family, if they were to convict one of these drug kingpins or crime bosses.

Jason knew that those on the jury had been warned that if any of their identities are ever found out by members of these drug gangs and organized crime families that their lives will be in serious danger.

He was very confident that his and the names of the other jurors would be sealed and kept in a secure place. Yet the possibility that his name along with the others would somehow get leaked out was always on his mind.

Sitting at his kitchen table, apprehension on his face as he tries to forget how cruel and viscous this particular drug lord was that was on trial. He and the other jurors had sat and watched via closed circuit T.V. from the safety of another room as the prosecution built its case. So many heinous and inhuman acts of violence were committed by these animals that he felt that they just had to be put away behind bars for a very long time.

He and the other members of the jury that he was on stuck together; and they were committed to putting this certain man, who went by the name of El Diablo, behind bars for the rest of his life. The stories of how other jurors and witnesses trying to convict this drug Kingpin El Diablo character had been murdered in previous trials were very unsettling. Jason nevertheless believed that all measures would be taken to secure their identities. His faith and trust was in the hands of the man that carried these sealed documents in and out of the courtroom. Because people's lives were entrusted in his hands, Jason believed that this one man must be of the upmost unswerving and reliable of any person in the courthouse.

Jason and the other jurors never spoke with this man, but they watched him closely as he went about his job. He was tall and skinny, perhaps early forties, with a small pony tail. Neatly dressed and always clean shaven. On his left ear dangled a small unicorn; and it struck some on the jury as odd, and as to why a man of his age and in this line of work would wear such a thing.

The man walked with a slight limp, but he did not need a cane. He looked to be in good shape so it was assumed that this limp was probably the result of an accident rather than a birth defect.

This trusted individual who had free access to the court rooms never spoke to any of the jurors. He never even glanced in their direction, and he showed no emotions as he walked past. Jason figured that the man has seen and heard enough of what goes on in a court of law that none of this bothered him anymore.

By protecting the jurors this way, it ensured that intimidation would not be a factor in their decisions.

Trying to forget those images, Jason now bows his head, and prepares to go to work. Taking the elevator down to the parking garage from his apartment, he always felt a little nervous. Others from his building had been mugged inside this very parking garage, causing him to breathe deeply as the elevator doors opened.

Cautiously sticking his head out and scanning all around he can see that no one else in here. A shiver runs up his body, as he hastily makes his way over to his car.

Getting in he quickly locks the doors, dejected over the fact that he too has let fear guide his actions.

A normal trip to the parking garage has now become something of a dare.

He has left the relative safety of his apartment, and has ventured out into the criminal invested streets.

Now vulnerable and exposed, a feeling of being watched causes him to shake. Looking in All directions, he still can see that there is no one else in the parking garage.

At one time, shortly after his jury duty he had thought of buying a gun for protection. However, the thought that he might kill someone went against his Christian teachings. As long as he minded his own busyness, he believed, that none of these gangs would have an excuse to hurt him.

He always went straight to his job, and after work he returned straight home. Like so many others going about their daily lives he pretended not to see what was going on around him. There was the selling of drugs on the street corners, to the man running down the street with a purse in his hand. At least twice a week gun shots could be heard, sometimes these disputes between gangs spilled out and onto the streets. Men would run into the street stopping the traffic while firing their guns at someone chasing them.

He like the other motorist dared not get out of their vehicles, all they could do was pray that they were not hit by any stray bullets.

Not liking this attitude of his of not getting involved bothered him greatly.

Jason felt over whelmed and outnumbered by the size of the gangs running the streets. That if he did report a crime that the police were unlikely to do anything about it. The gangs would then turn on him like they have so many others. Again his thoughts went to the idea of this avenging super hero, a vigilante that came from nowhere and cleaned up this city. Again he reminded himself that the days of brave men doing brave deeds are long gone. Chivalry, valor and complete disregard for one's own life when trying to save another are only in the history books.

After hitting himself in the head, he could only smile at such foolish thinking.

Now driving along his usual route to work, which takes him through several rundown districts, he is ever vigilant. With businesses boarded up and the streets in dire need of repair, it is a gloomy scene. The homeless and vagrant can be seen digging in the dumpsters for a meal or a piece of clothing. Trash and rubbish litters the sidewalks. Abandoned and stripped down cars dot both sides of the streets.

Gang members are standing on all the street corners, trying to sell their poison to anyone passing by. The prostitutes hang around the intersections hoping to entice a customer. Mixed in with these are the homeless and mentally challenged, who wonder aimlessly about the city.

The back alley clashes over drugs and money between rival gangs would often spill out into the streets. The innocent people caught in the middle of this mayhem and disorder has no place to hide and they pay a heavy price.

The gang members carry high caliber and automatic weapons, being out gunned the police rarely intervene in these street battles for money and turf. None of these gangs stay in one spot for very long, for safety reasons the members are constantly moving from one building to another. With so many gangs operating so close to each other it is safer for them to keep their enemies guessing as to where they are at.

The city is divided up into sections as if controlled by an occupying army. Each gang controls a certain number of blocks, with some ranging from a few to as large as a thirty block area. In these areas they sell drugs and other illegal goods. An invisible line separates each section and the gangs guard their turf very closely.

When one gang would dare cross this invisible line, then the shooting would start. Sometimes it looked like a scene from the old Wild West. These thugs and hoodlums would shoot randomly, whether running from or towards another gang member as they ran from one side of the street to the other. This is usually followed by cars racing by with several guns sticking out the windows firing in all directions. Many innocent bystanders are killed and many more are wounded, this only causes the people to become more afraid instead of trying to take their neighborhoods back.

It is the fear of retaliation by these street hoodlums along with the fact that the police did little to solve these crimes, that the people remained silent.

The residence in these crime invested areas walked about with their heads down, moving along at a good pace, there is certain urgency in their steps. This scene is becoming common throughout the city and any loitering by anyone could be fatal. No one stops to look in the shop windows any more, people no longer congregated on the sidewalks to catch up on the latest gossip. You moved briskly along minding your own business and you prayed that you would make it home alive.

In Africa the Zulu tribe has a saying, "Only the wildebeest that pauses to admire the scenery gets eaten."

Again recalling how, when he was a young teenager, he often would venture out late at night by himself. He walked several blocks to the nearest gas station to get a can of pop. Never did he fear that he might get mugged or worse, killed by a drive by shooting.

These days the gangs have lookouts that watch the city streets very closely. Any unfamiliar face in their territory causes them to be alarmed. The D.E.A. is always trying to infiltrate these gangs with the purpose to gain damaging evidence against the men who are in charge. Their job is to bring down the so called drug King Pins, the brains of these street gangs and their illegal operations.

Unfortunately many of these undercover agents would be found dead. The gangs keep a close watch on each other, and anyone showing the slightest sign that they may be informants are quickly killed. It was not unusual to find five to six bodies behind these abandoned warehouses on any given weekend.

These are the mean streets of Landore, and they rivaled any from the major cities like New York, Chicago and Los Angeles. A heavy influx of refugees from the poor Latin American countries only made things worse. These impoverished and often mistreated people had to fight daily just to survive in their native countries. Smuggled into the United States they brought the violence and ruthlessness of these street gangs to a whole new level.

As Jason drives further into these gang infested areas, he can see many of these sinister looking thugs and hoodlums standing in the doorways of abandoned and crumbling buildings. They stare long and hard at Jason as he passes by, causing him to speed up, hoping to be out of this part of town as quickly as possible.

He watches with distain as vehicles are broken into right on the street and in broad daylight. Despite their car alarms going off, no one walking nearby seems to notice. The people coward with their shoulders up, and with heads down and they continue their journey. Having grown numb to this type of crime, the people don't even slow down to stare.

With his window partway down, the sounds of screams can be heard, yet those walking on the street chose again not to notice. With their eyes fixed straight ahead, these zombies, these desensitized individuals march on. They seem cold and uncaring, but Jason knows that they feel as he does, asking themselves, "What can one individual do to stem the tide of this wrongdoing."

Sitting back in his seat he wonders if maybe he is just like they are, in believing that alone he cannot make a difference. He doesn't carry a gun or even a knife, what is he to do. He is no better than they are, afraid to take that first step. Fear rules everyone's lives and for that reason everyone has chosen not to get involved. If he jumped out of his car and tried stopping these criminals, he wouldn't stand a chance. All of these criminals carry guns and knives, and they out number him twenty to one.

Only a fool would risk such a venture, and Jason keeps telling himself that he is no fool.

He still believes that as long as he leaves these gang members alone that they will leave him alone. If he ignores what they are doing as does everyone else he will be allowed to pass safely through this section of town. He is no threat to them, and if he has to he is willing to change his route to work to avoid any confrontation. It did bother him as crimes are being committed and he doesn't even call the police. He has become one of these timid and cowardly citizens that he so despised. He would leave this city if he thought he could, to start somewhere else.

But from the news, he knows that nowhere in this city can he escape the crime that grips it so tightly.

With the police parked nearby they too ignore the screams and car alarms. He watches in dismay as money is exchanged between the police and the drug dealers. This money is no doubt a payoff, and the police simply get into their car and drive away.

It makes him sick, how at one time the police were so looked up to and respected. Now they are just criminals wearing a badge. He hopes that amid all the crooked cops, that there is still a few that hold their heads high. That these individuals will not be corrupted, that they will serve with pride and honor.

As his heart falls into despair at the misery that surrounds him, he senses a need to act, to bring about a change. But he is only one man, one individual among the populace of 200,000. Was he being rational in believing that he could make a difference?

What can he do? What could he say to them?

Maybe it will be a waste of time; perhaps it is too late to change society and the way its people are thinking and acting. Has man gotten to the point where everyday violence is acceptable, and the laws of nature have taken over with the old creed, "Only the strong will survive?"

It seems to Jason that those in society that are not prone to violence and acting aggressively will be bullied and stepped on by more assertive individuals.

In the old west of the 1880"s it was the gun that made everyone equal. With a gun on his side even a teacher or the town preacher could stand against the outlaws. In today's world the average citizen is forbidden to carry a gun, and without this equalizer he is fair game for the criminals that roam freely looking to take advantage of this.

The time for these wishful dreams will wait another time as the red light up ahead seems to be taking a long time to change.

Growing impatient at the long wait, Jason begins tapping the steering wheel. Getting the sensation that he's being watched, Jason gives a quick look over to his left. He sees two grubby dressed men standing on the sidewalk. They are unshaven, filthy and obviously up to no good as they warily look around. Jason cracks a smile, as he believes these hoodlums are preparing to steal some unlucky person's car.

He glances up ahead, his fingers tapping the steering wheel even faster now, hoping that the light changes very quickly. The unusually long wait for the traffic light starts to make him nervous. Turning again to his left, he notices that the two hoodlums that he had noticed just a moment before have left the sidewalk and they are now walking towards his car. Getting worried he swallows hard, and taking a glance in the rear view mirror, he sees a man standing very close to the rear of his car. Looking closer, Jason notices that this man has one hand inside his jacket, not a good sign.

Jason is tapping on the steering wheel very rapidly now, his skin beginning to tingle as if he were very cold. The sense of impending doom has his heart racing. Now beginning to sweat, he curses at the traffic not moving. The light ahead has turned green yet the cars ahead of him do not move.

Rubbing his smoothly shaven face, trying to remain calm, Jason doesn't know why these men are staring at him. After all he's not rich, and his car is seven years old. He has nothing of value. Surely these men can see this.

The two men from the sidewalk have walked in front of his car, here they stop. With their arms folded, and a scowl on their faces, they cast an ominous gaze at Jason.

Thinking hard, he can't think of anything that he might have done that would have provoked them. As his breathing increases one of the hoodlums, now standing only several feet away yells at him, "Drive your car into that garage," and he points to a nearby structure.

Nervously shaking his head no, Jason replies, "I'm on my way to work."

Now the man behind his car begins making his way up to the driver's window. Looking in front Jason sees that the traffic light has turned green again but the traffic still has not moved. This has a bad feeling about it, looking around he is hoping to see a police officer. With no police in sight, he puts up a brave front.

Hitting the steering wheel and cursing out loud, he tries to show some anger. Hoping to discourage these men, and that this poor bit of acting will show these men that he has a bad temper and they better not mess with him.

Now turning his head, he sees the man that was behind his car has walked up and is now standing right next to the driver's side window. With a black glove on one hand the man motions for Jason to roll down his window.

After rolling the window down and speaking in a firm voice, he tells the man, "You have the wrong guy; I was just going to work."

He follows this with a short laugh and a nervous smile, while this whole time his stomach is so upset that he feels nauseated.

Without saying a word the man reaches through the open window punching Jason a terrific blow to the mouth. Falling to the side and across the seat, Jason is nearly knocked out. His vision is cloudy, and for a moment he lay very still across the seat. Instantly blood is all over his shirt and the pain from his mouth is intense. While holding his mouth, the car door is opened and he is jerked from the car and thrown down onto the street.

Turning over and getting up on one knee, his head is spinning, he's confused. Thinking to himself, "I have done nothing to cause this type of treatment, I hope they will realize that they have made a mistake and let me go."

As he tries to stand to plead his case a man approaches him from behind and using a lead pipe he crashes it into Jason's right leg. The force causes him to buckle from the blow, and he falls face first down onto the pavement. He grits his teeth, the pain is intense and he holds tightly to his injured leg. As he rolls to the side suddenly he can feel a heavy boot pressing against his chest.

He is pinned tight to the ground, and despite all his efforts he is unable to move the man's boot.

Angry and feeling humiliated, he calls out, "I didn't do anything, just look at me."

By this time there are five men standing over him, each one has the crazed look of a mad man. They tighten up their faces and pucker their lips, some smash their fists into their hands.

Feeling like a wounded animal, Jason is at the mercy of these vultures standing over him.

Without saying a word, they grab him by his jacket and begin dragging him across the street towards the garage.

His body is limp as a rag doll and he is shown no mercy as his kidnappers forcibly pull him over the rough pavement.

Beginning to panic, he calls out to the people on the street watching all of this, "Please help me, call the police."

To his horror the people look the other way and continue walking as if nothing is happening.

Cursing under his breath, he guesses that this serves him right, as he too had often chose to ignore a crime that he saw happening. Instead of helping, he chose to mind his own business, believing that he would never be a victim of one of these crimes.

Now that he is a victim, he has a guilty feeling. Yes he should have helped others, he should have called the police regardless of if he believed they could help or not. Now finding himself in a very dangerous situation, his mind thinks of all kinds of worst case scenarios.

Maybe these men will cut him up into a dozen pieces, to show other gangs how tough they are. Will he be shipped to a foreign country and sold into slavery. His worst fears are that perhaps they will cut him open and remove his organs to be sold on the black market.

He still can't believe he's in this predicament, how could this happen, he was only on his way to work.

The pain by now is shooting up his leg causing his body to shake, unable to hold back he yells out in pain. However, the men dragging him across the street could care less about his condition, they laugh at his pleads for help.

Realizing that he's about to be an innocent victim, he claws at the pavement like a wild animal in a vain effort to stop. Despite his determination he is soon inside the garage and his heart skips a beat when the garage door slams shut. The noise echoes throughout the interior, giving him an ominous sensation of being trapped.

Laying on the dirty floor he quickly looks around, hoping that just maybe this nightmare will end when these men recognize that they have the wrong person. Jason wares no gang colors, nor did he flash any gang sings that would cause then to attack him.

• The five men, without blinking, stare at him as if he were their worst enemy. Their eyes are cold and lifeless, their faces rough and weathered. With a nod of a head from one of them they slowly make a circle around Jason. Sliding their heavy boots across the dirty floor the men make the circle smaller and smaller.

Breathing faster, Jason puts one hand on his jaw, feeling a sharp pain as he moves it the side tells him that it is broken. Cocking his head and looking at the man that hit him, he sees he has a pair of brass knuckles in his hand.

Cursing under his breath, "That would explain how he broke my jaw with just one punch."

Shaking his head and putting his hands out, he again pleads with them, "There's been a mistake, I don't know any of you."

To his disbelief one man pulls out a hand gun and takes several steps closer to him. He points it at Jason's head and says, "You will do as you're told or we'll kill you, simple as that."

Waving his hand, desperate to end this whole nightmare, "Just a minute, I have done nothing wrong to any of you so you need to let me go."

This feeble gesture only seems to anger them more and with a quick swing, he feels a boot strike the back of his head. Now hunched over and holding both hands on his head he begins to curse.

Very upset at this point, he mumbles to himself, "This has gone on long enough; they have no right to treat me like this."

With a fierce look on his face he manages to stand up despite the terrific pain in his leg, he now begins breathing heavily. Giving those around him a hard look, he tells these men sternly, "What you are doing is against the law."

Laughter erupts, as these men find these words very amusing.

Jason begins to sense that they don't really care about the law and the penalty for breaking it.

If he had to assemble the meanest looking, most disgusting group of criminals he could find this would be them. Each of these men carries a gun and a knife, a few carry baseball bats. Some have chains around their necks, and all are heavily tattooed.

This hideous laughter is the kind only made by evil and heartless men who have no feelings or compassion.

When the laughing finally subsides, one man approaches and gets right up into Jason's face and shouts, "Instead of punishing you ourselves, I think you should be introduced to Igor."

After hearing this, the other men get wide eyed, they are no longer laughing.

With a hint of caution in his words, "Are you sure you should turn Igor lose on him," asks one of the men, "we usually only send our most hated enemies to Igor after the boss has given us the go ahead."

Smiling, and walking around Jason, the man nods his head, "It has been some time since Igor got to enjoy himself, and I think this man will do just fine."

Not liking this talk at all Jason says loudly, "Okay, you had your fun, the game is over, open that door right now."

Secretly praying that his bluff will work and these men will let him go.

It is quiet in the room as the man who is obviously in charge turns his back. Jason looks at the others; they have a worried look on their faces, as if they know what is coming next.

Trying desperately to gain his freedom he pulls out his wallet, "Here is all the money I have, take it along with my credit cards."

Holding this out, he is surprised that none of these men move, they have remained exactly where they were.

He takes a quick glance at the door. Its distance he estimates is about 30 feet away. Thinking if he makes a break for it he might be able to get out of this mess. He knows the pain in his leg will be intense, but he will just have to endure. With possibly his life hanging in the balance he prepares for this last chance effort to escape this place.

As he looks back he sees a flash of light and instantly can feel a sharp pain in his stomach. Doubling over, falling to the floor his body convulses uncontrollably. The man holding the taser gun lets out a hideous laugh.

As the room begins to spin and his eyes become blurry, he knows he's on the edge of blacking out.

Grabbing Jason forcibly by the hair the man yells, "Don't pass out yet, you haven't met the boss," and he throws Jason forcibly back down onto the hard surface.

Trying his best to remain conscious, Jason struggles to sit up. Feeling a tremendous amount of agony, he tries to control his heart rate and breathing. Suppressing the urge to panic, he knows he has to stay calm if he is ever going to get out of this dilemma.

Lying on his side and wiping the sweat from his face he glances over and watches as the rear door opens. In walk two men, and they look like the others that are standing around him. Behind these men is another, and he walks with a certain swagger in his steps suggesting that he is the boss. Looking up he sees a man wearing very nice clothes, a broad hat with a single feather sticking out the top. Around the man's neck hanging from a gold chain is a medallion with the image of the devil on it. Looking up into his face Jason gasps, as he can't believe who he's seeing. This man with the broad hat is the drug king pin he helped send to prison only a month earlier.

With a sneer on his face this drug king leans over and says, "Bet you never thought you would see me again did you."

Still confused at seeing this man, Jason shakes his head several times. "You have me confused with someone else; I don't even know who you are."

But these innocent and naïve gestures fall on deaf ears.

Taking a white handkerchief from his vest pocket the man covers his mouth. He now slowly walks around his helpless victim, making short rude and vulgar remarks followed by laughter.

Outnumbered, cornered and injured, Jason feels very vulnerable and helpless, he finds himself in a very bad situation.

Now stopping and looking down with hatred in his eyes, "I know a great many things about you—Mr. Karsten."

Hearing this drug king pin call him by his name sends a chill up Jason's spine.

"You and four other jurors sent me to prison, or should I rephrase that, you tried to send me to prison."

Jason keeps thinking, "Why is this man out of prison, and how did he know I was on the jury that convicted him. We were told that our identities would be kept secret, because of the threats to our lives. We watched the trial via short circuit television from another room; only a few people in the court house knew the names and addresses of the jurors."

Quickly coming to the conclusion that someone on the inside must have been paid off, that's how this drug king pin named El Diablo got the names of the jurors.

Now El Diablo sits in a chair and he glares at Jason with those evil eyes. Those same eyes he had during the trial, and that same attitude. He believed he was untouchable, that no jury would dare convict him. He laughed throughout the trial as the prosecutor reminded him of the jail sentence he would receive after he is found guilty.

Trying to change the subject, Jason's next sentence may again fall on deaf ears but he had to try, "Hey, my leg is broken, I need medical treatment. You have to get me to a hospital."

Smiling, this ruthless drug king pin pulls out a piece of paper. Looking with a disgusting grimace on his face, he remarks, "A broken leg is the least of your problems."

Jason swallows hard, as this situation he's in keeps getting worse and worse. He realizes that at this point his life is in serious danger. These men standing around him are street thugs and muggers, and God only knows what else. By their appearance he would guess that brutality is a way of life for them. His show of pain and suffering has not altered their attitude towards him one bit. If anything they seem to delight in his suffering, and this gives Jason a bad feeling in the pit of his stomach.

Looking back at the piece of paper, "You are the last on my list," El Diablo states."

Holding up one finger he quickly says, "Let me rephrase that, you are the only one still alive that is on my list."

Wiping the perspiration from his forehead, Jason wonders what he is talking about. A list, what list?

Holding out the piece of paper out a little closer to Jason, El Diablo says, "This is a list of the five men who tried to send me to prison."

Obviously growing angrier, he says in a harsh tone, "They dared to stand up against me. I 'am the ruler of this city and all its miserable citizens. I call the shots here. I say who lives and who dies. The people of this city will bow their heads whenever I walk by. You should feel privileged by my talking to you."

Hearing the arrogant and conceited tone in El Diablo's voice, causes Jason to recall the days of the trial. This evil man thought he was someone special and that he was above the law. With an attitude that bordered on lunacy, El Diablo carried himself as if he were royalty.

Yes, Jason now remembers more about this man. He recalls his swagger, his attitude, and his belief that he was so much better than those around him. In truth, El Diablo was nothing more than an ordinary drug pusher. He sold his poison on the streets just like a common hoodlum. It was his ruthless and cold blooded tactics that enabled him to rise in the ranks and eventually take over the gang.

His brutality and disregard for human life soon got the attention of state and federal agents. Undercover operatives working on the case for years were confident that they had enough evidence on El Diablo to put him away for many years.

The jury did convict him and a sentence of 25 years was imposed on El Diablo.

To the surprise of Jason, here was El Diablo, barely a month after he was sent to prison.

Either he escaped and is on the run or somehow he managed to pay off the right people. Those that run this city are widely known to have taken bribes in the past, so Jason comes to the conclusion that money bought this man his freedom.

After a moment of silence, "Your fellow jurors seem to have run into some bad luck," El Diablo says with a slight chuckle.

Taking a moment before he continues, "Phil Garbish died when the brakes on his car failed; he ran a stop sign and was run over by a semi. Next would be Jim miller, you remember Jim don't you;

he's the one that dressed like a cowboy. Anyways, he had a mishap while fishing. It seems he fell over board and drawn. Number three on my list would be Harry Johnson, Harry slipped on a puddle of oil while working in his garage. He cracked the back of his head on the concrete floor; he was dead by the time they got him to a hospital. Next is Cory Wentworth, seems he had a very bad drug addiction that no one knew about. To make a long story short, he died of an overdose of heroin."

Breathing in short fast breaths, not for one second did Jason believe that each of these men had died as a result of an accident. He knew exactly who was responsible for their deaths and that person was sitting right in front of him.

Folding up the piece of paper El Diablo carefully places it back into his vest pocket. Rubbing his hands together, he wrinkles his forehead as if in deep thought.

"Through my resources I'm told that it was you that convinced the other jurors to find me guilty."

Jason is speechless, alarmed that this man knows those kinds of details. Thinking fast he tries to recall the people that were privy to this information.

Interrupting his concentration, "The question is," El Diablo calls out in a loud voice, "is just how you will die?" remaining motionless he stares intensely at Jason.

Doing his best at acting tough, Jason stares back at his tormentor. Not known for his courage or bravery, the timid young man now must call on a determination and fortitude he is not even sure he possesses.

Feeling his life is in jeopardy, a strange feeling over comes him. Deep inside he can sense that he is changing, no longer fearful, he grits his teeth, despite his broken jaw.

A moment later El Diablo comments, "I wish my brothers Razar and Mongul were here, they would know the proper treatment for you."

Thinking back, yes his two brothers, they were as devious and ruthless as El Diablo is. They were also about to go on trial for similar crimes. But it seemed the witnesses had just vanished, and the case was put on hold for the time being. Jason knows that these witnesses were probably murdered. Because of a leak at the court house he and his fellow jurors are now going to face the same ending.

At this point escaping seemed impossible, and with Jason being unarmed and suffering a broken leg and jaw it seems to him that he is facing certain death. Greatly outnumber, he wouldn't even be able to put up much of a fight. But the thought of giving up and bowing down to these bastards never enters his mind. If he is going to die than he will do it with dignity, he will spit in their faces with his last breath.

Looking up at El Diablo he can see the evil inside this man, and it causes him to shiver to think of what terrible things he has planned for him. Jason knows that soon he is going to face the same ending as his fellow jurors had met.

He now feels as if he is on trial, and these criminals are going to judge him.

El Diablo looks around the room at the assorted thugs and hoodlums that have gathered. He asks them, "Is there anyone here who can say anything nice about this man, this terrible man that tried to lock me up?"

The room remains quiet, as all eyes are concentrated on Jason.

Smiling at not getting a reply, he continues, "Who believes that this man should be punished for what he tried to do to me?"

Instantly the noise erupts into shouts of, "Guilty, Guilty," "Torture him," "Make him pay."

Several of these men move towards Jason swinging clubs and large knives. Holding one arm up as he tries to avoid being struck, Jason cowards back as far as he can until he is up tight against the wall.

El Diablo stands up and motions with his hands for everyone to calm down. As the eerie silence prevails, Jason can feel a cold chill race through his body. What did this butcher and his servants have planned for him. He is sure it isn't going to be a pleasant death, no; he feels they have something special in store for him.

He can only watch as this notorious drug king pin whispers something into the ear of another and this brings a smile to the man's face. As El Diablo is walking away he turns and says, "I will see you later."

Again pausing as he puts a finger in the air, "Let me rephrase that, I will see parts of you later," and he begins laughing which starts everyone else laughing.

After he leaves the room, the laughing stops. All eyes are once again on Jason. Feeling like a wounded rabbit about to be pounced on by hungry wolves, Jason prepares for the worse.

Putting his fists up, he is ready for their onslaught. It will be a feeble resistance but he will not go down without a fight.

From behind he is grabbed by the shoulders and forcibly picked up by two men and taken down a long narrow hallway. By this time he has no feeling in his right leg from the knee down. But the pain is intense up to his hip. He knows that several bones must be broken. The swelling has doubled the size of his leg.

While being constantly pushed he hobbles down the hallway the best he can. Using the wall for balance, he grimaces in pain with each step, knowing that if he falls he'll be kicked until he stands up again.

His eyes constantly scan all around, hoping against all odds to see a way out. But to his despair, he sees no windows or doors and the farther he goes down this narrow hallway his ever declining hopes of escaping grow more evident.

When the man in front of him reaches the end of the hall, a door to his right is opened and here they shove Jason inside. Landing hard on the floor he immediately grabs his broken leg. Biting his lip at the pain, the tears begin running down his face. Wiping them away he knows he has to put the pain and the fear out of his mind. Despite never having been in a life and death situation before, his instincts tell him to remain calm. To panic at this point will do him no good. Believing that there is a way out of every bad situation, he controls his breathing and concentrates. Realizing now that his captures do not plan on killing him immediately, this at least gives him something to be happy about, a small window of hope. Always positive in any situation he begins to get mad, and with this his determination increases.

Sitting up with his back against the wall, the first thing is to think of a way to escape this mad house.

His heart sinks when looking around he can see that he is in a room with no windows. Just the one door that he came in is the only way out. Unable to stand, he slides back away from the door, figuring that at any second men will burst in and beat him to death. However, as he waits, he is very tense and jumpy at any little sound. With his eyes glued on the door, the minutes pass by and still nothing. This is starting to freak him out, his sixth sense is telling him something bad is about to happen.

Finally relaxing, he lays down onto the floor. Rubbing his leg, he repeats, "Everything is going to be alright."

In a split second a deafening sound bombards him from the ceiling. Sitting up quickly and holding his hands over his ears he glances up to see four huge speakers mounted to the ceiling. The noise coming from them is so loud that they are vibrating the room and he feels as if his head will explode any minute.

He curls up into a ball, trying to lessen the noise. His eyes and face hurt so much from being pinched so tightly together. After what seems hours the noise is turned off, and he lay flat against the floor. Covered in sweat, shaking and with a small amount of blood coming from his ears, at this point he can't get his eyes to focus.

His head is still pounding; it is the worse headache he has ever experienced.

Just as he is relaxing, the door opens quickly and two men burst in. Trying to cover his face, he is dragged out the door. His body as limp as a rag doll and completely exhausted he can put up no resistance. Going down another narrow and nearly dark hallway, he is soon tossed into another room. Lying on the damp floor, with his head raised up just slightly he looks through blurred vision. He strains to focus his eyes, his head still pounds as if someone is hitting it with a hammer. A terrible stench forces him to pull back a short distance. The odor is so repugnant he has difficulty breathing. Shutting out the offensive smell he can make out what appears to be shackles hanging from the walls. It is a strange site, as it reminds him of some type of medieval dungeon the kind found in the lower chambers of castles.

Alone and defenseless, and his head spinning as if on a merry go round, he awaits for the inevitable. The different strange noises that echo from the dark corners of this room cause him to shake at the unexpected. Water is dripping from the walls in several places and he can hear the sound of rats running about.

Trying his best to stay focused, putting these terrible sights and smells out of his mind is not easy. He reaches deep into his soul for salvation, for the smallest ray of hope, an ounce of self-assurance; a chance is all he is asking. Yet, despite his setbacks, and the insurmountable odds facing him the anger inside of him grows. Revenge and retaliation now dictate his thoughts. He is changing from a mild manner person to one that needs to strike out at those that have done him wrong.

His fingers twitch, if only he had a gun he would get even with these animals. Not a violent person and the thought of ever hurting anyone has never entered his mind. Always able to control his emotions, he rarely showed the slighted signs of being upset.

However, this day is different, as these cruel circumstances put on him have been intolerable. These men, these barbarians have triggered something dark inside him that grows angrier by the minute.

Enraged like never before, and despite his injuries he curses out loud, "Dam you all!"

Making himself a promise that if God allows him to leave this place alive he will dedicate the rest of his life to extracting revenge on those that have hurt him and others.

Concentrating all his willpower and grit on finding a way out, he is discovering a toughness and resilience that he never knew he had. Anger has taken over and the fear of dying has left him. He now feels a certain confidence in his ability to overcome these horrific circumstances.

Despite being severely injured and without a weapon, Jason makes a fist and pounds the floor.

Taking a deep breath, he will not go down without a fight. This is surprising for him as he has always avoided any type of confrontation. Fighting was for those less educated he always thought. Now facing a foe that only knows violence and brutality, Jason is forced to fight or die.

His instincts for survival kicks into high gear, and an animal mentality takes over.

Reduced to a fight or flight response to what he has been through, young Jason Karsten prepares himself to meet death. The end he feels is not far away, and after saying a short prayer he relaxes, at peace with his God.

Hearing a faint voice causes him to instantly roll into a ball. With his arms across his face he shouts, "Come on you bastards."

Shaking in anticipation of the horrors that are coming, his heart races as the sweat once again runs down his face.

A moment passes and surprised at not getting a reply he slowly lowers his arms and glances around. Stunned that no one is standing in front of him, he turns around slowly fully expecting his tormenters to be there, but there is no one. Now looking across the room as his vision improves he can see two men shackled and hanging from the wall. Their heads are bowed, skinny and looking like skeletons it reminds Jason of pictures he has seen of people in German concentration camps.

Pulling his bruised and battered body across the floor he is curious as to who these unfortunate individuals are. Seeing no one else in the room he softly asks, "Who are you?"

All he hears in return are moans and groans from these two men that can't even raise up their heads.

The two men are hanging like deer waiting to be butchered; they are covered in blood, and deep gashes cover their bodies. It is obvious that have been severely tortured, and they look as if they are about to die.

Jason knows that this is where El Diablo tortures those that have disobeyed him. This devil of a man has chosen this dark and damp dungeon, far from the streets above to commit these acts of brutality.

Sick to his stomach and shaking his head in disgust at the thought of the countless victims that have been subjected to El Diablo's brutality and inhumanness now reinforces his determination to put an end to this nightmare place. Making himself a promise that if he ever gets out of here, he will see that the authorities know about this place.

Looking farther into the semi dark corner, he can see another man, this one is hunched over. He is shirtless and rags cover his body from the waist down, his hair is greasy and shoulder length. Making grunting noises like an animal, the man turns his head and glances at Jason.

Despite the pain he is feeling, the sight of this man's face causes Jason to recoil and shudder. Putting his hand over his mouth, the sight of this man's face temporally takes his breath away.

He sees a grotesque deformity, with eyes as big as his hands, and teeth that protrude beyond his mouth. One side of this man's face looks heavily scared, resembling a burn victim.

Before Jason has time to comprehend what he is looking at this man lets out a blood curdling scream and lunges at him.

Jason falls backwards narrowly escaping a vicious swing, as he lands onto the damp surface. Stunned and moving away quickly, Jason is dazed and shook up. The deformed man utters words that are all scrambled together not making any sense.

A large chain connected to this man's leg prevents him from getting any closer. Howling like an animal as he pulls relentlessly at the chain that binds him to the wall.

A glimmer of compassion and pity is felt by Jason of this tortured human being.

Wondering what cruel things El Diablo has done to him to cause this poor soul to act like this.

It is a sad spectacle, and the anger begins to boil once again inside of Jason. He makes another promise, to bring El Diablo and his henchmen to justice no matter what it takes.

Out of the shadows a man steps in and with a long belt whips the deformed man back into the corner. Turning and looking at Jason he remarks, "Later I will let Igor introduce himself to you." With that said the man laughs and claps his hands.

At this time a voice shouts down from above, "I said we would see each other again."

This rotten, winey voice he recognizes as El Diablo's. No doubt he has more punishment in store for him.

Looking up Jason can see a balcony about twenty feet up and here is El Diablo and some of his henchmen staring down at him.

Speaking as loud as possible, and determined to be defiant to the end, as his voice is hoarse and cracking, Jason calls out, "Just kill me and get it over with."

"Come on now, that's no way to act."

A slight laughter is heard by those above him.

"You brought me here for one reason, to get pleasure out of watching me die."

"That is true," replies El Diablo.

"But not just yet, we need to talk first. You have information that I need."

Thinking fast, Jason questions himself, "Just what information does El Diablo think I have? I'm not a cop or a judge, I'm nobody of importance?"

"If you think back to when I was being prosecuted," El Diablo says as he now leans over the balcony, "There was a man that brought in evidence that was used against me. It is this man I need to find."

Thinking as hard and as fast as he can, Jason does remember a certain guy that had very damaging evidence against this El Diablo. His name he can't remember, but he does recall what he looked like.

"So this is why they haven't killed me yet," Jason whispers to himself, "I have information that they need."

Standing up and leaning to the side to take the weight off his injured leg, Jason calls out, "Go to hell!"

Obviously those standing above him are angered by his comment, as he can hear yelling and cursing.

Soon the door opens behind him and several men rush in. Holding Jason firmly, they are followed by El Diablo. One rather large man grabs Jason by the neck and picks him right up off his feet. Being chocked Jason struggles to catch his breath. This man's hands are like a vise around his throat.

After a moment, El Diablo signals for him to release his grip, and Jason falls to the floor, he gasps for air.

With anger in the tone of his voice, "You will tell me what I want to know or you will end up like those two men chained to the wall," he tells Jason as he is fuming at the mouth.

Still holding his throat, he whispers back, "No way in hell am 'I going to tell you his name, not now not in a million years."

At that instant he feels a sharp weapon cut across his back and he grimaces in pain. Recomposing himself as he lay on the cold hard floor, angrier than he has ever been in his life. As the sweat once again begins running down his face, he looks up with stone cold eyes, "I will kill you someday, you can bet on that."

Laughing, El Diablo replies, "Dead men can kill no one, and believe me you will be dead very soon."

El Diablo motions with his head and again two men step forward and they drag Jason across the floor and out the door.

Trying to be brave, he tries bluffing these men, "I have friends in high places, they will be looking for me soon, so if you know what's good for you, you will let me go."

"Shut your mouth," calls out a gruff voice from behind him.

Groaning at the trouble he's in, Jason is distraught as he looks at his surroundings. Glancing up he sees an uncovered light fixture with several broken light bulbs in it. With only a single light bulb working it sways back and forth as it hangs down several feet from the ceiling.

The walls are made of brick and in several places some of these bricks have fallen to the floor.

With the light flickering off the crumbling walls, it gives the area a gloomy almost medieval appearance. The floor is cold and damp, and this tells him that he must be in the lowest part of this building.

The farther into this labyrinth of corridors they take Jason the more difficult it will be for him to escape. Having quickly lost his bearings he can't remember how many corners they have gone around. He has resolved not to give up any information, no matter how bad they torture him. He knows that if he ever did reveal the man's name that they will have no more use for him and he will be killed.

As he contemplates his life coming to an end, the two men let go of him. He is suddenly in a free fall, swinging his arms wildly in an attempt to stop. Immediately his body crashes to a sudden and hard stop. Lying on his side, trying to catch his breath, he coughs up blood several times. Slowly he gains control of his senses; he knows this is not the time to panic. Waiting a moment before trying to get up, as he listens for anything that maybe nearby. Doing his best to control his breathing, as each breath causes a sharp pain in his chest, this he assumes could be from a cracked rib.

Anticipating the unexpected, fists out he prepares himself. However it is quiet, too quiet.

Opening his eyes, and rubbing the sweat and dirt away, he finds himself in a round pit. The walls are at least eight feet high, and with the smooth sides, there seems to be no way of climbing out.

He can't image what they are going to do next, maybe they will throw down a few poisonous snakes. Shaking his head, "Anything but snakes, I hate snakes," he mutters.

He has nothing to use as a weapon, so removing one shoe he holds it tight in his grip, like a baseball pitcher about to deliver a fast ball.

Staring up he awaits the next surprise, hoping he can react in time.

To his surprise, the lights are turned off, and it becomes very dark. Now he won't be able to see what they throw down at him. He lay tensed and curled up, his fists ready to repel the unknown.

Feeling vulnerable, the worst images now begin to run through his mind. Maybe they will pour hot oil down on him and laugh as he suffers horrific burns.

The horrors range from being fed poisoned food to having a rabid dog thrown into the pit.

Perhaps they will fill the pit with water and watch him slowly drown.

Maybe loads of dirt will rain down on him and he will be buried alive. It is this image that makes him the most afraid. Being claustrophobic, the small confined space he's in is causing him to have a panic attack.

Breathing deeply, he wraps his arms around his legs tightly. Closing his eyes he tries not to concentrate on the present dangers. Trying desperately to picture in his mind more pleasant images, anything to calm his nerves and slow down his heart rate.

As he sits slightly rocking from side to side, the minutes drag into hours and still nothing has happened. There is no sound, not even a whisper. Nothing has been thrown down onto him as he had thought. Dumbfounded as to what atrocities El Diablo has planned for him he is sure it won't be pleasant.

For the next two days, nothing happens, and no one comes in to check on him. The room remains dark and totally without a sound. All Jason can do is to pray that this torturous isolation will end before he starves to death. On the third day the lights came on, holding up his hands, he must shield his eyes. He can hear voices, and they are getting closer. Finally he sees the image of a man looking over the top and down at him. Having had no food or water for so long, Jason's speech is hoarse.

"Can you help me," he calls out?

As he puts his hand in the air, desperately hoping that it is the police that have come to his rescue.

To his dismay, he sees El Diablo walk up and stand next to this man. His heart drops, as he was hoping against all odds that this was a rescue, that somehow a miracle had occurred and the police had found him.

"You look well," says El Diablo, "Most men would be begging for their life by now."

Managing to get up and lean against the wall, standing on shaking legs Jason replies, "You'll get no such pleasure from me you bastard!"

With his face showing anger, El Diablo answers as he points his finger, "I'll break you down, and then I'll kill you."

Jason is in a terrible situation and this monster above him holds all the cards. He could kill his captive at any time, and Jason is helpless to stop him.

But it seems El Diablo gets his pleasure out of torturing and breaking a man's will. To reduce an individual into a weeping, feeble shell of a human being is what this man enjoyed most.

Jason knows that he will have to be patient, that an opportunity to escape will come along. He must never give up hope of escaping this house of nightmares, and the chance to get even. The rage is beginning to build inside of him, and revenge is constantly on his mind.

It will be this belief that someday he will get even with this mad man and this is what enables him to endure all the pain and suffering.

A rope ladder is lowered down into the pit, and a man yells, "Get your ass up here!"

With no other choice, Jason climbs up one step at a time. His broken leg being almost useless, the climb is slow and agonizing

Once he reaches the top, two men grab him and throw him forcibly across the room. Landing hard, he rolls several times to help lessen the pain radiating from his injured leg.

He puts his hands out to protect his face expecting to be hit at any second. His body hurts all over, and the lack of food and water is only making things worse.

A bowl of what looks like oatmeal is sat next to him, the smell is terrible. He cautiously puts two fingers in it and tastes a small amount. It tastes like it smells, but he forces himself to eat it, as any food is better than none.

After finishing his meal, he's again led down a narrow hall where he is finally shoved into a room. The door slams hard behind him, causing him to cringe.

On his hands and knees he looks around, the room is completely empty except a single light bulb hanging down from the ceiling. There are no windows, no furniture, nothing, just four walls.

Refusing to submit to his pain, he forces himself to crawl, and he checks every corner, every square inch, hoping to find a way out. After circling the room he is dejected at finding no escape and there is nothing he can use as a weapon. He sits down in the middle of the room wondering what is going to happen next, what cruel and barbaric method of torture El Diablo will try next.

Just as he begins to succumb to the overwhelming need to sleep, the door burst open and two men step into the room, and without a word being spoken, again he's dragged forcibly out the door and down the hall.

Refusing to walk, he makes his tormentors drag him. If he is going to die he will not help these brutes in any way. Limp as a rag doll, he tries desperately to block out the pain that is ravishing his body.

Going into another semi-dark and gloomy looking room they strap him into a chair, and a bright light is put in his face.

A voice calls out, "This will all end if you just give us the name of the man that testified at El Diablo's trial."

Squinting his eyes, as the light is drying them out he replies, "Okay, you win, I can't take it any longer, I'll tell you his name."

Somehow despite his dire situation Jason manages to maintain a humor to all this, as he knows death is very near.

Sitting motionless, he lets a minute pass until someone grabs him tight around the neck and yells, "Tell me his name!"

Trying to keep a straight face he replies, "His name is Santa Clause."

His tormenters are not amused by this answer, and he can feel the chair leaning back. Suddenly water is being poured over his face. He gags and coughs, but the water continues none stop. He has heard of this torture method, it's called water boarding. The C.I.A. used it to get information from suspected Muslim terrorist.

Now he's being subjected to this same type of torture, and he can only guess how these men learned it.

Nearly passing out from lack of oxygen, the water is finally stopped. Breathing in deeply as he can feel that he is on the edge of passing out.

Again he's asked, "Give us the name of the man."

The bright light prevents him from seeing those around him, but he can hear several voices and again he defiantly replies, "His name is President Lincoln."

His tormentors react violently to his defiance and a whip is lashed across his midsection, causing him to hunch over. Gritting his teeth, Jason forces a smile, he will not let these bastards break him down, he will die first before giving them any satisfaction. This game of torture and questioning continues nonstop until Jason cannot stay conscious. Despite all their efforts at beating and whipping him, the lack of air is too much. After blacking out, he awakes as they are dragging him back to the room that he was dragged from.

After tossing him through the doorway the men say, "We'll be back shortly to continue this, so don't get comfortable."

Jason lay on the floor, bleeding and hurting all over, and his head is spinning around as if he were on a merry-go-round.

Forcing himself to stay awake, he lay on his back starring at the ceiling. He knows this could be the end, with the relentless torture and no possible way to escape this is as hopeless as it gets.

Mentally he knows he won't break down, but physically a body can only take so much punishment. With fortitude and resilience that even surprises him, he repeats, "I will not surrender, I will keep my pride and dignity, and I will spit in their faces on my death bed."

It isn't long and the men are back, and again they subject him to this water boarding torture. It isn't long and he blacks out, he awakes as they are dragging him back to the room. Lying curled up on the floor like a baby; he's cold and hurting terribly. His body at this point is shaking uncontrollably, and his heart is beating so fast he clutches his chest tightly. Suffering from shock and hallucinations, he knows that the strange things he is seeing and hearing aren't real.

Images of his mother standing several feet away force him to call out, "You are not real, go away!"

Another image is of a large creature with long tentacles and they are reaching for him.

Closing his eyes he prays that the visions have disappeared. At first afraid to open them, he slows his breathing and concentrates on where he's at, knowing that the images are just inside his head.

Trying to focus his mind, realizing that he can't take much more of this, as his heart will stop one of these times.

Lying lifeless on the floor, Jason awaits the end with supreme indifference; he has reached the limit of human endurance; but he is not afraid. He stares at the single light hanging down directly over him. Wondering if the light from heaven looks like this. He closes his eyes, and gritting his teeth, he knows there has to be a way out of this place. There is always a way out of every situation, no matter how dire and ominous it appears.

A person just has to expand his mind, use what is at hand. Jason digs deep into his memory, trying to recall anything that may help him now.

Opening his eyes quickly, he stares at the single light bulb hanging from the ceiling. Sitting up, he smiles a devious smile. Through the intense pain he manages to get to his feet, his leg muscles are aching from being hit so many times.

He has an idea, and he prays for just a little more time before the men return. Reaching out his hand, the light bulb is just out of reach. He attempts to jump, but with his right leg broken it causes a great deal of agony. Forcing himself to block out the pain, he again jumps.

This time his fingers graze the light bulb. Encouraged, he keeps trying, and finally he's able to grab and pull the cord down from the ceiling just a few inches before his hands lose their grip. Needing to rest, he summons up every ounce of energy he can muster. Jumping and grabbing the cord again he pulls and it begins to tare the plaster in the ceiling. He keeps pulling the cord which travels across the ceiling over to the wall. Continuing to pull, it finally leads down to the light switch next to the door.

Try as he might, he is unable to break the cord, he is just too weak. He now turns the light-switch off. Now he begins biting the cord with his teeth, stopping only when the pain from his broken jaw is too much. Repeating this biting and chewing until the bare wires are showing. He continues this until the electric cord is cut in half.

Stripping the rubber off the wires with his teeth, he next wraps the bare wires around the door knob. Taking off his wet shirt he lays it on the floor next to the door. With his head pounding, and feeling dizzy he must stay focused and alert. Jason waits, as he knows he will only get one chance, one opportunity to turn this crazy, far-fetched idea into a miracle.

Not a religious man by any definitions, but he does believe in a higher power, and it is this higher power that he now talks to. With his trembling hands pressed together, a nearly defeated young man looks up and closing his eyes prays that this God that can work miracles, this all mighty being that has created everything that exists, that he intervenes in this hopeless situation.

Breathing in very shallow breaths, Jason slumps back onto the floor, his eyes having difficulty focusing. Squinting several times, the door looks blurring, and he knows that he is losing his battle to remain conscious.

It isn't long and he can hear heavy footsteps approaching and they stop just outside the door. Mustering up yet another plea to his aching and throbbing muscles to perform just one more task, his body shakes as he attempts to stand. Stumbling, he moves close to the wall, with his trembling fingers on the light switch he nervously waits.

Knowing full well that if this idea fails, it is all over, he has no more tricks up his sleeve. Weak, battered and bruised, this will be his last hurrah, his whole life now rests on this million to one long shot working. If it fails to incapacitate or even temporally stun these men his life is over.

There is no time left to pray again, if it works he lives, if not he dies, simple as that.

Shaking his head he whispers, "It is not my time to die."

Opening and closing his eyes several times, he feels like he is about to pass out.

Looking up he whispers, "Not now Lord, please, just keep me awake a little longer."

He holds his breath as the door makes a clanking sound as it is being unlocked. As it swings open, the two men step just inside the door. With his hand shaking, he flips the light switch on. A crackling sound is heard as the faces of both men tighten up, they get wide eyed and clinch their teeth together tightly. Their bodies quiver and shudder, and in less than thirty seconds both men drop to the floor.

Remembering to turn the switch off or else he will meet the same fate as they have. Thrilled that his plan actually worked, and overcome with emotion it takes Jason a moment to grasp the situation. Controlling himself he wipes the sweat from his face, focusing on the two men now lying at his feet. The rage rushes through his body, here are the men that have caused him so much pain and agony, but now he is in control, their lives now rest in his hands.

Reaching down he next instantly grabs both their weapons. With hatred in his eyes he wants so bad to put a bullet in each of their heads. But he knows the noise from the gun shots will alert the others in the building. He can see that these men aren't dead, so his revenge will have to wait for another day. Looking out into the hall he sees that it is empty. Not knowing which way leads out, he must take a guess. He stays to the left and as the hall splits he goes to the right, switching back and forth, hoping this strategy will keep him from going in circles.

After what seems hours of walking and searching for an exit, his body is shutting down, his legs are having difficulty holding him up. Dizzy and sick to his stomach, he is determined to leave this house of horrors no matter what it takes.

He almost cries when he sees the rays of the sun shining through a window. He manages to make his way up three flights of stairs, stopping only when the pain in his leg becomes unbearable. Biting down hard trying his best to block out the pain he knows he must keep moving. With tears running down his face, he wonders how much more he can endure.

He had thought that his lack of guts to continue under these circumstances would have forced him to give up long ago, but he is discovering that deep inside there is a very strong and determined spirit that refuses to quit. He is no longer the mild mannered person he once was, he is now tough, determined and most of all angry.

His overpowering need for revenge drives him on like a powerful drug, it courses through his veins, it's constantly on his mind and it keeps him from failing.

Finally he spots a door, wanting to first rush out and be free of this place, he stops himself. Being reminded of where he's at, as this is a hangout for criminals and crooks. He takes a quick glance out the door window. Cursing, he sees two men just outside smoking cigarettes.

Time is critical, as he knows that soon this place will be franticly searching for him when the two men are discovered. He must think clearly and not rush any decisions, taking several deep breaths he concentrates hoping a plan will pop into his head.

As he leans back against the wall, hoping to come up with an idea, that's when something jabs him in the back. Lowering his head, he contemplates suicide rather than being subjected to more torture. With guns at the ready he turns around, fully expecting El Diablo and his men to be standing there. To his surprise there is no one behind him, and he at first believes that he is starting to hallucinate. With all that he has been through he knows that the traumatic experiences could cause a person to hear or feel things that are not really there.

Looking around he sees it's just the fire alarm control that he backed into. Lowering his gun, he shakes his head. He thought that this was the end of the road, that he had been recaptured. Despite the pain and misery he manages to laugh at this.

With his mental state at the breaking point, a shootout with the fire alarm seems too much for him to comprehend.

His laughter is replaced with crying. Sliding his body down the wall he sits on the floor running his fingers through his hair.

His mind jumping from one subject to the next, it is difficult to stay focused on the present situation he's in.

With nowhere to run, and seemingly out of miracles, Jason nudges the gun barrel up to his temple.

The cold steel barrel reminds him of the men that tortured him. Taking in one more deep breath he grits his teeth, "No. I will not die this way," he calls out.

Holding the gun with both hands he leans his head back and glances up at the ceiling.

Something just above his head catches his attention. Turning and giving it a longer look, he smiles.

"This just might work," he utters under his breath. Without thinking twice he breaks the glass and pulls the handle down. The fire alarm sounds, and he hurries as he hides just around the corner and under the steps. The two men that were just outside smoking cigarettes race inside and they run down the hall. Moving from his hiding place, he pushes the door open and hobbles down the steps. Limping down the sidewalk as fast as he can, Jason must grit his teeth to keep from yelling out in pain.

He ducks down several alleys, moving among the rubbish as quietly as possible. Finally after several miles he must stop to rest. Lightheaded and feeling nauseated from being malnourished, dehydrated, bruised and battered. His instincts tell him not to rest, that he must keep pressing forward, to put as much distance between that hellhole and himself.

He is again amazed at his newly discovered toughness. He never would have thought, before this nightmare began, that he could have withstood so much torture and agony and still be able to think clearly. A slight smile crosses his face. If he could pat himself on the back he would, but not at this moment. He is in too much pain, and has too little strength left to even clap his hands.

His body radiates in agony from his feet to his head. Dumbfounded at how well he is doing, a different person is emerging from the timid man he once was. Now anger and rage fills his thoughts. Vengeance is what is keeping him from faltering.

Needing a moment to rest he stops and leans against an old building, exhausted beyond anything he has ever endured. Taking a look around and with a deep sigh, nothing looks familiar; this is a part of the city he has never been in before. He must push on, by this time they must have discovered his escape, no telling just how close El Diablo and his men are.

He knows that El Diablo will be very upset at his men for letting this happen and he's sure that some will pay with their lives.

Staggering about like a drunken man he falls down several times. His body is at its limits, weak, dehydrated and suffering horrendous pain yet he somehow finds an ounce of determination to carry on. Spitting the dirt out from his mouth, he grips his hands tight. Pushing up on shaking arms he manages to regain his balance.

Summoning up more courage and drive, he staggers blindly across the alley. Holding onto a small railing his head spinning and vision blurred he is finally overcome by fatigue. Unable to hold himself up any longer, losing his grip he falls backwards down a flight of stairs. His mind now thinking back to when he was thrown into that pit, he prays this is not happening again. He tumbles and flops down the steps like a deflated basketball, finally stopping only when his head crashes into a door. Stunned, Jason's first instinct is to get up and keep moving.

He tries pushing up with both hands, however he's so weak that he quickly falls back down. With his head lying against the cold concrete, he doesn't see a way out of this situation, it's a dead end.

Unable to run, and with no strength left to defend himself, Jason will be easy for El Diablo's henchmen to recapture.

Suddenly the door opens, and as he looks up through blurred vision he sees a man with a long white beard. The scene begins to spin around and around, and everything gets as still as the night. He wants to stay awake but his body has been through too much. Despite all his efforts he slowly loses consciousness.

Waking with a jerk, he lay motionless, not sure where he is. Blinking his eyes, trying to get them to focus, he needs to see where he is. He can hear talking, and it's not far away.

It's several minutes before he finally gets his vision back, at first he thought his vision was permanently damaged. The bright light put in his face while being tortured he feared had damaged them severely. Now raising his head up just slightly, he takes a cautious look around. This room he's in he has never seen before. It is warm and dry here, and it doesn't stink. Trying to figure out where he could possibly be, he throws off the blanket and glances down at his broken leg. He's surprised to see a cast on it, and there are bandages all over the rest of him.

Holding his jaw he can feel some type of brace against it.

He knows that El Diablo would not have fixed him up. So the question is, just who came to his rescue, and why?

He knows no one from this part of town, and he's sure he's not in a hospital.

Trying not to panic, he takes several deep breaths and asks himself, "If I'm not back in that horrible building, than just where in the hell am 'I?"

His muscles are stiff and sore, and he gingerly eases his battered body to the edge of the bed. After tentatively placing his feet onto the floor, he needs to rest. Still feeling the effects of the traumatic nightmare he had gone through. Next he tries standing, still slightly wobbly, surprised at being able to put some weight on his broken leg.

Waiting a moment while his head clears, his muscles are stiff and sore. Now shuffling across the floor and through the doorway he cautiously peeks around the corner. In the next room he sees two elderly men playing cards. When they turn their heads and see Jason they each quickly set their cards down and give him a long look.

At a loss for words, Jason glances around, seeing if there are any more people here. He notices that this is a very small apartment, barely big enough for two people.

The old man with the long white beard puts is hand on his knees and speaks up, "It's good to see you up and about young man, you gave us quite a scare."

Speechless at first, Jason moves a little closer to the two, constantly looking around every corner. His fear is that this is all just an elaborate prank and that El Diablo is waiting just out of sight.

Pausing for a moment, he rethinks his last possibility. No, El Diablo would not have gone through this much trouble he now believes. There is not a helpful bone in that animal's body.

Still unsure of what is going on, he can see that the two elderly gentlemen are not part of any gang or criminal organization. Their eyes allude to warm and caring individuals.

He stares at the two for a moment, and a little hoarse, he must talk with his teeth clinched together, "I want to thank however fixed up my leg and my jaw."

Smiling and pointing across the table the old man with the white beard replies, "That would be Doc Morgan."

Jason looks at him, however, the man doesn't look at all like a doctor. His hair is rather long and unkempt, and his rumpled clothing sure doesn't look like something a doctor would ware.

Doc Morgan now stands and pointing he asks in a low voice, "How does the leg feel?"

Reaching down and rubbing the cast, "It feels okay," Jason replies with a smile. Still unsure about these two old guys, as they seem very laid back, like they have no care in the world.

Yet they have taken a very battered stranger into their home without knowing anything about him.

As his head starts spinning Jason begins to lose his balance. Doc Morgan pulls out a chair and motions for Jason to sit down.

Grabbing the back of the chair, he takes several deep breaths. After sitting down he needs a few seconds to clear his head.

Gingerly touching his broken jaw, Jason looks up to see Doc Morgan doing the same thing.

"It only hurts when you move it," states Doc, "I should know, see this scare." He points to a spot on his face. "My jaw was broken when I was a prisoner of war."

"Don't get him started on his damn war stories," states Edward. "Once he gets on that subject he won't stop for hours."

Seemingly upset by these remarks, Doc Morgan replies, "As if you never told anyone about your heroics during the war?"

"Not to the point where I bored them to death," answers Edward as he sets his newspaper down. "Why if I did tell someone about what I did during the war I'm sure they would find it fascinating."

Firing right back, seemingly forgetting about their guest, "You forget I served longer than you did, and I have more medals," shouts Doc Morgan.

Understanding the need for these old men to tell him their war stories, unfortunately he has more pressing things to get to.

Trying to ignore the pounding inside his head, he now needs answers.

He needs to know, where he is and just who are these two men? However, with his stomach growling loudly, he first needs to eat. These important questions will have to wait, as he feels he's on the verge of starvation. Catching a scent in the air, he looks to his right and sees several loaves of bread.

Smiling and giving Jason a wink, Doc Morgan says, "You stay right here," and he pats him on the shoulder as he walks by.

Jason sits quietly and watches as bread and mashed potatoes are put on a plate. Licking his lips, he can hardly control his urge to get up and grab the food with both hands. Bringing it straight back to the table, Doc Morgan sits it in front of Jason. On the verge of starvation he doesn't hesitate for a second as he stuffs the food into his mouth as if he were a wild animal. Nearly choking several times, he gasps for air in between bites. Unable to open his mouth, the soft bread and mashed potatoes are all that he can eat.

He wonders what these two men must think of him, maybe by the way he's acting is giving them second thoughts about helping him.

They bring another glass of milk over and sit it on the table. The two elderly gentlemen turn around in their seats and casually go back to their card game.

Jason finds this odd, why aren't they asking him any questions. Don't they even want to know his name or how he sustains his injuries? They have let a total stranger into their home, one that has obviously been in some type of trouble, but still no questions.

This should all raise a red flag to them, a warning that he may be a possible criminal. The two old men continue to bicker about their war years, oblivious to this stranger setting at their table.

By their actions and lack of interest Jason feels very comfortable here. He still watches both closely, waiting for any sudden move that may indicate trouble.

His suspicions will have to wait, first he needs to eat and that is what he does.

As he is devouring the meal, neither man looks at him, it's like he's not even here.

Finally after a second helping Jason sits back in his chair, it feels so good to have food in his stomach.

He has never been so hungry in all his life, and he never wants to experience a torment like it again.

Looking at both of these elderly men, he asks, "Why did you help me, you don't even know who I 'am?"

The two old men sit in silence, and then they give a halfhearted stare at one another.

Edward strokes his long white beard as he turns his head towards Jason and says, "You can call me Edward, and I don't need to know who you are to help a stranger in need."

"He's right," adds Doc Morgan, "You were in need of help, and that is all that matters."

Jason can see in their eyes and by their body language that they are kind hearted. They are just two old men sitting around enjoying old age.

Getting defensive, Jason speaks up, "What if I'm wanted by the police. You could be in big trouble for helping me."

The two old men laugh, and he can hear small talk between them.

Doc Morgan replies with a grin, "If we thought you were a bad person, we would have let those men find you. No, there is something about you that is different, and I'm not sure what it is?" Doc rubs his chin, turning his head from side to side as he studies Jason very carefully.

"You have been through a very traumatic experience," states Edward, "Would you like to tell us about it?"

The two old men seem to change their posture somewhat, and they turn towards their young guest with the expression only a caring individual can give.

Not wanting to give away all the details, he tells them, "I was mugged."

The two old men sit straight up, and by their facial expressions they are waiting for more of the story.

"I would like to tell you more, but I don't know either of you. How do I know you don't work for El Diablo?"

Hearing this, the two old men perk up and give a glance at each other. Rubbing his chin again, Doc Morgan says, "So, you are being hunted by El Diablo?"

Looking at his friend, Edwards comments, "That no good rotten bastard."

Jason gets the feeling that they these two old men have heard of El Diablo, and by their demeanor he is not a friend of theirs.

"What do you know of this criminal called El Diablo?" Jason asks with a sharp tone in his voice.

Doc Morgan is now standing, and showing some agitation, "We know a great deal about that individual, in fact I'm sure he would love to find us."

Edward nods his head in agreement, and his facial expression indicating that he too is upset by the mention of El Diablo.

Hearing Doc Morgan say this, it gives Jason the impression that they look at El Diablo as an enemy. That sometime in the past they must have crossed paths with El Diablo and the outcome wasn't good.

Feeling that he can trust these old guys, or else they would have either called El Diablo or the police by now. He needs to know more about them, and what they know about El Diablo and his criminal organization.

Still driven by a desire and need to seek revenge Jason lowers his guard, trusting his instincts that these two men can be trusted. With what they know could help him in his quest to find and kill El Diablo.

Beginning to open up, "I was on a jury that convicted him," Jason begins, "El Diablo was sent to prison for 25 years. But somehow he managed to weasel out of that and he then hunted down every member on the jury and killed them. I'm the last one still alive, he tortured me. He needed to know the name of one more person that testified against him. I would not tell him the man's name, so he continued to torture me, trying to break my silence. I'm not sure how many days I spent there, maybe four, I'm not sure."

The two old men lower their heads and breathe a deep sigh. He can see by their reactions how bad they feel for him. As Jason continues to go into more detail about the beatings, he sees Edward actually start to cry.

Shaking his fist and gritting his teeth, Doc Morgan proclaims, "If only I were younger, I would go after El Diablo and kill him with my bare hands."

The two old men are getting more upset the more Jason talks about El Diablo and his henchmen. It seems that they too have a score to settle with El Diablo. At this time Jason's head begins to hurt and as he is leaning forward the two men help him back to his bed. Lying down, face pale, he is exhausted and still hurting all over.

Holding out some pills, Doc Morgan says, "Take these they will help with the pain, then I want you to sleep, understand me young man?"

Forcing a smile, Jason feels that he is in a safe place, and these two elderly angles will watch over him as he sleeps.

"I'll see about getting a crutch for you," says Doc Morgan as he gives his young friend a wink.

Jason nods his head, and lifting a hand in a way that imparts thanks. He is now having trouble keeping his eyes open, still resisting the urge to sleep.

Swallowing the pills, he lays back, his body beginning to relax. The scenery around him is starting to fade. The memories of the last few days are running through his head like an old movie. The faces of the men that hurt him so bad are burned into his consciousness. Their faces he will never forget, he will get his revenge someday.

Waking up to the smell of coffee is a pleasant surprise, and Jason wastes no time in sitting up. Needing a few minutes to fully wake up, he stretches out his arms and legs. The scenery around is the same as before, it's a comforting sight. Easing out of bed he grabs a crutch leaning against the nearby wall. Standing and getting used to walking with a crutch, he makes his way into the kitchen. He can feel his strength returning and his thoughts are much clearer now, no more haze and confusion. The food and rest has helped him tremendously.

Once in the kitchen he sees Edward is reading a newspaper and he doesn't see Jason until he is right next to him.

Startled a bit at this sudden interruption he turns and smiles, "I didn't hear you approaching, I'm deaf in my left ear you know, an injury from the war. Anyways it's good to see you up young man, now let's get you something to eat."

Smiling, "I'm just a little hungry," Jason replies as he sits down.

Looking around with an inquiring glance, he asks "Where is Doc?"

Returning from the stove and setting a plate of toast and eggs in front of him, "He'll be here soon. He went out to get the latest news on the street."

Confused by this comment, Jason remarks, "You mean he went to buy a newspaper?"

Shaking his head no, "I mean what the word in the neighbor is, what all the excitement is about."

While eating Jason asks, "Did something happen last night that I missed?"

Lowering the newspaper and giving him a half grin, "The whole area is searching for someone special."

Jason knows that Edward is talking about him. He knows El Diablo has recruited every available body in the search for the prisoner that got away. Remaining silent, he waits to hear what news Doc will bring.

As he eats his food, he raises his head up and studies the room in more detail. The first thing that catches his attention is the several pictures of police officers that are on the wall. His first thought is that Doc or Edward or both were police officers or they have children that are cops.

If this is true than his time here will be short, as he no longer trusts the police. Looking closer at his surroundings he sees an apartment that lacks a woman's touch. It isn't picked up and kept the way a woman would have it looking. He assumes that their wives must have passed away, and these two old guys share this apartment.

He wonders how long they have been widowed, and why they have chosen to stay in this neighborhood. Two old men would be easy targets for the thugs and hoodlums that run this part of town. A simple walk down the street by either of them could result in a mugging or even death.

Jason jumps when the door opens causing him to nearly fall off his chair. He's surprised at how quickly Doc came through the door and reached out and kept him upright.

"You jumped pretty good young man," Doc utters, "you alright?"

Catching his breath, all he could think about is how those goons would come busting through the door and drag him out for more torture. The flashbacks are very unsettling.

Looking up and shaking a bit, "I'm fine, I'm sorry."

"Nothing to be sorry about, we all get spooked once in a while."

Jason nods his head and goes back to eating his breakfast.

He watches as the two elderly men now stand at the far end of the room. They talk to other in a low whisper.

Occasionally looking at Jason, this gets his heart racing. If for some reason they have decided to call the police on him he can't just run out the door. With escape out of the question, he must sit and wait to see what news Doc has brought.

His fate will be in their hands, if indeed the police are on their way he knows that El Diablo will soon know his whereabouts.

The two now casually walk back over and sit down at the table.

Smiling, "Seems you got El Diablo all upset with your miraculous escape," says Doc.

Jason remains silent; his business with El Diablo is no concern of theirs.

After a moment, "Looks like we made the right decision when we helped you," adds Edward.

Still not totally convinced about these two, he replies, "I did what was necessary to save my life."

Puckering his lips, "Very ingenious to use the electrical cord to take out those two men," says Doc. "I wish I had thought of that trick at one time or another."

The two old men stare at their young friend, both seem to be delighted with his company.

The quiet in the room is unsettling, and this causes Jason to become very tense.

"It's true that El Diablo and his henchmen are searching for you," continues Doc, "I promise that you will be safe here."

Now sitting back in his chair, a look of appreciation on his face, "You two have risked a great deal to help me, I hope you know what you're getting into," Jason replies.

"Oh we have been through some very tough times young man," answers Edward. "We know what we are getting ourselves into."

Giving his new friends a smile, Jason continues to eat, his head now lowered.

The two old men sit at the table, and while Edward taps his fingers in a nervous way, Doc rubs his chin. Jason is waiting for them to tell him that he has to leave. He understands if this is what they want, as their lives will be in great danger the longer he's here.

As Edward starts to talk Jason interrupts him, "If you want me to go I will."

Jerking his head back and making a face, he replies, "Heavens no, why would we do that?"

"I'm a wanted man, and El Diablo will not stop until he finds me."

Gritting his teeth, "He does not scare us," answers Edward with a snap of his head, "someday he will get what's coming to him."

Showing some emotion, "He's right," adds Doc. "El Diablo better stay far away from here." The two old men give each other a confident look, they seemed very agitated.

Jason has to smile at these to old men putting up such a brave front. Just what could they do if El Diablo's henchmen were to break in this apartment?

No, he does not feel safe here. This small apartment in this part of town and with its two elderly occupants is far from a safe haven.

He thinks they may have just read his thoughts, because now he watches as both men get an insulted look on their faces.

Grabbing his chair firmly by the arm rests, "You don't think we can take care of ourselves do you," demands Doc, giving Jason a long stare.

Hesitating before he answers, as he doesn't want to hurt their feelings, however, the fact remains that two elderly men will not be much of a deterrent if El Diablo's men break into this small apartment.

"I'll be honest," Jason says as he sits back in his chair, "I feel very vulnerable sitting in this apartment with two senior citizens."

By their reaction to this he can see that he has offended them, and standing up quickly Edward says firmly, "We'll show you who is vulnerable."

Both men reach behind them and pull out a revolver and pulling up their pant leg they each pull out another revolver. Not finished yet, in Edwards jacket pocket he has a Taser gun. Doc has a rather large knife on his belt, and opening up a draw in a nearby cabinet they pull out several more weapons.

Not finished with this array of weapons they each now produce a pair of brass knuckles along with a can of mace.

Jason sits wide eyed, astonished at the weapons these two supposedly defenseless elderly men carried.

Now looking straight at his young disbeliever, "We have other guns and various weapons hid throughout the apartment," comments Doc, "and we are trained in the martial arts, and vulnerable we are not."

Eating his words, a slightly embarrassed Jason replies, "I'm sorry I doubted you, my mistake."

Clearly Jason now knows that these two elderly gentlemen can take care of themselves, there is no doubt about that.

Continuing to make his point, "We both have military service, so we know how to shoot a gun," states Edward.

"We have seen some terrible things in our lives," adds Doc now sitting down at the table. "Edward and I served in the Korean war together."

Jason again must swallow his words, "Okay, you have made your point, I'm sorry for thinking you were just two ordinary senior citizens."

Wanting to change the subject, Jason says, "I can't stay here forever you know."

The conversation turns to Jason leaving, and nodding their heads both of these gentlemen advise him against that.

"You need to first recover from your injuries, besides the word on the street is that El Diablo has put a large bounty on your head," adds Doc.

"So you must know that every two bit hoodlum in this city is going to try and capture you."

Taking several deep breaths, Jason listens intensely.

"You can never return to your old apartment either," adds Doc.

"He's right, if you try and return to your apartment," states Edward, "El Diablo will have his men watching it. As soon as they spot you, they will most likely shoot you right there."

Insistent, "But there are things there that I need," replies Jason. "I do really need to go there."

Shaking his head, "With your injuries, it is best that you heal first."

Realizing these two old men are right, Jason must wait until he is fully recovered before attempting to retrieve anything from his apartment.

During the next month under the watchful eye of Doc Morgan Jason grows stronger, his meals consist of yogurt, pudding and bananas, as his broken jaw is still held in place. He still needs several pain pills a day to deal with the pain. His nightmares cause him to scream in the middle of the night and Doc has been giving him medicine for this also.

Over this time period Jason has become very close friends with his rescuers. He learns much about their families, and where they worked most of their lives.

Each day the old men confide a little more of their personal lives to Jason, who in return opens up about his own life.

A trusting and respectful bond is forming among the three. Jason feels relaxed and untroubled around his elderly companions.

Doc and Edward now begin to teach their young apprentice the skills he will need to survive on the streets. They have a secret agenda that they have not disclosed to their young friend yet.

Jason is taught about weapons, explosives, and the art of camouflage. He learns how to survive in the wilderness, and how to move about without making a sound. He is also taught how to disarm and incapacitate a man very quickly. He learns his most important lesson, that if necessary how to kill someone in the most efficient and effective way.

These two elderly gentlemen have hinted that they may have worked for the C.I.A., and have done covert operations in very dangerous parts of the world. Their knowledge of secret missions and tactical training is very impressive.

The two will not reveal just who they worked for, as they took an oath of confidentiality.

With such extensive training and knowledge in the art of warfare, Jason must assume that they were either Green Beret or special ops.

The weeks have seen him gain weight and recover his strength, although still heavily dependent on pain pills, Doc assures him that they will soon be lowering his dosage so that he doesn't become addicted to them.

Later in the day when he is alone in the apartment Jason goes into a room that he was told never to enter. Being curious as to what these two might be hiding, Jason opens the door to the secret room slowly. The small room is dusty and the air has a musty odor, suggesting that the door to this room has not been opened in a very long time. Taking a cover off a glass case Jason can see that it holds many types of decorations and medals while another glass case next to it has several pictures in it. Getting closer for a better look, he sees that the pictures show several soldiers holding up what appears to be a North Korean flag. The caption at the bottom of this second case reads, "To those we lost, you will never be forgotten."

Jason feels a slight chill come over him. To remember your fellow soldiers all those years ago really says something about Doc and Edward.

Startled when he is tapped on the shoulder, Jason turns around quickly. "I'm sorry if I looked at something that was personal to you," he says with hesitation in his words his face now turning red.

With a big smile, Edward answers, "They are personal, but they are meant to be seen."

Edward now gives the two glass cases a long stare, his mind going back in time to when the pictures were taken.

Swallowing hard, "They were good men, damn good men," he says as he wipes the dust from the glass. His hand quivers as it moves slowly from left to right.

Jason can sense that these pictures bring back memories that Edward would rather forget. The old man seems nervous. He breaths in and out deeply and his sighs suggest that time has not healed all wounds.

"You saw a lot of action during the war," asks Jason in an inquisitive manner.

Now looking up and seemingly at nothing the old man replies, "We saw too much."

Pausing for a few seconds, composing himself, he softly continues, "We experienced the horrors of war and witnessed the suffering of the innocent."

Jason is at a loss for words at the sight of this man on the edge of tears. He realizes he has brought back some disturbing memories to Edward. Not sure how to change the subject, he remains silent.

With his hand covering his mouth, Edward turns and walks away. His head slightly lowered, he shuffles his feet as he goes into the kitchen.

Not wanting to bring up any more painful memories, Jason decides to let this conversation end. He can see by the sad look on Edwards face that he must have seen some terrible things. He would like to know more about what Edward and Doc saw and did during the war but maybe it's best left in the past. When they decide to open up to him it will be on their terms.

The long weeks have turned into months, and Jason feels his body is recovering very well. Now able to put weight on his broken leg, and the brace on his jaw will soon be removed.

The two elderly men teach their young friend a great many things during this time and young Jason tries remembering everything he is taught.

His mentors seem to be training him as if he were a soldier about to go into battle.

The skills he has learned he is not sure how he will use. He has no plans to join the military or the police force. Still Edward and Doc continue to educate him in the art of self-defense and martial arts.

Honing his skills at breaking down a weapon blind folded and reassembly it, Jason has impressed his mentors.

He spends hours reading books on navy seals training, Green Beret survival skills and Special Forces search and destroy tactics. The art of disguise and concealment he practices every day.

It has now been a month and a half since his brutal ordeal, and he is relieved when his cast is removed. Jason is happy that his leg has healed so quickly. His jaw brace will take another week before it can be removed. The rest of his injuries are now only scares and bad memories.

With help from contacts he has been introduced to on the internet, he learns exercises that strengthen the muscles in his damaged leg and jaw.

He paces the floor constantly hour after hour in an effort to build up his endurance.

Taking several days to get the strength back in his leg, he feels confident that he is ready to move about the city.

His elderly companions have been somewhat distant from him these last few days. Jason suspects something, but isn't sure just what is going on.

While the three sit around the kitchen table, "You have learned a great many skills," states Edward. "You have been a good student."

At first smiling at this comment, Jason suddenly gets an odd feeling. His sixth sense is warning him, alerting him that the situation is about to change.

"We have a great deal of crime in this city," say Doc. "The criminals think they are in charge."

Sitting up Jason nods his head in agreement. "I wish the police could get rid of them."

Now with a look of anxiety on his face Edward says, "It would be so nice if someone just did what was necessary."

Speaking quickly, "Yes," adds Doc. "The police can't seem to do the job very well."

With a query look on his face, Jason replies, "What you are saying is that someone should take the law into their own hands, is that right?"

Now moving to the edge of his chair Doc answers quickly, "Yes, someone needs to exterminate the vermin that have turned this once peaceful city into a living hell."

"The street gangs rule this city with an iron fist. You know this first hand," he states as he gives Jason a pessimistic look.

Caught off guard by Doc's sudden use of these words, Jason gives the two a long look.

He can't believe these two nice elderly gentlemen are suggesting that a common citizen should take up arms and go out and kill drug dealers and muggers.

"Yes I have been the victim of an unwarranted assault, but that gives me no right to be judge, jury and executioner."

With a rough sound to his words, Doc replies, "Do you think that the police will arrest El Diablo for the crimes he has committed?"

Jason sits nervously, his eyes watching the two closely.

"Think about it," continues Doc, "they have done very little to stop the crime wave that is plaguing this city. No my young friend, the time has come for the good citizens in this city to stand up and fight, to take back the streets."

Jason understands how it seems the police and city hall has ignored the crime, but to take the law into one's own hands is vigilante justice. He has made himself a promise that he will even the score with El Diablo, but that is as far as he will go. He has no quarrels with anyone else, no matter what crimes that they have committed. He believes these two old men have been watching too many shows on T.V. that depict these vigilantes as hero's and defenders of justice.

In the end he knows the police will look at these vigilantes as just another criminal. Once arrested these vigilantes, these do gooders will be prosecuted and sentenced to jail just like all the other law breakers.

Shaking his head no, "It can't be done," states Jason. "Good people will not just pick up a gun and go out into the night and shoot the first drug dealer he sees."

"No," replies Doc. "But suppose this person had contacts on the internet that provided him with information and weapons that would help him carry out these acts without getting caught."

"This man would need special training," adds Jason. "He would also have to have a deep hatred for criminals of all types. Someone that has been a victim himself and he believes he will fulfill the like mined wishes of the community."

"I like your thinking," says a smiling Edward. "This person would also need a home base to operate from."

Smiling as he glances quickly at the two, "You and Doc have too much time on your hands," jokes Jason. "The fact is that no one is going to take the risk or the responsibility of taking the lives of others even if it is best for the city."

"Don't be so sure about that young man," retorts Edward, not once taking his eyes off Jason.

The mood in the room has changed, and the air is still and the tension is on each of their faces.

"Perhaps you are thinking about hiring a murderer to do these things," ask Jason, still not fully aware of what Doc and Edward have in mind.

With a sly look on his face, Doc adds, "No, not a murderer, but someone that is more reliable. A person that would not take pleasure in killing, however he would acknowledge that it is necessary. He would understand his role and listen to those advising him."

Jason is taken aback by these words. He knew that Edward and Doc always talked about the need to rid the city of criminals, but he had thought they were joking.

With the look on their faces it is obvious that they are very serious and are intent on putting their plan into action.

Jason guesses that the two have been waiting for just the right person to fill this role. A man that can kill and have no remorse for his actions and one that is well trained, this is who they want to carry out these so-called justified murders.

Before Jason can speak, "How do you feel about shooting someone," asks Doc in a firm tone, "to eliminate a criminal from the streets?"

Abruptly sitting back in his chair, "It is not my job to shoot criminals," replies an upset Jason.

Cocking his head slightly to the side, Jason is alarmed by the question. How dare these men think that he would just go out and start killing people.

Edward sees his young friend is confused, and leaning forward he says, "What Doc means is do you have a problem if we tell you to assassinate a person we believe no longer has the right to walk on the street again."

Nervous at where this conversation is going, "What you are asking me to do is criminal, to take the law into my own hands. I know nothing about such things. I rarely have ever fired a gun."

"You have a burning desire to seek out not only those that have wronged you but to avenge all those that have been wronged," states Edward.

Needing time to absorb all of this, Jason suddenly stands and replies in an angry tone, "So that is why you have taught me all about weapons and how to kill a man with my bare hands. You have been training me to fill this role of vigilante all this time."

Jason angrily paces the floor, he feels betrayed and used at this deception.

"You are the one we have been waiting for," calls out Edward. "We need you as much as you need us, think about it. You can never go back to your apartment or your job. El Diablo will be watching every place you ever visited, and once he gets his hands on you, your life will be over."

"He's right," adds Doc. "You are a marked man, there is no safe place for you to go except here."

Looking at the two old men, Jason shakes his head. "It seems for the time being I must stay here. But that does not mean I agree with you two, not for a second."

Laying out today's newspaper, Doc points to the headlines, "Crime wave engulfs city."

Flipping the page he points to several articles, "Here it says three innocent bystanders were killed by stray bullets from a gang fight. One of them was a nine month old baby."

Jason looks at the article, wiping his mouth he shakes his head.

Continuing on Doc says, "In the last five days eight people have been mugged, three stores robbed, 15 cars stolen, four rapes, a house set on fire and finally an elderly couple were tossed off the bridge by a gang for not bowing down when they walked by."

Now sitting down, Jason begins to read the paper more intensely, running his fingers through his hair. He had no idea that things were getting this bad, that so many innocent people were being victimized. Clinching his fist, he grows angrier the more he reads.

Finally it is the story about how a family of four were dragged from their car and assaulted in broad daylight. The two young children were forced to witness these horrific acts.

His stomach now tightening up, Jason grabs the paper crumbling it up he throws it across the room. He has seen and read enough, all the anger and hatred that he was keeping bottled up just for El Diablo now has boiled over.

He can't sit ideal while the crime goes unchecked, he feels a need to act, to right all the wrongs that have occurred.

"I need to know more about these plans you have of ridding the city of its criminals."

Smiling, Edward and Doc pat Jason on the back.

"Good to have you on our side," says Edward. "You won't be sorry for this decision."

"I'll first get the things I need from my apartment, but I can tell you right now I need no help in getting even with El Diablo."

"I'm no vigilante either, and I'm appalled at those that think they are above the law."

"Will you help us put our plan into action," asks Edward, his arms folded hoping for a positive reply.

"Your plan is nothing but a group of shut-ins playing out their fantasies on the internet. Killing people that you deem unfit to live is insane. You both need a wake-up call and get with the real world. The police are paid to risk their lives at arresting law breakers, not people like me."

"Young man," answers Doc, his actions showing how upset he is, "have you seen the violence on the streets. The police are corrupt, they are paid off by the drug lords. The good citizens in this city can't even walk down the street without fear of being mugged or hit by a drive by shooting. No, this city needs to be purged of the criminals and its corrupt officials. The time to take action is now, we can wait no longer."

Jason understands the need to clean up the city but he has no desire or yearning to be that person.

"No, you need to find yourself another comic book hero, because once I kill El Diablo, I'm moving to a safer part of the city."

Edward and Doc have remained seated, with their eyes not once leaving their young would be apprentice. The two have been waiting a long time to find just the right person, someone that has been trained and taught in the martial arts and self-defense. A young person that has not only seen but also felt the cruelty of the criminals in this city, a person with a burning desire to extract revenge on criminals. Doc and Edward along with all their internet contacts had all their hopes and expectations all on the shoulders of this one young man. He was their last hope, time was running out, they needed Jason to join them now. With him as their assassin these men calling themselves the F.L.O.C.K. (Freedom Liberators Opposed to Criminal Kingpins) could put their plan into action.

With their internet contacts they are sure that they can run a vigilante operation without getting caught. At their ages time is running out, they have put all their aspirations and pipedreams into this one person. He was the one they choose to fill the role of vigilante. They looked at him as if he were a white knight that would ride in and clean up the city and when his task was finished he would then just as quickly disappear.

Now that Jason has objected to this type of martial law, the two elderly men sit silently.

"I'm ready to go to my apartment and bring back some of my personal belongings," states Jason. "After that I'm not sure where I'll go."

"If you must go," answers a somewhat disappointed Edward, "at least wait until three in the morning, it will give you the best chance of not being spotted."

"Also," adds doc, "Only retrieve what you can carry, and be in and out in no more than five minutes, understood."

"I'll be as fast as I can," replies Jason.

Jason goes to his room, his thoughts center around this vigilante that Edward and Doc have talked about. Do these men really have a network of others that believe in their cause. Could all that they have told him be more than just a game played by a group of senior citizens?

The image of this vigilante going out into the night and eliminating the most vile criminal's does sound appealing to him.

However to elude the authorities would be difficult even if this vigilante has others helping him. No, Jason thinks that the idea that Edward and Doc have dreamed up of killing all the bad guys may be sincere and genuine, it nevertheless cannot succeed.

The odds that this vigilante will kill but a few before being killed himself are very high against him. This secret group on the internet that these men talk about, whose identities always remain unknown, will have to recruit another individual to carry out their dirty work.

Lying on his bed, Jason wishes he could help them. They have been very good to him, and he owes them his life. But they want a man with hatred in his heart and ice in his veins.

He has a score to settle with just one man, after that he plans to relocate to a different part of town.

No one else in his family has been a victim, not even any of his friends. So when he kills El Diablo his thirst for revenge will have been quenched. His need to see justice served will also have been satisfied. Looking forward to getting his life back to a normal routine, he drifts off to sleep.

The two elderly men sit quietly in the living room, obviously disappointed in their young recruit.

Sighing heavily, "I was so sure that Jason was our man," says Doc, with a long face.

Edward smiles at his old friend, "You have known me a long time, a very long time."

Looking at his friend Doc replies, "I have known you most of my life, and I trust you with my life."

"So listen to me carefully, this young man is not a lost cause. I feel in my heart that something will happen that will bring him back to us."

With a smirk Doc answers, "You always had this sixth sense, this ability to read a man's soul. That nose of yours has saved our lives on more than one occasion. If you believe that he will change his mind than I believe you."

Now sitting back in his chair, Edward continues, "There is something special about Jason. I sense a quality that I have not felt in anyone in a very long time."

"He is indeed a good candidate for the missions we would send him on," retorts Doc.

"Give him some time, I just know that he will be this cities savior," says Edward.

The two, guided by their uncanny instinct and intuition are confident that Jason will return. They contact several members of their network, informing them to prepare to put their plans in motion.

Waking up, Jason can see that it is nearly three in the morning. He has waited like he had been advised to do. Slipping out of the apartment as quietly as possibly, and from here he carefully makes his way across town.

Fearful of the thugs that roam the streets at this hour, he hides at the first sign of anyone. Hiding behind garbage cans, ducking under porches, he even climbs a tree just to avoid an encounter.

Feeling the need for back up, he calls several friends on his cell phone and asks them to meet him at his apartment. They are curious as to where he has been for the last month and a half. He tells them that he will answer all their questions when he meets them.

Reassured that he will be around trusted friends, Jason feels better about the situation he's in. He contemplates not even going back to Doc and Edwards's apartment. He is grateful for all they have done for him, but their talk of killing people bothers him. The network of others that they say will assist this vigilante makes him think that maybe his two old friends are losing their minds.

They have played too many video games, he believes, and being isolated in that apartment isn't helping them one bit.

Within a half hour he rounds the corner and there a short distance away are his friends cars parked in front of his apartment building. Feeling confident now that he isn't alone he proceeds up the three flights of stairs to his apartment, sure his friends will help him.

Looking down the hall he sees the door to his apartment open, and muffled voices can be heard coming from it. Getting an uneasy feeling he cautiously moves down the hall, sticking close to the wall.

Soon the voices are clearer, and he can hear that someone is crying and begging for help.

The voices sound like those of his friends. His stomach now tightening, he swallows hard as he moves closer to the open door.

Taking a glace into the room he is shocked by what he sees. Two of his friends are lying on the floor, blood all over them. Looking across the room his other two friends are on their knees and men have guns at the back of their heads.

Not wanting to believe what he is seeing, he is momentarily frozen. One of the gunmen asks in a loud voice, "You have one last chance to tell us where Jason is or you'll join your two dead friends over there."

"Please," one of them begs, "we told you we don't know where Jason is, we haven't seen him in weeks, you have to believe me."

Now growing angry as he believes the man is lying, the enraged gunman shoots the man in the back of the head. Like a sack of flour his limp body falls forward and he lays motionless on the floor.

Jason is stunned and horrified that he has just witnessed the execution of his friends. His stomach tightens up and he feels like vomiting.

Realizing how foolish he was not to adhere to his mentors warnings. Doc and Edward were right, that El Diablo had his men watching his apartment this whole time. His friends walked right into a trap, and he didn't even warn them that there could be trouble.

His heart aches, and on the verge of crying as he knows that he is directly responsible for their deaths.

Unfortunately for Jason there is no time to mourn the loss of his friends.

The man with the gun now notices Jason standing in the doorway. "That's him," the man yells.

Raising up his gun and pointing it towards the door he begins firing.

Reacting quickly, Jason covers his face as the bullets splinter the wood frame of the door very close to his head. He turns and runs, fleeing for his life. He makes it to the end of the hallway as bullets whiz past his head and shatter the window several feet away. He descends quickly down the stairs leaping eight to ten steps at a time until reaching the first floor. Despite his heavy breathing he can hear footsteps coming down the stairs behind him. Frightened and paranoid, he runs out the back door and up the alley breathing and sweating profusely.

He trips and falls several times as the image of his friends being shot dead causes him to hyperventilate.

Running scared, his heart is ready to pound out of his chest.

Shaking his head, he still can't believe what he just witnessed. His friends were murdered, they were innocent. "El Diablo had no reason to kill them," he mutters, "no reason at all."

Stumbling around in the darkness he suddenly sees the headlights of a car approaching from the far end of the alley.

Unable to go back the way he came, he feels trapped. He is so shook up that he doesn't know what to do next. Feeling helpless, he stops running and stands mute. Believing that he is about to die just like his friends did, he closes his eyes and says a prayer. As this mysterious car races ever closer to him, he is astonished when out of a side alley it gets hit broadside by another vehicle.

Both cars skid and hit the side of a building. A man quickly gets out of the second car and limping as he nears Jason calls out, "Come with me if you want to live."

Not having a choice Jason follows the man across the alley. Here they go down a short flight of stairs where an open door greets them. The two hurry inside and the door is quickly closed and locked.

Grabbing Jason by the arm the man says, "There's no time to get to know each other, you hurry this way." Through a maze of steps and corridors he is led until finally they are out the front door to a waiting taxi.

Once inside the taxi it races away, swallowing hard Jason is stunned at the speed of which things have just occurred.

Turning around in his seat, "You're safe now, so just relax," states the taxi driver.

Looking out the windows in all directions, a very upset Jason asks, "Just who are you?"

Waving his hand, "No names please, you can just call me Crow."

Thinking for a second, he begins to remember, this is one of the men that Doc and Edward had told him about, he is one of their internet contacts.

Glancing into the rearview mirror, and with a serious look on his face, "I take back what I just said," exclaims Crow, "we are being followed, that El Diablo is a monster, but he is very intelligent."

After rounding several sharp corners, sometimes on two wheels in their attempt at eluding El Diablo's men, Crow comments, "I need to hide you, so hang on."

With that said, the car increases its speed, and Jason is being bounced around like a ping pong ball. Holding onto anything he can grab, he prays that this harrowing race will end soon.

Suddenly the car sketches its tires, and Jason hangs on with all his strength yet he is still thrown hard into the seat. The door quickly opens and reaching in a pair of outstretched hands pulls a terrified Jason out of the car.

Completely baffled by these sudden actions, Jason is tense and beginning to panic. Yet his sixth sense tells him to trust these men that they are acting in his best interest. Without having time to even reach back and close the door the taxi speeds away.

Dumbfounded for a moment, Jason is jerked by the arm, and he stares at his new rescuer. A rather grubby looking man is leading Jason to the backside of a nearby large dumpster. Here the unshaven and wild haired man motions for Jason to get down. Doing as he is told, Jason crouches down, not knowing what to expect next. The man opens a small door at the base of the dumpster and motions for him to get in. Hesitant at first, but believing these people know what they are doing Jason ducks his head down and enters the dark interior of the dumpster. Pushing garbage out of their way, and after securing the door shut, the two men sit in silence. The strange man motions with his finger against his lips, "Not a word," he whispers.

With heart beating, Jason does as he is told, knowing that this man and the taxi driver are helping him avoid El Diablo's men.

The two can now here the sound of a car approaching, and it slows as it passes in front of the dumpster.

Wondering if they had been spotted as they made their way to the backside of the dumpster, Jason's knees begin to shake. Trying to control his Breathing, Jason closes his eyes. When the sound of the car fades away, he whispers a prayer. Too many narrow escapes, and putting his life in the hands of too many strangers has his nerves frayed. He wipes the sweat from his forehead, nervously waiting for the next harrowing adventure. The stench from the garbage is almost overwhelming, and Jason must cover his nose and mouth.

In the dimly lit interior, Jason cannot quit make out the man's face. This grubby man sitting across from him has a rather relaxed posture about him, and he seems not to notice the smell. With his head leaning back, and his eyes looking up, he seems to be listening intensely. Jason would like to ask him a few questions, but decides he better remain quiet.

After waiting an hour, the man signals by nodding his head that he is sure that it is safe to leave now. They cautiously exit the small door at the back of the dumpster, and once outside the man lays down on his stomach. Crawling on his hands and knees, he peeks around the dumpster. Waving his hand the man gets up on his feet and hurries away with Jason close behind.

Jason is led down several unfamiliar alleys, and again he must put his trust in this stranger, hoping his instincts are right.

A little surprised at how fast this man can move, Jason struggles to keep up.

Finally, after traveling several miles, they come to a high fence surrounding a warehouse. Following the fence until the two find a section where the fence has been cut. Pushing aside this piece, they quickly go through the opening. From here they sneak across an open area lit only by the moon. Moving as quickly and as quietly as possible, the two are soon right next to a building. Waiting a moment until he is sure the coast is clear, the stranger leads Jason through a back door and into a little room. Turning on a small light, Jason now can see the man who risked his life to save his.

Short and stocky, and slightly hunched over at the shoulders, the man seems very well built. Standing on a wooden crate, and looking out a small window, the man turns his head and says, "I'll have you back with your two old friends in no time."

Sitting down, his mind racing, Jason runs his fingers through his hair. Confused at everything that has happened in the last few hours, including his narrow escapes, and the strangers that helped him, Jason needs answers.

Looking up with eyes that beg for an honest reply, he asks, "Who are you?"

Pausing for a moment, as he himself studies the young man sitting on the floor, he answers, "Condor."

Tilting his head, Jason stares at the man for a moment. Waiting for perhaps a small laugh, or at least a smile, anything that suggests he is joking. However, the man keeps a stone cold face, his eyes cast upon Jason as if he were a ghost.

Before Jason can ask another question, the two hear a whistle. Condor now jumps from the window and hurries over to the door.

There is a faint knock, "Who's there," asks Condor as he pulls a revolver from his pocket?

"Red dog one," is the reply.

Putting the gun away Condor opens the door and two men step inside.

The three embrace as if they were old friends, and their faces show how happy they are to see each other.

Whispering among themselves, they point over at Jason, who is standing and obviously very nervous.

With a stern voice, Condor turns towards Jason, "It is alright, these men will take you out of this part of town, and you will be safe soon."

With that said Condor exits out the back door, not saying a word.

Nodding his head, giving a half smile, Jason has no alternative but to trust in these new strangers. There are no handshakes, and with an inquisitive look on their faces these two new men are as stern faced as Condor. One of them turns around and after sticking his head out the door he seems confident that it is safe. Motioning with a sharp jerk of his hand for Jason to follow them they step out the door, the three now hurry across the open area that Jason and condor had crossed to get here. After slipping back through the hole in the fence, here a car is waiting. Once inside they tell Jason, "lie down and do not show yourself until we say it is safe, understood!"

Swallowing hard, and sweating profusely, Jason shakes his head. With his head down he has no clue to where these men are taking him. Do they work for El Diablo, and is he once again a prisoner of that monster? Thinking that maybe he should try and escape, after all, he doesn't know these men. How can he trust them with his life, after all that he has been through, how can he trust anyone ever again.

Before Jason can act on his feelings, the car stops abruptly causing him to tighten up. Curled up like a frightened child Jason lays motionless, daring not to move, hoping that the end of this incredible journey is nearly over.

The car door opens quickly and looking up from his hiding place, Jason wonders what is going to happen now.

In a rough voice, "It is safe for you to come out now," the man says while motioning with his hand as he turns his head in all directions.

Gingerly stepping out of the car, Jason watches these two men very closely, waiting for any sudden movement that will signal that they are going to kill him.

"If you go in here," one of them says while pointing at a door, "Your two old friends are waiting for you."

Moving cautiously and slowly opening the door, a look inside reveals a flight of stairs. Turning his head towards the two strangers, they nod their heads and say, "Go ahead, you really are safe now."

A sense of relief comes over Jason. "Thank you, whoever you are."

The two men don't reply, and turning around they quickly get into their car and race away.

Once inside Jason must stop, so many things have happened so quickly that it all seems a blur. From the narrow escapes, to the strangers that risked their lives for him, he is amazed that he is still alive.

Climbing up the stairs, Jason is beginning to recognize where he's at.

Yes, he has seen this building before, and once on the third floor he hurries to a familiar door.

Opening it and stepping inside, he is greeted by Edward and Doc.

"I hope your adventure wasn't too nerve racking," says a chuckling Edward.

Still amazed at his narrow escapes, Jason replies, "If you have a beer I could use one right now."

Grabbing their young apprentice by the shoulders both men lead him into the kitchen.

Sitting at the table, they can see how shook up this young man is. With Jason having never been in trouble with the law or threatened by anyone before, the last few hours have taken there toll on him.

Wiping the sweat from his face, a haggard and confused Jason looks exhausted.

After calming down he asks, "You two know exactly what I just went through don't you?"

With their usual relaxed and laid back attitude, "Yes, we know everything that happened tonight."

"But, how?" A still confused Jason asks. "These things happened so fast."

With a smile, Edward answers, "Our contacts on the internet kept us constantly informed."

"He's right," adds Doc. "We have a great many eyes on this city. People help us that you wouldn't even begin to suspect. You were watched from the minute you left here until the moment you returned."

Jason is amazed, beginning to believe that maybe these two are part of a bigger network. This network is much more than a bunch of old men playing war games, they are sophisticated and clever. The men that helped him knew that what they were doing was very dangerous, but they were well trained and executed his escape perfectly.

Putting his hand on Jason's shoulder, Doc says, "We know about what happened to your friends and we are deeply sorry for you."

Swallowing hard Jason sits with his hands at his side. Looking up his face pale and his eyes sad he says, "My friends are dead because of me."

"Do not blame yourself," insists Edward. "Only one person is responsible for their murder and that is El Diablo."

"I should never have called them," an emotional Jason replies. "Now what am 'I suppose to do?"

His two mentors sit directly across from him. They stare intensely at their young savior.

They give him a moment to come to the conclusion himself, without being told.

"You can join us in our fight to clean up this city," Doc tells him in a stern voice.

Speaking up, Edward says, "You will get your revenge someday, and we will help you get El Diablo. But you must have patience, as El Diablo is very cunning and crafty. Finding him will be difficult, killing him will be even tougher. Work with us, and as a team we can do great things."

Beginning to realize that El Diablo and his men will stop at nothing to kill him, Jason's attitude is changing.

No longer passive about the crime on the streets, his inner feelings and state of mind grow angry and wrathful.

He is sick to his stomach over the very thought that he is responsible for the deaths of his four friends. If he is ever going to get the guilt and burden out of his head, he must avenge their deaths. He must punish all that break the law, he must execute those that he and the others deem are no longer fit to walk this earth again.

Thinking about what just went through his head, this taking the law into his own hands now seems just and proper. The time has come, the people of this city needs a white knight. Believing that the means justifies the end, his conscious tells him it is morally right and ethically acceptable. No longer existing as a timid member of society, Jason has quickly become bitter and hateful.

The need to strike back at the gangs that control the streets is his first priority. In time his score with El Diablo will be settled.

Gritting his teeth, and with an angry tone, "I'm in," he tells his two elderly mentors.

Happy that they finally have the man that will be the cities salvation, the two old men can barely contain themselves. They embrace Jason as if he were a soldier returning home from the war.

"We can waste no more time," Doc tells him. "You have much to learn."

Nodding in agreement, Edward leads Jason over to the computer.

Now confiding in their young friend, the two old men begin to reveal some carefully guarded secrets.

"There is a network of others, just like us," states Edward as he points to different areas on the map. "We stay in constant contact with each other. Information is passed around this network, but until now we could do very little with it. We lacked someone that could use this information. We knew when and where top drug lords would be meeting, but we had no one that could carry out a hit on them.

Calling the police about such a meeting resulted in nothing being done. The police are being paid to ignore such tips from the general public.

We grew more frustrated every day, and even thought about one of us going out at trying to get close enough to one of these drug lords and kill him. We knew it would be suicide, but at our age, time is running out. We were just about to go out on just that type of mission when you stumbled into our lives."

Jason sits up in his chair, his eyes and ears focused on what he is about to be told.

"We only communicate over the internet," continues Edward, "and we have never seen these other people, or do we know their names. We all have code words that identify each of us, the group consists of five main leaders, and under them are another thirty or so members."

Intrigued, Jason is very anxious to learn more about this secret group, and what their mission is.

"We use names of birds to conceal our true identities," says Doc as he joins them, "and you will soon learn how to contact them."

With his feet tapping the floor, Jason shakes his head, "Please tell me more," he almost begs his two elderly friends.

Giving him a quick smile, Edward says, "The group is called the F.L.O.C.K. Which stands for, (Freedom Liberators Opposed to Criminal Kingpins.)

With a half-smile, "Makes sense since all its members are code named after birds."

"We thought so," adds Doc as he gives a smile back.

"What we are about to divulge to you must be carefully guarded," declares Edward. "Our lives and the lives of so many others depend on secrecy."

"I understand the reason code names are used, and I promise to die before ever revealing this information to anyone."

Confident that Jason will not betray the F.L.O.C.K., Edward continues, "A man code named Sparrow is the one that works inside the court house, he is our eyes and ears there. Another code named Eagle works at the newspaper, he is usually the first to hear of any important news and he has many contacts out on the street. A very smart contact is code named Hawk, he is a professor, you could say he is the brains of the group. Crow drives a taxi, he tells us who is coming and going. Condor is our eyes on the street, he works undercover."

With a broad smile, Jason says, "I have met Condor and Crow, and if not for them I would probably be dead now."

"Yes," replies Edward, "our contacts kept us informed about everything that happened to you."

"This group you call the F.L.O.C.K. seems very organized," asks Jason.

"We have been practicing our make believe game for a very long time," adds Doc. "We are very good at what we do."

"You won't get any arguments from me," replies Jason as more information than he can comprehend flashes across the computer screen.

As the two continue to show their young apprentice more secret and highly guarded information, Jason cracks a smile, "I have to ask, what are the code names that you two go by?"

Giving his young friend a slight steer, Doc replies, "I'm called Parrot, and Edwards is called Starling."

Finding humor in this, "If I join your group, do I get a nickname also?"

"No," answers Edward in a stern voice, "this is no game. You will learn that lives are on the line almost every day. We are organized, but until now we have had no one to carry out our mission. All we do is simulate on the computer what he would like to do in real life. We formed this alliance years ago to vent our frustration on the declining social situation. Crime is on the rise along with corruption, the people have lost faith in the justice system.

We act out simulated attacks on these drug gangs that roam our cities, it is a kind of video game. Several years ago the other five leaders have discussed with us that someone needs to take the law into their own hands. We have made up a fictitious person who in our game goes out and avenges those that have been wronged.

Each leader contributes information that he has expertise in and feeds this information to our hero. It's just a virtual reality simulation type of entertainment; that is until recently."

"So what changed that caused you and the others to take this computer game and turn it into real life," asks Jason.

Taking a deep breath, Edward answers, "The streets have been getting more violent, the crimes more gruesome. We were about to pick one of us to be this hero, even though it would be suicide, it had to be done. Each of us is prepared to go down in a blaze of glory if need be, it is a more honorable way of dying than sitting around in a nursing home waiting for the end.

However, we are all too old to act on our feelings. But you Jason, you may be the one person we have been waiting on. We understand your need to seek revenge against El Diablo, and this we will help you with, in exchange that you also help us."

With the rage building up inside of him, Jason understands the need for the good people of this city to take back their streets. The lawless and anarchic behavior that rules so many lives must end. Going against his beliefs that the police and justice system will protect the citizens, his soft demeanor is changing.

Gritting his teeth, "I'm in," he tells his two elderly mentors.

As they sit in front of the computer, Edwards begins to reveal information that will be invaluable in the future. Noting places where safe houses are located and areas where weapons are stored.

They point out locations where he can get cash if the need arises

They point out a used car dealer that has made one of his vehicles available to them, whenever they need it.

"Sitting at the back of the car lot you will find a blue caviler," adds Doc, "a large sign on it reads scrape, Not TO BE Sold. The keys are located several inches up the tail pipe, and it will always have a full tank of gas."

Intrigued by the scope and complexity of this whole operation, Jason can only shake his head. These two elderly gentlemen have thoroughly thought out every detail. All night long the elders pass on information to their young apprentice.

"Knowing what you have gone through," states Doc, "we feel you can be trusted."

Late into the night Jason goes over the information several times, trying to remember names and places.

After Doc and Edward have gone to bed Jason now sits alone, he begins to envision these acts of vigilantism that he is about to commit. He will be breaking the law by serving out justice as he and the others see fit. Reaching deep into his subconscious, he looks for a sign that will tell him he is doing the right thing. To eliminate the drug gangs from the streets by whatever means possible, this he believes must be done. The end result will justify the means at what he must do to accomplish this task.

Making himself a promise that once the city is cleaned up and people can once again walk about without fear, that he will stop being a vigilante. He must let the police do their job, he prays that all the lives he will take will not haunt him the rest of his life.

Having walked into the room without making a sound Doc is able to stand only inches away from Jason without him knowing it.

Tapping him on the shoulder a startled Jason jumps away and falls to the floor. Looking up wide eyed he says, "How the hell were you able to sneak up on me without me hearing you?"

Smiling, Doc answers, "That trick and many more you will need to learn if you are to be successful."

Getting back into his chair, a little shook up Jason waits for this new knowledge.

Doc says, "We want you to be fully prepared to take on this task, there are things you must learn."

Jason has by now put his trust and faith in these two men, and if they believe that he needs more guidance before putting their plan into action, than that is what he will do.

"There is a man that will teach you valuable lessons, you must go to him."

"I will go where ever you tell me to go."

"Go across town to this address," Doc says handing him a piece of paper, "don't open it until you have left this part of town."

Jason accepts these orders as if they have been given to him by an army general.

Folding the paper several times he stuffs it into his pocket, as a nervous sensation comes over him.

"Once you reach the address you will go inside and ask for Falcon," continues Doc, "and that you were sent by Parrot and Starling."

Looking into Jason's eyes, Doc says, "I know you have always been a law abiding citizen, but things happen in a person's life that changes them. You must believe down in your soul that the mission you are about to embark on is right and it is necessary."

Biting his lip, Jason smiles, "I believe that the time has come to take the law into our own hands. I believe more now than ever that we are doing the right thing, and I will avenge those that have suffered for so long."

Patting the young man on the shoulder, Doc says, "You will need this."

Pulling out a hand gun, Jason recognizes it as Doc's favorite. This is the gun that the old man has always carried with him. It is the one in all the stories he told Jason, it is Doc's personal favorite.

Speechless at receiving such a personal keepsake, Jason bows his head. Overcome by this kind act, he is humbled like never before in his life.

The old man smiles, "I hope it brings you as much good luck as it did for me."

Not wanting to get emotional, Jason replies, "I will always keep a tight grip on it, and it will never leave my side."

Seeing the sun coming up, "There is no time to waste," Doc tells him. "Your mission begins now, good luck."

After the two shake hands the young apprentice exits the building and heads east along the main road. Pulling his hat down partially concealing his face and walking hunched over he moves swiftly across town.

When he has traveled several blocks, here he stops and pulls out the paper, and after memorizing the address he strikes a match to it. As he was instructed to do, as no trace of their activities can ever fall into the wrong hands. The direct route to the address is shorter but it will take him through a very rough neighborhood. Having heard the stories about how people walk into this neighborhood but they never walk out causes him to hesitate. The violence on these streets is the worst in the entire city. Murders happen on a daily basis here, and the police rarely patrol this section of the city as they too fear the violence.

Being daytime, he hopes it will be just a little safer that if it were at night, and Jason decides to chance it. He is armed, so he can defend himself if necessary.

He exits the alley and begins walking down the street, he tries his best not to draw attention to himself. No matter what someone says or does he knows he must keep on walking. He has seen and heard too many stories where a nod of the head or the uttering of a word can set these people into a violent rage.

Moving among the low life's that call this place home makes his skin crawl. The smell of marijuana is thick in the air, the people smoke it right out in the open.

Taking a glance in all directions there is not one police car in sight. What goes on in these inner city drug havens stays here. The people have their own rules, they decide what is right and what is wrong not the police.

Catching his attention, he hears a loud scream. It sounds like a woman's voice. Stopping to look for the source, a moment passes and all is quiet. Thinking that it was probably just a domestic argument, he continues down the street. Again these screams are heard as they echo up and down the street, but no one pays any attention to them.

The few people that are on the street don't even raise up their heads. They have totally ignored the screams. Wanting to see if he could help, he quickly remembers that he was firmly told by Edward and Doc not to interfere and do not stop to help anyone, no matter what.

He feels wrong for not stopping, but he knows he has a more important mission to carry out.

As he rounds a corner a man bumps into him, but Jason just shrugs his shoulders and keeps walking.

From behind a loud voice calls out, "Hey you!"

Still hunched over, Jason ignores the man and keeps walking.

He soon hears the sound of boots approaching him from behind, and reaching into his pocket he grabs his gun tightly.

"You there, what are you doing on our turf?"

Cursing under his breath, he realizes that these people don't recognize him as a local. Any outsiders are not welcome here, and many of them end up dead.

By now several other men have stepped out and onto the sidewalk and have blocked his path, and he can see they carry baseball bats and one has a tire iron.

Not looking for a shootout, he thinks fast, "Hey bro I came looking for some weed."

Laughter erupts, and after a moment the man says, "You are one lucking son of a bitch, we thought you were from another gang and we were about to dust you off."

Trying his best to smile, Jason says as he waves his hands back and forth, "No man, I just came looking for weed that's all, just want to get high."

"You came to the right place my man," and opening up his jacket the man pulls out several bags of marijuana.

"Just one bag for now," states Jason, "I'll be back later for more."

"This stuff ain't free my man, I need to see a 20 spot, you dig?"

"That's cool," a nervous Jason replies. "I got you covered."

Not thinking he pulls out his wallet, and this quickly gets their attention, and he knows he should not have showed them the money he has. The group of men begins to form a tight circle around him and one says, "How bout giving us some of that money?"

Outnumbered, Jason must think fast or else he may not make it out of this place alive. Knowing he must show them that he is not weak, that he is willing to fight, hoping that being tough will make them back off.

Jumping up and down, "Ain't nobody going to get my money. I'll bust them upside the head real good. If that don't work I'll rip their ears right off their heads."

To his disappointment, this doesn't cause the men to back away, instead it has caused them to become angry.

One of them points his fingers, "So you want to come into our hood and be a tuff guy," as he gets right up into Jason's face.

Swallowing hard, Jason stands stiff, his heart beating faster as the situation begins to look grim.

Waving his hands and taking several steps back, "I just came to buy some weed, that's all, no trouble."

Several of the men back away and talk quietly among themselves. Jason knows that they are not going to let him just walk away, not after they saw his money. Looking around, he counts twelve men, his gun holds nine rounds. He begins to ponder his odds of getting out of this mess. Will they kill him or just pummel him with the baseball bats?

This decision will never be known, because at that moment a car races by and its occupants spray bullets everywhere. Windows shatter in the shop directly behind Jason and these men sending glass fragments in all directions. The men scatter in all directions, some jump though open windows while others look for any type of cover they can find.

Reacting quickly Jason darts down the street, hunched over covering his head, he counts his blessing that he miraculously avoided being hit. Running scared until the pain in his side causes him to slow down. He wipes the sweat from his forehead, cursing at such a dumb mistake: He has learned a good lessen, that the shortest route isn't always the best route. Patience is something he never had much of, but he knows that acting to hastily can get you killed.

More cautious than before, he continues his trek through this dangerous jungle.

The homeless along with the drug users congregate at certain intersections, they wait here for their daily poison that they hope will make them forget the misery that surrounds them. These individuals have such a hopeless look in their eyes, as if the world is soon coming to an end. In most respects they are right, the way they live is horrendous. Their basic needs are neglected, unshaven and dirty and they wear rags for clothes. All they care about are the drugs that push them one step closer to death.

The closer Jason gets to the river the worse the living conditions get. These people that have withdrawn from society live in makeshift tents along the river. Needing to stop and take this all in, Jason had no idea that people lived this way. How could he have never noticed their plight, their subhuman way of life? He is ashamed at himself for not knowing, he has no excuses.

These desperate people bath and even drink the river water, which by its color and odor must be very polluted.

Jason now more than ever must change this city, to rid it of all its corruption and evil. Vowing to help these outcasts as much as possible, the scene is burned into his psyche.

With quickness in his steps he leaves behind this nightmare, and heads across a bridge. Once on the other side, he realizes he's in the section of the city called China Town.

With its pointed roofs and its many small shops that line the streets, it is a scene right from the movies. At least here the people seem friendly, and they smile as he walks by their tables adorned with fruit and vegetables. The men and women that make their living here hold up fresh cuts of meat or flowers hoping to entice him into buying them.

Needing neither, he smiles and moves farther into this section of the city that he has never been to. Again he asks himself why he never ventured here, what was his reason for not exploring this unique environment with its inhabitants that seem so far from his own world.

After searching down several streets, he finds what he came looking for. The address has led him to a Chinese bakery, the sign above the door reads, "Fu Wang's Bakery."

Going inside he can see only one other customer, it is an elderly lady. The old man behind the counter with a big smile asks in rough English, "Can I help you young man?"

Hesitant at first, still a little unsure about this sneaking around, he clears his throat and asks, "Just a couple of donuts if you don't mind?"

As the old man begins filling a sack with the donuts Jason looks around, he can see nothing that would indicate that someone here works for the F.L.O.C.K. It is just a simple bakery run by an old man, who by his estimate must be close to 80 years old. This elderly gentleman wears thick glasses and walks with a cane and it appears his left hand is paralyzed.

Thinking that perhaps he has the wrong address, that there must be another bakery close by with the man who he is seeking that will continue his training. The old man holds up the bag of donuts, still with a big smile.

"Do you need anything else," he asks?

Licking his lips, Jason isn't sure how to choose his words without giving away too much about his intentions.

Deciding to be straight forward, "I'm looking for Falcon, Parrot and Starling sent me."

The smile instantly leaves the old man's face, and he gives Jason a long stare.

Standing stiff, Jason isn't sure what to do next. It seems everything has gotten quiet, the noise that was radiating from outside has stopped. Strangely he does not hear the cars going by just outside, not even the wind that had been blowing the flags at full staff.

Concentrating so hard on the response he is expecting, Jason has mentally blocked out everything around him. His muscles tense up, and the loud breathing out his nose is obvious to those standing nearby.

"You were sent by these men?"

"Yes," he replies, "Do you know this person by the name of Falcon?"

Watching Jason closely the old man steps from around the counter and seems to be sizing him up.

"You are the one, the chosen one, the one that Parrot and Starling has sent here to be trained and tested?"

Standing stiff, his hands in his pockets, "Yes and can you lead me to Falcon?"

Waving his hand and removing his apron, the old man signals for Jason to follow him. The two go through the kitchen, and down a narrow hallway. The old man says something to those standing around and they quickly get out of the way. Following close behind, Jason grows more nervous by the second. He wonders if what he has agreed to with Doc and Edward could be way over his head. Is he the right man for the job, these and other thoughts race through his mind.

Going into the last room on the right, and once inside the elderly Chinese gentleman quickly closes and then locks the door. Going across the room he sits behind a large wooden table and on it are intricate carvings, they depict samurai soldiers fighting. Now sitting in a chair adorned with small stones of various colors the old man motions with his hand for Jason to sit down.

"How long have you known the two men that sent you here," he asks?

"Not long," he replies, as he further inspects the small room.

Staring intensely at Jason, he next asks, "You are much too young, why would Parrot and Starling trust you enough to send you here?"

Feeling intimidated by this man, Jason hesitates before replying, "I may be young, but I have been through a great deal of misery. Those two rescued me and have protected me. I owe them a great deal. They have confided in me things that very few others know. I trust them with my life, and I'm sure they feel the same towards me."

Sitting quietly, the old man seems to go into deep thought, while his eyes are closed and he remains perfectly still.

Swallowing hard, Jason begins tapping his feet on the floor, and this causes the old man to open his eyes.

"You have much worry and anxiety," states the elderly Chinese man.

"I don't like strange surroundings," replies Jason as he nervously rubs his arms.

"If you are to succeed at the task ahead of you, then all surroundings must not bother you.

You must focus on what has to be done at that moment and not be concerned with where you are at."

"This is all new to me," he answers. "I have learned a lot from my two mentors."

Sitting back with a big grin on his face, the old man utters, "Oh, you will learn a great deal more here, that is if you can take the training."

Jason is confused, Doc and Edward did not mention anything about training. Apprehensive about this, but he is still willing to go along with it if it will help him with what lies ahead in his quest to rid the city of its crime. If doc and Edward feel that he needs this training than that is what he will do.

Now standing up, "I 'am ready for this training that you have planned, let's get started."

"You are young and over eager. You have many flaws and weaknesses that I can see already."

Now standing and with his shoulders back and his chin sticking out, a defiant Jason state, "I'm tougher than you think."

Nodding his head and with a devious grin, "We will see, we will see."

Showing a lack of discipline and self-control, Jason demands, "Just show me this man named Falcon. I want to learn from him."

Sitting motionless the old man studies Jason for a moment, pulling out his cell phone he talks briefly, as it seems he is a man of few words.

"You will put on this blindfold," he says handing Jason one. "Do not ask where you will be taken, you must trust me."

Biting his lip, this whole situation gives him the creeps. Should he refuse and stop this game, and walk out as quickly as possible. Thinking of how Doc and Edward strongly urged him to seek out Falcon and learn from him. They would not send him into a dangerous situation. Despite his gut feelings, Jason nods his head. He will do as he is told and hope that this is over quickly.

Once the blindfold is on Jason is lead down a flight of stairs, the creaking sounds lets him know that these are old steps. The cool musty odor in the air is an indication that he is underground.

The surface under his feet has suddenly changed from wood to dirt. A hand is placed on his head, warning him to duck.

Bent over as the tunnel is not high enough to stand upright, he and the old man travel this way for nearly five minutes. A voice other than the old man calls out, "You can stand up now."

Finally he can stand straight again, his back was beginning to get sore.

The blind fold is removed, and his eyes need a moment to adjust to the light.

Looking around, the scenery is not at all what he expected to see.

It appears he's in a huge cavern that is big enough to hold a jumbo jet. The ceiling rises up nearly 100 feet. Scattered around are small wooden structures, many no bigger than a 10 foot by 10 foot shed.

In the middle stands a tall wooden tower that nearly reaches to the ceiling.

Various colored Lights of different sizes are strung along the walls providing light.

A sound from behind causes Jason to turn around and he can see a large set of doors is being closed. Two men struggle to move the massive twin doors. These are the ones he came through and looking around it appears it is the only way out.

Once closed, a loud sound can be heard indicating that very strong latches are securing the doors shut from the other side.

Glancing back over his shoulder he can see the old man staring at him. His eyes seem to penetrate into his soul.

Impatient, Jason demands, "When do I meet this Falcon character?"

"I do not see anyone here that fits the description given to me by Sparrow and Starling. They said he was fearless, strong, smart and cunning, and that I should never underestimate his wisdom."

The old man is still looking intensely at Jason, and he has a look of disappointment on his face.

The stillness is too much, he can't take the waiting and with his hands raised into the air, Jason calls out, "Falcon, if you are here, please show yourself."

The huge arena remains very quiet, and those that are standing nearby bow their heads.

Showing his immaturity and over enthusiasm Jason again calls out, "Do not be afraid of me."

At this time the old man steps in front of Jason and says, "I'm Falcon, and you are not worthy of this test."

Shocked by this, Jason looks closely at the old man, surprised that Doc and Edward would have such an old person train him. This didn't make any sense, there has to be a mistake.

"Let me get this straight," an arrogant Jason declares, "I 'am to be trained in the martial arts and other important things by a senior citizen?"

Not happy with his attitude, Falcon replies, "There is much you need to learn, first being, never judge anyone by their appearance. Just because a man may look weak or frail, does not mean it is so. Take the scorpion, it is small and does not move very fast, but if not shown proper respect it has the power to easily kill a man."

"Okay," answers Jason, "You have great knowledge, I want to learn from you then."

Pacing the area just in front of Jason, Falcon stares at the ground, his hands pressed together. Looking at his young student he says, "Your lessons will begin, but I have my doubts that you will succeed, you show a lack of discipline, self-control and most of all a lack of respect."

With an upturned lip, Jason shows his dislike for these words.

Trying his best not to show how unnerved he is, Jason calmly says, "So what is the first lesson?"

"Don't be so eager to rush into a situation before first examining it thoroughly is asking for trouble," replies Falcon.

"But I want to learn as much as possible," answers Jason as he steps about.

"Great knowledge cannot be rushed, it must be absorbed into your soul."

The two now walk over to one of these small structures, and Falcon motions for Jason to look inside.

Tentatively poking his head through a small window, he quickly jumps back.

His face pale white as he points with a shaking finger and udders, "There are hundreds of snakes in there."

Without changing his facial expressions, Falcon says, "Your first test is about to begin."

He takes Jason to a second structure, looking inside this one Jason is astonished to see jewelry and gold coins. His eyes get big, and a smile crosses his face.

"There is a small fortune in there," says Falcon.

"Who does it belong to," asks Jason.

"It belongs to you, if you decide that wealth is greater than life."

The pile of valuables before his eyes he knows is more than a person can spend in a lifetime.

"Your first lesson is very simple, pick up as much of this wealth as you can carry and it is yours."

Scratching his head a little cautious by this offer, "You say all I have to do is just pick it up and walk out and its mine?"

"Yes," replies Falcon. "No one will stop you and once outside you can spend it anyway you please."

Jason is thinking that this is too good to be true. What is the catch he wonders?

Standing to the side, Falcon now motions for Jason to go inside. Still amazed at what he is looking at, Jason puts the gold coins and jewelry into a leather backpack. Lifting it up to his shoulders he steps back out of the small structure and stands facing Falcon. The weight of the backpack causes Jason to stumble. Not being a man with an athletic build, he strains to stand upright.

Hoping his good luck doesn't run out, all he can think is that these men will at some time in the future ask him to assassinate someone. These gold coins and jewelry is a down payment. This he can understand, after all, he will be committing murder, so it does have a price.

With his hand up, "Just one catch," says Falcon. "You must not set the backpack down until you have left this place. If you should set it down, it no longer belongs to you, do you understand?"

Jason is ecstatic that he is rich beyond his dreams. Why on earth would he set this wealth down.

Smiling, "I understand," he replies as he walks towards the doors. Feeling like he has just won the lottery. "This," he whispers to himself, "Will pay for all the pain and suffering that I have gone through."

Waiting for the huge doors to open, Jason gets an odd feeling as the cavern gets eerily quiet.

Looking back over his shoulder he sees Falcon clap his hands together loudly.

He now watches as a young oriental girl is brought out from another of the small shelters. She appears to be in her late teens, with long black hair and wearing a brightly colored robe. Her hands are tied together, and she seems to be crying.

Two men escort her up the platform, and once at the top she is positioned out onto a small plank. With her head bowed, and knees shaking she stares at the ground that is nearly 75 feet away.

Puzzled by this, Jason gives a questioning look at Falcon.

Not returning his look, Falcon nods his head as a wagon is next wheeled out and it stops directly under the girl.

Looking closer, Jason is shocked that it has dozens of foot long razor sharp spikes sticking up.

Now he really has second thoughts about this, no way is he going to be witness to some sick human sacrifice.

"You have got to be kidding me," demands Jason, as he now begins walking towards Falcon.

With stone cold eyes, Falcon replies, "Her life is in your hands. She will either live or die, depending on your decisions."

"I have nothing to do with this, what you are doing is crazy."

"Very well young man, if you do not have the bravery to free the girl then she will die."

Knowing that he is trapped inside this cavern, Jason sees no way out but to play their game.

"Okay," he barks, not happy with this scene, "just what do I have to do to save the girl?"

"A lock is around the chains that bind her," replies Falcon. "You must remove the lock before the platform burns down and the girl will be saved."

Giving it a quick look, "But the platform is not on fire?"

Like a streak of lighting a flaming arrow hits the base of the structure which quickly begins to burn.

Frantic at this scene, Jason paces back and forth. Not believing that Falcon has actually set this platform on fire.

Obviously upset by what he is witnessing, "You have to get the girl down," insists Jason.

Waving his finger back and forth, Falcon answers, "No, you have a decision to make."

About to run towards the platform, Jason hesitates. Looking back he yells, "Where in the key to unlock the girl?"

With a half grin, Falcon says, "In the structure to my right." He points at the structure that Jason remembers seeing the snakes in.

Standing mute, Jason is dumbfounder by this turn of events.

"On the far wall you will find a key. This key will free the girl."

As Jason moves towards the snake invested shelter, the heavy backpack slows him down. Determined not to give up his new found wealth, he grits his teeth and marches straight for the shelter.

Peering in, again his stomach turns at the sight of so many snakes.

"Are they poisonous? He asks as his hands grip each other tightly.

"That is a question that only the bravest man can answer," replies Falcon, now standing a short distance away.

Angry at this ridiculous situation, Jason nonetheless must control his fear of snakes. Looking inside the small room, he sees a rope running several feet above the snakes and it leads to the far wall. On the wall he can see a key setting on a narrow ledge.

Being very agile, crossing the rope will not be difficult. The problem is he cannot do this while carrying the heavy backpack.

Looking at the girl who is now screaming for help, he knows he cannot let her die. His moral conscious will not let him stand ideally by while an innocent person faces death.

Having been told that once he sets the backpack down, that the coins and jewelry will no longer be his, he curses out loud, "You bastard, you tricked me!"

"No one has tricked you," replies Falcon. "I have simply given you a choice, the wealth or the girl's life."

Looking at the young girl, he sees the fear on her face and the panic in her eyes. The fire has begun to reach the halfway point on the platform.

Puckering his lips he gives Falcon a cold stare.

Throwing the backpack down he quickly grips the rope and pulling himself across as fast as possible to the far wall he grabs the keys. Placing them tightly in his mouth, he turns around and begins pulling himself across when the rope suddenly sages very low. Now only inches from the slithering snakes, he closes his eyes for a second. Concentrating on controlling his fears, he takes a deep breath, determined not to let this girl burn to death, he grips the rope tightly. With renewed vigor and like a man on a mission he begins pulling himself along the rope and is soon across the room. Taking the key from his mouth he once again gives Falcon a hard stare as he runs past him. Quickly running towards the platform he can't believe that Falcon is willing to let this girl die just to prove a point.

While looking up at the platform he nearly bumps into a man that steps out and with both hands up tries to stop him, but Jason angrily pushes him to the side.

He can now hear Falcon calling to him, but he cannot understand his words.

With the flames nearly as tall as he is, Jason races up the steps with his arms covering his face.

Believing that every second could mean life or death for this young girl, he endures the burns and with his clothing smoking he is stunned that when finally reaching the top of the platform that the girl is gone. Looking down he is stunned as he can see her standing beside Falcon.

"You set me up," yells Jason. Now franticly looking around for a way off this platform, he can see to his horror that the steps behind him have given way and have collapsed to the ground.

So he knows now that this is a test of his character, his integrity and most important his moral beliefs.

This was all just an elaborate game, an assessment of who he is. This ordeal was to show if he has what it takes to be a member of this secret society. Jason is on probation it seems and before Edward and Doc can reveal more about their organization, he will be tested.

Scanning straight ahead he sees a ladder extend out, for whatever reason this ladder is too short and it does not reach the edge of the top of the burning platform.

A man at the other end waves for Jason to climb onto the ladder. With the distance nearly eight feet to the ladder Jason backs up just as the flames begin to surround him. Urged on by the intense heat he runs and leaps for the ladder, his hands just catching the last rung. His feet swing back and forth but he does not let go. Pulling himself up he crawls across the ladder until he is safe.

Making his way down to the ground there is obvious anger on his face. "How dare these people pull a stunt like this," he mumbles.

He'll show this Falcon character that no one plays games with him.

Walking right up to Falcon, Jason says, "I should knock you on your ass."

"That would not be wise young man," replies the wily old man.

With a look of disbelief, Jason says, "Oh, I suppose you think you could stop me, uh?"

With a smile, Falcon says, "You have no training in the martial arts, you are not wise and your ego is too big."

Feeling insulted by these words and still upset at what was done to him earlier, Jason lunges at Falcon.

The old man leans to the side and quick as lighting delivers a punch to Jason's stomach.

Hunched over and surprised at the quickness of someone so old, Jason grits his teeth and comes forward again.

This time Falcon jumps into the air, his right foot striking Jason on the side of his head.

Now lying flat on his back, Jason seems stunned at being knocked around by this senior citizen.

Up on his feet again, determined not to be humiliated, he charges straight ahead like a wild man.

As before, Falcon easily dodges his opponent. He grabs Jason by the arm and twisting it he forces the young man down on one knee.

Cursing in pain, Jason tries to break free. Using all his strength, he is unable to break Falcon's grip.

"Have you had enough?"

"You will never force me to surrender."

"Very well young man," states Falcon. With that said he releases his grip and backs away.

Jason gets up holding his arm. Breathing heavy, and sweating the anger is on his face, he spits on the ground, he can see a small amount of blood, this infuriates him even more.

"I will wear you down old man," calls out Jason.

Falcon remains calm, his expression is peaceful.

Circling around, Jason looks for a weakness that he can exploit.

Falcon does not move, and as Jason gets behind him he sees his opportunity.

Rushing head first like a linebacker about to sack the quarter back Jason reaches out with both arms.

Sensing his opponent, Falcon is well versed in all types of self-defense. Unknown to Jason, Falcon holds several black belts in five different martial arts.

As Jason is about to pounce, Falcon leans forward. Catching a surprised Jason, who is thrown several feet through the air before landing hard on his back.

Starring straight up, he is dazed. Having the wind knocked out of him, he struggles to his feet.

Like a drunken man he waves his hands telling Falcon, "Come on, show me what you got."

Those standing around begin to laugh at his foolishness.

With a wave of his hand, Falcon silences the Crowd.

"You are untrained, undisciplined, and badly out of shape," comments Falcon. "You are a defeated man."

Unable to breathe through his nose, which by this time has swollen up, Jason staggers forward, determined to prove to Falcon and those standing around that he is a fighter.

Like a man with no common sense, young Jason Karsten feels he must prove his worth. Doubling his efforts, he manages to put Falcon in a bear hug.

Smiling Jason says out loud, "Now I have you old man. Let's see you break free?"

Closing his eyes Falcon seems to meditate for a moment.

"I knew you couldn't break free once I got my arms around you," says an over confident Jason.

As Jason gloats about his success he can feel the old man tense up. Expecting him to try and break his grip, Jason clamps down harder.

In the blink of an eye, Falcon jerks his head back catching Jason square on the chin. The blow sends him reeling backwards and onto the ground. His vision cloudy and head spinning it takes him a minute to remember where he's at. Unwilling to give up, he rolls to his knees, next he struggles to regain his footing. Stumbling around, Jason is bleeding from the mouth.

"I do not want to hurt you young man," states Falcon.

"As long as I'm still breathing," says Jason as he needs several seconds to catch his breath. "I will keep fighting, the question is, have you had enough?"

Shaking his head, Falcon must teach Jason the lessons he will need to survive if he is the one that will be taking out the criminals in this city.

So the battle continues, Jason is hammered and thrown about like a rag doll. Unable to admit that someone so old can defeat him, his pride now bruised, Jason continues the pointless and in vain fight.

Falcon admires his opponent for his constancy, his drive never to give up. He can see why Parrot and Starling had chosen this young man. There is a drive and determination in him that will serve him well in the future.

He can see that Jason is hurting, yet he refuses to quit.

Finally unable to stand, Jason concedes defeat. "You have made a fool of me," he says. "I should not have taken your age as a sign of a weak person, I apologize."

Helping the young man up, Falcon comments, "You fought valiantly, you have nothing to apologize for. A lesser man would have given up long ago, but not you. You would not admit defeat until you were unable to continue, this I admire."

Taking some sense of accomplishment from these words, Jason feels that he has proven to Falcon that he is a fighter. Also he hopes he has earned a certain degree of admiration from this man.

Sitting in a chair as a man patches up his cuts, the young girl approaches him. "Thank you for coming to my rescue, you are a brave man."

Falcon says, "You moved too quick to save the girl, we tried to warn you but you were head strong on going up that burning tower. This was a test and the girl was never in any danger."

Giving the old man a mean look, Jason answers, "I do not like to be tested in this way."

"It is the only way we could be sure about your beliefs. We needed to know if you valued riches over human life. You did not disappoint us, except when you continued to fight me. You must learn when you are outmatched, when it is better to withdraw and fight again another day, instead of continuing down a dead end."

Nursing his wounds, Jason understands these words. He must think before acting, that proceeding ahead too quickly can be a fatal mistake. He is learning that to be brave and fearless can be an asset, but it also can be a hindrance.

Over the next two weeks Falcon teaches the young apprentice all that he knows. Jason learns how to move silently in the night, and to blend in with his surroundings. He is taught how to kill a man with one blow. He is trained in everything that Doc and Edward said that he would need to know if he is to be a successful vigilante.

Jason is told stories of people being brutalized and subjected to unbelievable torture. His own memories cause him to have flash backs. These nightmares Falcon knows about and he puts the young man through a series of tests that will help him break free of these haunting memories. Any slight hesitation by Jason while sighting in on a victim could cost him a shot or worse his life.

With his mind clear and nerves of steel, a new man emerges from the shadow of the other.

Ready to leave this old master, Jason feels much more confident in himself. His knowledge of the art of killing is now much greater than he ever imagined. Vowing to keep this place and its occupants a secret he says his goodbyes.

Once back at the apartment, his two friends instantly notice a difference in him.

"You walk with your chin higher than before," comments Doc.

"And you no longer have a passive look on your face," adds Edward. "I can see a look of determination that was not there before."

With a slight smile, "It is good to be back. Thanks to Falcon I feel much more self-assured."

As the three sit around the table Doc asks, "I take it that your stay with Falcon was rewarding."

Jason hesitates before answering as he stares at his two old companions for a moment. "Yes, he taught me a great many things."

Waiting for more, the two sit wide eyed. Finally Edwards says, "You have to tell us everything that happened."

Leaning back in his chair, Jason again hesitates before answering. Choosing his words carefully, "Falcon is wise and astute in his teachings. But I'm sure you both know this, isn't that why you sent me to him?"

The two old men can sense a change in Jason, and they are not quite sure how to interpret this change. There is definitely something very different about him, they see that Jason carries himself with much more confidence.

A silence prevails in the room while both sides seem to study the other.

Leaving the room for a moment Doc returns carrying a gun case. Setting it on the table he looks at his young apprentice.

"We received this only days ago," he states. "We were sure that you would see things our way so I contacted an individual that provided us with this weapon. We have been keeping it hidden in a safe place waiting for the right person to come along that will make the best use of it."

Now curious Jason moves closer for a better look.

Opening up the case their eyes fall on a weapon the likes that none has ever seen before.

The three stare at this weapon for a moment and reaching down Jason picks it up. Lifting it up and down to get a feel for its weight, he remarks, "For a rifle this size it has almost no weight."

A piece of paper in the case is removed by Doc who reads it, "This is a one of a kind sniper rifle, it has a chrome-poly-vanadium 4519 barrel material, melonite barrel coating and lining, upper receiver-dry lubed and med-length carbine gas piston system, with a 4.5 lb. J.P. single stage trigger, Vitor Imod Mil-spec with ergo grip stock and forearm-free extended quad rail. Caliber is 22-250, the v-shok ammo provided are specifically made for this rifle, they are extra high velocity 210 grain fast burning powder infused. It has an effective killing range of 4000 yards."

After reading this Doc is completely in awe. Neither he nor Edward have ever seen or heard of such a weapon. Jason seems to be mesmerized by its sleek design and smooth appearance.

Edward grabs Jason by the shoulder, "This is the perfect rifle for the crusade that we have embarked on. With that kind of fire power and range it will serve you well."

Not taking his eyes off of this remarkable rifle for a second, he smiles and nods his head in agreement.

"We have a lot of work to do," says Doc. "You will need to know everything about this rifle, inside and out."

The three break down the rifle dozens of times, they show Jason its many intricate parts. They want him to know every square millimeter of this rifle, this will be his killing machine. He will be the only one that uses it, so it must never leave his side.

Over and over again the two teachers drill their young apprentice about his knew rifle. Nothing is left to chance he must know this rifle like he knows the back of his hand.

Jason is tested blind folded in his ability to tare down his rifle and reassemble it as quickly as possible.

Finally satisfied, Doc and Edward feel very confident in Jason. He now has a rifle that can kill a person from two miles away, making it difficult if not impossible that anyone will see or hear him.

"I have much work to do," says Jason as he walks over to the computer.

All Doc and Edward can do is nod their heads. They knew that after being with Falcon that his attitude would change. They know Jason is a more disciplined and better trained person that he was before.

With Falcon being a man of few words it seems Jason has picked up on this.

Having told the F.L.O.C.K. that their long awaited mission of cleaning up the city can now begin, they must wait for a target to be identified. With Condor and several others moving about the city in search of their first victim, the three show signs of worry. Their eyes are wary about this venture that they are about to embark on.

Taking the law into their own hands must be handled very carefully. Only the most vile criminals will be eliminated, and this is decided on by the members of the F.L.O.C.K. It has been agreed upon by all those involved that no mission will be carry out without their express authorization. The thought has been talked about by the members of the F.L.O.C.K. long before Jason came onto the scene that they may actually create a group of assassins that will eventually disregard their orders and begin killing anyone they deem necessary.

Because of this possible nightmare the elders have put into place several failsafe strategies. These failsafe strategies if needed to be used will do one of two things, first it will cut all ties with the person violating their orders. The violator will no longer have contact with anyone in the F.L.O.C.K., and the code words that are used to contact each member will all be changed. Without his contacts on the internet this individual will not get the support, the funding or the assistance from any member of the F.L.O.C.K. A rouge individual without this backing will be quickly caught by the police. The second and most drastic step that will be taken to stop this rouge assassin if necessary will be to kill him. Just who will do this killing will be randomly picked from the entire group, but most of the members of the F.L.O.C.K. have agreed that those that were instrumental in this individuals training and guidance must carry out the assassination.

The leaders of F.L.O.C.K. cannot let this rouge assassin be arrested by the police, the information that he has could seriously damage their organization.

All members have agreed to this doctrine, they have taken an oath that each will do what is necessary to keep the organization operating. The individual does not mean more than the mission, and therefore each member knows that he is expendable, that any signs of treason or betrayal by anyone one of them will be a death sentence.

This strict and firm directive is meant to keep the group from splintering, its harsh penalty will ensure unyielding loyalty.

At 2 in the morning the three are awakened by a sound coming from the computer. As the three hurry from their beds, each knows that this sound indicates that a target has been found.

As Doc sits down he focuses his eyes on the short message.

"Target will be at corner of 13th street and Galvin road at 4 A.M.—he will be wearing long black coat, hood covering his head and carrying a backpack."

"Operation Night Justice can proceed."

Operation Night Justice is the name given to their crusade, this ambitious and deadly attempt at reducing the crime in their city.

Giving a glance at the clock Doc says softly, "Well this is what we have been waiting for, it's your first mission Jason so be cautious and careful. Remember that if it looks too risking than abort the mission and return here immediately okay?"

Showing how nervous he is Jason doesn't answer, and instead he gives his two mentors a thumbs up.

"You better hurry," adds Edward, "you haven't much time."

Pressed for time Jason grabs his backpack, it has everything in it he will need. With his rifle broken down into three parts it fits nicely into the backpack and won't raise any suspicions. His other necessities that he always carries include : two percussion grenades, one smoke grenade and one army issue fragmentation grenade. Also in his back pack is three eight oz bottles, they contain gasoline, chlorine bleach and sulfuric acid. Other objects deemed vital to his missions according to Doc are one small 22 caliber hand gun, one large 12 inch knife, a 20 inch strand of piano wire and several road flares.

He has to smile at this assortment of objects, his mentors may be old but they have a diabolical side to them.

Pulling up the map on the internet, they choose the shortest route to their target. Estimating it will take Jason almost an hour to walk there, the extra hour will give him time to hide if the situation should arise that he is confronted by anyone.

Pausing for a brief moment in the doorway of the apartment as he is existing, he turns and gives a last look at Doc and Edward. They nod their heads, assuring him that they fully support what he is about to do.

Swallowing hard as his stomach begins to tighten up he leaves the security of the building and quickly makes his way through the narrow alleys. The night is quiet, and there is no wind to blow the garbage around. Looking up he sees there is only a partial moon, this he knows will help conceal him. At this time of night he also knows that the only ones out on the streets are the criminals. He moves silently, his foot strikes do not make a sound, he has learned this technique from Falcon.

Dressed all in black and with a mask covering most of his face, he is nearly invisible. Feeling confident in his appearance he is able to move right by several men as they sit in the alley drinking.

Knowing not to get over confident, he continues his trek to his destination. After an hour he spots a building that Doc had pointed out on the map. Its location is only two blocks from his intended victim. Slipping in through the back door he makes his way up the stairs until he is on the roof, at fifteen floors this will give him a good line of sight to his target.

After reassembling his rifle, he moves to the edge of the building. Mounting a large scope onto it he scans the area. He can clearly see the street signs, 13th street and Galvin.

This is where his contact has said that a man wearing a long black coat would be at 4:00 a.m.

Checking his watch it reads 3:37 a.m. He needs to take several deep breaths to calm his nerves. He attaches a silencer to the end of the barrel, this will muffle the shot, further confusing those around this man as to where the bullet was fired from.

Finding a small crevice between an air-conditioning vent and a wall he settles himself in and waits. Out of sight should anyone venture out here onto the roof at this time of night, he now focuses his scope.

Constantly checking his watch as time seems to have slowed down. A thought crosses his mind, he nor Doc and Edward know why this individual was targeted. What vile crime did this man commit that made him stand out from all the other criminals?

These questions are not for him to worry about, he has put his trust and faith into this group calling themselves the F.L.O.C.K., and he has to assume that they are positive beyond a reasonable doubt that this individual needs to die.

It is now 3:55 a.m. and he takes the safety off of the rifle. Putting the stock into his shoulder he aims his rifle and begins breathing in slow short breaths.

A moment later several men are now standing on the corner, tightening his grip he bites his lip. But none of them is wearing a long black coat, and milling around they seem to be waiting on a taxi, but in this neighborhood the taxi drivers don't dare come at night.

After several minutes the group of men now begins walking down the street and is soon gone from sight.

Wondering if one of those men was the one he was supposed to kill, and that maybe the man decided not to wear his long black coat on this night. If this is the case than the man has a guardian angel watching over him. Thinking more about this Jason is sure this man about to be executed has no guardian angel, most likely it was just pure luck on his part that he decided to dress differently on this night.

Not ready to abandon his mission just yet, Jason waits patiently. After ten minutes he spots three men round the corner and stop just under the sign that reads 13th street and Galvin.

A smile crosses his face as he can clearly see one of them wearing a long black coat, his face partially hidden by a hood and he's got a back pack slung over one shoulder.

This is the man he has been sent to kill, he is positive. Controlling his anxiety as this will be his first victim, Jason closes his eyes for a second. He believes in his heart that in carrying out this execution that he and the others are on the side of good and not evil, and that his task must be carried out, regardless of the risks.

They are not murderers, but instead they represent the moral right. He has been told over and over again that what this group of decent and righteous individuals calling themselves the F.L.O.C.K. is doing is appropriate action in the eyes of God. The members of F.L.O.C.K. are deeply religious, with at least one member being a preacher. This in their eyes validates their actions and they believe God will not hold them accountable for the scores of lives they will take.

Again his stomach tightens up, and he wonders how he will feel after pulling the trigger. Will he be happy that he has accomplished his mission and eliminated a criminal from the streets or will a feeling of guilt overcome him.

As the hooded man turns his torso in Jason's direction he puts the cross hairs of the scope on the man's head. No time to second guess his next decision, and with a jerk of his finger he watches as the man's head snaps back and he falls backward landing on his back. Those around him duck down and look in all directions.

A feeling of relief overcomes Jason, it is not what he thought he would feel like. Instead he feels proud of what he has just done. He has removed a person from society that the police could not. The streets are now just a fraction safer than they were just a moment ago.

Needing to leave the area as soon as possible he quickly breaks down his rifle and hurries down the steps. Jason moves swiftly across town and not stopping once until he is safe at the apartment.

His two mentors are waiting for him as he opens the door. Jason nods his head and softly says, "The man is dead."

Moving closer to their young apprentice the two old men are eager to learn how Jason is feeling after his first kill.

As the three sit in silence around the kitchen table, Jason says, "It wasn't as bad as I thought it would be."

"That's good," answers Doc. "You should not feel bad for doing the right thing."

Edward now says, "Your heart will always let you know if you have done something wrong. How does your heart feel?"

Looking at his mentors Jason replies, "I feel content and at peace with what I have done."

The three now go over his mission in detail, breaking down every step, they learn what they could have done differently, and what needs improving. Doc and Edward know that as this quest to clean up the city continues that the risks will increase.

Over the next several months Jason kills those that the F.L.O.C.K. deems no longer has the right to live.

The targets started out as one per week, but over the months this has increased steadily until Jason is going out nearly every night. His missions have taken him to almost every corner of the city, and his targets have varied. At first his targets were easy to identify, they were drug pushers and it seems that they all dress pretty much the same.

As time went by the F.L.O.C.K. began targeting criminals that were acquitted of various charges in a court of law.

When a man accused of murder is set free, and the F.L.O.C.K. did not agree with that verdict, they would contact Jason.

Jason would on occasion question several of these targets, having read the papers he wasn't totally sure that a man was guilty or not. However, his two mentors would fully back the other members of the F.L.O.C.K., and their orders were to be carried out immediately.

With the number of those killed by him starting to add up significantly, Jason begins getting a reputation. The drug gangs know that someone is targeting their members, they know that it is not the police, and it is not a rival gang. Behind closed doors the leaders of these gangs come together, they put a bounty on the head of this mysterious vigilante.

CHAPTER 2

In constant contact with his online associates in this deadly attempt at cleaning up the city Jason receives an alert.

He is emailed by Hawk that a price of $25,000 dollars has been put on his head.

"You should avoid any ventures out onto the streets," Doc cautions Jason. "I suggest a time of three weeks before resuming operations. This will give the streets a chance to calm down."

Not happy with this suggestion, "Three weeks is too long," he replies. "The job I do does not have a clause in it for a vacation. A great many acts of violence will occur if I sit and do nothing. I appreciate the warning."

"Very well if that is how you feel, but be very alert."

Turning and looking at his two mentors Jason can see a concerned look on their faces. Without a word spoken they imply that the young man should lay low for a while.

"Do you agree with Hawk," asks Jason.

Rubbing his chin doc answers, "Maybe not three weeks but a few days wouldn't hurt. It will give us time to prepare for the next mission, to let our informants gather information."

Glancing at Edward, who seems bothered by all of this, "If I were in your shoes, Edward says, "I would continue without a let up. Maybe the criminals are expecting the Vigilante Assassin to disappear for a while and this will be their opportunity to strike."

Doc casts a mean stare at Edward, who puckers his lips.

Smiling Jason says, "Your feelings for my safety is appreciated, but I have a calling, and until it is finished I must go out each night."

The two old men pat him on the shoulder, they know how dedicated he is at eliminating the crime in this city. Their young apprentice has vowed to hunt down every major drug dealer and murderer no matter how much danger he will be in.

Confident in him, the three go over details for the coming night.

Their target is a notorious drug lord, one calling himself, "The Demon."

This man is number five on a list of 15 drug lords in the city with El Diablo being number one.

El Diablo still remains too elusive to pin point so the next best thing is to take out his lieutenants. Having killed several of these lieutenants and lesser gang members already, Jason is none the less surprised that they still walk out onto the street unafraid.

Their ego being so big and their arrogant attitude putting caution to the side, these drug lords carelessly flaunt their ill-gotten wealth.

Their carelessness has made them easy targets, and Jason wastes no time as he is eager to put another notch in his belt.

As darkness falls, he loads up what he needs. Picking up his trusty backpack filled with its contents of a multitude of weapons along with his revolver that is always on his side.

Exiting out the back of the apartment building and avoiding the streets, as Jason knows that El Diablo has a great many people searching for him. The dark and gloomy alleys of the city late at night are his avenues at getting around. No innocent citizen would dare venture into them, not if they value their life.

Chancing a run in with drug addicts or a gang out looking for trouble is always a possibility in this crime invested city. Moving like a shadow towards his prepositioned outpost, Jason has avoided any encounters with the street hoodlums.

Going to the roof of an abandoned apartment building, he finds a small crevice to crawl into. Feeling comfortable that no one can see him here, he hunkers down.

The hours pass as he keeps a close watch on a drug house that one of his informants said a high ranking drug lord would be at. With his trusty rifle laying across his lap he waits patiently for his opportunity. The drug lords are easy to spot, they wear the most lavish clothes. They flash their jewelry around for everyone to see. Some drug lords are even accompanied to these drug houses by one or more girls.

They flaunt their ill-gotten goods as if they actually earned them. The truth is they are nothing more than thieves and bullies. They take by force what they want and they care little about who they rob.

But it is the poison that they spread on the street that bothers Jason the most. Drug use has turned so many good people into cowards, thieves and beggars. It has taken away a person's common sense of what is right and what is wrong.

With their minds weakened, their thoughts diluted, they fall victim to men like El Diablo.

These poor souls are now dependent on the drugs that the drug lords provide. In exchange for these drugs, the poor souls most do the dirty work for the drug lords.

They are forced to steel and rob and sometimes murder to appease their new masters.

These lost souls are now just a shell of their former selves. With nowhere to turn but the gangs, their lives spiral downward. Many of these people last only a few years. If the drug use doesn't cause their death, then the violent life they lead will.

It is what our society has become, the laws seem to protect the criminals more than the victims.

Regardless of how these people started out life, if they work for El Diablo or any other drug lord, Jason will not hesitate to end their meager existence.

After staking out the drug house for most of the night, he is disappointed that his target did not show. Often these tips of where a drug lord may show up are not always reliable. A great many nights he has sat and came home without taking a single shot. So many factors play into this game of cat and mouse, sometimes it's the weather, other times he is given false information and sometimes by betrayal.

With a large amount of money waiting for whoever identifies or kills the Vigilante Assassin Jason must not let his guard down for second. He trusts only two men, Doc and Edward, and this has kept him from being a victim himself.

Tired and annoyed that a night was wasted Jason crawls out from his hiding place and heads home.

The night is nearly over, and the moon is full tonight, and it casts long shadows from the tall buildings.

Although he feels a need to sleep, Jason knows the consequences if he should ever let his guard down.

In between these buildings is a network of narrow alleys that is used for garbage pickup and also delivery of goods to the different stores.

Feeling confident with the information he has gathered on the drug house, he plans to return tomorrow night. He has located an excellent perch overlooking the drug house, to which he can take out this notorious drug pusher.

Walking hunched over, his black overcoat concealing his rifle stock he begins the long walk back to the apartment.

Unknowingly, he has walked right into a trap.

Looking up he sees several dark figures step out from the shadows only ten yards to his front. With his rifle now disassembled into three parts there is no time to reassemble it. Reaching inside his over coat he grips his revolver tightly as he tenses up.

Taking several steps backwards he suddenly stops when a sound from behind him tells him that his escape route is now blocked. In the blink of an eye, Jason finds himself surrounded. Stopping, he counts ten men in front and seven behind him. Not waiting to find out what they want, but sure it is not good, he gets down on one knee. Keeping a careful watch on these shadowy figures he quickly devises a plan. Reaching into his backpack that he always carries with him, he pulls out two percussion grenades.

Removing their pins, he sends them sliding across the pavement towards the men to his front.

He can hear them laughing and pointing, it's obvious they don't know what these objects are. The grenades stop right in the middle of the group who has not moved one inch, and as one of them reaches down, the grenades explode simultaneously.

Three of the men fall down holding their legs, the others cover their faces as they scream and curse. With this group dazed, he turns around and fires three quick shots from his revolver, and three more scum have now gone to hell. Turning back around, he reaches down and pulls out a knife from his boot, and running towards the still confused men, the blade of his knife flashes through the air like a lightning bolt, and in the blink of an eye, two more villains have been removed from society.

Hearing heavy footsteps, he glances over his right shoulder to see a very large man coming at him swinging a chain. Remaining calm, again he reaches into his bag of tricks and pulling out a container of sulfuric acid he quickly throws it at the big man. The small bottle shatters against his chest and instantly the acid begins burning into his flesh. Screaming in pain he lowers his head and charges straight at Jason. Raising his revolver straight out, and one shot between the eyes and the huge man drops like a rock. By this time these dumb witted thugs have realized that they have chosen the wrong person to mess with. As they are running away, Jason fires his last three bullets, at them, and two more fall. Looking around, he counts nine bodies, "A good night's work," he says under his breath.

Moving like a shadow in the night, the mysterious Vigilante Assassin disappears into the darkness.

CHAPTER 3

Once back at the apartment, a delighted Jason can't wait to tell his two friends how his night ended. As after each mission the three always have a debriefing to go over what took place, however Doc cannot wait for Jason to tell them how things went, instead he anxiously informs him, "A professional hit man has been hired by the drug lords to hunt down and kill the Vigilante Assassin."

Now sitting at the table, Jason unlaces his shoes as he stares at the floor.

Giving a glance at Doc he says, "That doesn't change anything, I can take care of myself."

Interrupting, Edwards says, "We know you can take care of yourself, but this is different, this man that is looking for you is not a street thug or your everyday hoodlum, he's a professional hit man."

Taking a moment to think about this, Jason replies, "This hired gun does not scare me nor will I let it interfere with our mission."

The two old men now seem very worried, Edward is constantly rubbing his face and Doc is staring out the window, a look of dread is on his face.

Speaking in a stern voice Doc says, "Maybe you should suspend operations for a while, just until this assassin leaves town."

Defiantly shaking his head, "No, we have too much work to do."

Now moving closer to Jason, "No sense in jeopardizing your life," counters Doc, "don't be so stubborn."

Looking up as he tilts his head to the side, and cracking a smile he replies, "If I'm stubborn, than I learned that from you."

Taking a deep breath, Doc knows he's right, but still he wishes his young apprentice would reconsider.

"This assassin is not like the thugs on the streets," says Doc, "he's a professional killer."

"I can't stop what I'm doing just because someone is after me, the risks come with the job."

Going into the kitchen and sitting at the table, Doc remains silent while Jason fixes himself something to eat.

Waiting until Jason has food in his mouth, Doc says wide eyed, "We should go on vacation, maybe to Las Vegas?"

Jason knows how much Doc and Edward care for him, and he's happy that they want to protect him. But there is too much crime in this city to even dream about taking a vacation.

"I appreciate your concern, and if it makes you happy I'll be extra careful from now on."

"Edward won't be happy with your decision," states Doc, as he nervously taps his fingers on the table.

"You have both been like a father to me, but I must do what we started, and I won't stop until it's finished."

"If I were younger I would go with you," with that said, a sad look crosses Doc's face.

"I wish I had been born much earlier," Jason says, "the three of us would have been quit the team."

Looking up with bright eyes, Doc shakes his fist, "Nothing could have stopped us, why we would have cleaned up this city in no time."

The two laugh, as it had been some time sense laughter was heard in the apartment.

Later that day when Edward returns from a fact finding mission the three sit down to learn the latest news.

"My informants tell me that this assassin that is looking for you is called The Sandman," Edward says, his voice a little shaky.

"Sounds like a funny name if you ask me," pronounces Jason.

"Don't take this so lightly," an angry Edward declares, "funny name or not, this man has killed dozens of people."

Getting a serious look on his face, "You're right, I'm sorry, tell me more about this assassin."

"The Sandman got this nickname because of the dozens of people he has caused to take a permanent dirt nap," exclaims Edward.

"His preferred method of killing is to poison his victim. If he has to kill everyone in the room to get the one he was hired to eliminate, he will do that. The sandman is also a master of disguise."

Sitting up in his chair, Jason says, "Thanks for the information, I will keep my guard up, that I promise."

The room is now quiet, the only sound is the ticking of the clock on the wall. The three know that this business of eliminating the criminals in the city has just turned much more serious than it had been. The major drug lords have tolerated this Vigilante Assassin long enough, and now they want him eliminated.

What these drug lords will try is anyone's guess, and a city already plagued by extreme violence, could see it drastically increase.

CHAPTER 4

After sleeping the rest of the day, Jason wakes just as the sun is going down. He gathers the things he will need for the nights work. Memorizing the details of his next intended target given to him by his internet contacts he prepares to leave.

Waiting until Doc and Edward have gone to bed he quietly slips out of the apartment.

After traveling only a few blocks, Jason senses something isn't right. His skin tingles, and the air smells different. He hides behind a pile of lumber, sticking his head up just high enough to scan the area. The minutes go by slow and he neither sees nor hears anything unusual. Believing that maybe he is being jumpy because of what Doc and Edward told him. A professional killer hired by the drug lords is much more dangerous that the thugs on the streets.

Feeling confident that he isn't being followed, Jason continues his trek into the heart of the city.

Finding a rooftop with a good view of the streets below, he settles in like a deer hunter in his stand.

It isn't long and the screams of a woman echo from a nearby parking lot. Looking through his scope, he sees a man hitting a woman. The man grabs the woman's purse and begins running away. Quickly putting the cross hairs on the man's back he pulls the trigger. Instantly the man falls to the pavement.

Others come out to investigate, they comfort the hysterical woman.

Soon the police arrive and they begin questioning everyone hoping that someone may have seen who did this. But like all the times before, no one has seen or heard anything.

The police are growing more frustrated at never having a lead to catch this Vigilante Assassin.

The Mayor has assigned eight detectives to put an end to this person that is taking the law into their own hands.

With the area being searched Jason silently moves to another part of town. He knows that the police are after him, and one mistake could lead to his downfall. He always wears gloves, never leaving behind finger prints.

Sometimes he lets his beard grow for several weeks to help conceal his face. He never stays too long in one part of the city. Caution and patience is what he has been taught.

Moving several times from one concealment to another, as a feeling of being watched overcomes him. Getting jumpy at the slightest noise he is relieved that finally the long night is ending.

His score card reads, two robbers and a mugger killed.

As the morning sun is rising over the horizon this will make it too dangerous to go back to the apartment. He has committed a minor mistake, waiting too long before starting his journey home. Now Jason must find a place to stay during the day, only at night will he risk walking the streets and alleys.

He has heard the word on the street that a great many people are searching for him. Believing that if he is followed back to the apartment he will be putting Doc and Edward in danger. Realizing that he must lay low and let this search for him die down, his next decision is just where to hide.

Already at the edge of the city, the woods that stretch out to his left look as good as any place to go.

No one will search for him here he believes. As tough as these thugs portray themselves, muggers and murders don't like the woods.

After crossing a set of railroad tracks he cautiously walks through the thick foliage and up a small embankment until he emerges to a scene he has not seen in years. Tall trees that seem to stretch skywards for more than 200 hundred feet give the area a mythical appearance. Their broad limbs act like a giant umbrella blocking out most of the sunlight. Moving several hundred yards farther into this mesmerizing landscape he spots an idea location to set up camp. Under the overhanging branches of a huge willow tree halfway up a small hillside looks ideal.

He quickly gets to work building a lean to out of sticks, as this crude shelter will protect him if it should rain.

Jason lay inside a huge plastic garbage bag, this he buries under a pile of leaves and it is tucked up against the base of the tree. With just his head sticking out, he has a good vantage point. He can see in all directions without anyone seeing him.

This affords him concealment from anyone that might happen to be in this area. He will stay here for a few days, until feeling that it is safe to return to the apartment.

To Jason, now relaxed, these woods are isolated and it appears by the lack of trails that they rarely get visited.

Exhausted from the night before, he sleeps until noon.

Waking up, the sounds of nature are a pleasant change from the constant noises of the city. His memories go back to his youth, how he spent a great deal of his time playing in the woods not far from his home.

The pictures in his mind bring a smile to his face. Those were good times, as life was carefree and untroubled. Despite his parents objections he felt he had to move to a big city and experience the hustle and bustle of city life.

With his head lowered he wishes now that maybe he should have listened to them. His life since moving into his apartment has been anything but tranquil. From early morning to late at night it's a constant rush. Hectic and frenzied at times he was growing more impatient with his lifestyle. Bullheaded and determined to prove to his parents that he could make it in the big city he endured the chaos.

Snapping out of his trance, his stomach begins to growl letting him know that it has been some time since he last ate.

His only food is the mre's in his backpack. These small containers of food are light weight and they come precooked.

With nothing to do but stay concealed the hours pass slowly. He thinks about how his life has changed so dramatically since that fateful day he was dragged from his car and held prisoner.

Would he still be the mild manner guy he was then or would he have had enough of the crime and moved. The scenarios play out in his mind, how he never would have thought he would be a killer. The thought cause's him to close his eyes, the word killer sounds so wrong. To take another human beings life, to end someone's existence on this planet causes him to question his religion. Because of what he has done will he be denied entrance into heaven.

Will he be sent to hell to suffer alongside all those that he has sent there?

Thinking how Doc and Edward preached to him about what he is doing is right and justified in the eyes of God. "You are doing the Lords work," they would constantly remind him.

Still with so much blood on his hands, he has doubts.

A sin is a sin, and if he has to go to hell as a result of cleaning up the city then so be it.

Looking up at the thick clouds rolling across the bright blue sky, a sad look crosses his face.

Wondering if God is watching him, he swallows hard.

"Forgive me Lord," he says, "but I must continue the mission I'm on. After I'm dead you can judge me then but for now I must rid this city of its evil."

Feeling confident and self-assured, Jason is positive that God will not judge him harshly.

He is only doing the city a favor by eliminating these criminals. Only those that he and the others in his group deem unfit are killed.

They are no different that a judge and jury that convicts someone and then sentences that person to die.

The only difference is when his group feels that someone must die it is done immediately, they don't wait years and years before carrying out the sentence.

He and the others are saving the tax payers a lot of money. There is no trial, no jail time, just a quick execution. It makes sense in every aspect. The Mayor and the police should be happy that a citizen has taken up arms against the criminals.

He doesn't understand that they look at the Vigilante Assassin as a murderer and a serial killer. The Chief of Police has told the people not to assist or aid the vigilante. That he is a wanted man and anyone that renders him help will be prosecuted to the fullest extent of the law.

Jason knows that a great many people have voiced their opinion in what he is doing. Some strongly support him while others disagree completely.

Some people along with the police and Mayor believe that this Vigilante Assassin will not stop once the city is cleaned up. They believe he will continue to kill, that his thirst for blood will drive him to shot anyone for even the smallest violations.

The Mayor and Chief of Police have distributed flyers warning the people that the vigilante will shoot even petty crimes like j walking or littering. They have portrayed him as a mass murderer, a man that must be stopped at all costs.

Jason shakes his head, he is hoping that these stories do not prove true. Believing that when he and the others think that enough criminals have been eliminated that he will without hesitation put away his guns. That he will not have an overpowering urge to kill again and again. Wondering if the need to kill will be like a drug addict trying to quit his drug habit. Helpless to the adrenaline rush that urges him on, he can only pray that he is not a victim of his own doing. That deep inside his soul a voice will tell him that enough is enough, that it is time to stop. The thought that he may not be able to walk away from this life style bothers him greatly.

Holding the revolver with both hands he slowly brings it up until the front sight is against his temple. "I will not be an out of control killing machine," he whispers. "With your help Lord I will stop myself if it comes to that point."

With his eyes closed he breaths deeply, suicide is something he has always been against. But smart enough to realize that this crusade he is on must end at some point, the thought of tasking his own life is a very real possibility.

With the sun going down the darkness begins to cover the trees and the usual sounds of nature take over. As the thick dark clouds move overhead, he feels safer the darker it gets. It is always at night that he does most of his work, the darkness conceals his whereabouts quite nicely.

On the edge of falling asleep, he jumps when he catches the faint smell of cigarette smoke. This single smell is manmade, and it alerts him that he isn't alone in these woods.

Needing to know if the police have tracked him here or worse could it be El Diablo, Jason's sixth sense is telling him to get up and investigate. Opening up his backpack, he quickly assembles his rifle. He creeps out of his hiding place, and moves silently among the trees and bushes.

Following the scent, it leads him up a small hill, from which he can see the faint flicker of a campfire. Could this be just an ordinary camp he wonders, maybe teenagers are having a drinking party.

He needs to investigate further, and he needs to know if he is in any danger. Does he need to leave these woods as quickly as possible, or is he overreacting. Hoping that he isn't becoming paranoid, he pats the revolver on his hip.

Grabbing his rifle tightly, even if this is nothing to worry about, he never leaves his rifle behind.

Keeping low to the ground, he slithers over twigs and branches. Moving like this until he reaches a spot that makes it easy to observe who these people might be and what they are doing here. He suddenly hears the screams of a woman, and they are coming from the opposite side of this camp. From his concealment he looks through the rifle scope and quickly gets an accurate assessment of what is going on.

He counts three men, one is sitting with his back towards him, and one is sitting to the right. The third man is on top of the screaming woman. She is kicking and screaming, this is obviously a rape taking place.

The man on top of her hits her several times in an effort to quiet her down. The other two men laugh, and he hears them yell, "What's the matter is she too much for you to handle?"

Hearing this causes the man to become even angrier and he begins pounding the woman's head against the ground.

Jason slowly moves into a better shooting position where all three men are clearly visible.

After the one man is finished with the woman he gets up and walks a short distance, this is when the second man stands over the woman. She is pleading and crying for them to stop. The man smiles as he curses at her and kicks her legs. This man is now pulling down his pants, he moves on top of the woman.

This is all that Jason can stand; this terrible act of violence has to be stopped. Resting his rifle against a fallen tree, he puts the sights on the back of the man's head that is on top of the woman. Holding his breath, he slowly squeezes the trigger. With no silencer the shot echoes through the woods, and the man slumps forward. The second man, hearing the gun shot and seeing his friend lay limp jumps to his feet. Frantically looking all around trying to see where the shot came from, he now fumbles at trying to pull his pants up. This man stands still for just a second and Jason puts a bullet through his left temple. The man crumples to the ground, his body quivering and jerking.

By now the third man has gotten up and he pulls out a revolver and begins shooting in all directions. With fear on his face he doesn't know what direction the shots have come from.

Waiting for just the right shot, and when the man turns his back, Jason fires. The bullet hits him just below the left shoulder blade. His body twists around as if he were stung by a bee.

Cursing, he continues firing his revolver even as he is falling to the ground.

Once on the ground he lay motionless, and Jason stays where he is, watching to see how severely this man is shot.

The man's face is distorted in pain and with a quick jerk of his body he desperately tries to stop the bleeding. He rolls about the ground several times before finally laying still. Not believing he is dead, Jason dare not move. He watches closely for any signs that will tell him that this man is still alive. He thinks about a second shot, but he is positive that the first one had found its mark.

By this time the woman has managed to get to her feet. She looks around, hoping to see her rescuer. Half clothed and bleeding from her face, her body trembles uncontrollably.

As much as he would have liked to get up and go to her he knows better. No one can ever know his identity. Even though this woman would promise never to tell anyone what he looks like, Jason cannot risk it.

For what he has done in his life, if ever he is captured by the police, he will surely be severely punished. To be incarcerated with the low lives from society will be a harsh punishment in its self.

The woman begs, her arms holding the side of her head, "Please, whoever is out there, I beg you to show yourself!"

Jason lay still for a moment, his mind torn between going to this woman who has just been violated, and retreating back into the solitude of the woods. Watching her move about, he knows she is able to walk.

After several more attempts at trying to coax her unseen rescuer from the shadows, she begins running down a path towards the city.

Happy that this woman is able to flee, Jason knows it won't be long until the police are here.

These woods had been a safe haven for him up to this point. Now he will need another sanctuary, another hideout. After the woman runs away, the thought crosses his mind that he should go and take from the three dead men what money and valuables they have. It would be taking a risk, and up to this point he has been able to elude the authorities by not getting greedy or over confident.

Estimating the time it will take the woman to make it to town, and how long it will take the police to arrive, he believes he has enough time. Walking into the camp, Jason now holds his revolver in his hand, it is better suited for close range verses his rifle.

Turning over the first man, he is shocked and surprised. Recognizing this man as one of the men that tortured him, a sense of relief comes over him. It felt good to kill this man, as the nightmares still haunt him.

Searching his pockets he relieves the man of his wallet and revolver. Moving over to the second man, he is surprised that he is still breathing. Instantly the man rolls over and fires a shot that narrowly misses Jason's head. Falling backwards with cat like reflexes, Jason fires three rounds as fast as he can pull the trigger. Two of the bullets strike the man in his neck, and the man frantically covers his throat with both hands. Caught off guard by this near fatal mistake, Jason scrambles to his feet.

Aiming his revolver at the man, he waits for any signs of life, not wanting to make the same mistake twice.

Lying face down, the man remains motionless. Blood can be seen pooling by his head, an indication that this time there is no escaping death.

Slightly shook up from this near fatal encounter, Jason keeps the revolver pointed at him, needing a minute to collect his thoughts. After calming down, he takes a closer look at the man that nearly killed him. Wondering why his first shot didn't kill him, however, looking closer It is obvious now that he was wearing a bullet proof vest. Jason can see that the bullet did penetrate the vest, but it didn't travel far enough into his body to be fatal.

At this time the faint sound of police cars can be heard in the distance.

Leaving the dead men where they lay, Jason hurries through the woods to his campsite. Gathering up his belongings, he moves deeper into the woods. Not sure just how large an area encompasses these woods, but hoping they are large enough that the police won't try and search all of it.

To his misfortune, he is soon standing on a ridge overlooking several houses. These woods barely cover four square miles. No time to brew about this, Jason descends down an embankment and crosses a set of rail road tracks.

More sirens fill the night air, and it seems they are coming from all directions. Keeping his head, Jason remembers that there is a safe house in this part of town. As he begins running swiftly along the tracks it begins to rain.

Undeterred, getting wet is the least of his concerns. Finally after what seemed miles he spots an old junk yard. Remembering its location on the map, the safe house is not far away.

Breathing heavily, "Yes," he utters, "Only a short distance to go."

Rounding a bend he can see the river, it is here that he will find refuge. Leaving the railroad tracks he must next cross a large open field. Walking through waist high grass his eyes scan in all directions.

A road is very near, but he knows he cannot use it. His safety will be here in the tall grass.

Half way across he must duck down quickly as he sees the flashing lights of a police car approaching.

Tensing up, he lays flat with his face against the cool wet ground. His senses heightened, he closes his eyes for a second and listens. The police car is getting closer, and by the sound of is engine it is slowing down.

A spotlight flashes right over his head and for a second he pulls the hammer back on his revolver. This is not a good place to have a shootout with the police. He has no cover, no protection. He would be a sitting duck and in a matter of minutes this whole field would be surrounded by the police.

Having thought about how his life might end, he always envisioned a shootout with the drug dealers not the police.

To his relief the lights move on, and lifting up his head he can see the police car traveling farther down the road.

Up onto his feet he hurries to the edge of the tall grass, here he must cross another road. It seems deserted, and in a flash he is across and sliding down an embankment, stopping right at the river's edge.

To his right he can make out the silhouettes of a row of boats tied to a dock.

Having memorized the location of every safe house shown to him on a map, he must search for a boat called, The Lobster.

Being cautious as he nears the marina, a feeling of being exposed has his heart racing. If he is going to be spotted by someone, this would most likely be the place. The area consists of retired people, which means they have a lot of time just sitting and watching the area.

To his relief, he finds the docks deserted, believing that the rain has kept everyone indoors. Now to find this boat that will give him a measure of protection. Moving down the wooden dock, it creeks and cracks with his every step. It isn't long and he spots the boat he's been searching for.

A 50 foot fishing trawler tied at the end of the pier. Climbing aboard, he glances back making sure he was not spotted or followed. Quickly going below he is relieved that it is empty.

With no way to contact Doc and Edward and inform them of the situation, he must sit tight until the police have exhausted their search.

Glad to see a refrigerator, opening it he is delighted to find half of a left over pizza. With the boat hooked up for electrical power he quickly warms up his meal in the microwave. Searching the interior he finds a change of cloth along with several weapons. These safe houses scattered throughout the city and even along the river are maintained by contacts. These citizens have answered the call for justice and they do what they can to help.

All of their identities are unknown, with the only contact being over the internet. This method of secrecy ensures that the group as an operating unit will not be shut down if one of the contacts decides to inform the police. The leaders of this vigilante operation have built in several failsafe procedures that will quickly alert the others in the event someone should go to the police.

All passwords will be changed, and for the first 48 hours all operations will cease.

There is one man that controls this whole organization, his name and identity is a well-guarded secret. Doc and Edward refused to tell Jason anything about this person. This one individual is the key component to the whole operation, without him they would be forced to shut down immediately.

Jason has always wondered just who this individual could be. Is he rich or is he a politician. His status in society has to be of great importance, he is taking a risk getting involved in such an organization. Wondering if this individual even lives in Landore, perhaps he lives in another state. Jason was not happy that his two friends would not reveal this man's identity. But he does understand the need for secrecy. This clandestine mission that all of these people have chosen to get involved in is dangerous and risky. Each must know that given the opportunity that the drug lords would kill them without a second thought. Perhaps it is best that he doesn't know this man at the top. This group will continue its mission even if Jason is killed or captured.

This way he cannot reveal anyone's name or whereabouts, that is except Doc and Edwards.

With his capsule of poison, he will not let the authorities take him alive, he owes these men that much.

Feeling safe, Jason makes use of the shower and puts on clean clothes. Further searching reveals maps, flashlights and a G.P.S. system. Whoever stocked this boat was ready to leave at a moment's notice.

Watching the door as he lays on the sofa he is nearly asleep when he hears footsteps. Jumping to his feet, he looks out one of the small portholes. A shadow walks by, causing him to step back. Moving to the far corner and crouching down he points the revolver at the door.

The creaking of the steps tells him that someone is coming down and will be through the door in a matter of seconds.

Now leaning to the side he braces himself against the side of the boat. The door opens slowly, his heart begins beating faster. With no place to run he quickly moves closer to the door. Jason must be prepared if this is the police. The door opens halfway and then stops. Jason can hear breathing and the scent of a cigar fills the air.

Curious, he reaches out with his left foot, hooking the bottom of the door. In one swift action he swings the door wide open.

Pointing his revolver straight out, his hands sweating profusely, he grits his teeth in anticipation of what could come next.

To his surprise it is an old man.

"Don't shoot, don't shoot," the man begs as he waves a hand in the air.

Not seeing any weapon, Jason lowers his revolver. "Who are you," he demands as he looks behind this man.

Peeking out from the arms that cover his face the old man replies, "I own this boat, but if you want it, then it's yours just don't shoot me."

Forcing a smile, "you don't need to worry, I'm not going to shoot you or steal your boat."

Lowering his hands, the wide eyed old man gives Jason a long look. "Am 'I your prisoner." He asks in a feeble why.

Looking past him, Jason asks, "Are you alone?"

"Yes yes," he quickly replies. "No one but me."

He motions for the man to come the rest of the way inside. The old man hobbles as his cane taps the floor. Closing the door quickly, Jason looks out the small port holes. Finally satisfied that there is no one else he sits in a chair facing the man.

With his eyes straining, the old man leans forward for a better look. Puckering his lips several times as he carefully studies this man in his boat.

"Don't believe I have ever met you before young man."

"I don't get out much," replies Jason as the tension slowly eases.

"Hiding and carrying a gun," says the old man, "you must be hiding from the law."

"You have it partly right, but the law is the least of my worries."

"I never been one to pry into another man's business," states the old man, "looks like you been through a lot."

Shaking his head, Jason remains silent, not sure what he should do next now that he has company.

"Might as well be on first names, you can call me Isaac."

Hesitant at first, Jason answers, my name is Ronald."

Isaac gives him a long look, makes a face and then says, "You don't look like a Ronald, no, I have known fellows named Ronald and they all looked like a Ronald, but not you young man."

Smiling at such an assumption, Jason replies, "You can't tell a person's name by what he looks like."

Now sitting back in his chair, one arm resting on the table Isaac says, "With that answer you have just confirmed that your name is not Ronald."

Growing frustrated, Jason throws his hands into the air. He paces back and forth, his thoughts are on where the police are at this moment.

Not liking this confined space with no way to escape if he is discovered, Jason contemplates finding a new hideout.

Isaac by this time has begun opening several cabinets. He sets two plates out on the table and glancing over his shoulder says, "Pull up a chair and I'll fix us something to eat."

Jason is confused that this old man isn't afraid. He acts so calm and relaxed, but why. He just found an armed man in his boat, he should be scared for his life, but he isn't.

"Why aren't you afraid," states Jason. "I could be a serial killer."

Without turning around Isaac says, "Your eyes tell me that you won't kill me. You may have killed others, but you don't have any intensions of killing me."

Flabbergasted by these comments, Jason is at a loss for words. This old man seems to know him very well even though they have never met before.

"If you think you know so much," demands a slightly nervous Jason, "tell me other things about me?"

Facing his young friend, Isaac pauses for a moment, his eyes scanning every inch of Jason's face.

Tilting his head to the side, he gives the rest of him a quick look over.

"You are about 25 years old, you have been subjected to some type of torture and the need to seek revenge is the driving force in your life."

With mouth agape, Jason is stunned and shocked. How could this man know this about him just by looking into his eyes. This doesn't make any sense, there has to be a logical reason how this man could have known these things about him.

Taking several deep breaths, "I don't know how you knew these things, but yes, you are correct."

"I may be old and need a cane to get around, but I can read a man's soul very well."

No arguing with that as Jason can only shake his head.

As the two eat their meal, Jason can see several scars on the old man's face.

It looks as if he too has been through some sort of torture.

Glancing up Isaac says, "I suppose you won't tell me anything about yourself or where you're from?"

After chewing his food Jason replies, "The less you know about me the better off you will be."

Lighting up another cigar and calmly sitting back in his chair, "Your actions say that you're running from someone. But they also say that you have a lot of confidence in your ability to deal with this threat."

Unable to figure out how this old man knows so much, Jason asks, "You have an uncanny ability to see a lot from so little. I don't believe in E.S.P. and we have never met before so my conclusion is that you must work with the network."

A smile crosses Isaac's face, "You are wise and you catch on quickly. Indeed I do work with the network. I have been kept up to date on all that you have done for us. The network owes you a great deal for stepping into the role of vigilante."

Feeling a lot better about the situation, Jason relaxes knowing that this man is part of their organization.

"I work closely with only two members," Jason says. "They are the only ones that know my identity that is until now."

Pouring himself a drink Isaac motions if Jason would like one.

"I normally don't drink but this time I will make an exception."

With his face showing delight he pours his new friend a drink.

Not having had any alcohol for so long the first drink causes Jason to squint his eyes and he coughs several times. This reaction causes Isaac to laugh out loud.

Jason has to crack a smile, "That is some drink," he says in a low whisper.

"Just some of the finest whisky in the whole city," answers Isaac as he offers Jason another drink.

Waving his hands, his face still red, "No thanks, one was enough for me," Jason replies as his voice cracks.

The old man seems to delight in watching his young companion struggle to talk.

Looking at his watch, Isaac says, "I told the guys at the bar I would only be a few minutes, I don't want them to come looking for me."

Standing up Jason finds himself in an odd position. Should he let this man just walk out, after all he now knows the identity of the Vigilante Assassin.

Seeing the worry in Jason's eyes and his body language tells Isaac that he needs to reassure him that all is okay.

Putting a hand on Jason's shoulder Isaac says, "We are in a dangerous business, and one mistake could be fatal. You have my word that your whereabouts and your identity will remain a secret."

Jason must make a life or death decision, should he trust this man and let him leave. Although Isaac did say he was part of the network, still he must be sure.

"You have reservations about letting me walk out this door don't you," asks Isaac.

"Yes I do," Jason answers quickly.

"I can assure you that if I were not trustworthy my two old army buddies would not have allowed me to be part of the network."

Hearing this answers a lot of his doubts. So Edward and Doc are old friends with Isaac, this is something he will have to bring up when he returns to the apartment.

"What else can I say that will convince you that I'm on your side. I want to see the crime in this city reduced. I want all the drug gangs and the poison they sell out of Landore. I would love more than anything to see El Diablo and his two brothers dead."

A wide eyed Jason is stumped, this is another person that has a grievance against El Diablo.

"You also have been wronged by that butcher,"

Holding his cane tightly and gritting his teeth, "Oh I could tell you some stories but I doubt you would want to hear them. Let's say I won't rest until he and those worthless brothers of his are long dead in the cold ground."

A moment of compassion and empathy over comes Jason as he has an idea of what El Diablo and his brothers may have done to Isaac.

Standing tall Jason says, "I trust you, I feel confident that you will keep our meeting a secret."

The old man pats his friend on the back, "You take care, and don't forget you always have a place to go if the need arises."

Turning and walking up the steps Isaac is soon walking back down the docks. Jason watches as the old man disappears and is gone from sight.

Needing to concentrate on getting out of here and back to the apartment, he must devise a plan. Although he knows he can stay here as long as he wants, it is just too easy to be trapped here. He must find a place that offers at least a slimmer of hope of escaping if he is discovered.

He spends the next two days holed up in the boat, until late on the third day he decides the time is right to make his way back to the apartment.

Retracing his steps he hugs the river bank traveling several miles towards the city until he finds himself in front of a make shift tent city. He remembers this place, with its homeless and outcasts' people, and the substandard living conditions.

Stopping he stares wide eyed, his heart sinks as these vagrants walk about as if in a daze. Wearing rags for clothing, unshaven and dirty they remind him of pictures he has seen of prisoners of war from a German P.O.W. camp.

To his surprise an elderly woman approaches him from behind, she softly says, "Are you okay young man, you seem lost?"

Jason swallows hard, he can see the suffering in her eyes that she has gone through, the years have not been kind to her. Putting her frail hand out she says, "Come with me,"

Doing as he is told he followers the old woman into this tent city. Others now come out to see who this stranger is, they stand and stare just as Jason stands and stares at them. A man humped over and using a walker speaks up, "If you are hungry please have a seat."

The man motions for Jason to sit down on a tree log that these people use for a chair.

This odd collection of individuals now gather around Jason, some touch his clothing while others try to sit as close to him as possible. Speechless, Jason feels like an adventurer that has just discovered a long lost tribe in South America.

The humped over man brings out a bowl and hands it to Jason. The gray colored substance has a bad smell to it and Jason wrinkles up his nose.

Several of those around him laugh at his reaction, one says, "It may smell bad but it will keep you alive, so go ahead and eat it."

Not wanting to hurt their feelings Jason tastes a small amount, and to his surprise finds that it isn't so bad after all.

Patting him on the back the old man says, "We have more if you like, just say the word. No one ever gets turned away that needs a meal, not anyone."

Jason is humbled that these people that are living in such squalor conditions have such big hearts.

"Thank you, but this will be enough."

The people are very quiet, and they huddle tightly together. They are skinny and have a pale complexion, this Jason knows means that they are not getting the proper nutrition that they need.

The old man now sits across from Jason and asks, "Why have you come into our camp, you do not look like the others that have wandered into here."

Choosing his words carefully, "I was on my way home and decided to take a short cut," he answers.

Those around him have a look of skepticism on their faces, hinting that they don't believe his story.

"No one but the most needy and destitute would dare venture into here." The old man says as he too doubts this young man's story.

"By your looks I would say you are definitely out of your element," he continues, "and from your clothes to your clean face, you are not here seeking a meal. Perhaps you are being chased by someone, maybe one of the street gangs that control this part of town?"

Jason has to give the old man credit, he can read a face very well.

Realizing that these simple people don't buy his story, "You are right," Jason answers as he glances around, "I'm being chased."

"We can hide you until this threat is gone, no one will find you."

Their wiliness to harbor a stranger despite the dangers again surprises Jason.

Not wanting any of these kind hearted people to suffer on his account, "I will be on my way," he says as he stands up.

"I appreciate everything you have done for me, but I must go."

As Jason turns to leave the old woman grabs his arm, turning him around. In her hand is a small plastic bag containing several cookies.

With eyes that display kindness and compassion she places the bag into Jason's hand.

"It isn't much," she whispers, "But it is all I have."

Overcome by these acts of caring and kindness Jason is speechless, he can only look at those around him, seeing that they of all people can ill afford to part will even the smallest scrape of food. Yet they selfishly give up their meager morsels to a stranger.

Unable to speak as he wipes the tears from his eyes, he reaches into his pocket and pulls out the money that he took from the three men he recently killed.

Handing it to the old man and woman, who at first seeing the money cover their mouths, now begin to cry.

"You take this money," Jason demands. "You need it more than I do."

The people are all now standing and they begin hugging each other, it's as if Christmas has come early for them.

Choked up, Jason hurries out of the camp. Proud of what he has done, it lets him know that yes he does kill people, but he still has a good heart. His soul has not turned black and the need to kill has not taken control over his common sense and compassion.

Still at peace with his God, and truly believing now more than ever that his mission is righteous, honorable and necessary. Jason begins looking at himself as a savior sent from heaven, the redeemer, the guardian of the weak.

His psych is changing, and at times he begins to think that maybe he is invincible. Having God on his side, this crusade he has begun must continue, it must be completed and most important, all the evil in this city must be vanquished.

Catching himself as his delusional thinking at times surprises him, nonetheless he feels empowered to carry on and not stop. If his own life is to be sacrificed, he is content knowing he did what had to be done. The needs of the many out weight the needs of the few or the one.

No longer self-centered, no longer afraid, confident in his actions, a new Jason is emerging from the old.

A sense of worth and meaning now fill his life, and purpose driven to the point his own life often hangs in the balance, a young man begins to realize that he has a destiny. This quest to eliminate all the criminals in the city has now taken on a biblical conviction.

Urged on by a faith he previously never new and awakened by the misery that people endure has enlightened his attitude.

After each mission he now takes the time to say a silent prayer, thankful to be alive.

Before all of this began his religious beliefs were sparse and at times he rebelled against the notion that a higher power controlled our destinies. Looking back he feels that a hand has been placed over him, protecting and guiding his every move.

This change in attitude greatly pleases Doc and Edward who have from day one insisted that God was on their side. Deeply religious themselves, the two constantly pushed their beliefs onto Jason, hoping to change his mind set.

As time has gone by Jason looks more and more towards the bible for guidance and direction. His two mentors had placed a bible on the night stand next to his bed the day he arrived. Ignoring it until recently, Jason has begun to read it more and more. The passages in the bible help him stay focused, and they teach him of the glory of enteral life.

With so much blood on his hands and more to come in the future, he must without a doubt believe his work is right and justified.

One slight hesitation on his part while executing a target could cost him his life and the mission that the F.L.O.C.K. has organized will end. There is no one else to take his place, the future of this city rests in his hands. He must keep the faith, believe in his convictions and never lose sight of his goal.

Arriving at the apartment his two mentors greed him warmly.

"We have been worried about you," says Doc.

Still thinking about the people in that tent city all Jason can do is smile.

As he relaxes Edward asks, "We know that these missions that you venture out on are stressful and demanding, but you still need to talk to us about them, it's not good to keep things bottled up inside."

With a half grin, "The mission went well, I met some remarkable people."

They can see the change in their apprentice, his eyes seem calm, his movements easy and untaxed.

Over the following hour Jason opens up about the previous days actions. Doc and Edward are happy that he has turned more and more towards God and the bible. They sense a peace in him that they have not seen before.

The weeks have stretched into months, and despite his success at eliminating dozens of criminals from the streets, his main target constantly eludes him.
El Diablo has proven a very weary opponent. His whereabouts are carefully guarded, and he moves frequently from one location to another.
Tired of waiting for his pray, Jason turns to a more direct and lethal approach.
He now tries getting information out of several drug pushers that he knows does business with El Diablo.
Concealing himself in the thick brush next to a train trestle, he waits for one of these men to make a pickup of drugs.
At a predicted time the unlucky man walks right into the trap set by Jason.
After subduing this man, he drags him out to the middle of the bridge. Hanging him upside down tied to a long rope from this railroad bridge, he begins to swing him back and forth. Despite the man pleads that he doesn't know where El Diablo is, Jason constantly threatens to cut the rope.
After several hours of this torture he realizes that the man is telling the truth. With a cold and callous look in his eyes, Jason cuts the rope and the man falls into the river far below.
If this man should survive Jason hopes that he will spread the word that El Diablo is a marked man. Hoping to put fear into that devil, causing him to constantly look over his shoulder, make him think that he is always in the cross hairs of the Vigilante Assassin.
With the night young, he kidnaps another drug pusher, this one he stakes out over an ant hill. This man also pleads that he has no information as to the whereabouts of El Diablo. Believing the man is stalling, Jason pours syrup over him, this causes the ants to come out

of the ground and go into a frenzy. With his mind so set on revenge, Jason has lost his compassion for his fellow man. Despite the man's screams, and pleads for mercy he turns and walks away.

The next night he forces two street hoodlums into the nearby woods. After tying them to a tree he fires several shots right next to their heads. But despite these efforts these men plead and beg that they do not have any idea as to the where El Diablo is. Confident that they know nothing he also leaves these men tied to the tree to fend for themselves. Their welfare he could care less about and again hoping that they spread the word that someone is hunting El Diablo. His need to find and extract revenge on El Diablo is clouding his thinking.

Again he sneaks into the center of the city and finding a spot on the roof of a building that has a good view of the streets below, he now waits.

It isn't long and several men can be seen making their way up the street. Anyone they encounter they knock to the side, these men must be very tough criminals Jason suspects.

Looking through the scope on his rifle his heart skips a beat, he can't believe who he's looking at. Here is Mongul, one of El Diablo's brothers and he is walking right towards Jason.

Besides El Diablo he has also been after his two brothers, but they too have proved a hard target to find.

But now one of them is in the open, and Jason can't believe his good fortune. Because Mongul keeps moving around Jason can't get a shot. The men have turned around and now have begun moving farther down the street and only their legs are visible because of the advertising signs sticking out from the buildings. Sensing a lost opportunity Jason removes a bottle of chlorine from his backpack. Tossing the bottle through the air it lands several feet in front of these men. The glass bottle shatters spreading its contents over the sidewalk. With its pungent odor this causes the men to stop, with only their legs showing it is his only shot.

Wasting no time he fires and the bullet strikes Mongul in the left leg just below the knee. Not a fatal wound but it will inflict a great deal of pain and that in itself is a measure of success.

As the men on the sidewalk duck for cover Jason cautiously makes his way down and very quickly is out of that part of town.

Going back the apartment, he barks out, "I shot Mongul tonight."

Quickly getting up from their chairs they hurry to his side anxious to hear more.

A little out of breath Jason continues, "I only wounded him."

"That will show that dam El Diablo that we are getting closer to him," states Doc.

"You have done good tonight young man," says Edward, "regardless of if you were successful at killing anyone or not the fact is you made it back here safely."

Even with wounding Mongul Jason is not happy, his main target is still out there.

His two mentors can see how upset he is, the strain on his face is evident.

"You must have patience," says Doc. "When El Diablo slips up and makes a mistake, you'll be there."

"He's right," adds Edward. "You can't forget the bigger picture. Our mission is to clean up this city. If you can't control your anger, it will be your undoing not his."

With his head lowered, Jason can feel the anger build up inside of him. Lashing out at his mentors he demands, "You don't know how I feel. You couldn't possibly understand what I'm going through. The pain, the nightmares, the need to get even with that bastard."

Unable to sit Jason now paces the floor, he mumbles to himself.

His two companions feel for their young apprentice, they know what he is going through. Believing the time is right, they motion for him to sit. Jason objects, telling them, "I have no time to sit, what is wrong with you two. There is a man out there that must die, do either of you know what it's like to hate one man so much that you dream each night of killing him with your bare hands."

The two elderly men take in a deep breath, they begin to worry about the sanity of Jason. They wonder if maybe they have pushed him too hard. That killing night after night has begun to decay his thinking. They must reel in this young gun now or risk losing him, and without Jason their hopes of cleaning up this city is as good as over.

Still fuming, "You two sit in this apartment day after day, you talk a lot, but still you can't fathom what goes through my head. Why do I even take advise from you, you don't know my pain, so just leave me alone!"

A stern look from both causes Jason to stop, he can see on their faces that he has stepped out of line. Regaining his composure, embarrassed that he let his temper show, he does what he is told and sits down.

The two elderly men pull up their chairs and sit directly in front of Jason. With a firm tone in his words Doc says, "What I'm about to tell you no one else knows about. As you know Edward and I fought in the Korean War. We both know and understand what you are going through, so don't belittle us with your ranting and complaining. The scares we carry are as real today as when they first happened, we have been able to set aside those feelings, to control our tempers, something you need more practice doing."

Now feeling like a child being scolded, Jason sits with his arms crossed, the look on his face says that he is willing to listen to their story but doubts it will do any good.

"You need to listen carefully," demands Doc. "We don't want to lose you."

After taking in several deep breaths, "Okay," Jason replies, "I'll listen."

Now needing a moment to collect his thoughts Doc begins, "Edward and I were in the special ops unit during the war which operated behind enemy lines. We were briefed on a mission to go deep behind enemy lines and rescue a group of U.S. soldiers being held at a prisoner of war camp.

We were the third such unit to try this rescue, the first two failed. Those men were either killed or captured, as we have not heard from them.

Our group consisted of myself, Edward and three other men. These men were battle hardened and they would without hesitation risk their lives to save you.

During the night a helicopter dropped us several miles behind enemy lines. We traveled for three days, constantly on the watch for enemy soldiers. The terrain was terrible, but the insects were even worse. The black tete flies stung us right through our clothing and the poisonous snakes were everywhere. The heat was repressive with the temperature soaring into the 90s. As we got close to our objective, Edward said that his sixth sense was telling him that something wasn't right. I had gone on more than two dozen missions with him and when he said something wasn't right, it put me on alert. We had encountered very few enemy soldiers up to this point, this was unusual. This deep inside enemy territory we should have seen hundreds of soldiers.

The absent of these soldiers told us that our mission may have been compromised. This could be a trap, and we were walking right into it just like the first two units did.

To assist us we were all given names of villagers that would help us if we were to get into trouble. We wondered if maybe one of these villagers had informed the local authorities, and they were on the lookout for us.

The Central Intelligence agency was working with a double agent from North Korea, this person gave details of where this prison camp was located. Unknowing to them or to us, the double agent was feeding them false information. The first two special ops units walked right into a trap, and we were going to be next.

Thanks to Edward's uncanny ability to sense danger we stayed hidden for an extra day. Deciding to take a different path to the prison camp than the one ordered by high command, hoping this would help our mission if indeed we were being set up.

Finally reaching our objective, we crawled up a hillside and we could see the outskirts of the camp. Between us and it was a low flat area consisting of knee high grass, there was no cover and nothing to hide behind if we were discovered by either a passing patrol or someone in the guard towers. Just in front of the camp was a small section of trees, if we could make it there we would be safe.

Without resting we proceeded towards the camp. It would take us eight hours to cross the open area even though it was no more than 100 yards wide.

Staying low to the ground we moved an inch at a time. At one point a patrol of ten soldiers walked within feet of us. We were ready to start shooting if they spotted us, and I thought my heart would beat out of my chest I was so nervous.

Finally we reached the safety of the woods that were maybe 30 yards from the prison fence.

Here we rested and planned our next move.

It seemed those enemy soldiers around the camp were on heightened alert. There was a lot of movement, as soldiers were constantly rushing from one end of the camp to the other.

It gave us an ominous feeling that they were expecting trouble, and we were hoping that this constant activity would subside after a while giving us an opportunity to execute our mission.

We stayed hidden and watched and studied the camp closely. We learned when the guards changed shifts and what time they ate. Looking through binoculars, it was clear that a frontal assault on this camp was out of the question. Guard towers were situated only 50 yards apart, each one contained three men. A double fence 15 feet high strung with barb wire circled the entire camp.

My plan was that Edward and I would sneak onto a supply truck entering the camp, the other three men had their own idea. Their plan was to kill several North Korean soldiers out on patrol and then steal their uniforms. Disguised as camp guards they hoped to walk right through the front gate. I quickly advised them against this plan, stating that it was too dangerous. The men reminded me that our rescue chopper was due to pick us up at 1800 hours tomorrow. Time they said was something we did not have much of, there was no time to come up with another plan.

We said our goodbyes, Edward and I staked out a spot just inside the woods not far from the road. Here we waited for a supply truck to pass by.

We didn't have to wait long, we could hear the churning of the diesel engine as it struggled down the bumpy road. It is at this time we heard gun fire coming from the far side of the camp. This is where the other three men were, we knew something had gone wrong.

The area was soon swarming with enemy soldiers. I had an idea, instead of running, we should stay close to the camp. This is the last place they would look for us.

We watched as truckloads of soldiers went out the front gate. I was hoping that the commanding officer would think that if there are any more American soldiers in the area that they will try to get back to their lines as quickly as possible. I had gambled, and for the time being we could breathe a sigh of relief.

Our orders were that if something should go wrong that we were to abort the mission at once and return. We talked about this, and we both agreed that we couldn't leave our brothers behind. We would do whatever it takes to rescue them and bring them home.

The mission had quickly turned from dangerous to nearly impossible. The enemy knows we are here, and they have blocked all our escape routes. We both knew at that point that it is highly unlikely that we will come out of this alive.

As the last truckload of soldiers rumbled past, it left the camp thinly guarded.

If we were going to attempt a rescue it had to be soon.

Moving farther back into the thick woods I perched myself in a high tree that had a good view of the camp. I watched prisoners being marched from one building to another, their hands were bound and a hood covered their faces.

I focused on one enemy soldier that appeared to be in charge, when I saw his face a cold chill went through my body. This was Major Yun Van Ru, a North Korean zealots known for his brutality towards prisoners. I had heard the horrible stories of the atrocities that this evil man carried out. His reputation was well known, even his own soldiers feared him.

I watched as he ordered several prisoners brought out to the center of the compound. The men had their heads lowered, and they dragged their feet as they walked. Major Ru showed his impatience right away by stepping close to them and viciously whipping them with a long metal cane.

When one man fell to the ground he refused to let the others help him, instead I could hear him screaming at the soldier to get up. His English was fragmented and irregular, but his message was clear. He counted to five and at which time he pulled out his revolver and shot the man in the back of the head.

I gripped my rifle tight, I so wanted to put the cross hairs of my rifle on this man's head and pull the trigger. Taking a deep breath I knew that if I did it would alert them of our whereabouts. I needed to stay focused if we were going to have any chance of rescuing these men.

For the next several hours I watched as this Major Ru continued to savage my comrades and there was nothing I could do about it. My stomach turned and I hit the tree with my fists, to sit and be a witness to this cruel and inhumane treatment was almost more than I could take.

I made myself a promise that given the opportunity I will kill this man even if it costs me my own life.

Edward and I stayed concealed while the North Korean soldiers continued to look for us. On the second day, still without a plan of action, the situation was now getting worse. We had missed our deadline to meet the helicopter. It would be a long trek back, that is if we survived.

While watching the camp I saw two of the men that had come on this mission with us. They were tied to posts in the middle of the compound and left in the hot sun.

By now they were showing the signs of being tortured and malnourished.

Sitting on the ground with Edward, we discussed what had to be done. We could wait no longer, making a pact, we were going to hijack a truck entering the camp. We would kill as many enemy soldiers as we could before being killed ourselves.

It was a suicide pact, there would be no going home.

At that instant we heard a noise from behind us. Quickly Lying close to the ground we listened intensely. The sound was getting closer, and raising my head up I could see the tall grass moving. Whispering to Edward I told him I didn't think this was an enemy soldier, whatever it is it was too low to the ground to be a person. My next thought was that it was a dog, and it had followed our scent here. But again the sound was not that of a dog either, there was no barking or growling.

Parting the tall grass just slightly, I got the shock of my life. Not more than a few feet away was the biggest snake that I had ever seen. Unable to get up and run for fear we would be spotted all I could do was to lower my head and stay face down.

The huge snake sniffed the air around me and then continued to crawl over me. I was always petrified of snakes and having one this large crawling across my back was very unnerving. As its huge weight pressed down onto me it became difficult to breath. I glanced over at Edward whose eyes were as big as saucers. He had his rifle pointed at the snake ready to shot it if it decided to make a meal of me. Putting my hand up I signaled him not to shoot, I knew that the sound would attract the guards to our location.

After what seemed minutes the huge snake finally finished its trek across my back. Taking a deep breath all I could do was smile. We estimated that this huge snake was 25 feet long and its weight was close to 400 pounds. Needing awhile to calm down we couldn't delay this suicide mission any longer.

Edward and I made our way along the road staying just inside the woods and when a truck approached we jumped out and shot the driver dead. Quickly getting behind the wheel, I drove as fast as the truck would go. It seemed we were hell bent on dying, I gritted my teeth and Edward began yelling at the top of his lungs.

We burst through the front gates, and just as quickly soldiers began firing at us from all directions. The tires blew out causing the truck to veer hard to one side, it flipped several times. I felt like a rag doll as I was bounced helplessly around inside the cab.

When I next opened my eyes I was looking down the barrel of a rifle. We were both pulled from the vehicle and a dozen soldiers surrounded us. Edward and I were uninjured except for a few cuts and bruises. They quickly bound our hands behind our backs and forced us to our knees.

Major Ru stepped up and said he had been searching for us. He demanded to know if others were still hiding nearby. Of course we refused to answer. Major Ru was used to getting information from his prisoners, and with a cruel smile he directed that we be taken to a small structure on one side of the camp.

Refusing to walk we made the enemy soldiers drag us across the compound.

We were next thrown through the small opening of one of these structures, and found ourselves chest deep in mud. The small door closed and only a small amount of light came in through several small cracks in the ceiling.

In the semi-darkness we sat in silence not knowing what to expect next but preparing ourselves for the worst. The voices just outside grew dim and after a few hours it was apparent that they intended to leave us in here for an extended period of time.

We searched along the walls of the interior of our new prison but found no way out. The smell was wretched, as the rotting bodies of several small animals lay nearby. With the sides too steep to climb out we could do nothing but wait and see what Major Ru had in store for us.

In this relentless heat the wet mud was beginning to dry quickly causing our skin to develop rashes. As the mud got thicker we managed to keep our heads above it, and we dare not doze off, the mud would have swallowed us up. We stayed inside this structure for two days, during which time we could hear the horrible screams of men being tortured. We wondered if that would also be our fate, or would we die in this dark smelling pit.

On the third day the door was opened and it took several soldiers to pull us out of the nearly dried mud.

Being in this semi-darkness for so long the bright sun light caused us to shield our eyes.

After a few minutes we recognized the voice of Major Ru, his broken English now sounding comical.

He demanded that we give him not only information about if other American soldiers are nearby but also the names of the villagers that are helping these soldiers.

Looking at him, Edward cleared his throat and said, "You can go to hell!"

This of course infuriated Major Ru, he knocked Edward to the ground and began kicking him fiercely. Each time Edward tried to stand one of the soldiers would strike him in the head with the butt of his rifle. Falling to the ground each time, but as stubborn as he is Edward refused to stay down. I attempted to fight and strike out at Major Ru but was held securely by several soldiers.

Edward was taking a terrible beating, I pleaded with him several times to just stay down, but gritting his teeth, he replied, "This bastard doesn't know who he's messing with."

The more he inflicted punishment onto Edward the happier Major Ru got. I could see the evil in his eyes, he loved to cause pain and suffering.

Finally the beating stopped, Edward lay motionless on the ground, and for a moment I feared he was dead.

A groaning sound reassured me that he was alive, barely but at least he was alive.

He was ordered to get up, but physically he was unable to. Major Ru but his revolver next to Edwards Left ear and fired a shot. The percussion from the blast shattered his ear drum. He rolled about in agony holding both hands against his head. Blood from his damaged ear was now running down his neck, but to his credit he did not scream out in pain. Edward knew by now that when a prisoner cried out in pain and agony that this only made Major Ru happy, and he was determined not to let that bastard have any pleasure from this incident.

Again he asked for information, but we both refused.

He was determined to break our spirit, and we were determined to remain silent even if it cost us our lives.

A smiling Major Ru next put us into two separate tin sheds. These sheds were not tall enough for us to stand up in nor were they long enough for us to lie down. As the sun rose in the cloudless sky the sheds began heating up. I could hear Edward in the next shed, in severe pain he was mumbling and not making any sense so I called to him to hang on, that we'll get out of this mess, that I promise.

The temperature in the sheds must have reached 140 degrees, and soon our bodies stopped sweating. This I knew was a sign of dehydration, and if we didn't get water soon our vital organs would begin to shut down. The sides of the sheds were so hot they burned my fingers when I touched them.

The only relief was when the sun finally set and the darkness cooled our surroundings.

I continued to reassure Edward not to give up, however I knew he was a strong willed man and the thought of giving up never entered his mind.

The following day we were removed from these ovens and taken to a barracks where other U.S. soldiers were kept.

We were given a small bowl of watered down rice. I tended to Edwards injuries, and I was thankful that he appeared not to have any broken bones.

Several prisoners came near us warning us not to make Major Ru angry.

They said he has killed many prisoners, his thirst for blood has no limit.

Pointing my finger at them I said we are getting out of this mad house. They laughed, no one has ever escaped this prison camp they said, and anyone that is caught trying to escape is shot immediately.

I saw the two men that had come on this mission with us, they looked like they had been through hell. Their clothing was ripped, cuts covered their faces, one of them was missing hair on one side of his head. It didn't appear that it had been cut but rather pulled out.

Crawling over to them as my legs had trouble holding up my weight I was told that the third man was dead.

The two men were shook up and in shock as they told me that the guards had strung the third man up against the fence and used him for target practice.

I was so angry, the hatred was building up inside of me and all I wanted to do was kill every one of those North Korean bastard soldiers.

Hearing these horror stories I vowed to get even, I didn't know how I was going to do this, given my present situation, but get even I was going to do.

All day we lay trying to recover our strength, I was expecting that at any moment we would be subjected to more torture.

I soon could see the reason that we had been given this short reprieve, coming through the front gates several villagers were being forced at gun point into the compound. Soon Major Ru was confronting them, he wanted names of the collaborators that were helping the Americans.

These old and frail villagers looked frightened, and they insisted they knew nothing.

Major Ru by his actions obviously didn't believe them.

He next ordered all the prisoners brought out of the barracks. Helping Edward to his feet we managed our way until we were told to stop. Standing in the middle of the compound gave me an ominous feeling. Were the guards going to shoot all of us, was this going to be one of those mass killings I had heard about. Our bodies would then be dumped like garbage into a deep hole. Once covered over no one would ever know of our tragic ending.

The guards then instructed us to tell them which villager was working for the U.S. inelegance.

As a group we remained silent, no one uttered a single word. These men were in terrible shape, tortured beyond imagination, deprived of adequate food and water, yet they stood firm and would not betray any collaborators. It was a proud moment to be standing next to men with such conviction, dignity and honor. If I were going to die I couldn't think of a better group of men standing around me when that time came.

Growing agitated by this lack of progress, Major Ru had one prisoner removed from our group. The man's feet were bound, and a long rope was next attached to the back of a jeep. I watched horrified knowing what was next, the rope was then tied around the man's legs. With the wave of his hand, Major Ru signaled for the jeep to begin driving in circles. The man clawed at the ground in a vain attempt to stop as his body twisted and rolled from side to side.

Turning towards us Major Ru said that if we don't tell him who the collaborators are that he will have the man dragged until he is dead.

Not a single one of us said anything, and we stood as straight and defiantly as we could. Our chins up and chests out we stared at this evil man that delighted in brutality. The sight of our comrade being slowly ground into the dirt was heart wrenching.

Having watched this long enough I had to do something. Later I regretted my decision, which got me and the other prisoners no reprieve from the torture.

Taking a step forward I called out that I know who the collaborator from the nearby village is. Motioning for the jeep to stop, Major Ru stood in front of me, his wicked grin belying his foul demeanor.

Swallowing hard, and is a hoarse voice from lack of water I told him that the person he was looking for was Santa Clause.

The smile quickly left, and his face snarled up tightly like a cat about to pounce on a bird.

Swinging his cane he caught me on the right side of my jaw. The crushing sound was followed by intense pain. I dropped to the ground, my jaw obviously broken. Getting back to my feet I stared him in the eyes.

Again he struck me, this time across my forehead. I reeled back, falling to the ground again. Shaking my head, and despite the flow of blood running down my face I again stood and stared at him.

This repeated defiance angered him greatly.

Pulling out his pistol he aimed it at my head and pulled the trigger. Click is all we heard, I was sure my life was over. Surprised that the gun had missed fired, I took a deep breath.

Cursing at the pistol failing to fire he turned to one of his guards. He grabbed a rifle and putting the end of the barrel right between my eyes he told me to beg for my life.

Knowing I would be dead soon anyways, I would not give him the satisfaction.

I told him he was a coward and a bully.

Tossing the rifle to the ground he threw his arms into the air. He screamed like a wild man, unable to comprehend that someone dare speak to him this way.

I turned towards the other prisoners, they nodded their heads for me to stop. One whispered that I was only making the situation worse.

Looking at Edward, he grinned and gave me a thumbs up. "Show that bastard he can't break us."

Turning back around, Major Ru was now consulting with several of his guards.

Because of my defiance, he said, one villager will be made to suffer.

An elderly man was taken to a spot not far away, and I wondered just what type of punishment they had planned for him.

A guard appeared carrying a gas can, and once near the old man he doused him with the gas. Another guard then tossed a burning stick at the old man. The flames immediately covered the old man's body. He attempted to pat out the fire while screaming in agony but it was no use. He soon dropped to the ground and in another moment there was no movement.

I couldn't believe what I was witnessing, I knew this Major Ru was a brutal man but this was beyond that. He actually smiled as this horrible scene unfolded.

Now more than ever, I swore that before I die I would make this man pay dearly for what he has done.

Turning towards us, Major Ru again demanded to know who was helping the Americans.

I thought about coming up with another smart reply, but I kept my mouth shut.

The Major paced back and forth, occasionally he would strike one of us with his cane.

I could see that his evil brain was thinking of some gruesome type of torture to try on us.

For the next several days he denied us sleep. Guards forced us to march around the camp non-stop. He was trying to break us mentally, having realized that physical torture was getting him nowhere.

Several of my comrades fell from exhaustion, and they were kicked and punched in an effort to get them back on their feet. Those that were unable to stand were dragged away, we never saw them again.

On the third day my legs were burning and I couldn't keep my eyes open. The need to sleep was so overwhelming. Earlier in the day Edward had collapsed and couldn't get back to his feet. When the guards approached him I pushed them away. I carried Edward on my back, even though I myself could barely stand.

The pain and agony was almost too much to bare, but I endured because the thought that if I can't carry my friend he will be killed. So finding strength and determination I didn't know I possessed I blocked everything out of my mind. Staggering about like a zombie, in a daze I walked.

If I could have cried I would have, but my body was too dehydrated. Finally we were allowed to rest at which time Major Ru once again demanded the names of the villagers that were cooperating with the American forces.

One man, both physically and mentally broken crawled on his hands and knees towards Major Ru.

Standing over the man like he was a king, Major Ru grabbed the man by the neck.

He looked at us and with that devious grin and pronounced, "So you filthy Americans do have a breaking point." This was followed by a hideous laugh.

Calling the guards to come closer, he announced, "This is your enemy," as he pointed to the soldier on the ground. "He is weak and a coward. The Americans are not soldiers they are nothing more than frightened children. "

The guards now joined in his laughter. Major Ru seemed to get pleasure from his degrading remarks.

Putting his hands in the air, the guards stopped laughing. Pointing towards me, Major Ru said, "I have broken his will, and I have reduced him to nothing more than a spineless excuse for a man."

Pausing for a moment, he continued, "All of you will meet the same fate."

Now grabbing the soldier by the neck again, forcing him to his feet, he shouted "Now tell your fellow prisoners that they are losers, and that they have no choice but to cooperate."

We all stood waiting for this soldier to join Major Ru, to turn his back on his comrades. Yes, the man had been through a great deal of torture and deprivation, but no matter, you still do not join the enemy and desert you comrades and your country.

The soldier looked at us, and I could see a half grin cross his face. Looking at me he winked, and he gave me a slight nod of his head.

I knew at that instant that he had not betrayed us or his country.

Turning towards Major Ru the man called out as loud as he could, "All you North Korean bastards can go to hell."

Those of us that could speak echoed his words. It was a great moment in a hopeless situation.

This one act of defiance, this rebelliousness seemed to renew our spirits.

The soldiers around me uttered the words, "Bastards, Bastards!"

The look on Major Ru's face was priceless. Here he was so sure and confident that he had broken our spirit and temperament that for a moment he was speechless.

Enraged and furious, he shot the soldier dead right there on the spot. His body lay at my feet, and looking up I gave Major Ru a hard stare.

"Someday I will kill you," I told him.

With the wave of his hand he signaled for a prisoner to be tied to the back of the jeep again. The unlucky soldier kept a stern face, he knew his fate and he uttered not a word. They continue to drag the man around the compound for the next hour. We were forced to stand and witness this cruel and barbaric torture.

Finally the jeep stopped and we were allowed to go to this soldier. I kneeled down next to him, I could see that most of his skin had been torn from his body. It was a sight that burned in my mind for years and years. To my surprise the soldier was still alive, and as these other men have shown he was going to be defiant to the very end. With his last breath he uttered, "Don't give up!"

My heart sank as his body went limp, this man had been subjected to horrendous and unspeakable type of brutality and yet he smiled at me as he died.

I took in several deep breaths, talking to God I vowed that I would find and kill Major Ru. I had to avenge these men's deaths, and I was not going to let anything stop me, this I vowed to my dead comrades.

Looking back at us Major Ru said, "You are not broken yet, but you will be."

All of us were next tied together in a large group in the center of the compound. Here we sat, not knowing what heinous type of torture this evil man was planning next.

The daily and constant brutality is slowly breaking down each man. One man became delusional and began screaming as he ran towards the fence. Climbing half way up he was shot and killed, his body dangled from the barbwire.

The guards did not remove him from the fence for several days. Major Ru wanted this to be an example, he refused our request to take our brother down. It had gotten to the point that we knew we were going to die. Each man was aware that there was no escaping this hell hole.

Our only chance of salvaging some dignity from this terrible situation before we die was to attempt a breakout. We knew it would be suicide, but we couldn't sit and wait for death to come to us.

There were five of us strong enough to walk, and it would be just us that would attempt the impossible. We devised a plan, it was reckless and without much hope for success, but it was all we had. Our only weapons were several pieces of splintered wood that we removed from the walls of our shelter.

We waited for just the right time and one night during a heavy rain storm we put our plan into action. The rain continued to come down in buckets with dark clouds obscuring the moon. The wind at times was so strong that it appeared that the guard towers would be blown over.

This weather was actually to our advantage. We knew the guards were crouched down inside their guard towers protecting themselves from the weather. With no one was watching the compound we put our plan into motion.

Crawling on our stomachs across the compound the first thing we did was to free the man tied to the stake. Untying the ropes he fell to the ground, holding him on my lap and with his last breath he whispered, "Kill every one of those bastards."

It was heart wrenching, this was a proud and dignified man, and he did not deserve to die this way.

We next crawled back over to a small shed, and pushing a board to the side we slipped inside. The dark interior was eliminated by a single lantern. We spotted the guard, and to our good fortune he was sleeping. Sitting in a chair with his face and arms lying across the table his snoring echoed inside the small shed despite the howling winds outside.

Holding the splintered piece of wood tight, Edward drove it with all the strength he had left into the guards neck. The guard quickly raised up his head and that's when I jabbed another piece of splintered wood into his throat. He convulsed and jerked about before lying motionless. Grabbing his rifle, we felt a little more secure now that we were armed.

The urge to seek revenge was now more powerful and overwhelming than the need to escape.

The five of us debated briefly what we should do next. But in quick fashion we agreed to kill as many of the guards as possible. If we did manage to get through the front gates our chances of getting very far in our condition was slim to none.

If recaptured we all knew that death would be slow and severe. Major Ru would not show us any mercy.

We then decided not to try and escape instead we would inflict as many casualties on our enemy as we could before dying ourselves.

Each of us was fully prepared to die this day, and being young men this was not a decision we looked forward to. To know you are going to die is a gut wrenching moment in a person's life, one matures very quickly under these circumstances.

My outlook on life changed that day, I was at peace with myself and my God.

Adding to our good luck we were able to acquire several more rifles, and now our spirits were rising. Still looking at a suicide mission, but with the extra rifles we now knew that a great many of the guards would be killed.

We made our way back over to the shelter housing our comrades.

I could see that these other prisoners were so malnourished and beaten down that they could not even stand. To escape and leave them behind is something I and the other men could not do. Our fellow soldiers are like family to us, if they cannot leave this hell hole . than neither can we.

At this point we knew for sure that this day would be our last. With death inevitable, the thought of dying no longer bothered us. We were happy to be going out in a blaze of glory. There is no better, more honorable way to die than to die fighting your enemy.

I looked at each man, in his eyes I could see pride. I sensed he was at peace with his decision.

I shook their hands, knowing we would see each other again in heaven. None of us cried, we were so proud, our heads up high. These were my brothers, my friends. How I wished this nightmare was over, that a miracle would ascend from the sky, and we would live another day.

As the weather outside intensified it was now or never, our one chance to put our plan into action. This would be the night.

We gave several of these men the rifles we had found earlier, they would cause a distraction by shooting at the guard towers further confusing the enemy.

Crawling back over and searching the dimly lit shed we found the one truck with keys in it. In the back of this truck was a container with a few more rifles, our luck was turning.

A good friend of mine named Roger got behind the wheel, starting it up we wasted no time. Our plan was simple, inflict as much death and destruction on the enemy as possible before we are killed. Too weak to slide open the heavy double doors to this shed, we braced ourselves, ramming the truck straight ahead. The old wooden doors shattered as if they were made of match sticks. Driving by the barracks that housed the other prisoners, we tossed them several more rifles. They may not be able to walk but they could still shoulder and fire a rifle. This extra firepower would help distract the guards.

Turning the truck around we now headed straight for major Ru's quarters. The sound of gun shots could be heard, and soon bullets were ripping through the thin canvas that covered the truck.

Despite being hit several times, Roger never let off the gas. We crashed through the front door just as a soldier appeared in the doorway. He managed to get several shots off before being hit by the truck. His body bounced off the hood and up and over the truck.

The truck continued another ten yards before stopping. Despite being shook up, we managed to exit the truck just as it exploded.

The blast was so strong that it knocked us through the thin wall of the building. Laying on the ground all I could here was rifle fire and soldiers yelling. As I was crawling away from the flames I looked back to see one of us lying on the ground not moving. I called to him to get up, but there was still no movement. Risking the flames I went back and grabbing him by the shoulders I dragged him away.

Trying to catch my breath, I laughed and told him that that was a close one.

He still did not move, I felt for a pulse and there was none. I felt so bad for this man, and I held him for a moment.

The sound of heavy machine gun fire followed by mortar rounds exploding inside the compound startled me. I was confused by the chaos all around me, as enemy soldiers were running in the opposite direction. Suddenly I saw men running into the camp through the front gates, to my surprise they were wearing American uniforms.

Bullets were whizzing past my head, and several explosions shook the ground. It took me a moment but it finally dawned on me that this was a rescue mission. I was so pleased to see the men.

I could only sit and watch as I knew I had several broken ribs and a deep laceration across my legs.

The enemy was in full retreat, and helicopters with more American soldiers were landing nearby.

A soldier named Isaac helped me to my feet and yelled that we have to leave at once before the enemy regroups and comes back. I knew he was right, as a barracks of several hundred soldiers were stations only a few miles away.

As I hobbled across the compound I spied Major Ru, he was with a group of guards that were attempting to stop us.

Grabbing Isaacs rifle I pulled hard against his grip, I wanted to kill Major Ru before we left.

At that instant two enemy soldiers charged at us firing their weapons. Isaac was hit several times causing him to release his grip on me. Apparently out of ammo both enemy soldiers jumped at Isaac who at that moment put himself between me and these enemy soldiers. He pulled a knife from his belt quickly striking down one man. The other soldier knocked Isaac to the ground and was choking him when I managed to crawl close enough to pull him off. This gave

Isaac enough time to grab the soldier and put him in a head lock and with a quick twist he broke his neck.

I could see the blood covering Isaac's clothing from the bullets wounds, and the grimace on his face told me he was in severe pain.

To my surprise Isaac picked me up and tossed me into the chopper. In a stern voice he said that we have no time to seek revenge, we are leaving right now.

The chopper jerked upwards causing me to fall backwards. I was fuming at this man for not allowing me to go after Major Ru.

He could see how upset I was and tapping me on the shoulder he pointed to the ground. Leaning over I could see a large column of trucks about to enter the compound. Knowing that there must be a hundred enemy soldiers in them, we had no chance if we were to stay any longer.

Cursing, I knew he was right, but still I wanted to remain behind.

Now feeling the effects of my injuries, everything began to spin around me. This had been a daring and very risky rescue mission, I along with the others owe our lives to them.

Edward and I spent several months in the hospital, and several high ranking officers along with the Secretary of Defense came by to congratulate us on our rescue. This was all very nice but the visit we got from Isaac was the most rewarding.

This man had risked his life to save us, and in return he just wanted to see if we were okay and if there was anything he could do for us.

Our friendship with Isaac started that day and it has never ended.

Five years after the war ended, my need for revenge sent me back over to South Korea. The two countries were divided, and access to the north was forbidden. Despite Edward telling me to let it go, to forget about the war, I had a promise to keep. I swore I would get even with Major Ru, and I was going to keep my word. This payback was for all the soldiers that he tortured and killed. Nothing was going to stop me, I was hell bent on finding this man. There was no power strong enough to stop me, an anger burned deep inside of me and I could not rest until this job was completed.

I would first search on this side of the border until I was sure he wasn't here. I knew he was cunning so I predicted that he would sneak into South Korea to hide. It would be the last place that the international court would think to look for him.

Major Ro was wanted on charges of genocide, atrocities against prisoners of war and cold blooded murder. If he is caught by the authorities he would receive the death sentence so it was in his best interest to disappear into society.

I went among the people for three months asking if anyone knew of a man called Yun Van Ru. No one had heard of that name, and even given his description was met with disappointment. It was beginning to look that maybe he had stayed on the north side. I was hoping that I would not have to go back into that god forsaken country.

Finally my persistence paid off, a local market vender said he knew of a man by that description. He said the man lived in a rundown apartment building only a few blocks away. He also said that this man rarely goes outside, and often his meals are delivered to his apartment. My spirits were lifted, and I quickly got the address and was soon standing across the street from this apartment building.

As the wind blew a cold chill came over me, my senses were telling me that an evil man was near.

I had to be sure it was Major Ru, so I rented an apartment directly across the street. From my room I watched the front door of the apartment building day and night. Something inside me said that Major Ru was indeed inside that building. Call it a sixth sense, but I could feel the evil in the air.

On the fourth night a man appeared in the doorway. His posture and the way he turned his head looked familiar. The man was wearing an over coat and he walked with the aid of a cane, his face tucked partially inside the coat.

The man moved swiftly down the street. I hurried from my apartment, but not too fast as to draw anyone's attention. Once on the street I moved in the direction the mysterious man was going.

I looked cautiously around every corner, knowing that Major Ru would be wary. He was aware that he was wanted by the international authorities for atrocities committed during the war.

Hiding in South Korea would be the last place the authorities would think to look for him. It is where I would go to avoid detection if I were him.

After walking several blocks it seemed that the mysterious man had vanished. Maybe he knew he was being followed. Perhaps he was waiting for me, to add another murder to his long list.

I returned to my apartment, still feeling that this could be the man I had come so far to hunt down.

My luck was changing as two nights later this same man dressed in the overcoat and walking with a cane appeared on the street. But he was not leaving but returning to the apartment building. Somehow he had managed to exit the building without me noticing him.

Before he went through the door I noticed that he carried two burlap bags. Their contents I didn't know, but I knew exactly where they had come from.

During my recon of the area, I remember that just a few blocks away a vender put his sold vegetables in burlap sacks. The other venders used straw baskets. This was the lead that I had been waiting for. Knowing that this mysterious man only goes out once every fourth night I waited patiently in my apartment.

During that time my mind constantly thought of the ways I was going to kill him. Should I shoot him without saying a word or should I let him know who I'm. I wanted to look him in the eyes, to see the fear that he had put into so many others.

I was anxious and restless, but I knew to bid my time and wait, after all it had been more than five years since I last laid eyes on him, a few more days I could wait.

When the predicted night arrived I left the apartment early and hid only yards away from the vender that I had noticed was the only one that used burlap sacks. My stomach was tightening up, and I felt a little sick. Was this a sign that tonight I was going to come face to face with Major Ru?

My hand quivered as my fingers rubbed the handle of my revolver. For a moment I closed my eyes, I could still picture this man brutalizing so many and his total disregard for human life.

It was a dark night, and with only a few street lights it would make identifying him from a distance very difficult.

Being this close, I also would be putting myself within his reach. I'm sure he was armed, a man with his reputation always carries a weapon. If he saw me I'm sure he would not hesitate killing me right on the spot, regardless of anyone standing nearby.

The risk was worth it if indeed this was Major Ru.

As the crowd thinned out I saw a man wearing a long overcoat walking with a cane coming in my direction. He stopped several times and scanned the area, his eyes carefully watching those nearby. He waited, his face hidden, his one hand inside his coat. If this was not Major Ru, than it was someone that was hiding from the law.

Approaching until he was only ten feet away this man spoke so softly that I couldn't hear what he was saying to the vender.

Peering out from between the wooden crates I spied the one object that sent a shiver through my body, the cane this man had was the same one that Major Ru broke my jaw with. Its distinctive medal tip and the engravings of dragons on it left no doubt in my mind.

Touching my jaw and the scar on my forehead, the memories came flooding back, it took everything I had not to jump up and empty my revolver into him.

When his sack was full he turned and began walking in the direction of his apartment. This was my chance, I had to make my move now or risk losing him.

He walked a block and then turned around, seeing someone so close to him caused him to turn back around and now he began to walk briskly.

I'm sure with my disguise that he didn't recognize me.

I watched as his right hand went inside his coat and bringing it out I could see a black object.

The street light flashed just briefly off of this object, letting me know that it was probably a revolver.

Now more than ever I was sure this was Major Ru. His walk, the cane, the way he turned his head, and the revolver, yes, this was him alright.

But I couldn't strike at him from the back without seeing his face first. I wanted him to see who was about to end his life, it was important for me and for those that he killed.

I quickly ran down an alley going up two blocks hoping to be ahead of him.

Trying my best at controlling my breathing, I peeked around the edge of a building. Coming up the street was the same man I had been following. To my good fortune he did not change his course, this wary and evasive man was losing his touch. He was known for avoiding capture by the police and staying out of sight, maybe it was the guilt that was on his mind from the atrocities that he had committed, or had he simply grown tired of running, whatever the reason he had made a grave error in not taking a different path back to his apartment.

This was my chance to find out for sure if my instincts were right, that I had traveled so far and searched diligently for the right man.

The streets this late at night were nearly deserted only an occasional car would pass by. I moved back into the shadows and pressed myself up against the stone wall. I could hear his footsteps, he was wearing army boots. The heel of these boots was striking the sidewalk with a sharp snap. This was an indication that this man had been in the military.

As the mysterious man stepped in front of me I reached out and grabbed him by the shoulders tossing him to the ground. Lying on his back and stunned by my quickness this man was wide eyed and he slide backwards trying to move away from me.

My gun was pointed at him and I motioned with my hand for him to release his revolver.

At first he pretended not to understand me, he shook his head and had a confused look on his face.

I could clearly see his face, and he stared at me with those same cold eyes I had seen in the prison camp. This was indeed Major Ru, the man that routinely tortured and maimed at will.

Here he sat, like the coward that he was fearful for his life. Reaching down I yanked the revolver from his hand.

Backing up a few steps I told him to stand up.

Major Ro slowly got to his feet, not once taking his eyes off me. I stared at him the same way he had stared at me all those years ago. But now I was in control, I called the shots here.

There was a moment of silence before he spoke.

"So we meet again," he uttered.

He had recognized me very quickly this I was not expecting, seeing that he must have tortured and killed hundreds of people. I wondered what I had done that would make him remember me.

"You will not kill me," he said, "the war is over go back to your country."

But inside my head the war still raged, the pain and torment were still very fresh.

"You have escaped the authorities for a long time," I told him, "for your freedom is about to end."

"Very well," he said, "I was growing tired of always running and looking over my shoulder. I will go with you to the nearest police station, I'm sure there is a reward for my capture."

These words meant nothing to me, to have this man spend the rest of his life in prison was a crime itself. No, this animal did not deserve any humane treatment, he needed to suffer.

Taking a step forward I placed the end of my revolver against his temple.

I could see him begin to shake and the sweat was running down his face.

"You cannot kill me," he said in a shaking voice, "you must turn me in it is the right thing to do."

I had no intention of turning him in to the authorities, but I was going to do the right thing. I would make sure that he never had the opportunity to hurt another human being, not now not ever.

As I pulled the hammer back he began to tremble, this is what I waited so long to see.

Holding the revolver like this for several minutes, this once mighty bully was quickly reduced to a sniffling coward.

I eased the hammer forward and removed the barrel from his head. This gave him a false sense that I had changed my mind. I could see relief on his face and he let out a big sigh. I quickly lowered my arm and stuck the revolver into his side and pulled the trigger. His knees buckled as he staged away from me. A quick death is not what this butcher deserved, he was going to suffer and feel the pain that he has inflicted on so many others. I let him lay in a pool of his own blood, and by the look on his face he knew that death was but a short time away.

In a zombie like state, I pulled out my knife and slit his throat. Taking several steps back I put a bullet into his head. As God as my witness, I had to make sure that this butcher, this tyrant that brutalized helpless men would never again walk this earth."

A young Jason is spellbound by this story. He had no idea the terrible things that Doc and Edward had gone through. Now humbled and embarrassed, he wipes the tears from his face.

"I had not right to talk to either of you the way I did, I apologize a hundred times over."

With his usual smile, Doc answers, "It's alright, maybe we should have told you this story long ago. After all you have proven yourself to be trustworthy and a key asset to this organization. We promise that from this day on there will be no more secrets."

It had been a learning ordeal for Jason who again was taught not to judge a person on looks alone. People can hide their feelings very well, and what someone has gone through in life is not always obvious.

He is learning a great many things, not only about his two mentors but also about himself.

One being that regardless of what terrible things that have happened in the past, they can and should be forgotten at all coasts. His two mentors are good examples of this, as they have led normal lives since those nightmarish days.

CHAPTER 5

Walking into his office at the 38th precinct, Lt. Wilson throws his hands into the air. On his desk is a stack of papers. He has been put in charge of tracking down and arresting the Vigilante Assassin. A 17 year veteran of the police force, Lt. Wilson knows that this will be his toughest case. As more and more criminals are found shot to death, public opinion has begun to sway in favor of this modern day robin hood. This silent killer is doing what the police could not, that is to make the streets a safer place to walk.

Despite the publicity from the police Chief and Mayor that this vigilante is nothing more than a mass murderer, and a serial killer, the people have looked at him as their savior, giving him the status of guardian angel. Each criminal that is found dead and the police attribute it to the Vigilante Assassin his urban legend grows.

Lt. Wilson knows he will get very little help from the general public, so he must rely on informants for tips and leads. Searching through the daily pile of papers, he desperately hopes that someone has seen a glimpse of this vigilante. Just a quick sighting of him to give them his height and race is what he's looking for. But each day is always the same. Another victim found, there are no witnesses, and no physical evidence at the scene.

Lt. Wilson is beginning to think that this man he is after is more ghost than human. He has the ability to penetrate a heavily populated area, takeout his victim and then seemingly disappear into thin air.

No one ever sees him coming or going. But the m. o. of the victim is always the same, a single gunshot to the head. His victims are always drug dealers or other criminals, and he always strikes at night.

The authorities know that this vigilante uses a 22-250 caliber rifle to kill with. They now suspect that he is using the tops of tall buildings, this is maybe the reason he is never seen.

They search the data base for any military snipers living in the state, this vigilante they suspect must have gotten his training this way.

Glancing at the calendar on the wall, Lt. Wilson can see by this date the body count is over 75.

This self-proclaimed savior is quickly becoming one of the most notorious murderers in the country. The pressure from the Mayor and even the Governor to find and stop this madman is increasing more each day. Frustrated at working with so few clues, Lt. Wilson has begun taking pills to calm his nerves. A nagging ulcer is also hampering his efforts.

The common person in the city seems not afraid of this Vigilante Assassin, but it is the law breaker that now must constantly look over his shoulder.

Knowing that on one hand this Vigilante Assassin is reducing the crime rate, but on the other hand a citizen cannot take the law into his own hands. To the Lieutenants dismay, even criminals are calling the police station demanding that this man be arrested.

The detectives have spent months searching for evidence, they thoroughly examine each crime scene. Despite all their efforts very little is learned. Like a mythical avenging angel, this vigilante extracts his vengeance on those that break the law and then just as swiftly he retreats back to the safety of the heavens.

As small amounts of evidence are pieced together, the detectives realize that this Vigilante Assassin is not working alone. He may be the only one carrying out the murders, but they suspect that a sophisticated network of others is helping him. With the help of the FBI and DEA they have begun to monitor the internet.

Minor and insignificant pieces of data are beginning to point to a group that operates on the wet. Just as the authorities seem to get close the group will switch code words and the process starts all over again.

They know they are dealing with very intelligent people, and their only hope is that one of them will make a mistake. Just the slightest error, the smallest miscue, the most insignificant of slipups is all the detectives need. Ready at a moment's notice a specially trained team has been assembled. Their orders are to stop the Vigilante Assassin and his accomplices at all costs. They are told if any of them resists than they are to kill them immediately.

Working long hours Lt. Wilson and his men have started to get a profile of this person. They estimate him to be a white male in his mid-twenties. He is of average height and weight, perhaps unemployed and no education beyond high school. This man is surely a victim of a crime, thus his reason for wanting to eliminate all the criminals he can. The police records are searched, and any person that had been mugged, robbed, assaulted or victimized in any way is investigated. The detectives start by looking back as far as ten years, it is a long and grueling process, but they are hoping that it will pay off with new information.

CHAPTER 6

Sitting alone in the solitude of the apartment, Jason wonders if all that he has done up to this point has done any good. Illegal drugs are still sold everywhere, however the crime rate has dropped but not nearly as much as he and the others had hoped.

He ponders if he should be more bold and daring in his attempts to rid the city of these criminals. Also, maybe others should join him, more vigilantes will definitely help.

But his thoughts keep going back to El Diablo, he is the source of all the evil in this city. But El Diablo's ability to avoid being seen in public, and his caginess and shrewdness have made him a challenging target. On more than one occasion Jason knew the whereabouts of this man, but he seemed to elude him every time.

Growing frustrated at being unable to eliminate his nemesis, Jason ponders his next move.

"If I can't eliminate El Diablo," he utters with content, "than the next best thing is to take his money."

He sends out dispatches via the internet, asking his contacts to find the location where El Diablo stores his drugs and money. This will be risky, as only those closest to El Diablo are privy to this information. Nevertheless he instructs his fellow conspirators in this war on crime that this is of the utmost important.

Telling them that it is a code 13, this is the highest code that the group has. The numbers represent varying degrees of alarm. The lower the number the less important the situation and the higher the number the more serious and dangerous it is. Code 13 is the groups highest number, this highest of emergencies has never been used up to this date.

Going behind Doc and Edward's back, he sends out this code 13, knowing that the two would never approve of using it just to locate a stash of drugs and money.

Using the code without their permission, Jason knows that he has done wrong. But his need to strike at El Diablo is too overpowering. All he can do now is wait and hope that he gets a lead.

Several days pass and yet his contacts come up empty. Jason understands that only a trusted few of El Diablo's henchmen know the whereabouts of this secret location. It is the hub of most of the drug trafficking in the city. Learning of its whereabouts and shutting it down would be a major blow to the drug gangs.

Night after night, Jason monitors the computer hoping that someone will send him a message, a clue, anything that will point him in the right direction.

Growing wary and nearly abandoning this vision of dealing a crippling blow to El Diablo, until a late night message flashes across the screen.

Wide eyed, Jason sits up and copies down the short sentence. Its sender is unknown, but it doesn't matter, as long as the address is correct.

Forgetting what time of the night it is, "I think you need to read this," he calls out.

A moment later a tired and slightly perturbed Doc stumbles into the room.

"This better be good," the old man mumbles as he looks over Jason's shoulder.

Adjusting his glasses, he reads what is written down on the paper. Clapping his hands, "Oh my God," he exclaims. "This is what we have been searching so long for," a jubilant Doc shouts out.

"We now know where that bastard keeps his drugs," states Jason. "We must devise a plan of attack. Alert everyone in the F.L.O.C.K.

to assemble at a predestined location, from there we will storm the location."

Doc shakes his head, "No my young friend, you will get no help from anyone. Those that comprise the F.L.O.C.K. have clearly stated that they will not pick up arms and do battle with the criminals in this city. I'm sorry, but this mission you will have to go on alone."

Disappointed and angry in hearing this Jason begins to lash out, "What are they a bunch of..." but stops himself mid-sentence.

Looking at doc he knows that the others members of the F.L.O.C.K. are also senior citizens, and at their age there is little they can do. Recomposing himself Jason says, "I'll go this alone, one man has a better chance of getting in and out without being spotted."

A smile crosses Doc's face, this was a very good answer from his young apprentice.

Looking at the piece of paper again Doc is unfamiliar with the address. Jason pulls out a map and he traces the route with his finger, until he knows the exact location of El Diablo's lair.

Still amazed at this stroke of good luck, "I'm not familiar with that area," states Doc, as he rubs his chin "we will need to find someone to help guide you once you are there."

Ecstatic at this good fortune, Jason wastes no time and prepares his backpack with the necessary things he will need.

Meanwhile Doc has contacted Eagle, asking for someone to guide Jason while in that part of the city. Before the morning sun comes up, he gets an answer.

Writing down the instructions, Doc passes them on to Jason.

Anxious to leave at once, Jason is stopped at the door, "You know you can't travel about during the day," demands Doc, now standing with his hands on his hips.

Taking a glance through the window, Jason cracks a smile, "I was so eager that I didn't notice it was day outside."

"We have much to prepare before you set out on this mission," states Doc, as he guides his young apprentice back into the room.

The two wake up Edward, who can't believe they actually have the location of El Diablo's hideout.

"We have been searching for it for years without any luck," says Edward. "A good many of our contacts have disappeared during the search. They no doubt met a cruel ending at the hands of that monster."

"You must be extremely careful," states Edward. "This will be the most dangerous and risky undertaking that you have attempted. If you should run into any trouble we will be unable to come to your assistance. You must be prepared to fight your way out if necessary, and die if there is no escape. Do you understand this?"

"Yes, I have been waiting for this opportunity for a long time. I will go into this mission fully prepared to die it necessary."

Grabbing the young man by his shoulder, Edward can only nod his head. He has grown very close to Jason, and looks at him as his own son. The thought that Jason may not come back from this mission bothers him greatly. He glances a look at several pictures on the wall, his eyes begin to tear up. He has lost loved ones in the past, and their memory causes him to sit down.

Jason looks at Doc, who whispers, "Edward feels partly responsible for the deaths of some of his family members."

"Tell me more," begs Jason. Feeling that he needs to know more about Edward's personal life and about these family members, he urges Doc to confide in him.

Taking the young man to the side so they will not be heard, "When Edward was new on the FBI, he was known as a fearless and bold officer. His skills at catching criminals and quick at defending himself with his service revolver were becoming well known. He would come upon a situation where other police officers might be out numbered or out gunned. Not waiting for more police to arrive he would take care of the situation his own way. Sometimes he would drive the squad car right into a barricade that was protecting a drug gang that was having a shootout with the police. Other times he was known for sneaking to the roof of a building and jumping right down in the middle of a group of criminals.

He carried two revolvers with him at all times and there were many times when I and other officers would arrive on a scene only to hear multiple gun shots coming from inside a house. Knowing that Edward was in there, we waited until the shooting stopped. A moment later he would come walking out, and a big smile was always on his face. These daring forays often got him wounded. Most of the time he was reprimanded for going against direct orders and wait for the backup to arrive. His citations for bravery and heroism nearly equaled his number of reprimands and warnings. But he only knew one way to do his job, and that was always with a disregard for his own safety."

Jason seems very intrigued by this information, this he wished he had known earlier.

"Getting to the point of this story," Doc says, "a gun battle was taking place between the police and mobsters. In those days we didn't have street gangs, the mob ruled the city.

Edward arrived on the scene and quickly saw that the mob was not going to surrender. The house they were in was heavily fortified, and the mob was prepared for a long shootout with the police.

Seeing that this situation needed to end soon, Edward again went against orders to wait for state troopers to arrive. He managed to get close enough to the house where he found a way into the basement. Once inside he made his way up the steps, here a mobster jumped out and shot Edward in the right arm. Falling back he fired three quick shots, killing the mobster. Now wounded and knowing that the mobsters would be coming down the steps in force to get him he had to come up with plan. With his escape route now being watched by these mobsters, he prepared himself for a shootout to the death.

Despite the pain in his injured arm Edward stayed focused and soon came up with an idea.

Disabling the fuse box, this cut the electricity to the whole house. With no lights the mobsters would have to move about in the dark.

Barricading himself behind several tables that he tipped over he hunkered down to wait for these men to come down the steps.

To his surprise one of the mobsters called him by name. Edward was well known among the mobs running the city. They had put several contracts out on his life. His ability to outsmart these gangsters at their own game infuriated them. He had arrested or killed a great many of them, and they were eager to get revenge.

They told him that they were going to kill him.

Looking to his left Edward noticed a propane cylinder. It was about three feet long and picking it up it only weighted about 15 pounds. Always quick with a plan, he knew with the blood running down his arm that he couldn't wait for the state troopers to arrive. He would be dead from lack of blood before they got here.

At the top of the steps he could hear the mobsters talking as they were preparing to come down and he estimated that perhaps there was about eight of them just around the corner at the top of the steps.

Firing several shots at the top of the steps he next threw the cylinder. Luck was on his side as it hit a wall and rolled back where it stopped just at the top of the steps. Waiting a moment until he could hear the mobsters talking again, this let him know that they had moved closer to the steps and were about to come charging down. Despite the pain, he waited until he was sure the time was right. Leaning out from his cover he fired at the cylinder. The bullet caused the cylinder to explode, and instantly the house was on fire.

Several mobsters ran out the front door to escape the fire. Here they were either shot or arrested by the officers waiting there.

Hoping that all the mobsters had fled the house, Edward made his way up the steps.

Avoiding the flames he went from room to room looking for anyone that may be injured. Confident that everyone had gotten out he headed for the front door. Jumping from his hiding place was a mobster named Rocky. Edward knew this man, and he was not going to let him escape.

Rocky had stayed when the others ran, his face and arms were severely burned. With a revolver aimed at his head Edward quickly fell to the side, a bullet grazed his head.

Returning fired, Rocky was hit several times and collapsed to the floor.

Kicking the gun away from the injured man, Edward felt he had the situation under control.

Rocky pleaded for his life, saying he was unarmed. Feeling compassion, Edward went against police policy, putting away his revolver he bent down to help the man up.

Quick as a flash, Edward was hit in the head with a steel pipe. He lay on the floor semi-conscious, he felt his service revolver being removed from his holster.

The shadowy figure uttered the words, "It's payback time." With that said he ran out the back door.

Despite being severely injured Rocky managed to shoot his way through the police line. Commandeering a car on the street he quickly sped away. With the police close behind it seemed that this mobster's days were numbered.

When Edward was taken outside his first question was where is Rocky headed. The answer he got sent a shiver up his spine.

The mobster was headed directly for Edwards house. His wife and two young sons were there alone.

Refusing medical help he drove his police car as fast as he could.

When he arrived at his house he could see police cars everywhere. Stopping him several officer's told him that they were sorry.

Getting a bad feeling in his stomach he could see his wife in the doorway holding their youngest son in her arms. Rushing to her side, she was crying. The little boy lay motionless, his clothing soaked in blood.

Rocky had extracted his revenge before the police could stop him. To this day Edward blames himself for this tragedy.

Swallowing hard Jason is speechless, he had no idea that Edward carried this burden around with him.

"We'll leave him alone," says Doc.

Edward sits at the kitchen table, his eyes are tearing up, and his hands are now shaking.

Jason has never seen Edward like this, he always put on a tough guy image. But now he looks broken, a man mourning the loss of someone very close.

The two leave Edward by himself, as they now discuss their next mission.

With the story about Edwards past on his mind Jason's mood changes quickly.

With a renewed sense of vigor and drive, Jason feels anger. He knows what he is doing is right, and he is determined now more than ever to complete his task.

Sitting in front of the computer, "Show me what I can expect when I get there," requests Jason.

Tapping into the city archives, they find the blue prints for the building that El Diablo keeps his money and drugs. Going over every floor and every entrance and exit, Jason must learn the inside of this building like the back of his hand.

They search hallways and the location of stairwells, from the basement to the roof, nothing is left to chance.

Several hours later they have devised a plan, "You must use the ventilation shafts," states Edward now recovered from his earlier emotions. "It will get you access to any part of the building without being seen."

Happy with what they have come up with, Jason feels confident that he can pull this off.

Looking at his watch, "In six hours it will be dark," states an excited Jason, "I will then go and meet our contact."

"You have his name," a worried Doc says, "just watch your back."

Seeing the worry in the faces of his two friends, "I will be extra careful, say a prayer for me when I leave."

Patting Jason on the shoulder Doc says, "We always do."

After pausing a moment, "Just go there and do what has to be done and get out as quick as possible young man, no time to loiter."

Laughing at such a suggestion, "You worry too much," answers Jason, "I'll be back, you can count on that."

The rest of the day the three pack the weapons Jason will need, and what other supplies to take along. They try to think of all the possible things that could go wrong, all the worst case scenarios. They go over ways to counter any glitches or problems that Jason may encounter, as this will be his most dangerous mission to date. They remind him that he can expect no backup if he should run into trouble.

As the sun begins to fade, Jason grabs his backpack, and halfway out the door he turns and looks at his friends. Doc and Edward are standing by the kitchen table, Edward with a newspaper in his hands and Doc preparing supper. The two elderly men stand mute, their facial expression says it all. With a look that a parent gives his son before he leaves to go off to war, they know it is the right thing to do, but they also wish he would stay.

With his chin up, Jason nods head, not saying a word he walks out the door.

Not wanting to waste time walking across town, Jason waits for Crow to pick him up.

The taxi pulls up right on time and after getting in Jason tells Crow the address.

Without turning around Crow replies, "That is the worst part of town, why on earth would you want to go there?"

Taking a deep breath, "I can't tell you that, but I will say that if my mission is successful, the crime rate in this city should drop significantly."

"Sounds like a very dangerous plan you have," Crow hesitates for a moment, "can you use some help?"

Smiling at his suggestion, Jason replies, "Thanks for the offer, but I must do this alone."

Glancing in the rear view mirror, "If you get into trouble, don't hesitate to call me, you understand!"

"I'll call if I need you, just wish me luck."

Mumbling to himself, Crow is obviously not happy with Jason going on this mission alone.

Sitting low in the back seat, Jason watches the streets, hoping it is a quiet night.

Going down several dark and foreboding alleys, the two are on edge. There have been many murders in this section of town, with very few arrests and even less convictions.

This is El Diablo's turf, and he has shown in the past that he is willing to kill anybody that tries to do business here. His goons are stationed at several key locations in this part of town, and they monitor all traffic that comes in and out of here very closely.

The taxi is a good cover, as gang members use their own cars to travel about.

"This is far enough," calls Jason, as he sees a sign hanging from the back of a building that reads, "Al's liquor store."

Not liking this area at all, Jason steps out of the taxi, he leans over and tells Crow, "This is where my contact said to meet him."

Shaking his head, Crow replies, "It looks like you picked the worst place to meet this contact, I hope we don't get shot while we wait."

Moving several steps away from the taxi, Jason replies, "You don't need to stay."

Giving him a puzzling look, Crow says, "I can't just leave you here."

"I'll be alright, the contact is expecting just me not anyone else. If there are two of us he may think it is a trap and not show."

Taking deep breath, "I hope you know what you're doing," says Crow, "people die here every day."

"I appreciate your concern," relies Jason while scanning the eerie and creepy surroundings.

"If I'm not back in twelve hours, Parrot and Starling will contact you. We have gone over several scenarios in case I get myself captured. They will need your help then, but let's hope I can get in and get out without getting caught."

Understanding this, Crow reluctantly agrees, "You just be careful," he says as he slowly drives away.

Now standing alone in this dangerous place, Jason backs up against a building. Not wanting to expose himself, he must wait patiently until his contact arrives. The wind howls as it swirls around the buildings, and the familiar sound of violence can be heard in the distance.

Sitting beside several empty containers, the hair on the back of his neck suddenly stands up. His eyes quickly look both ways up and down the semi dark alley.

His senses alerted, he grips his revolver tightly.

He sees a figure approach from his right. Dropping down on one knee, he pulls his revolver out of his coat pocket.

His heart is starting to beat faster, as the memories start flashing in his mind of the last time he was a prisoner of El Diablo's. Closing his eyes, his body shudders at the thought of going through that torture again.

Trying to focus on the present, Jason grits his teeth, he has a job to do. He must concentrate on this very dangerous task that lies ahead, nothing can distract him, this mission is just too important.

The man in the alley walking towards him has slowed down, and he carefully places each footstep as he walks closer.

Stopping only twenty feet from Jason, who has moved a few feet and is now concealed behind a pile of rubbish. The man looks in all directions. Putting his hand to his mouth, the man makes a bird sound, this is the signal that tells Jason that this is his contact.

When Jason stands up, the man at first jumps back, not knowing who this is.

With his hand tight on his revolver, Jason calls out, "Blue dog one."

This is a code word and if this is his contact the man will respond with the correct answer, if he doesn't Jason may have to kill him.

"Mountain sky," is the reply he gets.

Loosening his grip on the revolver he is relieved that this was the correct answer.

Stepping out and into the middle of the alley, Jason asks, "Are you Billy the Kid?"

In a high pitched voice, "Yes, are you the Vigilante?"

"Yes, I 'am, and we must hurry."

As this contact guides Jason up the alley, he can make out what this man looks like. Wearing a scarf that partially covers his face, a beard and mustache protrude out. His long hair hangs down to his shoulders, and his clothes are rather baggy. The man shuffles his feet as he walks, the noise echoing up and down the quiet ally.

Arriving at the rear of a rundown building, the two begin moving several old and broken wooden crates out of the way.

Pointing at a spot, Billy the Kid says, "Here is a hidden panel."

Jason is thankful for his help, as he never would have found it on his own. The panel measures only about eighteen inches across by maybe twenty inches tall. Taking a screwdriver from his small backpack, Jason removes the four screws holding the panel in place.

At this time a very nervous Billy the Kid says, "This is as far as I go, you are on your own my friend."

Giving him a long look, "I won't forget this," answers Jason, "I owe you one."

Quickly looking around he replies in a nervous voice, "You just finish this job without getting yourself killed."

Pausing a moment, "El Diablo's men patrol this alley every thirty minutes, check it carefully when you are exiting," warns Billy the Kid.

With that said the mysterious contact wastes no time in leaving this area and his shuffling echoes off the tall buildings.

Jason wonders if he will ever see this man again. Will they only meet like this, to help each other and then disappear?

Getting back to business, Jason pulls several of these wooden crates closer to the opening just in case someone was to walk in this area. He doesn't want one of El Diablo's goons to notice that these crates are out of place. Now he squeezes through the opening, and is pleased to find that the ventilation shaft did expand a little wider on the inside.

With his backpack in tow, he begins a slow crawl through a maze of corridors. Trying his best to remember the directions that he had studied on the blue prints, however, it isn't long and he is lost.

He is determined to locate El Diablo's storage room no matter how long it takes him. He has brought enough food to last several days if that is what it will take to find what he came here for.

He runs into quit a few dead ends in this network of ventilation shafts, and some of them lead him in circles. But he presses on, knowing that eventually he will find what he came for. Each time he looks through a ceiling vent or a wall vent, his heart jumps. He thinks, "Yes, this has to be the room."

But each time he is met with disappointment.

The hours continue to go by, and so is his confidence in finding this room.

A dark thought crosses his mind, perhaps Billy the Kid was wrong, and this isn't El Diablo's liar.

Perhaps this is a trap, as there is a sizable bounty on his head. Fully prepared to shoot it out if necessary, he has made himself a promise not to be taken prisoner. With his rifle and revolver, along with ample ammunition, he will take out as many of El Diablo's men as he can before they kill him.

He has begun to mark the sides of the ventilation shafts with a piece of chalk. Hoping this will keep him from searching the same shafts over and over again.

Finally, exhausted and on the verge of giving up, there through a high wall vent, he sees what has taken him so long to find.

Across the room he can see several bags of money lying on a table. But what disturbs him more are the hundred or so boxes of drugs. Bags of cocaine and other drugs are piled to the very top of these boxes. They are arranged on pallets, ready to be shipped out like flower from a mill. Doing a quick guess, Jason estimates that there must be millions of dollars' worth of drugs and money here.

He can see only one man sitting at the table; this man holds a rifle across his lap. He sits motionless, his eyes staring at the door.

Scanning the rest of this room, it is apparent that this is the only door to this room. He can see several small windows, but they are located nearly to the top of the ceiling.

As ideas are running through Jason's head, as to just how he intends to carry out his mission, he hears a loud knock. The man at the table gets up and walks over to the door. Jason can hear him talking with someone on the other side of the door.

After a moment, the man opens the door and three men come in. These men are well armed, and saying very little they pick up several boxes of drugs. Before these men leave Jason can hear one of the three telling the guard in a rough voice, "Lock this door behind us, if anything happens to this stuff while I'm gone, you're a dead man."

Doing as he is told the man closes the door and begins latching it shut. He now puts two large pieces of wood across the door into brackets on each side.

There is no way anyone is getting through that door unless they have a tank.

Jason watches as the man goes back to his seat, here he puts his feet up on the table.

Jason knows he isn't going to be able to sneak up on this guy. He pulls out his wire cutters and begins to cut out a small hole in the vent. Ever vigilant, as one brief sound, one minor slip up, and his mission will be compromised. He works without taking his eyes off the man. As he cuts each strand of wire, it makes a slight twang sound. Hoping that this noise does not travel very far, and after each cut he is relieved that the man never moves or looks in his direction. When the hole is big enough he puts away the wire cutters and gently pushes the small screen opening out and to the side.

His preferred weapon for this mission is a simple 22 caliber rifle. A small caliber, but effective at this short range, and it's not nearly as loud as the bigger more powerful guns he normally uses. He uses a special bullet made by one of the many mysterious and nameless figures that assist him in this war on crime. A hollow point armor piercing bullet that has sharp edges that resemble a deer hunting arrow, it is a wicked looking projectile.

He must give credit to those individuals that provide him with such things. These members of F.L.O.C.K. maybe old but they have some very devious ideas.

Moving back a few feet, he pulls from his backpack the three parts of his rifle. Jason quickly and as quietly as possible assembles his weapon. He screws the barrel in, next the stock folds forward. The three pieces are quickly put together and the magazine inserted. After crawling forward, he eases the barrel just a few inches through the small hole. He now sights in on the man, bringing the cross hairs of the sight up from the floor and slowly raises the barrel. He thinks about shooting him in the heart, but the man is wearing a black leather jacket. There is the possibility that he might be wearing a bullet proof vest under his jacket, if that is the case than the bullet may not be powerful enough to penetrate the vest.

Not wanting to take any chances, Jason continues bringing the barrel up until the cross hairs are on the man's forehead. A head shot is always the quickest and most effective way to kill a person, as he was taught by his two old friends. Holding his breath as he steadies himself, he slowly squeezes the trigger. The rifle kicks slightly, with the bullet striking the man right between the eyes. Already leaning back in his chair, the man's head falls to the side as his body goes limp.

Using just a twenty two caliber rifle, Jason knows it is strong enough to kill at this distance. He is hoping that it didn't make too loud of a noise that others will be alerted and come to investigate.

Jason waits several minutes, ready to exit quickly if necessary, if indeed others did hear the gun shot.

Taking a sigh of relief when no one comes to the door, it is all still very quiet. He now cuts the rest of the vent and shoves it out of the way. Having learned many tricks over the years, he pulls a pipe out of his backpack and wedges it inside the vent. Next he ties a rope to the pipe and begins climbing down until he is standing on the floor. From here he moves very cautiously, carefully placing each foot step. His eyes dart back and forth, looking for the slightest movement that may suggest there is someone else here that he did not see.

He had seen only the one man, but in this line of work you can never be too cautious. Moving around these boxes that are stacked on pallets until he is very close to the door, he is confident now that there is no one else in the room.

Walking over and standing next to the table, he is still amazed at the amount of drugs and money sitting around him. Before starting this mission, he had to come up with a plan for destroying all these drugs. He has to thank Hawk for helping him out, with a PH.D., Hawk knew just what chemicals it would take to destroy these types of drugs.

Jason now pulls out a plastic bottle from his backpack, in it is sulfuric acid. Just a little of this on each box is enough to ruin its contents. He wastes no time and as fast as he can move he makes sure every single box will be rendered worthless. He watches as the acid bubbles up causing an irritating odor as it destroys the drugs.

Looking back at the table, a smile crosses his face. He helps himself to all the money he can stuff into his backpack. There is no need in leaving anything to that butcher El Diablo. One last thing before leaving, Jason decides he will leave El Diablo a message. Grabbing a marker from the table he writes in big letters on the wall to make sure El Diablo will see it.

"Thanks for the money, your enemy Mr. Karsten."

Jason knows this will send El Diablo into a mad rage, and oh how he wishes he could see that.

Watching the door closely he backtracks across the room and quickly climbs back up the rope, and after pulling it up he closes the screen shut. Hoping it will be some time before anyone can figure out how someone was able to get into this room without going through the door.

Anxious to leave this place, Jason makes his way back out through the ventilation shaft the same way he came in. Stopping just inside at the panel that leads outside he waits and listens, as he remembers Billy the Kid saying El Diablo's men patrol this alley every half an hour. It is a nerve racking wait, and the longer he stays here the greater his chance of getting caught.

Several minutes pass when he hears voices, it sounds like three or four people are walking down the alley.

By their words and heavy foot strikes he believes they are El Diablo's men.

Waiting another ten minutes after these men have passed, Jason feels the time is right to leave this place.

Opening the panel, he gingerly pokes his head out. Not seeing or hearing anything, he breaths a big sigh of relief. As he makes his way through the dark alleys, his spirits are high, he can't wait to inform his two mentors how smoothly this mission has gone.

Before going directly back to the apartment he needs to make a drop off first. He travels a few miles until stopping at a dumpster that is directly behind a certain bakery. After looking around, making sure that no one sees him, he stuffs some money into a brown paper bag, and puts this it into a container that is in the dumpster. This is one way he communicates with his contacts, this container is all he ever sees of these contacts, as they rarely ever meet face to face. This money is his way of saying thanks to these people who also risk their lives fighting crime.

Not wanting to take a chance in walking through this part of town at night and with this much money, he calls Crow to pick him up.

His trusted friend arrives within minutes, and they waste no time in leaving this bad part of town.

Sitting in the back seat with his head down, Jason is showing the signs of the mission he has just accomplished. Tired, his nerves on end and grateful that he wasn't caught, a sense of relief overcomes him.

"You have done well my friend," says Crow, noticing the pale look on Jason's face.

"I never said if I completed the mission or not so how can you say that I have done well?"

With a smile, "You are alive," replies Crow.

Glancing ahead, "I'm glad this is over with, this part of town gives me the creeps."

"Me too Brother, Me too," answers Crow as he speeds down the street.

Once back at the apartment Edward and Doc congratulate Jason not only for completing the mission but for making it out alive.

"Tell us," inquires Doc, "How much of El Diablo's stuff were you able to destroy?"

With eyes half closed, a fatigued Jason answers, "Everything."

Sitting back in his chair, a jubilant Edward comments, "You were able to destroy all of his drugs, that's great!"

"The acid worked just like Hawk said it would."

Pumping his fist in the air, "What a great day it is for the organization," calls out Doc, now on his feet and marching around.

Opening up his backpack, "I was also able to take this money."

The two old men stare at the stacks of cash, their eyes as big as saucers.

Covering his mouth and laughing Doc says, "And you took his money too, fantastic!"

They want to hear about the details, but Jason is so tired they must wait until he is rested.

While Jason sleeps the city is abuzz, cars are racing up and down the streets. The drug gangs are out in full force, they seem to be searching the neighborhoods.

Doc and Edward know that El Diablo is angry that his drugs were destroyed and his money is missing. He has sent every able body member of his organization on a man hunt.

Cars driving by on the street are stopped and searched by El Diablo's men, and the driver's lives are threatened. People walking are randomly assaulted by these gangs in the hope of getting the whereabouts of the person that destroyed their drugs.

The whole area is in chaos, it is a near riot.

It is hours before the police can restore order, and many people are killed during this time.

Waking up in the late afternoon, Jason walks into the kitchen and begins fixing something to eat.

"Hello Doc, Hello Edward," he says as he wipes the sleep from his eyes.

Doc and Edward are playing cards, and Jason notices a rifle leaning next to each of them.

"Expecting trouble?"

With a look of worry on his face, "While you were sleeping," says Doc, "this city has been turned upside down. A massive search is taking place, one like I have never seen before."

With a stern tone in his voice, "They are looking for you," states Edward, "your life is in great danger."

Sitting down at the table, Jason wants to hear more of just what is going on. The three knew that El Diablo would be furious, so Jason doesn't understand the panic in their voices.

"So El Diablo is angry," says Jason calmly, "this was expected."

Looking up, Doc replies, "We were not expecting El Diablo to react this way, yes we knew he would be upset, but it is anarchy out there."

The sound of police cars continue to echo from one end of the city to the other. The news on T.V. shows a city under siege. Businesses have closed, looting has broken out and the death toll is rising. State troopers along with the National Guard have been called in to quell the disturbance.

Walking over to the window, Jason is appalled at what he sees.

"It looks like El Diablo has declared war on the city, and he won't stop until he finds me."

With his head down, a solemn Doc answers, "It appears that way, so maybe you should think about leaving town, at least for a while, just until things calm down."

Turning around quickly a perturbed Jason replies, "I will not run from that monster, I will continue to disrupt his drug dealing every chance I get."

Edward now steps closer, "They outnumber us, if they find where you are staying, we won't be able to stop them."

Looking at his two mentors, Jason doesn't like what he is hearing. He had thought these two men would stand next to him no matter how bad the situation.

Feeling slightly betrayed, he asks, "Do you want me to leave, just say the word and I'm gone."

The two old men now stand close to their apprentice. They have looked at him as if he was their own son, and they would do anything for him.

Speaking with a crack in his voice, "Our home is your home for as long as you want," says Doc.

"We are only thinking of what is best for you," states Edward.

Now angry, Jason says, "I thought you two would never coward down from anyone, that nothing scared you. Now you stand here suggesting that I leave, to run away like a frightened child. No I will not leave, I will continue to fight crime in this city and if that means putting myself in dangerous situations, than that's the way it has to be."

The two men smile at Jason, "You have spoken with what is in your heart," says Doc.

Confused by this, Jason shakes his head, "What is going on here?"

"We had to know your true feelings," says Edward, "to know that you are willing to die for this cause."

"So you were testing me," asks Jason, "and how did I do?"

"We had no doubt that you would react this way, that is why we will always stand by you," replies an emotional Doc.

Not happy with this test, Jason nonetheless understands their reasoning. This crusade that they have embarked on calls for absolute devotion; there can never be one second of doubt about what they are doing. Trust, faith and unity are what will see them through this time of great danger and self-sacrifice.

"We must be prepared for the worst, as El Diablo will search for you forever," says Doc.

With a smile, "Not if I kill him first," counters Jason.

"You have tried several times," replies Edward, "but each time he manages to elude you, he is very sly, a hard target to hit."

"That day will come, and when it does this city can get back to normal, along with our own lives," states Jason.

"You have dealt El Diablo and his organization a crippling blow," says Doc, "but not a fatal one."

"El Diablo has contacts with the Mexican drug cartels," states Edward, "they will be very unhappy when they learn of what happened. El Diablo will blame you, and I fear that they may send more professional hit men to kill you."

Undeterred, Jason replies, "There is too much at stake to stop our mission now, we will just deal with this new threat when it happens."

The three now celebrate a great victory, they sit at the table and raise a toast. The two old men envy their young crusader, wishing they could join him in this battle of good versus evil. But monitoring the situation from the safety of their apartment, they give Jason valuable information. Without their guidance they know that Jason would be just another short lived hero. He would be just another innocent man trying to stop the violence only to be killed for his efforts.

Their greatest contributions to this cause are their contacts on the internet, they are the generals leading this battle.

Within a few days the chaos on the streets seems to have lessened somewhat. The traffic is nearly back to normal, the people have begun to walk in the open again.

Anxious to resume ridding this city of all its criminals, Jason begins to plot his next endeavor.

"You have a message," says Doc, sitting in front of the computer.

Looking over his shoulder, Jason reads the short message.

It is from Billy the Kid, he has left a letter at their usual drop off and pick up spot.

Rarely is any information given over the internet, it is all done in person. This letter will contain information vital to helping fight the gangs and other lawbreakers.

Standing up, Jason says, "I must go."

With a look of concern on his face, Doc says, "Be extremely careful, there is a hefty price tag on your head. Trust only those that you have dealt with before, and don't assume they won't turn on you. Money makes devils out of good men, so never turn your back on anyone."

Feeling touched by his words, Jason nods his head.

"I will be cautious and vigilant, and I will be back as soon as possible."

Slipping out the back door of the apartment building, Jason moves warily among the garbage cans and debris that litter the dark and deserted alley.

The night is unusually dark, there is no moon tonight. The wind is blowing discarded newspapers high into the air. A weird sensation causes him to shutter, hoping that it is not a bad omen.

A window is heard slamming shut, and Jason ducks under a stairwell. His sixth sense is telling him that he is not alone in this alley. Wondering if one of those assassins has tracked him here, and now they have him in their sights.

Controlling his breathing, he waits. His eyes scan in both directions, trying to catch the slightest movement that will let him know what he is up against.

An hour passes and nothing, he neither sees nor hears anything out of the ordinary.

Scratching his head he hopes he isn't getting spooked by so many people wanting to kill him. Needing to focus on the task at hand he gets up from his hiding spot and continues down the alley.

At that instant he hears a loud growl, and dropping down to the pavement he holds his revolver straight out. His heart is racing, and the sweat is now forming on his forehead. Just in front he sees a set of glowing eyes, this is where the sound came from.

Swallowing hard, he envisions some horrendous madman striking at him with a pick axe. Ready to repel this enemy sent by the drug cartels to assassinate him, Jason prepares himself.

Scooting back so that no one can get behind him, Jason now waits.

Gripping the revolver so tight that his knuckles turn white, the fear of what is out there has him on edge.

He can see a short figure in the partial glow of the night light, and it is moving back and forth, almost like it is stalking him. No time to assemble his more powerful rifle, he must rely on the revolver to stop this menace. He can hear the sound of a chain as it is dragged back and forth on the brick pavement.

Lifting his head up, he moves forward hoping to get a better look at what this thing is.

Whoever this man is he hasn't come any closer, this causes Jason to creep slowly forward.

To his surprise he can see that in the semi darkness that it is a dog, and it has a chain wrapped around its body so tight that it can hardly move.

Putting away his revolver he slowly approaches the poor animal. Jason can see that it is a very large German Shepard, and he estimates that it must weight close to one hundred and twenty pounds. It has the usual black and brown markings for this type of breed with one oddity. Behind its right ear is a small patch of white fur, this odd color on this breed is indeed rare. With its massive teeth, mesmerizing eyes and a loud growl it is a very intimidating beast. Taking a chance, as he has always loved dogs and with his hands extended out he tries calming it down, but it lashes out at him, its claws narrowly missing his face.

Jumping back, Jason knows that the dog is scared and hurting that is why it tried to bite him. He knows the pain it is in is causing it to strike at anyone that comes near. Trying again, he gets a little closer, this time talking in a calm voice, 'It's going to be alright boy."

Sniffing the air, the dog seems to sense that Jason is not going to hurt him, and he lowers his head. Inching forward, ready in a split second to jump back, Jason puts a hand out and the dog sniffs the stranger. A few seconds pass until the dog begins licking his fingers.

Happy that he isn't going to be attacked Jason begins to cautiously untangle the chain from this poor animal's body.

He can see that the chain has cut into its flesh, and it looks to be infected.

As gently as possible he is able to free the helpless dog, who at once jumps to the side and turns with its teeth showing.

Pulling out his revolver, Jason stands straight, hoping that he doesn't have to shoot this poor dog. After a tense few seconds the dog lowers its ears and walks right up to Jason, rubbing its head against his thigh.

Happy and relieved, Jason strokes the coarse hair on its back. Believing that he has just made a new friend, "I think I'll call you Duke."

The animal seems at peace around its new master, as it freely lets Jason touch him.

Now the problem is to take the dog back to the apartment, so that he can get on with the mission. Hoping that Doc and Edward won't mind sharing their living quarters with such a big animal, Jason prepares to take Duke home. He is sure that Doc can fix the cuts on the dog's body.

This dog, he believes, will warm him and the others if anyone tries breaking into their apartment. A dog he knows will hear someone's footsteps long before any person could.

It will be nice to have Duke around, as Jason has grown bored talking to his two elderly companions. He dreams of a day when he and Duke can walk the streets and go to the park.

Interrupting this dream, and to his surprise the dog suddenly bolts away and continues running down the alley despite his attempts at calling it back. Stopping a short distance away, Duke turns his head. Eyes fixed on Jason, it seems to signal how grateful it is for its rescue. With his head held high Duke barks once. Now turning he continues running and disappears into the darkness.

Sadden by this unexpected turn of events he nonetheless hopes the dog finds a good home. He was hoping for a companion, one that he would one day take on his outings. Needing to forget that thought, as a more important mission lies ahead he continues up the alley.

Soon he is at the place where information is secretly exchanged between him and his contacts. It is a dark and secluded place, tucked far back into a dead end alley, and void of any street lights. Gazing upwards the tall buildings seem like they will touch the sky.

Jason now blends in with his surroundings, he waits hidden among the rubbish that is piled up against the buildings.

Watching both directions, he must be sure that he was not followed. If the location of this exchange site should fall into the wrong hands it could be disastrous for the organization.

Not taking any chances, Jason is content on waiting.

After three hours of sitting motionless he is sure that he is alone and next he removes several bricks from the side of a building. Reaching inside this space he pulls out a small metal box. This is what he came for, the information inside will guide him on his next task.

He removes a letter from the box, it is how he and Billy the Kid communicate back and forth. There is no time to read it now, as he knows the sun will be coming up soon. He must not be caught out during daylight hours, in his line of work the less people that see him the better it is.

With a great many people looking for him the darkness is his friend, it conceals his face and provides cover as he moves about the city.

Arriving back at his base, he quickly opens the letter. Billy the kid informs him that a vicious biker gang is preparing to distribute drugs in the city. This gang is filling the gap left when Jason destroyed the warehouse full of El Diablo's drugs.

He even gives Jason the location of where this biker gang is staying. It's in a church of all places out in the country, just to the north of the city is where they have gathered. Further invaluable information is the name and location of a bar where this biker gang just happens to be gathered at. This information is invaluable, and Jason begins immediately to prepare a plan of action.

One of his contacts over the internet informs him that this biker gang consists of nearly one hundred members. They call themselves the Demons of Discipline.

Doing a little research, he tracks this gang as they have spread their violence and mayhem from one state to another. He also finds out that their bitter enemy, a gang calling themselves the Brute Force, just happens to have a club house on the outskirts of the city. These two gangs are the equal of each other, as murder, robbery and selling drugs is all they know. Being this close to each other could start a turf war, and this gives Jason an idea.

Waiting until dark, Jason once more slips silently through the deserted and dark back streets. Finally leaving the relative safety of the alleys, he ventures through an old abandoned railway station. Its creepy structures resemble those from an old western ghost town. Doors are falling off their hinges and most of the windows are broken out. Jason keeps a safe distance from them, not knowing who or what could be lurking just inside. He knows many of these empty structures are havens for gangs that make their living by robbing and stealing.

He makes a mental note to come back here and rid the area of any such trouble makers.

Moving farther down the railroad tracks and after crossing a railroad bridge, he locates the bar that the Demons Of Discipline frequent. Being 3:30 in the morning the bar is closed. Taking a look at the parking lot he can see that it is empty.

He now cautiously goes around to the rear of the bar. Locating the back door, he next spots an overhanging piece of wood protruding about ten feet up a nearby wall. Removing a long length of rope from his backpack he loops one end of the rope around it. Making a hangman's noose on the other end, he now tucks this out of the way so that no one will see it.

With the help of other contacts, he also knows the location of the club house where the Brute Force hangs out.

Given the great distance it is from here to there, he must once more call on Crow for his assistance. Who like an efficient and obedient soldier arrives within minutes of his call. After giving him the location, Crow once again shakes his head, "You pick the worst places to visit, you know that."

Forcing a smile, "I appreciate the chances that you take helping me out. After dropping me off, I don't think you should hang around and wait for me, I'll find my own way back."

Turning his head around, "And I appreciate that I don't have to hang around an area that will get me killed."

The two laugh, but they each know just how dangerous this area is. Numerous people have been killed here, and several of those were police officers.

After entering a rundown part of town, the taxi stops a short distance from the Brute Force club house. Jason exits the taxi before it even comes to a stop and with his head down, he hurries over and hides next an abandoned and stripped down vehicle.

He watches as the tail lights of the taxi fade in the distance.

Lights are on in the club house, and he can hear voices. A great many motorcycles are parked everywhere. Guessing that the party is over and most of these bikers are probably sleeping. This will give Jason an opportunity to scout out the area. There is really no houses on either side of the club house that would afford him any type of protection should he choose to take out some of these bikers.

However, he sees a row of abandoned houses directly across the street from the Brute Force Club House. These vacant houses are two stories and look to be in very bad shape. No doubt used by drug addicts and the homeless.

Its location will work perfect for what he has planned, and he is hoping it will be a bloody night.

After several hours of watching the gang members move about, he is satisfied that his plan will work.

Now he will go back to the apartment and wait until the next night. His plan is to get these two biker gangs to fight each other.

Having already told Crow that he won't be needed, he sets out for his long journey back. As dangerous as it is to walk alone in this city at night, he can't risk putting Crow or anyone else's life in jeopardy. To call Crow back to this location may arouse suspicion, it is best that he travel alone as much as possible.

The trip back to the apartment ends up being a journey that takes nearly all night to complete.

After leaving the area controlled by the Brute Force, he hopes the solitude of the railroads tracks will be uninteresting.

After going only a mile he encounters several men on these dark and lonely tracks. Standing under a street light where a road crosses, these men form a line across the tracks. Slowing his pace, Jason carefully studies these men. They look exactly like the type that would be out here in the middle of the night. Long hair and holding a can of beer in their hands, they have trouble standing straight. Jason moves to the left side of the tracks hoping to avoid a confrontation. However these men also move to that side and they refuse to let him pass.

Jason can see that they carry only baseball bats and one has a knife. This tells him that they aren't murderers, but just muggers and robbers.

Feeling confident that they appear to have no guns, he stops and gives them a hard stare.

The biggest one in the group steps forward and pointing his finger says, "Give us all your money little man."

Remaining perfectly still, Jason doesn't blink an eye, he stares at these fools who don't have a clue of who he is or what he is capable of doing.

After not getting an answer, the big man, his face showing anger, now pulls out a knife.

"I'm going to cut you real bad," he says as he steps closer to what he thinks is an easy victim.

With his hand on his revolver, Jason decides to have some fun and he replies, "I have a better idea, I want you and your ugly friends to give me all your money instead."

The five men begin to laugh, as they find this amusing that one man against five would say such a dumb thing.

After the smiles leave their faces, one of them lunges at Jason, the knife slicing harmlessly through the air as he simply leans to one side. Reacting quickly, Jason delivers a punch to the man's jaw, causing him to fall to the ground. Getting back quickly to his feet, disturbed and embarrassed at this, the man again lunges forward, only to encounter another punch to the jaw.

As he lay on the ground dazed his cohorts makes jokes, asking him if he has forgotten how to use his knife. Now more upset, the man is back on his feet and has the look of a madman in his eyes. Breathing heavily, he motions for the others to circle around behind Jason.

As the four begin to spread out, Jason motions with his hand, "I wouldn't do that if I were you."

Stopping, slightly confused by this man that is outnumbered five to one, they wonder why he doesn't coward down like so many of their other victims.

Speaking up, one of them asks, "Just what are you going to do to stop us."

Waiting a moment before he replies, as Jason can tell that this makes the group even more nervous.

"I'll shoot each of you in the foot, to start with," he answers as he gives them a devious grin.

Now clearly agitated that someone dare threaten them, one of them calls out, "Let's all get him at the same time."

Dropping to one knee, Jason fires five shoots in a matter of seconds. The men all fall down holding their foot and screaming in pain.

Standing back up Jason says, "Let this be a warning to all of you, the next time you try and hurt someone, I'll track each of you down and put a bullet in your head."

The men coward away, frightened at nearly being killed. Two of the men get up and limp away looking back over their shoulders to see if this mad gun man is following them.

Finally realizing who this gunman is the other three begin to beg for their lives, they cry like little children. Jason has taught them a good lesson, and he hopes they remember this the next time they decide to rob someone.

Turning and walking away, Jason pays them no more attention as his mind has more important things to worry about.

Finally reaching the city limits, he must carefully avoid the crack houses that infest this area.

The lowest of the low gather here and they are so doped up that they have lost touch with reality. He has heard some unbelievable things that have happened here, so he wants to get through this area as quickly as possible.

With no alleys in this part of town he must walk for a short distance on the sidewalk. The streets are nearly deserted, the exception is a lone drug pusher standing on the corner. Not far from him are the prostitutes, three of them wait for any cars that may drive by. Crossing the street Jason does not want to get near these people that he despises so much. These drug pushers and prostitutes have a very short life expectancy. Most are dead before they reach the age of 30, the rest end in up in prison.

Suddenly he hears a loud commotion, he stops dead in his tracks. Leaning hunched over he hurries and hides behind several empty metal containers. Looking around the corner he sees a group of men standing beneath a telephone pole. They are obviously out of their minds on drugs, Jason watches is amazement as they attempt to throw a rope with a steel hook tied on one end up and over the power lines.

What they hope to achieve by this, Jason can't even guess.

With the street light on, Jason knows that there is power going through the lines. Most of these power lines have thirty to fifty thousand volts of electricity running through them.

"What a bunch of idiots," he says to himself.

The men stagger about as they continue to throw the rope, only to have it fall short.

Needing to continue his journey, Jason slips past the men without them even noticing him.

Making it only about half a block, that is when he hears a loud crackling sound and a flash of light from behind. Turning around he is shocked by what he is seeing. It appears that the men were finally successful in their attempt at snagging the power line.

Sparks are flying in all directions, and on the ground lay two of the men, their clothing on fire. Screaming and running around in circles the third man is also on fire and is obviously in severe pain. He eventually stumbles and falls to the ground. Unlike his two friends he isn't dead yet, and he rolls from side to side in an attempt to smother the fire.

Knowing that this is going to draw a large crowd of spectators very soon, Jason hurries down the first alley he finds.

Crossing each street, he is ever vigilant. The city is not what it once was, its core now rotted and decaying like a flower without water. It seems that the muggers and thieves outnumber the good people in this city.

Successfully avoiding any more trouble along the way, he is relieved to make it back to his apartment.

Going over his plan with Doc and Edward, the two agree with him that it is a sound plan. It is a chance to take out a great many trouble makers in just one night.

"The best thing about this plan," states Edward, "is that the police will think that it is just a fight between two rival gangs. Maybe it will take some of the heat off the man hunt for the Vigilante Assassin?"

"You must be extremely careful," Doc says, "any number of things could go wrong."

"I did a thorough recon of the area," replies Jason. "I spotted several escape routes if the need arises for me to make a hasty getaway."

Discussing the plan in detail, the three now look for any flaws or weaknesses that may be a problem. Weapons are selected, and a time is chosen to put their plan into action.

Several contacts on the street are alerted in the event that Jason finds himself in need of help. These contacts will provide transportation and can cause a diversion if necessary, but they will not be armed. The killing will be left to Jason, as a lot of individuals believe in this cause, yet they refuse to commit murder.

Only one man can be responsible for the deaths of so many, and that one man will be the Vigilante Assassin.

Jason has taken on this role as sole executioner; however he does not take pride in what he does. This extreme form of justice was thrust upon him by El Diablo himself. If not for the cruel torture and humiliation he suffered, he too would not commit these acts of violence.

No, this is not the life that he set out for himself, his plans included going to college and getting a teaching degree.

How his world has been turned upside down, and his future is anything but promising. The fact is that the police will continue to investigate the murders that he has committed. They will continue to investigate long after he has put down his guns and resumed a normal life. There is always the possibility that one day he will be arrested and charged with these murders.

The crime of murder, especially the ones committed by a serial killer, will continue to be investigated forever. The city has tagged the Vigilante Assassin as just that, a serial killer.

Regardless of the fact that the Vigilante Assassin only killed those that deserved to die, his act of taking the law into his own hands will label him a murderer. There is a good chance that someday one of his contacts will turn against him. For this reason, Jason has long ago planned on leaving this city as soon as his mission is done.

He has not told Doc and Edward about this, and he plans to keep it that way. He will travel as far from this city as possible and try to start a new life. But the fact remains that his past may someday catch up to him. Worried about being arrested and facing a trial, he has decided to end his life if he is caught.

In the heel of his shoe is a cyanide caplet that he keeps in case he is ever captured. One bite into the caplet and he will be dead within two minutes. Not believing in suicide, as to him this was always a cowards way out. But also fearing that he will be put on death row, this would be worse than taking his own life.

His two mentors have no clue as to his plans, he is sure that they would strongly disagree.

The fact remains that by the time he is done cleaning up this city that he will have a great many deaths on his hands. The people will think of the Vigilante Assassin as an urban legend, the people's savior.

His heroics and daring feats will be admired and revered, and some will even say he was sent by God.

The authorities will take a very different look at the Vigilante Assassin, and instead label him a criminal of the state. A killing machine that knows no boundaries; and a man that kills for pure joy.

They will try and dispel the belief that this person is doing good, that he only wants to help. No, the authorities will track him down like a dog, and he will be prosecuted to the fullest extent of the law.

As the sky turns dark, Jason gathers up his backpack. Not bothering to say good bye to his friends, he slips quietly out the door. He prefers it this way as Doc and Edward show too much emotion when he goes out on these missions. Their closeness to him means that they are being too cautious. That what was once a routine night of assassination is now looked upon by them as being very dangerous and perilous. The two old men have even hinted that maybe Jason should hand these dangerous assignments over to someone else.

However Jason knows that no one else will take his place, the members of this organization have already strongly stated this. That is why they waited years while planning out these missions, there simply was no one that would step up and assume these duties. Not until he came along, and either by chance or by God's will he had filled the roll of Vigilante Assassin.

Jason knows that when people become too close emotionally that it affects their judgment and decision making.

He feels a tremendous amount of respect and admiration towards his two mentors, but he doesn't look at them as a father figure. They on the other hand look upon him as a son, and it is this reason that they caution him so much. They have gone from a mentor and adviser on the art of killing to something close to a Boy Scout leader. Jason can sense a softening in their approach to these missions, to them it is getting too violent and risky. In the beginning there was no target or mission that they would not shy away from, even missions that Jason himself questioned as being too treacherous, often got a laugh from Doc and Edward.

These two old tuff dogs knew all the nasty ways to kill someone and they eagerly taught their young apprentice without giving it a second thought. Their priority was following the orders given by the F.L.O.C.K., regardless of the risks involved they sent Jason out the door as quickly as possible. By this date Doc and Edward were starting to change their attitude, maybe it is the flash backs from their army days, and what Jason is doing might be stirring up these long forgotten nightmares. It could be that they are just getting too old for this game, the daring and bravado in their actions and manners is waning. Whatever the reason, Jason will not let it deter him from completing this mission that he has embarked upon. He will see this crusade through to the very end or die trying.

Jason decides to walk across town instead of getting a ride from Crow, as his instincts are telling him to be very cautious this night. Although Crow has never given him the slightest sign that he may be untrustworthy, or unreliable, still in this line of work one can never be too cautious. If Crow should ever be apprehended by the police or El Diablo, Jason is not 100 percent certain that he would not turn on him.

For these reasons he has decided to go alone across town, it will take longer and be more dangerous but he has learned from Falcon that the easiest and shortest route is not always the best.

At two in the morning he leaves the apartment, and safely making his way through rundown neighborhoods, crime infested streets and roving gangs he returns and stakes out a hiding place behind the bar that the Demons of Discipline are partying at. He watches as groups of two and three gang members will come outside to either urinate or to do drugs.

Bidding his time, as patience in his line of work could mean the difference between life and death. Finally a lone gang member staggers out the back door and as he is leaning against the wall Jason quickly springs from his hiding place and puts a rope around the man's neck. The man is next dragged into the shadows, and the rope around his neck is pulled tight, causing him to gasps for air. Having earlier prepared this trap, Jason now puts his plan into action. Pulling the rope, he hoists the man up into the air about fifteen feet. The stunned biker kicks his legs and tries desperately to remove the rope that is taking the life from him. After several minutes he hangs motionless, Jason is thankful that no one else had come outside during this time.

Now he pulls out a piece of paper, and on it he has written, "Let this be a warning, you are on our turf, Brute Force."

He attaches this to the man's shirt, sure that the others will see it.

He knows this will send the gang into a mad frenzy and they will seek revenge. Jason, still a little unsure about calling Crow, has decided to get in touch with another contact.

Needing a vehicle less suspicious than a taxi, this new contact arrives at a location only blocks away.

As he approaches the driver, nervous at never having had contact with him before, Jason holds his revolver tight. The two exchange code words, satisfied that he can trust this man Jason quickly gets in on the passenger side, still holding tightly to his revolver.

Riding across town in a milk truck, Jason smiles, here is the most wanted man in the state and his method of traveling is in a milk truck.

As funny as it looks Jason is confident that neither the police nor the drug gangs would suspect that the Vigilante Assassin would travel this way.

Not a word is spoken between the two, and not knowing this man before tonight Jason keeps a tight grip on his revolver. Giving the man the address, he doesn't flinch one bit about driving into such a dangerous part of town. Jason is dropped off several blocks from the abandoned houses he had seen a few nights earlier, which are not far from the Brute Force clubhouse. Moving silently from one yard to the next, his heart rate is increasing. This night he knows could dwarf any mission up to this point. In sheer numbers of casualties it will definitely put a dent in the crime wave sweeping this city.

Taking a look at the tops of these structures he believes they will provide him with the perfect vantage point. It is a rundown section of town, and many of the houses and buildings are boarded up and abandoned.

Directly across the street from the Brute Force club house Jason slips silently into an abandoned apartment building.

He has to be very quiet as these abandoned structures are often used as crack houses. Not being from around here, if he were to come upon these people doing their drugs they will at once assume he's the police. This is why he always carries a hand gun, for any sudden surprises. With no lighting, the interior of these structures are dark and gloomy, only small rays of light coming through are from the street lights. He must step over the trash and debris that is scattered everywhere. The pungent smell of mold and wood rot permeates the air. As he makes his way up the stairs heading for the top floor, a slight noise in front catches his attention.

This causes him to stop dead in his tracks, and he remains perfectly still as if he were a mannequin in a store window. Cocking his head to the side he listens intensely, hoping that it is just a cat or a rat.

At the top of the stairs a man staggers out from a room, he stops momentarily when he sees Jason. Jason can see that this person is just another typical drug user, filthy and disorientated.

The man stares at Jason for a moment and with a frightened expression on his face he reaches inside his coat. Without hesitating Jason pulls his knife from its sheath and throws it as hard as he can.

The knife sticks in the man's throat, preventing him from calling out. This is another of many deadly lessons he learned from Falcon, a master at martial arts.

Jason quickly races to the top of the stairs, here the man is lying on his back, dead. Putting his boot on his face he reaches down and pulls the knife out.

Looking at this sorry individual, Jason can only guess at what crimes he has committed in order to feed his drug addiction.

He drags the body back into the room he came out of. Surprised, he can see three other people in here, however they are lying on the floor. Looking closer it is apparent that they are doped up and unconscious.

He leaves them as they are, they are not on his hit list. Continuing up the steps he finally makes it to the top floor, and from here he makes his way out a window. Standing on a small catwalk he still needs to get higher. Not having a rope he must climb up the old rain spout hoping that it will support his weight.

Cautiously a little at a time he manages to move up the spouting until he is on the very top of the building. Now he moves along the peak so to be in a perfect position to see the house across the street. He stops halfway across to survey the area and without knowing it he nearly walks right into a power line. Jerking his head back at the last second, whether it is a live wire or not, he doesn't want to find out the hard way.

Ducking down he continues to move along the peak until he is up against the old brick chimney. This should afford him cover as well as a place to steady his rifle. Crouching down, he quickly assembles his rifle, all the while watching the activity across the street.

He can see that the Brute Force gang is in high spirits, as he can hear yelling and loud music.

Most of the gang is outside, and this is a warning to everyone that this street is now off limits to any traffic. The police are so intimidated by the gang that they to avoid this area when the gang is having a meeting.

Jason can see several blocks up the street the headlights of a great many motorcycles. He had wondered if the Demons of Discipline would come charging in, guns blazing or would they seek another way to handle this matter.

A moment later that question is answered, as he looks through his binoculars he can clearly see the lead biker waving a flag with the Demons Of Discipline logo on it.

As the roar of 100 or so approaching motorcycles grows louder it gets the attention of the Brute Force. Several members hurry inside and quickly come out with arm loads of weapons. Jason now waits, poised for these two gangs to start killing each other.

The Demons of Discipline ride four wide, and he can clearly see guns being waved in the air. The Brute Force began congregating in the street, Jason estimates there are seventy five of them.

Without slowing down the motorcycles run directly into the men standing in the street. Bodies go flying through the air and bikes skid sideways and crash into parked cars. Gun fire is now coming from everywhere, it sounds like a war. Several groups of men are fighting with knives and baseball bats. It is sheer carnage as these two gangs violently attack each other.

This is his opportunity, and Jason wastes no time in ridding the Earth of this scum.

Firing from the concealment of the roof, it is like shooting fish in a barrel. Jason makes only head shots, and he tries to kill an equal amount from both gangs. The clip in his rifle holds eight rounds, and he goes through three clips so fast that it surprises him.

In a matters of fifteen minutes there are bodies lying everywhere. It looks like the aftermath of a bomb explosion. Doing a quick count, he can see thirty two bodies lying in the street as well as the yard.

Having done his good deed for the day, it is now time to for him to leave.

After descending the spouting and slipping in through a window he starts going down the steps when he sees two men fighting in the doorway. With this exit blocked he turns and departs the building out the back door. The sound of police sirens begins to fill the night air.

He knows this whole area will soon be surrounded by the police, swat teams and state troopers. Wishing for a little luck that with all the excitement out in the streets that he can make a quick retreat without anyone spotting him.

Jason only gets a few feet across the yard when he is suddenly confronted by a member of the Brute Force gang. The man's face in grimacing in pain and he is holding his side. In his other hand is a gun and as he points it at Jason's head, "You're going to die," he says.

Caught at a disadvantage, Jason has to think fast.

His gun is in his right jacket pocket, no time to pull it out. No time to reach down and grab his knife either.

With hatred in his eyes, the gang member pulls the hammer back on the gun and says, "I'm going to count to three, and them I'm pulling the trigger."

Prepared to die, Jason has no choice but to reach for his gun. He knows he doesn't have time but he will try anyways. However a shot rings out and the man falls to the side and onto the ground. Looking to the right Jason can see a member of the Demons of Discipline leaning against the building, he too is injured.

He had fired the shot killing the man, and at first Jason is at a loss for words. Here is a member of a vicious biker gang, and he saved his life.

As he fumbles for the right words to thank him, the man points the gun at Jason.

Surprised, he waves his hands and shouts, "No, I'm not a member of the Brute Force."

The biker smiles, he too had been shot, as blood is all over his clothing.

Gritting his teeth he replies, "Doesn't matter who you are, as long as you're not a member of the Demons, I have no choice but to kill you."

So this man is living up to the creed of the gang. Everyone else is an outsider and they are fair game. Jason needs a rouge to distract this man, and he looks past him and yells, "Here comes members of Brute Force."

As the man turns his head just slightly, Jason quickly reaches into his jacket and pulling out his revolver he puts a bullet into the man's head.

Seeing no other gang members around, Jason turns around and hurries into the darkness. He is feeling happy about the recent events, despite his close encounter with death. There are now thirty some less criminals walking the streets terrorizing people.

CHAPTER 7

It wasn't long before the police began to suspect that a vigilante was operating in the city. They would find the usual suspects dead, they were murderers, drug dealers, muggers and rapist. The method of killing these people was always the same, a shot to the head, primarily the temple. Ballistics showed that this vigilante's preferred weapon was a 22-250. It is a small caliber bullet but it has an effective killing range of two miles. It actually can penetrate a steel plate better than a thirty odd six.

On most nights, Jason would perch himself on top of a high rise building and shoot a target that was three to four blocks away.

The victim would be dead before they heard the gun shot. Shooting from this distance was another reason there was never any witnesses.

As the number of people the vigilante killed began to increase so did the urban legend. The newspapers called him the "Vigilante Assassin."

At first this name bothered Jason, he didn't look at himself as an assassin, but more like an exterminator. He is riding the city of those he and the members of the F.L.O.C.K. deemed morally and socially unfit.

In Jason's mind the police and the justice system was turning a blind eye to the corruption that was tearing apart this city.

He felt an obligation to take the law into his own hands, to dish out punishment as he saw fit. Yes some innocent people would die, but looking at the larger picture it could not be avoided. He believed in what he was doing, and the needs of the many out weighted the needs of the few or the one.

The rampant violence is disrupting the social network. Many parents are afraid to send their children to school for fear that they may get mugged or shot. Grocery stores, as well as most other businesses now have armed guards standing at the doors. No one dare venture out at night, this time belongs exclusively to the drug gangs. They march through neighborhoods with near immunity, striking at anyone that dare be foolish enough to be out.

People boarded up their houses, with steel bars on the windows and doors, they are a prisoner in their own homes.

Social events like little league baseball games, and parades are a thing of the past.

Jason had to stand up, he had to make things right. Things will be as they once were, people will walk about and go where they pleased. No more fears of drive by shootings, no more crazed drug addicts terrorizing the populace. He is determined to purge this city if he has to do it one block at a time.

This taking of lives is brutal and barbaric, and it is not what Jason set out to do in his life. Because of circumstances beyond his control, he is thrust into this role. By this time he has reached a point of no return, meaning if he were ever caught by the authorities, he's sure he will get the death penalty.

So he has no choice but to continue this mission of trying to remove as many criminals from the streets as he can. This task Jason quickly found out is not going to be a fast or easy thing to do.

The lawbreakers outnumbered the law-abiding, and there are more goons than good guys.

As the squad cars race out of the parking lot the police station is on heightened alert. They just received word of a violent gang fight across town. Dispatchers are receiving reports of dozens of dead. Units of the swat teams are briefed as they ride across town in armored vehicles.

An hour later an officer hands detective Wilson a note. After reading it he slams his fist down onto his desk.

Several other detectives enter the room, their mood changes as they also read the note.

"We all know who is responsible for this." Lt. Wilson states in a firm voice.

Looking at his superior one detective says, "Do you really think that the Vigilante Assassin could have killed this many people?"

Crumbling the note up and tossing it into the trash can, "Oh, it was him alright," he answers.

As the detectives sit in chairs in front of the desk, Lt. Wilson continues, "At last count there were 43 dead and 18 wounded. 24 of the dead were shot in the head, and after we get the ballistics report it should match all the other victims. I believe this Vigilante Assassin is behind these two gangs fighting each other. He took advantage of the chaos to turn this into his personal slaughter house"

"If this is true," states one, "Than this vigilante has changed tactics. He has gone from shooting single criminals to now shooting dozens at one time."

Shaking his head, Lt. Wilson replies, "This madman must be stopped, and we have to search the crime scene for the smallest clue. If you have to apply pressure to the street thugs in order to get information, than do so. The Mayor has given us the green light to use all means available, even if our methods break the law."

The detectives sitting around the desk are shocked by this approach.

Standing up, Lt. Wilson says, "From the Mayor himself, the man that breaks this case and arrests the Vigilante Assassin will receive a medal and a promotion."

Now the detectives seem to be energized, as this could make them famous.

"How could he have orchestrated this type of ambush alone," asks one of the detectives.

"Just how we don't know yet, so I need all available men working this case," replies a frustrated Lt. Wilson.

The men hurry out of the room, the thought of catching the most wanted man in the city has them excited.

Lt. Wilson, waiting until the room is empty makes a phone call.

Speaking softly he is in direct contact with the Governor, informing him of the progress they are making.

"I can assure you Governor," Lt. Wilson states, "We are close to finding and putting behind bars this so called Vigilante Assassin."

In a rough voice, "I'll give you and your department just three more weeks," the Governor says. "Then I turn this whole case over to the feds, do I make myself clear!"

With his head lowered Lt. Wilson answers, "We are doing everything possible to catch this guy, we just need more time."

"Time is something you don't have much of, in three weeks I'll put another agency in charge of this case. The people of Landore and this entire state are demanding that we stop this madman right now."

"I understand Governor, we'll double our efforts. I'll see to it personally."

"You do whatever it takes, how you find and arrest this person I don't want to know. This is a statewide emergency of the highest priority. Just get this man behind bars before it costs you your job!"

With that said the governor hangs up. Now frustrated and perturbed Lt. Wilson is beside himself with what to do. He's getting pressure from all sides, and this only worsens his ulcers.

Calling in his detectives he informs them, "You have a green light, use whatever means are necessary to get information. The clock is ticking, we need clues. Go out and put pressure on anyone you think may give us a lead."

The detectives have never seen Lt. Wilson this upset. Usually very calm and orderly, he fumbles with the stack of papers on his desk. Cursing at the smallest thing, with a wave of his hand he ushers the detectives out of his office.

Looking out the window he mumbles, "I'll find you, you can't hide forever. Somewhere someone knows who you are, and when I find that person your days will be numbered."

CHAPTER 8

After returning from his most successful mission Jason stays inside the apartment for the next several days. With so much excitement on the streets he doesn't want to chance taking out another criminal. The T.V. is constantly updating reports of the worst murder spree in the city's history. Not even when the mob was operating were so many people killed in one day.

Letting the city calm down after so many deaths, Jason must wait patiently.

His two mentors are shocked and astonished by what he has done. Yes they knew he would kill more than just a few that night, but for Jason to kill this many at once even amazes them.

They never would have thought that one man could kill so many criminals in such a short period of time. They are proud that he has rid the city of these criminals, but on the other hand, they are worried that they may have created a monster.

The two old men talk quietly among themselves and they wonder, "What if Jason doesn't put his gun down when it is deemed that the city has been cleansed?"

How are they going to stop him, but the more important question is, can they stop him. After all this young man is very well trained and disciplined, they should know they are the ones along with Falcon that taught him these deadly lessons. Jason is a skilled killer, and he will not be easy to stop. Perhaps if he should find out that his two mentors are plotting against him he may kill them before they have a chance at killing him first.

Once this task of eliminating all the criminals from their beloved city has been completed, they worry that the killing machine that they helped create won't stop. That the need to kill again and again is permanently programmed into his head.

The two old gentlemen have discussed just such a scenario. If indeed Jason refuses to put his gun down and return to a normal life, they will force him to even if it costs them their lives.

Having looked at him as their son, the thought of using force to stop him bothers them greatly.

Each knows that if it comes down to it, one of them will have to kill Jason. It is a gut wrenching decision, and they pray that it doesn't come to that.

The murders that Jason has committed are also on their hands. They were instrumental in the planning and preparation of his missions. If Jason is ever captured, they will have to evacuate the city very quickly. There is a slim possibility that the D.A. will make him a deal that if he turns over the names of those that helped him, than the judge may go easier on his sentence. Although Jason has repeatedly told them that he will never be taken alive, that is not a guarantee. Edward and Doc must prepare themselves for the worst case scenario.

That worst case scenario being that their apprentice and adopted son Jason may turn on them to save his own neck. Because of this possibility, the two have made preparations to destroy all of their computers and all the documents that would tie them to the Vigilante Assassin.

They are old enough to know that the best laid plans sometimes can contain a hidden flaw. In their line of work, it is not wise to trust anyone 100 percent. Secretly Edward and Doc have begun measures to dismantle the organization. If they feel at any point that Jason is out of control and he no longer takes their advice they will shut down all operations. His contacts will be told not to have any further dealings with him. Hoping that without this support network he will be forced to stop the killing. If he doesn't stop, he'll be alone and the risk of getting caught will increase greatly.

A week has passed and from the window of their apartment they have noticed an increase in the number of police cars in the area. Sparrow has sent emails saying a special undercover police unit is operating in the area. This unit is very good at infiltrating any group or organization. The units plan is to monitor the city closely, tracking anyone suspicious. Random searches and pat downs of people walking the streets are a common sight.

With the bounty on his head increasing almost daily Jason knows that someone will break ranks and turn him in. The money will simply be too much to ignore.

He will begin limiting his face to face meetings with his contacts, more will be done on the internet. His codes will be changed more often along with where he meets his contacts.

Feeling at times that the walls are closing in on him, Jason has been taking pills provided by Doc that will help him sleep. Although Doc prescribed only one pill a day, Jason has been secretly taking as many as eight. His hands twitch for no reason and he has begun hearing voices.

He prays to God that this crusade be over soon, and he can return to a more normal existence.

Now more than a week has passed since the killing of so many, and he has an itch to get back to work.

The streets are somewhat back to normal and he can wait no longer.

"I must go," he calls across the room.

Looking up from his paper, Edward nods and gives him a half grin.

Doc says, "Why don't you wait another few days, let things calm down a little more."

Putting extra ammo into his backpack Jason replies, "I have waited long enough, I must continue our mission. The criminals are reeling from what I have done, we must keep the pressure on."

Doc glances over at Edward and the look on his face says it all. They both know by listening to Jason talk like this that it may already be too late for this young man.

The longer Jason talks about the need to kill more people the more exited he gets.

Now getting up and walking across the room Doc confronts Jason, "I'm going to be honest with you, I think you need to take a break from this mission you are on."

Looking up as he puts things into his backpack, "You and Edward are becoming too cautious. You two should just let me do my job."

Now angry at this reply, Doc sternly says, "You listen to me young man, you are getting obsessed with all this killing you're doing. It is affecting your thinking, and it's going to get you killed."

Taking in a deep breath, "It's too late to stop what we started, we must continue regardless of the risks."

Shaking his head, Doc is beside himself with what to do.

"The people in this city need me to rid it of all its criminals," Jason says in a mocking tone. "I'm their only hope, without me this city will be overrun with thieves and murders, and don't forget the drug dealers."

Hearing this, Doc knows that Jason has now crossed the line. His mental state is becoming clouded with visions of him being this white knight, this savior of the people and that when his mission is completed he will be honored as a hero.

Now standing and heading for the door, Jason pauses, "God will protect me, and in the end the people of this city might even erect a statue of me."

"You are becoming delusional," an angry Edward calls out. "The authorities look at you as a serial killer, no different than any other. You will not be looked at as a hero, don't be a fool."

Tossing his backpack over his shoulder, Jason gives the two a long stare.

"Maybe it is you two that has become delusional. You are the ones that started this whole thing, it was you that recruited me, don't forget that."

"We still stand behind what we started," says Doc. "But you are becoming infatuated, even fanatical with all this killing. You need to listen to us when we say it is time to temporally stop this crusade. Too much is going on, you have killed too many. Let things calm down, we can start this up again when the time is right."

Showing displeasure after hearing this, "I will stop when I feel the time is right. I'm the one doing all the dirty work, don't forget that." Slamming the door shut on his way out.

The two old men are sad by these turn of events, they never thought their young apprentice would turn out like this.

"We will let him go just a little longer," states Edward. "Then if he doesn't start listening to us, we know what we have to do."

Sitting down, Doc runs his fingers through his hair, the look of complete bewilderment is on his face. He and Edward have discussed this before, and they know what it will take to stop Jason. It is agonizing for both of them as they looked at Jason as a son.

Patting his friend on the shoulder Edward says, "I pray that he will see the light, and that he will break free of this need to kill."

With a slight smile, "I hope you're right. I pray that you are right."

Suddenly the computer begins beeping, they know a message is coming in.

Typing in the correct code they can see that it is from Sparrow. From inside the court house, this unknown man has given them valuable information time and time again over the years. The two know that any information from Sparrow means something important is taking place.

Sparrow always keeps his messages brief and to the point.

"A helicopter will begin patrolling the sky at night, they will be using infrared scopes to search the top of the buildings. F.B.I. agents disguised as the homeless will be positioned around the city. Undercover agents will be trying to infiltrate the drug gangs in an attempt to get information on the Vigilante Assassin. Sparrow out."

With their heads lowered, each knows that Jason is in great danger. They have no way of contacting him, there is nothing they can do.

CHAPTER 9

Viewing the alley from the concealment of a dumpster, Jason watches as the citizens walk by on the street. Nameless and faceless, they are ordinary people going about their lives. He wonders how many of them have been victims of a random crime. How many even had the guts to report that they had been attacked, robed, or raped?

Maybe they have been a witness to a crime, but fearing retaliation they refused to testify. A grip of fear and dread has taken hold of this city. What was once a descent place to call home now is nothing more than a lawless town right out of the old west.

Jason was hoping that before he died that he could change this city, and restore it back to the way it was.

Breaking his concentration he sees a man jump out of the shadows and grab someone off the street. He drags the poor soul a short distance and then hits him in the head with a small club. The man falls to the ground, wrenching in pain and calling out for help. Others on the street slowdown to take a look, but they do not stop. These ordinary citizens choose to ignore what they have witnessed, not wanting to get involved. It makes Jason's stomach turn at this cowardly behavior, how they can simply ignore the man's plea for help.

He cannot and will not sit idly by while this terrible act is taking place. He moves from the concealment of the dumpster and moves quickly along the old brick walls of the buildings. After robbing the man this thug begins kicking and stomping on him. To Jason this is unnecessary; he has already robbed the man. There is no need to continue punishing him, there is nothing to gain by this cruel act of brutality.

His blood begins to boil and the rage is building at this senseless act.

Moving closer he pulls out his revolver ready to exterminate him. This thug must have spotted Jason, and with a quick glance the thug turns and starts running.

Jason hurries after him, but the man is zig zagging in such a way that it is impossible to get off a shot. He is unable to shake Jason, and now begins knocking over garbage cans in an attempt to slow his pursuit. Realizing that Jason isn't giving up the man climbs up a fire escape ladder, Jason quickly follows. Now with the steps between the two, Jason is again unable to get a shot at him.

As the man reaches the top, Jason is only twenty feet or so behind him. The man disappears over the top and Jason slows his ascent, figuring that the man may be lying in wait for him. Moving up slowly, the gun pointed above his head Jason can now hear pounding. He knows instantly what it is and moves without haste up and over the top. There halfway across the roof is this thug trying with all his strength to get the door open. He kicks and hits it with his shoulder several times, but the door does not budge.

As he must have sensed that someone was very close he turns to face his pursuer. That's when Jason shoots him in the stomach with his taser gun.

The man tightens up and convulses as he falls to the roof. As he lay on his stomach, Jason pulls out a pair of handcuffs and secures his hands behind his back. Next he pulls a piece of rope from his pocket tying one end tightly around the man's ankles. He is now hog tied, and next a handkerchief is put around his head and across his mouth to prevent him from calling out.

Jason now sits down to catch his breath.

Looking over at this poor dumb soul, he has to laugh.

"You moron, if you had only turned the door handle and pulled the door towards you it would have opened."

Jason now drags the man over to the edge of the roof, glancing down, he can tell that they are up nearly eighteen floors. His first thought is to just throw him off, he deserved nothing less.

But a pile of discarded junk at one corner of the roof catches Jason's my attention, and this gives him an idea. Finding some heavy rope, he ties one end around the man's ankles, the other he secures to a plastic pipe sticking up through the roof. He isn't sure if this plastic pipe will hold the man's weight, but if it does break and the man falls to the pavement far below, no loss he figures.

This whole time this low life of a human being struggles to get free. Jason sits and waits patiently until the man has tired himself out, than he eases the man's body up and onto the small edge of the building. He lets him take in everything that is happening, and by the panic look on his face he is not liking it at all.

With a hard kick from Jason, the man tumbles over the edge. A second later the rope springs tight, and looking over the edge, the man is dangling only ten feet away.

His eyes bulging and face turning red, it is apparent that this man is scared to death.

Jason thinks about cutting the rope and ending this scum bags worthless existence.

The world will not miss him one bit, but he suddenly has a better plan.

Looking at this man, Jason calls out, "When you are set free, I want you to inform all the other criminals out there that someone is watching them. I don't work for the police department, so punishing and killing criminals instead of sending them to jail doesn't bother me. One more thing, you will live this time, but make no mistake that if I ever catch you again committing a crime I will end your life in a heartbeat."

With shock and freight still evident in his eyes, the man nods his head as Jason walks away. He knows that in the morning that someone will notice him hanging from this building. He wonders if he has done the right thing, will this act of kindness come back to haunt him.

The back alleys are quiet, but they were not always this way. The thugs and hoodlums routinely patrolled the alleys looking for some poor soul that had lost his way. But that all changed when the Vigilante Assassin appeared on the scene. Most of the criminals have taken to doing their dirty work on the streets. They fear this unknown assassin, he has become somewhat of a ghost figure.

The stories about the Vigilante Assassin have grown into epic proportions. Some say he is a phantom, a spirit sent by God while others think he may have mythical powers. With his ability to kill and never be seen or leave behind any trace that he was even in the area has many of these criminal scared for their lives.

The streets are quiet, even the hardcore gang members have made themselves scarce.

After walking several miles he finds himself at a usual place where he receives information from various sources.

Picking up an envelope from the dumpster, Jason reads it.

"Urgent, meet me behind Eli's bakery. Information that several individuals will attempt to hijack a school bus, you must intercept."

Jason knows how important this is, and the lives of innocent children are at stake. With quickness in his steps, he hurries through the darkened alleys.

Ever vigilant of muggers and trouble makers he watches for any movement that may suggest an encounter. Stopping as the sound of an object ricochets down a nearby fire escape ladder, until it hits the pavement. Scanning the roof tops, he crouches down, expecting some hoodlum to jump out and try to rob him. To his surprise all is still, a slight wind blows a newspaper all around.

Not seeing or hearing anything, however his sixth sense is telling him to beware.

Arriving behind the bakery, he finds it vacant. "Where is Condor, has something happened to him?"

Getting an odd feeling as he stands in the semi glow from the lone light hanging directly above the back door, Jason tenses up. Backing up against a building Jason reaches for his revolver. His heart now beating faster and his senses heightened. Still unable to see or hear anything, he knows something isn't right.

Just as he notices a slight movement to his right, it's too late.

Instantly an object shoots through the air pinning his right arm tight against the wall. Just as quick, a second object pins his left leg to the wall. Surprised by the suddenness of this attack, Jason is momentarily stunned. These horse shoe shaped objects have penetrated several inches into the brick wall holding him firmly against the building,

He struggles to free himself, conscious of someone very close. Out of the shadows a man walks towards Jason, helpless and trapped, Jason tries to remain calm. Stopping several feet in front of him, Jason can see who has done this to him.

The man's eyes are cold black, his face showing multiple scares, hair down to his shoulders and wearing a black cape. Cursing at being trapped like some wild animal, Jason knows who this man is.

He had been warned earlier about a man calling himself the Grim Reaper that would come seeking him. Nevertheless Jason considered this assassin no more of a threat than any of the others that have tried to kill him. The Grim Reaper stands perfectly still, his head leaning slightly forward, the caped man does not say a word.

Jason can hear a hissing sound as this man's breathing is labored, and a pungent odor fills the air.

Pretending that he doesn't know this man Jason calls out, "Who are you and what do you want?"

However, the mysterious man doesn't answer, he continues to stare at the ground.

Bothered by this, Jason knows that this assassin is different than the others. The man does not gloat or laugh at having caught the famous Vigilante Assassin. Instead, he slowly raises his head and stares at Jason, studying him, from bottom to trop.

Breathing faster, Jason finds himself in a very unusual position, being sized up by a very dangerous person.

"You are the Vigilante Assassin," a grovel voice utters.

This man's words sound like that of a long time smoker, rough and coarse.

"That is what the people of this city call me," replies Jason.

The caped man again remains motionless, his eyes not blinking, and this sends a chill up Jason's spine.

With his right hand pinned he tries reaching across his body with his left hand, hoping to grab his revolver. At that instant, the Grim Reaper steps forward, seizing Jason by the wrist.

Jason can feel the incredible strength this man has, and his grip is like a vise. He twists Jason's arm back, the pain causing him to grit his teeth. Quick as lightning, a fist catches Jason squarely on the jaw. His head is knocked back against the wall, and blood now flows from his mouth.

Not expecting this, Jason's mind begins to race. Is this man going to torture him or is he going to take him back to El Diablo. Hurting and confused, Jason struggles to hold his head up.

Again the Grim Reaper steps back, not once taking his eyes off his victim.

As his breathing increases Jason looks at this man, "Go ahead and kill me, that's what they have paid you to do!"

Slurring his words, slacked jaw and shaking his head, "I will kill you, but first you will tell me the names of all those that help you fight crime in this city."

Jason now realizes that El Diablo not only wants him dead, but also those that have assisted him. El Diablo knows about this network of vigilantes, they have caused him much trouble and pain.

"You will get no such information from me," a defiant Jason replies.

Taking a quick step forward, the Grim Reaper gets right in Jason's face, "I always get what I want."

Jason is repelled by the man's pungent odor, it is the smell of a rotting corps, causing him to gag.

As the Grim Reaper steps away, Jason pulls on the horse shoe shaped object that has his right arm pinned to the wall. He can feel it begin to loosen. The Grim Reaper turns around, aiming a pistol at

Jason, he fires and a pencil sized steel object penetrates the wall just inches from Jason's face.

Without lowering the pistol, he says, "The next one will be in your shoulder, I will continue this until you tell me their names."

Mustering up his courage, Jason replies, "Go to hell, back where you came from."

In an instant he hears the sound of the gun, and the steel object slices into his left shoulder.

His knees buckle, his face grimacing in pain. This Grim Reaper is living up to all that Jason has heard about him. Some say that the Grim Reaper isn't human, others have suggested that he's a zombie, and he can't be killed.

The stories and myths of this man go back decades, his trail of destruction and brutality is legendary. It dwarfs anything El Diablo or his henchmen could come up with.

If Jason has ever felt pure evil, it is at this moment. Trying to buy some time, he says, "How much are they paying you to do this."

The Grim Reapers eyes flash back and forth, he seems to be having trouble thinking of a reply.

Getting more nervous at not getting an answer, Jason continues to loosen the object pinning him to the wall. The Grim Reaper stands mute, his head down with his arms at his sides. He is a menacing figure, one that seems very unstable. From the left Jason can see a homeless man making his way down the alley in his direction. The man stops occasionally to rummage through the garbage cans.

Tilting his head to the right, the Grim Reaper also has seen this man. Stepping back into the darkness, where he cannot be seen, this hired hit man waits silently.

Jason must warn this man, to get him to go the other way.

Speaking as loud as he can, despite the pain in his jaw, "Don't come any closer."

Looking up the homeless man glances in Jason's direction. Putting his head back down as he continues searching the garbage cans.

"You are in great danger," Jason pleads.

Now doing a slow walk the homeless man walks right up to Jason and says, "You say something to me?"

"Run away now."

Looking over the man's shoulder, Jason can see the Grim Reaper move out of the dark and towards this old street beggar. Jason knows the outcome and with his right leg he kicks at the man in an attempt to get him to leave.

It is too late, a thin cord is wrapped around the man's neck. Jason is frustrated at not being able to help save this man.

The homeless man is picked up right off his feet, showing the incredible strength of the Grim Reaper. A moment later his lifeless body is tossed to the side like a sack of potatoes.

If ever there was a time when Jason felt his life was about to end, none was more imminent than at this moment.

Jason watches as this devil pulls from his pocket a long knife. Jason still has his revolver, a little confused why this man didn't take it from him. But counting his blessings as this is a mistake that may prove fatal for this hired assassin.

Holding the knife against Jason's throat the Grim Reaper says, "I kill you now."

Needing a miracle, Jason has one last trick. Clicking his heels together, a sharp blade sticks out from the tip of his right shoe. With all his strength, he kicks the Grim Reaper in the groin. Instantly reeling back, the Grim Reaper doubles over, groaning.

Knowing that the Grim Reaper won't die from this assault, Jason franticly pulls at his right arm. The horse shoe shaped object is beginning to loosen, just a little more and he'll be free. Looking up his heart skips a beat when he sees the Grim Reaper coming towards him. Sputtering words that don' make any sense, the wounded and angry Grim Reaper holds the knife high in the air.

Just as the knife comes down, Jason slips his arm out of the metal object and jumps to the side. The steel blade crashes into the brick wall sending pieces of brick in all directions. Turning with the rage of a mad man the Grim Reaper lunges at his victim again.

Jason quickly pulls out his revolver and fires three rounds in quick succession. The Grim Reaper is momentarily stopped, and he touches the places on his chest where he is shot.

Crawling away, Jason is stunned that this man is still on his feet. The bullets clearly penetrated his chest, yet there is no blood. Positive that the Grim Reaper is not wearing a bullet proof vest, he doesn't understand how this can be.

With the Grim Reaper coming towards him again, Jason fires three more rounds. One striking the man in his right knee, another his right shoulder and the third in his throat.

Stopping, the Grim Reaper seems to go into convulsions, his body shaking, he throws his hands into the air. The Grim Reaper drops to his knees, his head slumps forward. Jason wipes the sweat from his face, thankful that this nightmare is over.

Getting to his feet and hobbling away, he braces himself against the buildings to keep from falling down. His jaw broken again and blood running down his shirt, he needs medical treatment immediately.

A sound from behind causes him to pause and look back, what he sees he can't believe. Shaking his head in disbelief he is shocked to see the Grim Reaper getting to his feet. What kind of man can still be alive after being shot six times he asks in amazement?

With one bullet left in his revolver he takes careful aim and when the Grim Reaper lifts up his head, Jason puts a bullet right between his eyes. Falling back and landing hard on the ground, the Grim Reaper lay with his arms and legs spread out.

Waiting a moment, just to make sure that this time that indeed this monster is really dead, he watches him carefully. After seeing no movement, Jason takes a sigh of relief, positive that the Grim Reaper will no longer kill anyone ever again, he is now just an old legend.

Despite having this steel object in his left shoulder Jason needs answers and he makes his way down the alley and to the dumpster where Condor stays. Angry that a trusted confidant betrayed and set him up, he reloads his revolver. After opening the lid to the dumpster and looking to the back of it he makes a gruesome discovery. His friend has been murdered, and it appears he was tortured first. With an ear and an eye missing, Jason knows his friend held out to the very end before giving up any information.

Piecing together what happened, Jason surmises that Condor was forced to write that note, then he was killed by the Grimm Reaper.

Staggering into the apartment, Doc and Edward are appalled at the condition Jason is in. laying him on the floor, Doc injects Jason with pain medication along with a tranquilizer.

In shallow breaths, "The Grim Reaper is dead, in the alley behind the bakery, and so is Condor."

Shaking his head doc says, "You must be more careful, one of these days," stopping doc can see that Jason is now unconscious.

"So," says doc, "than the Grim Reaper is human after all, so much for all those stories about him being supernatural. That bullets couldn't kill him because he was already dead."

Realizing that he must go and remove the bodies before the police find them, Edward heads out the door.

After removing the steel object from Jason's shoulder Doc manages to stop the bleeding and he then wires his jaw shut. A short time later Edward returns, standing next to Doc, they both stare down at their wounded warrior. Running his fingers through his hair, Edwards says, "There was no body behind the bakery, I took Condors body to the morgue."

Swallowing hard, Doc is at a loss for words. Turning and looking at his friend he asks, "Do you think someone came and dragged him away?"

Shaking his head, Edward replies, "I saw the spot where he lay, and I did not see any heels marks suggesting that he was dragged away. It just doesn't make any sense."

With a wild look Doc says, "Than maybe the stories about this Grim Reaper are true, that he can't be killed."

It is a frightening though to think that these drug lords are using some type of voodoo or black magic to kill the Vigilante Assassin.

Neither believes in any of that stuff but the fact remains that somehow this Grim Reaper disappeared from that alley and it looks like no one helped him.

CHAPTER 10

During the next two weeks Jason recuperates, his last outing nearly costing him his life.

He is troubled when told that the Grim Reaper was not in the alley as he said he would be.

"Someone must have removed the body," suggests Jason.

Drinking his morning cup of coffee, Doc replies, "Nobody seems to know what happened to him, my contacts have all reported that they have heard of no one removing the body from that alley that night."

"Are you sure he was dead," asks Edward, "Did you feel for a pulse?"

With a weird expression, Jason answers, "I shot that bastard seven times. With the last one being in the head, there is no way he could have survived. To answer your question, no I did not feel for a pulse, I know a dead man when I see one."

"Then someone must have removed the body," says Doc. "I trust your judgment Jason, let's just forget this whole thing."

Nodding his head, Jason wants nothing less, as he can still see the evil in that man's eyes and feel his cold fingers around his neck.

Several more days pass and Jason feels he is recovered enough to resume his duties despite his jaw still being wired shut. His inactivity is too much, he can't wait any longer.

Seeing their young apprentice begin to put things into his backpack, they each flash a worried look at each other.

"You need more time to recover," states Doc, "So put that stuff away."

"He's right," adds Edward. "Give yourself just a few more days, what's the rush?"

"The people may begin to think that the Vigilante Assassin has left town," says Jason in a guarded voice. "If the criminals also think this than it will renew the crime spree."

At this exact moment a message comes across the computer screen. Setting aside their disagreement they casually walk over to the computer. Typing in the code, a few seconds pass until the words come across. Someone has just given these three, and especially Jason, an early Christmas present.

The message reads, "Know location of El Diablo, will send address in next message."

The three can barely contain themselves, and throwing his arms in the air, Edwards says, "Praise the lord."

Nearly crying, Doc is speechless. He like so many others has a score to settle with that man.

Jason pumps his fist into the air, "It's about time," he calls out in a confident voice.

The network of people calling themselves the F.L.O.C.K., have been trying to locate El Diablo for a very long time, but without success. Now to their disbelief, someone has come forward, who it might be is anyone's guess.

Perhaps it is from someone that has been tortured or robbed by El Diablo or his men. It also could be someone close to him, and they have grown tired of his ways and this is their way of getting rid of him. Most of the drug gangs know that the Vigilante Assassin is looking for El Diablo, and now one of his goons has possibly turned on him. Sense Jason has been eliminating criminals, El Diablo has been rarely seen.

He knows how effective the vigilante is and he has taken precautions to avoid being killed like so many others of his kind.

It isn't long and an address is on the computer screen.

Standing up, Doc says, "I know where that house is located, it is out in the country and it is surrounded by thick woods. How are you going to drive anywhere near it without being spotted?"

Sitting back in his chair, Jason taps his fingers nervously on the wooden desk, his mind in deep thought.

"You could parachute in," Edward suggests, "but that will be very dangerous, I'm sure they will spot you right away."

"What about just driving a car towards the house at a high rate of speed, and catch them by surprise," suggests Doc.

Not happy with any of those ideas, Jason now begins to pace the floor. The two old men can only watch, at their age they cannot participate in this daring adventure no matter how much they wish they could.

Pulling up a map on the computer they locate the address, and it is indeed surrounded by thick woods. There are no other houses within miles of it, and only a single road leads to it. The driveway must be nearly a mile long. El Diablo is sure to have the entrance heavily guarded.

Making a fist, Jason confidently says, "I'll start several miles away from the house, at the far end of the woods. Being dropped off so far away should keep me from being spotted. I'll travel as quietly as I can across these woods until I spot the house. Once I find a perfect location overlooking the house I'll wait until I have a good shot and then that will be the end of El Diablo."

Shaking their heads, Edward and Doc like his plan.

"For once we agree with your first plan of attack," says Doc, "it sounds like the best opportunity we'll have and it affords you protection and an escape route if you are spotted."

Feeling very confident in this mission, the three begin preparations.

Besides his usual weapons he packs several M.R.E.'s, these will sustain him if the need arises that he has to stay in those woods for an extended period of time. They all know that this opportunity to eliminate El Diablo will not come again.

Jason prepares himself for a long stay if necessary. He packs only what is needed and nothing more. He will travel light and fast, hoping to reach a spot overlooking the house just as the moon is at its brightest.

After everything is checked and double checked, there is nothing to do but wait for night fall. The three sit around the kitchen table eating supper, an eerie silence permeates the room.

Occasionally looking up, Jason can see the worry on their faces. These two have always had his best interest, and he knows they care about him a great deal.

When their eyes meet, Doc says, "You know, maybe it's time I went along on one of these missions."

This causes Edward to nearly chock on his food.

"Are you nuts," Edwards states firmly. "You can hardly walk from here to the street and back without needing to stop and rest three times."

Now tossing his fork onto his plate, "If this is going to be Jason's last mission, I have every right to go along."

Sitting straight up, Jason remarks, "What do you mean, my last mission?"

Now the two old men look at each other, they have let this slip out.

"We have been discussing that if El Diablo is killed, we believe that the crime rate will drastically drop," states Edward, now slightly embarrassed at this slip of the tongue.

Needing to back up his friend, "That's true," adds Doc, "our need to continue this crusade will be over."

Clearly unhappy about this, "Just slow down," utters an upset Jason. "Neither of you ever talked to me about this. You had no right to make this decision without talking to me first."

"We have consulted with the other members, and they all agree that maybe after El Diablo is gone, that the group can then disband," says Doc.

Shaking his head defiantly, Jason angrily replies, "We have much more work to do, with El Diablo dead it will indeed curtail the crime rate, but we cannot stop there. There are so many more that need to be eliminated, this mission that we started is far from being over."

Edward and Doc knew that Jason would react this way. They were hoping against all odds that maybe just maybe his attitude would change. But as he rants and raves about the need to keep killing, their worst nightmare is coming true. They have created a killing machine, and deep in their hearts they know only one way to stop him.

With the talk changing to another subject, as Jason believes he has made his point.

One more thing he does that disturbs his two mentors, Jason drills out the ends of the bullets and next he pours in several drops of mercury, finally sealing this over with wax. Giving a glance across the room he says, "This is to insure that if the bullet does not kill El Diablo than this poison will."

Their faces say it all, long and drawn, at a loss as to what they should do next. They remain silent, and biting his lip Doc starts to say something when Edward nods his head against it.

The two go into another room and continue their discussion of how and when to stop this out of control killer. The two can't believe that Jason is making these types of bullets. They had agreed at the beginning of this crusade that a single bullet would be used to kill. Never did they imagine their apprentice concocting such things, in their minds it didn't seem right.

To kill a person with a clean shot is one thing but to add poison to the bullet that is something they were totally against.

What other devious and dishonest ways have Jason come up with to kill, the two dare not ask.

As the sun begins to set low in the sky, the apartment once again becomes very quiet.

With his backpack at the ready, Jason must wait just a little longer before going out on this mission.

Unable to sit, Doc crosses the room and standing in front of Jason he demands, "When this night is over regardless of if you have killed El Diablo or not it will be your last mission."

Waiting a moment before replying, Jason looks at his two mentors, he does not like the look in their eyes.

"If you will not help me continue this crusade, then I will find another member of F.L.O.C.K. who sees things my way."

Now upset to the point where Edward has to restrain him, Doc lashes out, "You have gone too far, you have become a renegade, killing is all you think about."

Still sitting calmly, "I had trusted your judgment in the beginning but now a higher power is directing me."

Throwing his hands into the air, Doc must sit as he grabs his chest.

"I must agree with my old friend," utters Edward. "You have lost your common sense, it's like you have become a totally different person."

With a quick response, "You are right, I'm different, I'm not afraid anymore, I have a calling that I must fulfill."

Shouting across the room Doc yells, "You are losing your mind if you think God is guiding and protecting you. If you go against our orders things will change around here, you can bet on that."

Trying his best to hold back what he would like to say, as he still has a tremendous amount of respect for both of these men, instead Jason replies, "This mission, this crusade we have all embarked on is right and justified. You two feel this way because you cannot accompany me on these forays, and you now resent me because of this."

Taking a deep breath, Edward strongly replies, "That is not why we are trying to stop you, we believe that you are unable to stop yourself. Something evil has taken hold of your values and it is causing you to go down a dark and deadly road. We are only trying to open your eyes so that you can see that you seem to be hell bent on killing everyone and also getting yourself killed in the process."

Standing and putting his backpack over his shoulders, and showing the confidence in himself that he has gained over these months, "I know my limitations, I know how long I can play this deadly game, and it will be my decision as to when the Vigilante Assassin will put down his rifle."

The two old men stand mute, as here is the one person that they and all the members of the organization have come to look at as the savior. In the beginning this whole operation worked like a well-oiled machine, things went smoothly and efficiently. But sense Jason began to get the idea that he is protected by a guardian angel and that God himself is guiding him there have been a lot of close calls.

His brushes with death are getting more frequent, and his narrow escapes are leaving him paranoid and mistrustful. The strain of so many people looking for him has caused Jason to need a great many sleeping pills to get through the night. The nightmares wake him nearly every hour and it takes Doc a long time to calm him down. He can see the change in this young man and it bothers him, he knows that Jason needs to see a psychiatrist.

With the tension high Jason leaves the apartment without any more words being spoken.

In the alley, Crow is waiting, and like an obedient servant he will take the Vigilante Assassin wherever he wants to go.

Crow is the one person right now that Jason has the most faith in, he has always been there when Jason called. Always putting himself in danger, Crow never refused to pick up or drop off Jason no matter how dangerous the area. Crow has been a loyal member of the organization and a trusted friend.

However, in this fight against evil young Jason must not get too attached to anyone.

Getting in Jason gives his trusted friend the directions.

The car races to the edge of the city and is soon going down several dirt roads. Pointing out a spot not far ahead, "That looks like a good place to let me out."

With an inquisitive look on his face, Crow asks, "Why on earth would you want to be dropped off way out here in the country?"

"I can't tell you that," answers Jason. "This mission I'm on is a secret. I can't even tell you, so don't ask me again."

Crow has been helping the organization for a good number of years, and he knows when to stop asking questions.

"You take care young man," and with that said he gives Jason a wink and begins driving away.

Waiting until the taillights have disappeared, Jason enters the dark woods. Following his compass readings he now embarks on what could be his shining moment as the Vigilante Assassin. This one act will be payback for so many, and when word spreads of El Diablo's death, he is hoping that it will be a catalysts for the people of Landore to rally around.

Maybe the people will regain their nerve and take back their city.

Of course these are just dreams, perhaps it will take much more bloodshed to reunite this city.

Remembering the promise he made to himself when he joined this organization, that he wouldn't stop his crusade until he was completely confident that he had made a difference. When the crime rate drops significantly, and the people can once more walk the streets without fear, then and only then will he stop this crusade.

He is troubled by what Doc and Edward said before he left on this mission, and he begins to think that maybe they are plotting against him. He can't imagine their reasons for stopping what has been so successful up to this point, are they losing their nerve and has old age finally caught up to them.

Whatever their reasons Jason has decided that now is not the time to stop, and sense he does all the killing it should be his decision as to when to stop not theirs.

He does respect them and he listens to their advice but it seems lately that they have gotten cold feet about this crusade. He would like to talk to the other members of F.L.O.C.K. but that is not aloud. Only Doc and Edward have their code words and they have not given them to him. Their reason is that secrecy, confidentiality and remaining anonymous has kept this organization going this long, the fewer that the know the inner workings the safer it is.

Butting heads with his two mentors on this subject has resulted in much arguing, with Jason demanding to be included, but each time he is denied access.

This feeling of being used has caused him to resent the members of F.L.O.C.K. and he has thought of leaving the group and organizing his own faction. But who would he recruit, who can run an operation as smoothly as these unknown people do. For the time being he will work with these men, but there will be a day when he will run this show, and he will be in charge, but that day will have to wait as a more important target awaits.

Having traveled several miles through the woods with just a small flashlight, and his compass pointing him in the right direction, he knows he is getting close to his objective. Getting down on his hands and knees, he crests a large hill, with his binoculars he can see in the distance a two story house sitting at the end of a long driveway. A chicken coop sits to the left and a small shed is directly in front of it. Recalling what the unknown contact had described, he is positive that this is the house that he has been searching for. Turning off the flashlight, as to not give away his whereabouts Jason slowly proceeds to make his way closer. Being careful to be as quiet as possible, fearing these drug lords may have listening devices all around. He stops every few feet to look and listen, but all he hears are the sounds of insects. Moving as stealthy as possible is a key factor if his plan is to succeed; this mission is one he has been waiting on for a long time.

Jason is in no hurry, and looking at his watch, as the time is just after midnight. This will give him at least another six hours before the sun comes up, he can be as cautious as he deems is necessary.

The night air is still, and a partial moon shines down through the trees. He was expecting a brighter moon but the thick cloud cover is partially blocking it. However, this small amount of light is just enough to see by, perfect for an ambush. Feeling like everything is going as planned Jason must keep his emotions in check. As bad as he wants to put a bullet in El Diablo's head, he must still treat this like any other assassination. To be calm, quiet, and most important, keep your guard up at all times.

As he has learned many times, mostly the hard way that the most thought out plan can go wrong, so he must be ready to beat a hasty retreat if necessary.

Going only a few feet from the concealment of one tree to the next, he stops each time and waits a moment before continuing.

His senses are telling him that this night will be special, and it will be one that he will remember the rest of his life.

To finally rid the city of its most notorious drug lord will be the shining moment in his long crusade. But most important his need for revenge will have been satisfied, and he is hoping that the nightmares will end shortly afterwards.

Looking up into the night sky, he whispers, "Look over me just one more time Lord, this mission I must complete. There are so many others that have prayed for this night, I can't let them down."

Feeling a little more confident, Jason continues his slow and methodical advance towards his ultimate target.

The faint aroma of cigarette smoke stops him dead in his tracks. He knows it didn't come from the house, as it is at least two hundred yards away.

He knows that someone is very near, and he tenses up. Now believing that he may have walked into a trap, he pulls out his revolver. With his ears straining to hear the faintest sound, he covers his mouth to quiet his breathing. Ten minutes pass and nothing, still his senses are telling him that he is in danger. Another twenty minutes passes and still no movement anywhere near him, the smell of cigarette smoke is no longer in the air.

Jason is beginning to think that maybe he is overreacting. Is he getting to the point where he is now hearing and smelling things that aren't there?

Perhaps the thought of what will happen to him if he's caught by these drug dealers is creeping into his subconscious. He always tries to think that he will manage to get out of any situation that he may find himself in. To be calm and not panic, think first before reacting.

However this uneasy edgy feeling he has will not subside. Thinking that maybe he has been spotted and should leave, and come back and try again another night.

"No, that is not an option," he reminds himself.

This drug lord will be leaving the country in the morning; this job has to be finished tonight.

With his life in possible danger, he will not retreat. Regardless of what lies ahead he is determined to see it through to the end.

Just as he is about to move forward a small flicker of light catches his attention. Looking down the hill, his eyes are glued to the spot he had seen the light. The waiting is terrible, but he knows patience is everything. Sure enough, about forty feet in front of him he can see that same small flicker of light. The aroma of cigarette smoke once again fills his nostrils.

Exhaling just slightly, Jason knows instinctively what this small flicker of light is.

By the light of the moon, he can see the outline of a small three sided structure. It is open in front and on top. Jason moves to his right, every inch of ground is carefully covered. Knowing that a snap of a twig or the rustle of a tree branch will give him away, he must meticulously place each foot step. Arriving at a spot that gives him a better view of what he is up against, Jason sits motionless. The outline of a man's head sticks up just above the top of the structure. Each time this person takes a drag on his cigarette the small fireball would glow. The man is guarding the house below, and Jason wonders how many other men are also in these hills surrounding the house.

Jason is now in a bad spot, unable to sneak away for fear he will be heard. Not sure how he is going to close the gap between them without alerting this man of his presents.

The man's undoing is his addiction to cigarettes, if not for that Jason would have walked right in front of him. Looking up, all Jason can do is whisper, "Thank You."

Jason must now sit and wait, hoping this man makes a fatal mistake. Maybe this unknown man will need to get up and stretch his legs, or perhaps he will be bitten by a bug and need to move around in order to dislodge the creature.

The sky begins to cloud over even more, and the moon slowly disappears, making the woods very dark.

Jason can no longer see the outline of this man, and his immediate whereabouts are unknown.

Jason listens carefully, hoping the man will make some noise. He gets a disturbing feeling with the thought that this man may be aware of his presents already and is at this time is maneuvering to come in from behind him.

Knowing not to panic and get up and run, Jason remembers what Falcon taught him. "You must be vigilant, ever watchful, become an object. The art of stealth is the ability of not being seen, even though you may be in plain sight."

Heeding that advise, Jason slows down his breathing and heart rate. His arms lay at his sides, his eyes almost shut, he is as still as a rock. Remaining this way for what he estimates to be two hours, and the woods have remained as still as ever.

He now knows that the men hired to guard these drug lords are professional killers. They are trained in concealment and the art of ambush.

These men are hired guns, working for the highest bidder, killing is a way of life for them.

With no movement for over two hours Jason realizes that his adversary is skilled and experienced. In this deadly game of hide and seek, his own skills will be tested to the fullest.

Jason needs to draw him out of his concealment, to draw him into a position that will be at his advantage. But how without giving himself away is the question. Firing his rifle is not an option as it will alert those in the house as well as others that maybe hiding nearby. The night will be ending soon, and with the coming sunshine Jason will be exposed. He needs to do something soon or else the drug king will get away.

Suddenly he hears several light footsteps moving in the dry leaves. Jason grips his rifle tightly, anticipating a showdown with this man.

Listening he can hear the sound of water hitting the dry leaves that covers the ground. This is the moment he has been waiting for, his chance to move and act. Ever so quietly Jason moves in the direction of this sound. Peering from behind a tree, there not more than ten feet away is his opponent. The man has made the first foolish mistake, and this long game is about to end.

Jason watches as the man finishes urinating and he steps back into the safety of his shelter.

As this man moves around inside his shelter to make himself more comfortable, that is when Jason moves closer. With just the thin sheet of plywood separating the two, Jason closes his eyes for a second. Realizing that his next move will take another human life, and he asks the Lord to forgive him.

Not a religious person, but not an atheist either. Jason believes in a higher power, but he is also distraught as to why this higher power would allow such violence to ravage our societies.

Maybe there is a reason, a purpose to all this madness. Who is he to question how a God should run the world.

Quickly getting back to the situation at hand, as he must not dwell on the things he can't change.

How is he going to dispatch this man, as there are many options he can choose from?

It must be silent and swift, a lethal strike the very first time. This man can have no opportunity, no chance to call for help. Any noise, even the slightest rustle of leaves will give Jason away and halt his plans to stop the drug king.

There are several small holes on the backside of the plywood of the structure and this gives Jason an idea. The man has his head pressed against the plywood as he tries to conceal as much of himself as possible. Pulling out his knife, Jason puts the edge of the blade at the opening to one of these small holes. Not sure what part of this man is on the opposite side, he believes this is his only and best opportunity. Drawing in a deep breath Jason plunges the knife through the hole with all his strength. His knuckles hit the plywood so hard they bleed. He hears the man's boots hit the sides of the structure only once, and then all is still. Jason listens intensely, wanting to know if anyone else has heard this noise.

Waiting patiently, it is several minutes until he is sure that he was not heard. Pulling his knife back through the hole, he wipes the blood off on the dry leaves before putting it back into its sheath. Cautiously he makes his way around to the front, ever wary that this man is a trained assassin and that he just might be playing dead. Lying flat on the ground, Jason creeps forward and around to the right side of the shelter and peeks inside.

He is relieved to see that indeed the man is dead. The knife had gone through the back of his neck and out his throat. This would explain why he didn't call out and alert those in the house below.

Several thoughts now go through Jason's mind as he looks down at this man. How many men has he killed during his life, and what is his reason for doing this type of work. Money is the root of all evil and no doubt this man was lured by the large amount of money offered to him to perform these tasks.

Scanning the hillside Jason notices a narrow path leading down through the trees until it reaches the open field. From here the tall grass extends roughly one hundred yards all the way to the house.

With his rifle slung over his shoulder, he lies on his stomach and carefully crawls down the path. Constantly on the alert for any more of these hired guns that maybe hiding nearby, his hand keeps a constant grip on his rifle. Every twenty feet or so he stops and raising his head takes a quick look around, he must be constantly at the ready for whatever may happen. The thought that this trail could be booby trapped adds to the strain and tension now cursing through his body.

It would be like El Diablo to do this, to set multiple traps and snares, as this monster knows that there are a great many people trying to kill him. To be constantly on the move, not staying too long in one place, this type of tactic is what has kept him alive for this long. His contacts are of the most trusted, and his brief outings are only to the most secure and secluded of places.

The one that has betrayed him this time by giving the F.L.O.C.K. El Diablo's whereabouts this night will never be known. This person is most likely a close confidant in the drug cartel, and for whatever reason he has chosen to betray his boss. This cowardly act is by a man who does not have the nerve to kill El Diablo himself, instead he will rely on others to do his dirty work. This is the creed of the drug dealers, to look out only for yourself and to eliminate those that stand in your way. El Diablo must know this as he like those around him is nothing more than thieves and murderers. They live by the gun and that is how they will die, either from the police or from one of their own.

Jason along with Doc and Edward have always suspected that for El Diablo to have survived so long in this lawless organization called the drug cartel that he must be killing those that have been with him too long. Any member that he suspects is learning or knowing too much about the comings and goings of the drug deliveries is killed. This method assures him that no one but he controls his drug empire, he is the only one that knows the contacts from the Mexican cartels.

It is a ruthless and brutal way of running an operation such as his but it has worked very well up to this point.

El Diablo has obviously overlooked one of his disgruntled lieutenants, and this mistake will cost him his life.

Jason continues his slow and methodical advance down the narrow path, and once he reaches the tall grass he pauses to scan the area. With just his eyes above the grass he has a good view of the house and this is when he notices a light on in one room.

For the next twenty minutes he doesn't take his eyes off of this light, remaining motionless as he considers his next move.

Several scenarios race through his mind as to why a light would be left on. Perhaps someone is reading a book, or maybe a late night phone call. Worst case scenario, El Diablo is about to leave this safe house, and Jason's one and possibly his last chance to kill this man could be soon over.

With just the one light on, he assumes that it was left on by accident, as he can see no movement inside or outside of this house suggesting anyone is about to depart. Satisfied with this final conclusion he lies back down on the moist ground.

Taking in a deep breath he begins crawling forward his movements are slow and relaxed. Every inch of ground is carefully covered, this is one mission he does not want to abort.

Not taking any chances whatsoever, his mind is totally and completely focused on his objective. He has dreamed of this opportunity for a very long time, and knowing that being over anxious about killing El Diablo maybe fatal he must stop several times to control his anger.

As slow as a turtle at times it takes him nearly an hour to cover the one hundred yards through the tall grass to the house. Choosing to remain flat against the ground, it was the only way of not being seen. Getting up and walking the ten feet or so across the neatly cut grass and peering through the window, he discovers that this room with the light on is the bathroom.

He could wait here and hope that the drug king comes in, at which time he will then have his shot.

But the odds of that happening are too low, and his chance at being discovered is too high. Besides the glass window may deflect the bullet enough from administering a fatal wound. Jason must think of another way to take out this drug king pin.

Lying flat against the ground next to the house he notices a shed almost directly in front of the house; and its door is partly opened. If he can make it to this shed he has an idea that just may work.

Standing and pressing himself up against the house he moves along until he's to the corner. Lying back down onto the ground, he peeks around the edge. "Dam," he says under his breath. Sitting in a chair on the front porch is another hired gun. This will make things more complicated, so Jason retreats back, needing to come up with a new plan. Looking to his right he notices a chicken coop not far away.

He smiles as another crazy idea has entered into his brain. Going back to the tall grass he slowly makes his way over to this chicken coop. Once there he reaches over the fence and lifts up the latch holding the gate in place. Going inside this small enclosure he next finds a hole in the wall, here he reaches through knocking several chickens off their roost.

Quickly moving back a short distance he conceals himself next to a pile of lumber. It isn't long and just as he had hoped; the rooster comes strutting out the gate. This is what he was hoping for, now he will wait to see if his luck continues. With the morning not far off, the rooster begins to let out its morning ritual.

Jason watches as the man from the front porch gets up and strolls across the yard in his direction. Walking right up to the rooster the man kicks it so hard it flies several feet through the air before landing. The injured rooster now begins to flop around, annoyed by this, the man walks up and presses his boot against its throat. He seems to be getting pleasure out of inflicting pain on this helpless animal.

From his hiding place Jason springs into action, racing over he hits the man in the head with a large rock. The man's facial expressions indicate just how surprised he is as he is falling backwards. Laying on the ground the man is still conscious, and Jason can see him reaching and fumbling for his gun.

But the injured man is too slow and Jason delivers another crushing blow to his head. Lying on the ground the man doesn't move, Jason stands over him with the rock held high over his head. Waiting for any sign that he may try getting up, his heart is now beating very fast. However the man doesn't move, and feeling for a pulse, and not finding one, Jason breathes a sigh of relief, confident that the man is dead.

Taking a quick glance towards the house, Jason can see no movements, and no other lights are on except the one in the bathroom.

Sure that this commotion didn't wake anyone, he drags the man behind the chicken coop, hoping that no one will find his body until long after he's gone.

Jason now walks around the perimeter of the yard until he reaches the shed. Slipping inside he sees what he came for. In the corner are several cans of gasoline. On the wall is a bundle of rope, this he will also need.

A quick look out the door and all is still quiet. With a five gallon container of gas in each hand and the rope in his mouth Jason hurries over and stands next to the house.

Next he puts several bales of hay up against the house and begins soaking them with the gasoline. When this is finished he tucks one end of the rope under the bales of hay and lays the rope out about twenty feet.

Not finished yet, he will need a way to slow down those inside if they rush out too soon and try to drive away before he has gotten into a shooting position. Going back into the shed he finds several boxes of nails, tearing open these boxes he scatters the nails all over the driveway. As it is becoming lighter out he has no time to spare. Lighting one end of the rope, Jason quickly runs across the open field and makes his way up the narrow path. The rope will burn slow enough to afford him time to get in a got shooting position.

Now at a point overlooking the house and resting his rifle against a tree he doesn't have to wait long. The burning rope has reached the gasoline soaked bales of hay and instantly there is a large fire. Almost immediately lights come on in the house. He can hear shouting and several people are outside trying to extinguish the fire. He holds his shot until he can see the drug king; that is who he came here to kill.

Unfortunately, El Diablo is too wise to expose himself this easily. Jason watches as several men race to their cars, and one of these cars backs right up to the front door. El Diablo runs out and is in the car before Jason has an opportunity to get a shot off.

He curses at missing the one shot he had, this was supposed to be a special night. His dreams of Killing El Diablo were just that, dreams. Thinking about shooting the car that El Diablo is in crosses his mind, but the odds of hitting him are too low. He suspects that the windows in the car are probably bullet proof anyways, as he knows that El Diablo protects himself very well. Disheartened over these cruel turn of events Jason can only hope that an opportunity in the future presents itself and he prepares to disappear into the woods. The two cars squeal their tires as they race for the road leading out. Still fuming at this missed opportunity, however his attention is quickly drawn back to the two cars.

He watches as the cars now begin to swerve as first one tire and then another goes flat. Jason had forgotten about the nails in the driveway. Feeling a jolt of excitement he leans against a good solid tree, easing the rifle into the pocket of my shoulder. After driving a short distance and stopping the men begin to exit the cars, running around throwing their arms into the air. Again, Jason doesn't panic, confident, he remains motionless, and waits patiently.

Finally after all these years, the man he has been searching for steps out of the car. Wearing a broad hat with a long feather sticking out the top he is easy to spot. The most hated man in Landore stands and yells at the men around him, oblivious that his life is about to end. Taking careful aim as he focuses the cross hair of the scope Jason holds his breath as he gently pulls the trigger.

The bullet hits El Diablo in the back of the head. Lurching forward and collapsing to the ground he is dead before the others even hear the sound of the gun shot. Panicked and shocked at seeing their boss dead, the men huddle down next to their cars, expecting more gun fire.

Jason feels there is no need to kill any more of them, as he has accomplished what he set out to do.

He knows if these men continue the life they have been leading, than he's positive they will face a cruel death.

CHAPTER 11

    The tid bits of information are starting to trickle into the police station. Working day and night the detectives are slowing narrowing down the whereabouts of the Vigilante Assassin's hideout. Lt. Wilson along with the Mayor have begun a public information campaign that they hope will turn the people against this killer. Flyers dot the city, they read, "This vigilante is a serial killer the likes that no one has ever seen before. He must be stopped at all costs. No one is safe from his wrath, soon he will begin targeting teachers, mailmen, the elderly even the local pastor. Please come forward if you have any information, you may remain anonymous." The reward money being offered for any information leading to the arrest and conviction of this Vigilante Assassin has steadily risen over the months until it is at $500,000 dollars.

    Exhausted from the long hours, Lt Wilson is hopeful that this case will break very soon.

    Running into his office an out of breath a detective utters, "There's been another killing by the Vigilante Assassin, this time out in the country."

    Jumping from his chair, "who and where? Why do you think it was the Vigilante Assassin, he has never ventured out of the city to do his killing."

    Catching his breath, "It was a head shot sir, and from the initial reports the shooter was a great distance away."

    His face lighting up, Lt. Wilson pumps his fist into the air, "We got that bastard this time for sure."

"You're not going to believe this," states an excited detective, "The dead man is El Diablo."

His eyes wide open, a big smile crosses his face.

"Finally someone killed that S.O.B., well than it is a great day after all."

The young detective still excited about this news says, "All the preliminary results point to the Vigilante Assassin as the killer."

"This could be the break we have been looking for. I want every available man combing that area."

Turning back around Lt. Wilson quickly has the Mayor on the phone. "Mr. Mayor, I have good news, the Vigilante Assassin has struck again. This time he has taken out one of the top drug lords in the city."

"As good as that sounds," replies the Mayor, "We still need to stop the Vigilante Assassin at all costs."

"I have every man working on it as we speak. I have a positive feeling that something will be found that we will finally be able to apprehend this mad man."

"Let me know immediately when you do," answers an eager Mayor. "The city is counting on you and your department to break this case and stop the Vigilante Assassin before he kills again."

"We will do our best."

After hanging up another detective walks in, "We have a witness," he states.

Grabbing the detective by the arm, his face lighting up like a kid on Christmas morning, "Take me to this person right now," he demands.

The two hurry out the door as Lt. Wilson can barely contain his excitement. Meeting a third detective just outside his office they are lead down a hall and into a small room. Sitting like a frightened child is a woman crying, she is surrounded by several police officers.

Taking a seat across from her Lt. Wilson asks, "Tell me what this man looks like."

However the woman says as she shakes with fear, "If I tell you he will find me and kill me."

"We will protect you," answers Lt. Wilson. "This police station has more than 50 officers in it at any given time. This is the safest place in the whole city."

The woman wipes the perspiration from her face, her hands are shaking terribly.

Leaning forward, "We need you to give us a description of the man you saw that night."

Quickly sitting down beside the woman a sketch artist begins to draw as she gives him details.

Going a short distance away, Lt. Wilson asks, "Give me the details of how this woman was able to get a look at the Vigilante Assassin when no one else has been able to."

An officer says, "It seems that this woman was in the house not far from where El Diablo was killed and early this morning she saw a man walk by her window. She said that she went to another window to get a better look. All she saw was a dark figure until he walked close to the light pole. She said she could see his face very clear and she knew he wasn't one of El Diablo's men."

Clapping his hands together, "You keep asking her for details," says an excited Lt. Wilson.

"I have to inform the Mayor of this news."

CHAPTER 12

Beside himself with joy and pride, Jason feels as if a ton of weight has been lifted from his shoulders with the killing of El Diablo. It had been a long time coming, and now exhausted, both physically and mentally, he must return to the apartment. This assassination is the highest profile individual that he has taken out up to this point.

He is hoping that the killing of El Diablo will send a clear message to the criminal gangs operating in his city. That it is a sign of things to come, that their time is up. No more will they be allowed to openly commit crimes without the fear of being punished. After word gets out that the Vigilante Assassin has killed possibly the top drug lord in the city if not the whole state, his status as a savior and hero will surely increase.

As Jason continues his long trek through the woods he ponders if someday he will ever reveal to the people that it was he who was the Vigilante Assassin. Perhaps a day will come when the need to tell his story arrives. He knows it will not be any time soon, no not until he is an old man and facing death will he tell the world.

By then all those that helped him will have passed away and no retribution can be brought against them. He will keep quiet, as silence is his best friend.

Most of those contacts were on the internet, so he really has no way of identifying any of them.

Maybe the identity of the Vigilante Assassin should remain a mystery, something the authorities can guess at for years and years to come.

Now leaving the tall trees of the woods, he can see the first rays of the sun as they peak over the horizon. He must put a great amount of distance between himself and these woods. Knowing that when the police arrive and start to investigate El Diablo's murder, it won't take them long to figure out who is responsible.

He is hoping that perhaps a few days will lapse before the authorities are called to this location, enough time for those people staying at that house to clean out any drugs and weapons that he is sure is there.

Once called, this whole area will have hundreds of police officers searching every inch. They will pick this place apart, but as always they will find no trace of the Vigilante Assassin.

Smiling Jason is confident that he has left nothing behind, no finger prints, no gum wrappers, he didn't even spit the whole time he was in these woods or near the house.

Pulling out his map he locates a safe house only a few miles away. This safe house will provide him with food and transportation.

Needing to hurry as each minute that passes the sky gets lighter and he doesn't want to be outside during the day. Running as fast as he can and after rounding a curve in the road he spots an abandoned shack set just back inside the woods. This is what he is searching for, and wasting no time as he needs to get off the road he continues to run as fast as he can. Just as he is nearing the shack the faint sound of police sirens can be heard in the distance. Startled by this, he was positive that no one at that house would call the police this soon.

Now cursing, he was hoping to rest awhile before moving on, now that won't be possible. The note he has along with the map says that a four wheeler would be available for him to use at this old shack.

This contact is another unknown person that has provided this shack and the four wheeler for the Vigilante Assassin to use.

Getting closer and looking all around, there is no four wheeler. Stepping inside, the shack is empty. His sixth sense suddenly comes alive. His skin gets cold, and his breathing increases. On an old wooden table in the middle of the room he sees a walkie talkie, and the small red light on it is flashing. Now his instincts are warning him to get out, that something is not right here.

A voice calls out over the walkie talkie, "This is Officer Burrows of the Landore police department, come out with your hands up."

Realizing at that moment that he has walked into a trap, he knows that one of his contacts has betrayed him. Pulling out his revolver he peers out the window, there standing behind a tree not more than thirty feet away he can see an officer pointing a gun in his direction. Scanning the rest of the area, he is surprised that there are no others police officers. This lone police officer has taken on the job of capturing the Vigilante Assassin all by himself.

Jason speculates that this Officer Burrows is a rookie and he wants all the glory and fame to himself of capturing the Vigilante Assassin.

This young and inexperienced officer has set this up and thinks he can arrest the Vigilante Assassin that easily. Jason goes over several ideas on how to get out of this jam. It's not the first time he has been cornered, and he has learned a great deal of tricks over time.

Reassembling his rifle, he keeps a close eye on the officer. He can see that this is a young man, obviously scared by the way his hands are shaking.

"I'll count to five and you better come out with your hands in the air."

Jason has to laugh at this, just what is this officer going to do if he doesn't come out?

In one quick motion Jason has the rifle pointed out the window and fires a shot. The bullet hits the tree just inches from the officer's head. Stunned, he falls backwards at which time he loses his gun. Awkwardly scrambling to his feet he races over and as he is about to pick up his gun, a bullet ricochets off it causing it to be knocked several feet from him. Now sitting down with his hands covering his ears, the frightened and shaking police officer sits sobbing on the ground. He believes that the next shot will kill him, as he also knows that the Vigilante Assassin does not take prisoners.

Now leaving the shack, Jason quietly comes up behind the officer. Holding the barrel of his rifle against the man's head he says, "This was a very foolish thing that you tried. All those that have tried to either capture me or kill me have all ended up dead."

The young officer has trouble getting his words out, "I realize now just how stupid I was. I got greedy and wanted all the glory of capturing you to myself, please don't kill me."

Jason lets several minutes go by before saying, "In the future I hope you use more common sense, another foolish mistake like this one will get you killed."

The young police officer can hardly believe his ears, mumbling to himself, "Did he just say in the future?" He knows by these words that for whatever reason, that this cold blooded killer has decided to spare his life.

"I'll need your car keys," demands Jason. "Do not look up at me, do not raise your head is that understood?"

Shaking his head, "I understand perfectly."

Now reaching down Jason takes the officers handcuffs and secures his hands behind his back.

Jason backs up keeping his eyes on the officer the whole time.

He can see hidden just inside the woods is the officers patrol car. Getting in he must hurry and get out of this area, the sun is already out and high in the sky.

As he races down the dirt road he is alarmed by the sound of police sirens now echoing all around, and the sound of a helicopter can be heard overhead.

Now realizing that his whereabouts are being radioed to every law enforcement agency in three counties a sense of urgency has his mind racing. Somehow either the officer he just tied up had previously informed his superiors of his actions or someone in that house panicked and called the police.

How the authorities know he is here is not the problem, his biggest concern is to get off this road and find a safe house to wait out the search.

Driving as fast as he dare it isn't long and he sees several police cars approaching him. Not known for his driving skills, he knows if they realize that he isn't a police officer they will turn around and give chase.

Sweat is running down his face, trying to remain calm, and as the police cars go by he waves at them.

Two of the three police cars continue down the road however the third one stops and turns around.

Very quickly the police car is right behind Jason and he can see from his rear view mirror that the officer in on his phone.

"Damn it," he yells.

Increasing his speed hoping to outrun this officer, but in a flash the police sirens are turned on and his lights begin flashing. Jason knows he's in a bad spot, rarely does anyone ever outrun the police. They have radios and can call for road spikes to be placed across the road miles ahead.

Knowing that letting himself get captured is not an option, he prepares for the worst.

He does not want a shootout with the police, so he must think of a way to escape this mess. Cursing at his bad luck he continues to accelerate and he hits speeds of 80 miles an hour. Rounding a curve he balances on two wheels, nearly flipping the car over. Looking in the rear view mirror he now sees that several police are right behind him. Looking ahead he spots a bridge, but he can see that it has been blocked with several police cars.

With no other roads to take except this one he swallows hard, his hands grip the steering wheel very tight. He continues to drive right at the police that are blocking the bridge, and thinking fast he has run out of options.

Deciding very quickly that trying to bust through this road block will not succeed, and it will no doubt kill a few police officers, and this he can't do.

Taking in a deep breath and just as he is about to hit the police cars he suddenly steers the car hard to the right at the last second. Bullets begin shattering the windows and he must duck down across the front seat to avoid being hit.

Busting through the guardrail the car is in a free fall, holding onto the seat Jason braces himself. In a matter of seconds the car crashes into the water causing him to be thrown forward where he hits his head against the dash. Bouncing around and momentarily dazed Jason quickly shakes off the confusion as water now begins entering the car through the broken windows.

Looking around and surprised that the car did not sink immediately and that it is actually floating down the river. Behind him he can see dozens of police officers lining the bridge, and he knows they will quickly give pursuit.

It had been a God send that the river was swollen from the recent rains. Now the fast moving current is carrying Jason away from the police, but for how long. Each minute that passes it seems that the car is sinking a little deeper and soon it will be completely submerged. Climbing out the window and onto the hood he spots several low hanging tree branches just ahead. Praying that with a good jump he thinks he can grab onto one of them and make it to shore.

Balancing himself on the car hood as the car bobs up and down in the turbulent waters he waits for the right moment. Just as he is about to jump the car bounces off a rock causing him to fall backwards and into the water.

Struggling to keep his head above the torrent waves, he begins swimming towards the shore. However, the current is too strong, despite his best efforts he can't break free of the strong undertow. Going under several times he manages to make it to the surface and coughs from swallowing so much water.

This is definitely not the way he pictured that he would die.

He would have preferred a more honorable way, like being killed while fighting criminals.

This would indeed be a sad ending for the mighty Vigilante Assassin, and despite his predicament, he has to laugh.

All of his marksmen skills and his training will not get him out of this mess. To have faced the vilest criminals that society has to offer and always come out on top will do him no good now.

With his strength waning he can't keep his head above the water much longer. As the scenery around him begins to blur something touches the back of his head. Turning around he can't believe what he's seeing. He is about to be run over by a massive tree trunk, and taking a big breath of air he ducks under the water just as the tree is crossing over him.

As the massive tree bobs up and down he reaches out and grabs a root. Pulling himself up, he gasps for air. Now with something to hold onto all he can do for now is drift down the river.

Being hidden by the massive size of this tree it affords him great protection, no one can see him.

Deciding to stay where he is, he will follow the river until he is sure that it is safe to head for the shore. Constantly maneuvering around so that he is always on the side of the tree that is facing the middle of the river, this will afford him some protection from being spotted from anyone on the shore. The river twists and turns many times, and this causes the massive tree to also turn. Jason must anticipate when the tree is going to roll or risk being pulled under. Mile after mile he drifts with the current, with his eyes just above the water line.

He must be vigilante and always watchful as other debris is floating past him. Most are sticks and branches washed into the river by the heavy rains but there are also smaller trees anyone of which could snag onto is clothing and pull him into the dangerous under currents.

He has also seen a few large poisonous snakes in this river and occasionally he pushes them away with a stick. With the undulating motion of the waves, the muddy water occasionally splashes over his head getting into his mouth. Having swallowed some of this water it isn't long and his stomach begins to turn.

Throwing up several times eases the cramping in his lower gut, despite this inconvenience he has not let go his grip on the huge tree that continues to carry him farther down this river.

The hours pass and his hands are beginning to cramp up. Having had a death grip on the tree roots for so long his hands are starting to go numb. He knows that in his exhausted condition if he loses his grip he doesn't have the strength to swim to shore.

Every time he approaches a bridge he submerges himself under the tree and holds on for dear life. He must hold his breath as long as he can until he is ready to blackout before resurfacing for air. Hoping by that time he has floated a good distance from the bridge, and won't be spotted by the police that he is sure is manning every bridge.

Several times while peering up through the thick roots he could see a helicopter fly overhead, and each time he would disappear under the water.

But what worries him the most are the dogs that the police are using to track him. No doubt they got his scent from the old shack and now they are combing both sides of the river, looking for the spot where he came out of the water.

He wonders how far down this river the police will search before finally giving up. Not knowing this answer, he has no choice but to continue this long ardent journey.

Nearly falling asleep several times, he knows his body is growing weak and he must get to the shore. Looking around, he sees nothing but thick forests on both sides of the river. The tree that has been his life line has by this time gotten close to the shore on his right. Summoning up all his reserve strength, he pushes off from the tree. Not a good swimmer even when healthy and rested he struggles with each stroke of his arms. Little by little the shore gets closer until his feet begin to touch the muddy bottom.

Climbing several feet up and onto the dry river bank, Jason collapses. He lay exhausted and sore but grateful to be alive.

Believing that he has managed to slip by the police, he now wonders just where he is.

Suddenly realizing that he no longer has his backpack, his face turns pale. He left it in the car, and his finger prints are all over items in it. With his finger prints and other objects in that backpack, the police will be able to identify him very quickly.

His only salvation is that the car sunk to the bottom of the river and the police are unable to locate it. But another nightmare inters his thoughts, with the windows shot out of the car, his backpack may float to the surface. With so many people searching the river banks, it is most likely that someone will find it.

Those worst case scenarios will have to wait, his first priority is to get back to the apartment.

With the sun going down he knows that at least the air and water searches will be suspended. The ground searches with the tracking dogs will go on all night. Climbing up the bank until he reaches the crest, he spies an open field. On the far side is a farm house, it looks run down and deserted. Feeling that he has nothing to lose by investigating it, perhaps he can even find something useful. If it is empty he can hang his clothes up so that they can dry. He walks with stiff legs as the long period of time spent in the cold water has caused his leg muscles to cramp up. Choosing to keep close to the edge of the woods, he avoids the open field. As he makes his way closer to this old house, faint noises can be heard.

Quickly lying flat on the ground, he remains this way for several minutes. Having not heard these noises again he slowly raises his head up, there is no one in sight. Beginning to get spooked at the slightest sound he knows he must control these emotions.

The long shadows begin to creep across the landscape as the sun sets lower in the sky.

Annoyed that he is blinded by these rays, he covers his eyes. Only by slipping just inside the woods is he able to see in the distance. The trees block most of the sun's rays, and as he gets closer to the house he uses them as cover.

Finally at the edge of his cover, he runs across a small field and presses himself up against the barn. Waiting a moment to see if he was noticed, he now slowly moves to the corner. A quick glance reveals a dilapidated house that is ready to collapse. The roof sags in the middle and a lot of the shingles are missing. The grass in the yard is knee high and the fence circling the property has fallen down in several places.

Confident now that no one is living here, it will give Jason some time to rest. Spooked by the voices he heard earlier he assumes it was from the stress and tension. Walking up to the front door it makes a loud creaking noise as he pushes it open. To his surprise an old woman is standing not more than ten feet away from him.

Leaning forward, "Is that you Floyd," she calls out, straining her eyes as she stares at Jason.

Caught off guard by this Jason doesn't move, should he run or just stay put?

A voice from a side room calls out, "Are you looking for me Harriet?"

Not sure what he should do as he was sure this house was empty. An old man approaches the woman and again says, "Did you call for me?"

The old woman squints her eyes at the man and then back at the stranger standing in her doorway. The old man turns and noticing the stranger quickly stands in front of the woman.

Shaking as he puts up his fists, "You ain't going to do no harm to my wife, I'll fight you till my last breath."

The old man wrinkles his face, his body trembling. Old and frail but yet he puts up a brave front.

"I mean neither of you any harm," Jason says. "I didn't know anyone was living here, you see I'm lost."

As he lowers his hands the old man replies, "Why in tar nation didn't you say that in the first place, you nearly scared us to death?"

With a quick wave of his hand he motions for Jason to come into the house.

Each step Jason takes causes the floor to creek and crack, and added to this noise his wet shoes also squeak. He cautiously follows the old man over to a table that appears to be held together with duct tape. The old man now motions for his new quest to sit.

Turning his head, "Ma could you bring our new friend something to drink?"

With a wave of her hand she shuffles into another room.

Jason can clearly see the shabby surroundings that this elderly couple lives in and he is appalled.

The place looks as if it has been recently ramshackled by a bunch of hoodlums. Furniture is in dire need of repair and the paint is peeling off the walls. Most of the pictures on the walls are hanging crooked and some pictures have even fallen to the floor.

Dust covers everything, and in the top corner near the door a bird has made a nest. On the table it appears these two old people were trying to put together a puzzle. A lot of the pieces are missing and noticing Jason looking at this the old man says, "Yep, me and the misses have been trying to finish this puzzle for a long time but as you can see we are missing a lot of the pieces. Looks to me like whoever put it into the box at the factory where it was made left out some pieces."

Taking a glance down to the floor Jason can see the missing puzzle pieces under the table.

At that moment the old woman returns and she hands Jason a glass with a cloudy substance in it.

The old man lowers his head and says, "I know it aint the cleanest water, but it's all we have, I'm sorry."

Jason can see how embarrassed these two are, the pride and dignity is all over their faces.

Before he can say anything the old man speaks up, "I guess I plum forgot to introduce myself, I'm Floyd and the misses is Harriet."

The old man pauses for a moment as he contemplates his next sentence, "But you can call us Ma and Pa, same as everyone else around here."

Debating if he should tell them his real name, and decides what harm could it do.

"My name is Jason, and I appreciate your kindness."

Floyd leans forward to get a better look at Jason, obviously the two old people have very bad eyes. It takes him a moment as he looks up and down his new house guest.

"A young feller you are. You say you are lost?"

"Yes, I guess I wondered too far into the woods and got turned around."

Floyd now accompanied by his wife give Jason an odd look.

"Now looky here young feller," Floyd says as he rubs his chin, "Me and the misses may be old and we can't see only a few feet in front of our own faces but we ain't no dummies."

Taken aback by this response, Jason realizes that they aren't buying his story about being lost.

Tapping his fingers on the table Floyd says, "You ain't dressed to be huntin in these woods and you ain't got no backpack, so you ain't no hiker either."

"Trying his best at a quick reply, "How do you know I'm not hunting?'

Floyd sits back in his chair, his wife patting him on the shoulder.

She has the look that a mother gets when she knows her child is lying to her.

Now leaning forward again Floyd says, "If you be huntin, where's your dang rifle?"

Now Jason bows his head, yes these two are old and frail but like Floyd had said earlier they ain't no dummies. Looking at the two Jason can only smile, they caught him in a lie.

"You are right," he says, "I'm not hunting or hiking, truth is my car broke down several miles up the road and I was hoping to use your phone."

Now Floyd is smiling, and tapping his wife on her hip says, "We got us a real story teller here ma, yes sir, he can tell some whoppers can't he."

"I'm telling you the truth," insists Jason. "I have no reason to lie to you anymore."

"Do you always drive around soaking wet?"

Biting his lip, Jason is stuck for an answer.

Now with a scowl on his face, Floyd rubs his chin, "I think you are runnin from the law, yep that's what you're doing alright. Your arms and legs are all scratched up pretty good, like you been runnin through the woods"

The two now back away from the table, they hold onto each other tightly.

"If you came here looking for something to steal, you're plum out of luck," says Floyd. "All we have is each other, and you'll have to kill me before I step aside and let you take my wife."

Totally caught off guard by this, Jason waves his hands, "No,no, you have nothing to worry about. I didn't mean to scare you, I should have been honest right from the beginning. Please sit down, I'm very sorry for upsetting either of you, I apologize."

Hearing this the two gingerly sit back down at the table, they still hold tight to each other.

"My name is Jason, and I'm running from the police, you were right about that. Except they are chasing the wrong man, I was framed for a crime I did not commit."

Nodding his head, Floyd utters, "Now that is an honest statement if I ever heard one. The dang police are always chasing the wrong man. I know that for a fact. Well I remember must be 30 years ago or was it 40, don't know exactly but I suppose it don't really matter, the point is that they once come here trying to arrest me for something I never did."

Jason would first like to get something to eat before he has to listen to Floyd tell his story.

Harriet speaks up, "We got some rabbit stew, it ain't much but you're welcome to it."

Feeling humbled by this kind jester, "I would love some if you don't mind."

Quickly getting up Harriet shuffles away waving her hand, "I'll be back in a jiffy young man, you just stay sittin right where you are."

Floyd says, "We don't get many visitors out here in the sticks."

"Just where are we," asks Jason, knowing that he floated a great distance down the river while holding onto that tree before coming to the shore. Guessing that he was in the water at least eight hours maybe longer, and judging by the speed of the river, he estimates that he could be nearly 50 miles from Landore.

Scratching his head, Floyd thinks for a moment, "We call this place paradise but on the map its half way between Willow Point and Old Man's Bluff."

Cracking a smile, Jason has never heard of either of these places and he suspects that Floyd just made up those names.

"I've never heard of those places," he tells the old man. "Can you tell me the name of the nearest city and how far away it is?"

Perking up, Floyd answers, "I sure can, you take this road out in front of the house and go due east I reckon maybe two miles maybe a little further. When you reach a fork in the road go left not right. If you go to the right you'll end up in Miller's swamp. Let me tell you, with all this rain we've had lately, that ain't no place to be. No sir, it's got snakes as big as your arm, and the mosquitoes the size of a golf ball."

Jason sits back and takes all this in, he is amused by the way Floyd talks. It is a mix of southern draw and backwoods slang.

Interrupting her husband, Harriet brings in a bowl and sets it down in front of her guest.

Jason gives it a long look and then glances at her.

She nods her head, "Go ahead young man, it ain't gonna bite you."

The two old people begin laughing, and soon Jason joins them. It had been some time since he laughed, and it felt good.

Taking a small amount and putting it into his mouth, he was not sure just how this was going to taste. To his surprise it tastes very good and not remembering when he last ate he quickly devoured the entire bowl.

"My oh my," says Harriet, "you must have been starving, don't move and I'll get you another bowl."

Floyd gives him a wink, "She likes cookin, so eat all you want."

Again Jason is humbled by their generosity. He can see that they have very few possessions, and he's sure that sharing their food with a stranger is a strain on them. Yet they are happy to help, these are good people he knows.

Clearing his throat, Floyd says, "Now getting back to how to get to the nearest city. I already told you don't go into the swamp, so if you go left you'll go a couple of miles, here you'll see an old bridge, don't cross it. That old bridge has been ready to fall for more years than I can count, why if person were to step just one foot on it the dang thing would collapse.

Yes sir she was a goodin when she was first built, yes sir the Orville brothers was the ones that built her. Let me tell you when them boys built something it last forever, yes sir it sure do."

With a long face Jason raises his eyes brows, and with a twirl of his fingers Floyd gets the hint to continue his story.

"You just keep going down the road till you see three large boulders to your right. I suppose they be about the size of a good size horse, maybe a little bigger. Old man Wilkins lives just behind these boulders, so be very quiet goin by them. He don't take to kindly to strangers, fact I hear tell he once shot a man that got too close to these boulders. I reckon that was back in 1942, or somewhere around that time, don't know for sure, don't really matter I suppose. Just heed my warning young feller, stay clear of them boulders, understand?"

Trying his best not to laugh at this story, Jason must lower his head to hide his broad smile.

"I'll be sure to avoid it Floyd, you can bet on that," Jason replies with his hand covering his mouth.

The room is silent as Floyd seems to gaze at nothing.

Leaning forward Jason says, "Where do I go after passing the three boulders?"

"Sorry young feller," replies a confused Floyd, "I was a thinkin about doin some fishin tonight. You much on fishin?"

Not caring about fishing as he needs to find a way home, Jason replies, "I have done a little not much."

Before he can say anything else Floyd speaks up, "Then young feller we be goin fishin tonight. I'll take you to a special place where nobody else knows about. The fishin there is the best around these here parts."

As the sky turns dark, Jason decides for safety's sake that he must stay here until morning. Already lost, he will be in even more trouble if he tried walking out of here in the dark.

Now with a second helping of rabbit in front of him, he settles in for a long night of storytelling.

Thinking about some of the places he's been and the terrible situations, this place isn't bad. Looking out the window, he believes that he is so far away from any city that it is unlikely that the police will find him here.

The hours pass and Floyd continues to give directions, and Harriet puts bandages on Jason's cuts. Some may need stitches once he gets home, but that is the least of his worries. Finally unable to stay awake any longer, Jason tells his host, "I need to rest is there somewhere I can sleep tonight?"

Standing next to her husband, Harriet replies, "We got only one bed, and as our guest you are welcome to it, Floyd and I will sleep out in the barn."

Wide eyed Jason can't believe that these old people are willing to give up their bed to a stranger.

"No way," insists Jason, as he gets up from his chair. "You two have been so kind to me I would never let you give up your bed for me. I'll sleep in the barn."

The two smile at their young guest, "Follow me young feller," says Floyd as he pats Jason on the back.

The two walk a short distance to the barn, and Jason is hesitant about entering it. This barn is in worst shape than the house. The walls along with the roof have gaping holes big enough for a man to crawl through. Holding a lantern Floyd leads Jason over to a corner where a group of chickens have bedded down for the night.

With a wave of his hand, Floyd gets the chickens to move several feet away.

"This is as good as any spot in the barn," Floyd says. He picks up an old blanket and sets it down on the straw.

Needing a moment to take this all in, Jason answers, "This will be fine, I'll see you in the morning and thanks for your hospitality."

Giving a quick nod of his head, Floyd begins walking away, and the barn grows dark as the only light was the lantern that Floyd had and he took that with him.

Lying on his back, Jason has to smile at his surroundings. Thinking of the tale he will tell to Doc and Edward when he sees them again. This whole ordeal is like something out of the movies, it is almost like a dream.

Looking over to his right, staring at the chickens he whispers, "You better fear for your lives, cause I'm the Vigilante Assassin."

He rolls back and forth as he laughs at his own humor.

Feeling that he won't be bothered the rest of the night, he removes his wet clothing, hanging them on the stall next to him. Wrapping up with the blanket, it is only minutes and he's fast asleep.

He dreams that he is falling backwards into a dark and seemingly bottomless pit. Flaring out his arms and legs in an attempt to stop, but it does him no good as he continues his rapid descent. He can see the light above his head getting smaller and smaller until it is nothing more than a pin point.

The evil presence that surrounds him is pulling him deeper into the abyss, down into its lair where he will be trapped forever. Just as the light fades completely he sits up with a jerk, out of breath and sweating profusely. He clutches one hand to his chest leaning forward with his head down.

These recurring nightmares are getting worse, and he doesn't have any of the pills with him to calm his nerves.

He believes that during one of these nightmares that he will be unable to return to the present. His mind will be trapped in the dark void of this horrible pit for all eternity.

The thought causes him to shake his head, he knows he must break free of this torment, this misery that is clouding his thinking or it will tare him apart.

Lying back down, the night is still, not a sound, and this has a calming effect on him that no pills could match. Praying that his mind can rest as well as his body he closes his eyes and is soon asleep.

Waking with a start, he opens his eyes to see a chicken sitting on his chest. The two stare at each other for a moment, and it reminds Jason of a scene from a movie he once saw. Thinking to himself, "Doc and Edward aren't going to believe this."

Shoving the bird to the side Jason stands up and is pleased that his clothes are dry. After getting dressed he takes a cautious look out the barn door, the area looks deserted. He walks to the house and finds Floyd and Harriet putting that same puzzle together they were on yesterday.

"I thought you were missing some pieces?"

Without looking up, Floyd replies, "Won't know if we're missin any pieces till we get it together." Now wrinkling his forehead the old man stares at Jason. With his face blank, he asks, "That's an odd thing to say young feller."

"I mean you seem to have had it nearly completed yesterday, and you told me that a few pieces were missing then."

Giving Jason a peculiar look, "You sure are a story teller," says Floyd. "Why me and the misses just opened this puzzle box not more than 15 minutes ago."

Jason can clearly see that it is the same puzzle the two were working on yesterday. For them not to remember this is an indication they may be suffering from Alzheimer's disease.

Harriet now looks at Jason and says, "Better get your books together, you don't want to be late for school."

Jason is saddened by this, as these two are so open and generous, it's a cruel thing for them to end up like this.

"Best get something to eat," calls Floyd still not taking his eyes off the puzzle, "We got 40 acres to plant and nearly a 100 head of cattle to milk."

He watches as Harriet hurries into the kitchen and begins frying eggs. There is nothing Jason can do for these two, he'll eat breakfast and then he'll be on his way.

At the table Jason listens as the two talk as if it is the 1950's. They talk about electricity coming into these parts, and maybe they'll go see a picture show. They mention names like Clarke Gable and Betty

Davis and how President Eisenhower is going to throw out the first pitch at the World Series.

With his head down, Jason feels so sorry for them. To mentally think it is decades earlier these two must be in the latter stages of the disease.

Deciding not to tell them he's leaving, as this may cause some kind of panic attack. He'll sneak away when both are busy.

Still not sure where he's at, Jason asks, "Do you have a map Floyd, I'd like to see where we are."

Scratching his head, Floyd needs a moment to think. "Ah yes," he says, "I got one right here in the desk."

Opening up the draw he pulls out an old leather pouch. Brushing off the dust he lays it on the table.

"Haven't used it in years," he says. "No need to since I spent my whole life in these parts."

Jason unfolds the map, the color is badly faded, and it tears in a few places as he straightens it out.

Now taking a deep breath, Jason is disappointed. In the lower right hand corner the date reads, July 14 1967.

This map will do him no good, it is so outdated that most of the roads and bridges now in use are not even on this map.

Floyd can see the grim look on Jason's face, and he moves closer to see if he can help.

"You forgot how to read a map sunny?"

Now sitting back in his chair, Jason says, "Your map is too old, it's useless."

With a perturbed look on his face, Floyd says, "You're a city boy alright. Why there ain't nothin wrong with my map, only the way you are lookin at it."

Growing annoyed, "This map doesn't even list the names of the roads on it, how can a person figure out how to get somewhere?"

With a big smile, Floyd replies, "If you want to go east you wait till the sun comes up, that way is east. If you want to go west you wait till the sun starts to set, that way is west. That young feller is how you read a map, any more dumb questions?"

Biting his tongue, Jason wants to scream, but he catches himself. He realizes that the old man means well, it's not his fault that his mind is fading.

Standing up, and putting out his hand, "Thanks for the directions and also for the good food, I owe you for this. I'll be on my way now."

Floyd and Harriet stand close to each other. She has a bowl of water in her hands and he is holding the puzzle box. They seem confused by what Jason has just said. He can see in their eyes that they are not sure what is going on. He would very much like to stay and help them in any way he can, but with the authorities on his trail he must keep moving.

Walking out the door he can hear the two talking to each other.

A moment later Floyd calls out, "You come back from that war, you hear me son."

With a lump in his throat Jason forces himself not to turn around. Through the tall grass and around the barn, he walks until he's on the dirt road.

He feels for these two kind heated people, it saddens him to experience this first hand.

But this chapter in his life he must put out of his head, he has a long ways to go to get home.

Now the real problem begins as he is not sure where he's at and how far he may be from Landore. Still estimating that he drifted 50 miles down the river, walking back to town will take days. If only he had a car, or even a cell phone he could call Crow to come get him. A smile crosses his face, even if he had a cell phone he wouldn't know where to tell Crow to come pick him up.

All he can do for now is to start walking, hoping that he spots a familiar landmark, anything that will narrow down his location.

Suddenly getting an odd feeling, he ducks just inside the woods. Lying on his stomach, he carefully watches the road. He soon hears the familiar sound of a helicopter and just like a falcon swooping down on to its pray the helicopter fly's low over the road.

He can clearly see the police emblem on the side of it. Within seconds it is out of sight. So the police have set a drag net over a very wide area, using the roads is now out of the question. Moving slowly through the thick growth of the woods he must come up with a plan or else he'll never make it home. As the hours pass and still no master plan he watches as the sun now begins setting behind him. Hoping that he is going in the right direction, but that is only a guess.

How big of an area these woods may span and if any other roads go through them Jason doesn't know.

He envisions walking around in circles in these woods until dehydration and malnutrition cause him to collapse. It is an agonizing and slow way to die, but the reality is that this worst case scenario just may happen. Determined not to perish in the middle of nowhere, he searches for a road.

With the darkness creeping all around, Jason must find a place to sleep the night. Figuring that he can just lay on the forest floor, he searches out a good spot. Under a large oak tree looks the best. With its overhanging branches it will not only conceal him but also protect him if it should rain. Unable to start a fire as this would attract anyone that may be nearby, especially the authorities. Jason is sure that the coming of nightfall will not stop them searching for him.

Now lying down, thinking about the day's events, he is relaxed.

In the morning he is confident that a way home will present itself.

As his eyes go closed, a sharp sound to his front springs him to his feet. Grabbing a large stick, he stands prepared as he strains to see in the semi darkness. To his front he can see a shape, it is moving back and forth in the thick brush.

Cursing as he believes that the police have tracked him here, he can only surmise that Floyd must have pointed them in his direction.

With no other option he turns to run, it is then that a loud growl causes him to freeze in his tracks. In an instant it is apparent that this is not the police that have found him. Looking back over his shoulder he can clearly see the outline of a large bear. Knowing that a man cannot outrun a bear, his only option is to climb the large oak tree.

Hoping that he has not lost his tree climbing skills that he used so effectively while playing tag as a child.

Jumping and grabbing the lowest branch he pulls himself up and with heart racing is quickly 15 feet off the ground. Looking down through the branches he can see the bear is now standing just below him, and raising up onto its hind legs it reaches out with a big paw just missing Jason by inches. Jerking his head back, a very frightened Jason begins climbing higher. Breathing heavily and not stopping until he is at the very top of the tree.

The small limbs sway back and forth under his weight.

Now with so many tree branches in the way he cannot see the bear. His fear is that the bear will come up the tree after him, and if it does he has no place to go. No weapons to defend himself with and no way of getting down without first encountering this beast. He is in another bad situation, and the odds are once more against him.

He waits patiently, trying to devise a plan of escape if this beast decides to start climbing. He can hear its heavy breathing, and it seems to be pacing back and forth at the base of the tree.

The night grows black as dark clouds move in to obscure the moon. A slight wind begins blowing and soon he can feel the first rain drops. Cursing at his bad luck, with the thunder and rain he won't be able to hear if the bear has started climbing up the tree.

With this constant noise it could be on him before he knows it, and any plans of escape will be gone. Holding himself close to the tree he has no alternative but to sit and wait. As the hours pass it is getting more difficult for him to stay awake. Several times he doses off only to catch himself falling backwards.

He knows that a fall from this height could be fatal, and if the fall doesn't kill him he's sure the bear will. Still not sure why this bear is so aggressive towards him, normally bears shy away from people. Unless it has a cub with it, than its motherly instinct will look at anything as a threat and she will protect her cub.

Taking off his belt he wraps it around the tree branch and then around his waist. Pulling it tight,

as this should keep him in place as he leans forward to get some sleep. Despite the rain and wind, Jason doesn't wake until the morning sun begins peeking over the horizon.

Taking a glance down, he cannot see the bear anywhere. Putting his belt back on he begins a slow descent, carefully placing each foot just in case he has to quickly climb back up.

Reaching the large branches, he looks in all directions. Breathing a sigh of relief that the bear is nowhere in sight he jumps down to the ground.

Examining the animal's tracks, they tell him that this was a very large bear, perhaps weighting more than 500 pounds.

Now he must not only worry about the police chasing him, now there is a bear that has his scent. Not sure why the bear would show so much interest in him, perhaps it was the smell of chickens on his clothing. Looking at his clothes he can see that the rain has soaked his bandages and has caused his cuts to bleed. That would explain why it stayed for so long. This bear could also be injured and it is looking for any kind of food it can find. Knowing that the smell of blood carries a long ways in the wind, he must move as quickly as possible away from this area.

Hoping he has seen the last of it, he continues walking in an easterly direction. The thick underbrush hinders his progress until he finds a deer trail, this will make his trek a little easier.

By midday the sun is shining down through the trees casting a pleasant scene.

Flowers have begun to peek up through the thick green foliage, and the chatter of birds now fills the air. Needing to rest, he sits against a large tree. Leaning his head back, it is so peaceful and tranquil here, nothing like the hustle and bustle of the big city. The sounds around him are very calming, and the thought of going back to that crime ridden city causes him to close his eyes.

Knowing he has a job to finish, and despite his desire to stay right where he's at, he forces himself to continue walking. He wonders just how large of an area do these woods cover. He thought by now he would be seeing signs of civilization, telephone lines, train tracks anything that would indicate that he is getting closer to the city.

By night fall he still has seen no sign of civilization, hoping he has not been walking in one big circle, he searches for a place to bed down for the night.

A small clearing catches his attention, getting closer he can see a tent set off to one side. His first instinct is to run in the opposite direction, but his need for food and water overrides this emotion.

Crawling on his stomach he inches right up to the edge of the clearing. Peering over the brush he can see a man sitting next to a fire pit, he seems to be cleaning a rifle.

He wonders if this man is part of the search party out looking for him or is he just a hunter out here for a few days of hunting. Thinking for a moment, he must make a critical decision, being unarmed he will be easy to capture if he just walks into this man's camp. Waiting until dark, he could sneak up on the man and overpower him. But night is hours away, he must act now.

Watching the actions of this man, he seems very relaxed, not like someone on a bounty hunt.

The man even whistles a few times, his boots are off and he pokes the fire a few times with a stick.

Jason is positive that this in no law man, and he is not a part of the search.

Getting up off the ground and standing he calls out in a loud voice, "Hello there."

Turning his head the man gets to his feet, still holding the rifle. He gives the intruder a long look, and he looks past Jason to see if there is anyone else.

"I hope I didn't scare you," says Jason, now stepping slowing into the camp.

The man answers, "You look to be lost, come on over," and waving his hand he signals for Jason to come closer.

The two meet and instantly the man sticks his hand out, Jason is a little unsure but does the same. The two shake hands, "My name is Tony."

Trying to look calm, "My name is Jason, nice to meet you."

"You say you are lost?"

"Yes, I've been walking for two days."

With a smile, "You'll be happy to know that another twenty minutes and you'll be out of these woods."

Happy to hear that finally this trek is almost over, he returns the smile.

Jason now studies his new friend, estimating him to be about 60 years old. With a receding hairline and a gray mustache Tony is very fit for his age.

Now sitting around the small fire Tony asks, "I see you don't have a hunting rifle, so what brings you into these woods?"

Scratching his head, "I was just on a hike and I guess I got turned around. Next thing I knew I lost my bearings and have been walking trying to find a way out."

Tony reaches into his backpack, and this causes Jason to quickly get to his feet. Tony pulls out a

brown bag and opening it up he hands Jason a beef stick.

With his heart racing, this was not what he was expecting and by the look on Tony's face he is also a little shocked by Jason's actions.

Holding out the beef stick, "It's okay it won't bite."

Jason smiles and soon breaks out into a laugh. The two laugh for a moment, as Jason sits back down and starts chewing on the beef stick.

"You seem awful jumpy," says Tony. "Is anything wrong?"

Shaking his head, "I'm sorry but yesterday I was cornered up a tree by a bear, I guess I'm still a little on edge."

Holding up his rifle, Tony says, "Nothing to worry about, I got my lucky rifle with me. This rifle has killed more bear and dear than I can count."

Nodding his head, Jason eyes the rifle. He could take the rifle and leave the man here, or he could use him as a hostage. But these thoughts quickly fade as Tony talks about how nice it is to get out of the city a few times a year and go hunting. The two talk for hours and Jason realizes that Tony knows very little about the Vigilante Assassin, or the manhunt that is searching for him.

Tony doesn't even live in Landore, and his knowledge about the Vigilante Assassin is what he has read in the newspapers.

As the sky begins to turn dark, it is agreed that Jason should spend the night here and in the morning Tony will guide him out of the woods.

As the two are sitting around the fire a low flying helicopter races across the sky just above the tree tops.

Jason immediately dives for the cover of the thick brush while Tony remains sitting giving his new friend an odd stare.

Jason can hear that the helicopter has not gone far, no doubt they have seen the camp fire and will soon circle around to investigate.

Now pinching his forehead tightly, Tony rubs his chin. He looks at Jason, not sure why this man was so frightened of the helicopter.

Cursing at his bad luck, Jason walks back over next to Tony.

"I guess I owe you an explanation for why I jumped when the helicopter flew over."

Still sitting, Tony remains silent, as he now studies his friend in more detail.

In the blink of an eye Jason grabs the rifle and takes several steps back.

Rubbing his hands nervously together Jason begins, "You seem like a good and decent person, and I don't want you caught up in my troubles. The fact is that the police will be here soon, you see they are looking for me. I don't want you injured or killed in the cross fire, so I'm taking your rifle and leaving."

Getting to his feet, Tony motions with his hand, "Give me back the rifle."

Taking another step back, "I can't do that, the police have orders to shoot me on the spot."

"What crimes have you committed?"

Swallowing hard, "Let's say I was doing the city a favor but they didn't look at it that way."

"You still need to give me the gun."

"That's not going to happen," and gripping the rifle tight he now points it at Tony.

Tony is a man that is not easily scared, and standing straight he says, "You don't scare me, in fact I'm going to walk right up to you and take back my rifle."

Jason doesn't want to shoot this man, he has done nothing wrong. But giving up the rifle is something he just can't do, so sliding his feet back he braces for a fight.

Stopping only a few feet from Jason Tony asks, "I can see that you may have committed some crimes but you are not an evil person. If you had wanted to hurt me you would have done that in the beginning, no, you seem like a righteous man. God has a way of directing all of us through life, some of his commands we don't fully understand.

But he is the savior and the Lord, he only means what is best for his children."

After saying this Tony pulls down his shirt revealing the white square on his neck that symbolizes that he is a man of the cloth.

Wide eyed Jason can't believe that this man is a preacher. Taking a deep breath, Jason fumbles his words. Not sure how to react to this unexpected revelation.

"I'm sorry father," he says with hesitation, "I didn't know you were a man of God."

Smiling at this, "You have nothing to be sorry for my son, there was no way for you to know. Believe it or not we preachers do like to hunt and fish, it does not go against the teachings of the bible."

Now caught in a tricky situation, Jason ponders his next move, should he turn and run. He's sure once the preacher realizes who he is he will alert the authorities. If he stays, he will be putting the preacher's life in great danger, as the sound of the helicopter can still be heard.

'I need this rifle to defend myself with," Jason almost pleads. "The police are looking for me and when they have a shot they will take it, so I must leave or else you may get injured."

Calmly walking up to Jason, Tony pats him on the shoulder, "You need not worry about me, the Lord watches over me, he'll protect me."

Jason has never been a religious man and hearing this causes him to bite his tongue.

"You don't understand," he insists, "The police will swarm over this area, probably shooting first and asking questions second, so I must leave at once."

Staring at Jason, Tony looks deep into his eyes. "You have a good heart, and your soul is pure, I don't know what crime you have committed, but for some strange reason I feel that you were justified in doing it. Call it a message from God or a preacher's intuition, but I feel compelled to help you."

Again Jason is confused, here is a man of faith and he says he is willing to help him. Thinking about his odds of escape as by now the area should be completely sealed off and the police will begin tightening their noose.

With just one rifle a shootout with the police will be suicide, and he doesn't want the preacher caught in the cross fire.

Handing the rifle over, Jason says, "How can you help me?"

Reaching into his backpack he pulls out some clothing and a pair of glasses.

"Put these on, do it quickly, I can see flashlights heading this way."

Doing as he is told, Jason dons the same attire as Tony, along with the neck band showing the small white square.

"Put these in your mouth," Tony says as he hands Jason several marbles.

Hesitant at first, Jason does as he is told, not sure what purpose they will serve.

"I'll do the talking," Tony says, "you just follow my lead, and don't act nervous. Remember we are out on a hunting trip."

The two can see multiple lights coming from all directions, and the sound of the brush being trampled grows louder.

Taking a glance at the rifle, Jason feels very vulnerable without a weapon in his hands.

Looking up Tony gives him a wink, "It won't do you any good, it's not even loaded."

Jason has to laugh at this, he should have known that a hunter never loads his rifle until he is about to go hunting.

At that moment several men jump over the tall grass surrounding the camp. Wearing black masks over their faces, and guns at the ready they begin ordering the two to lie down on the ground.

With weapons pointed at their heads they do as they are told. While lying on the ground they are handcuffed and searched for weapons. With eight officers surrounding them, three others begin pulling things out of the tent. When this is done both men are helped up to their feet, neither has said a word.

Showing frustration, Tony says, "Is one of you going to tell me what is going on here?"

The officer in charge replies, "You will shut your mouth until I say you can talk, understand."

His heart racing Tony puts up a brave front, "We have done nothing wrong."

Opening up Tony's wallet, the police first check his I.D., they compare his photo on his driver's license, they are satisfied that it is a match. Next they ask for Jason's I.D.

"I lost my wallet yesterday while hunting."

The officers ask again, this time in a harsh tone, "Show us some identification."

"I'm telling you the truth, I lost my wallet yesterday while hunting, is that too hard to understand?"

Jason now realizes that these police officers do not have the description of the Vigilante Assassin, and the clothing he was wearing or else they would have recognized him immediately. He can only guess that there was a gap in the information being shared by the different law enforcement agencies. The officer that cornered him in the shed and those on the bridge got a good look at him.

It is a stroke of pure luck, and maybe a little divine intervention. Whatever the reason for this blessing, he knows it will be short lived.

The confusion that caused this will soon be rectified, and every police officer will know exactly what the Vigilant Assassin looks like.

The police will soon be forwarding his description to every newspaper, T.V. and radio station. Flyers with his picture will be on telephone poles and in the post offices in every city for a hundred miles.

Speaking up, "I can assure you we have done nothing wrong," states Tony.

Looking closer at the driver's license the officer in charge utters, "My apologies Father Tony, I didn't know."

"That is alright my son, all is forgiven."

"We are searching for a wanted fugitive," states the officer. "We spotted your camp fire and thought that he may be here."

"We have seen no one for three days," replies Tony. "I do not fear this wanted man, with the Lord by my side, he will protect me."

"If this fugitive were in these woods," the officer says, "You and your friend would be dead right now."

Tony now looks at Jason, a concerned look is on his face.

"What has this fugitive done that is so terrible?"

"I would rather not go into details," states the officer. "But I can assure you he is dangerous and hot tempered, so if you see anyone else in these woods you must contact the police immediately."

"I will do that, yes I'll call right away, we can't have that evil man on the loose."

After taking the handcuffs off of Tony, the officer now turns towards Jason, "We still have no way of knowing who you are."

Stepping between the two Tony says, "This young man is training for the priesthood, his name is Alex Whitting. I have known him since he was a small boy, and now he wishes to devote his life to the Lord."

The officer gives Jason a long look.

"The two of us decided to go on this hunting trip slash religious retreat to get closer to our creator. We will fast for 24 hours, at which time we'll begin another 8 hours of prayer. If you and these other officers would like to join us we would be very pleased."

Now turning his head and giving Tony a long look, and then back at Jason he steps to the side to talk with the other officers.

Tony gives a slight wink, Jason cannot believe what he has just heard. Here is a man of faith lying to the police and for a stranger that he knows nothing about.

With his hands still cuffed together, Jason leans forward and whispers, "You are risking a great deal by helping me. If they find out you are lying, you'll go to jail."

With a confident look on his face, Tony replies, "The lord works in mysterious ways, some we understand and others we don't. Sometimes it is best to just go with your heart, the lord speaks to me this way. If you are a righteous and honorable man, the Lord will let you walk out of here."

Jason can only shake his head, if indeed he somehow manages to get out of this jam, he has promised to start going to church.

After several minutes the officer walks back over and confronts Tony, "These woods are preventing our radios from contacting the station, and verifying your story. We will check out your story in the morning, in the meantime don't go anywhere."

With his hands pressed together, "We will not leave this place until we hear from you again, you have my word on that."

Taking the cuffs off of Jason the police begin their trek out of the woods. The two stand silent as the flashlights fade in the distance and are soon gone.

Needing to sit down after this encounter, Jason wipes the perspiration from his forehead. Sitting with a gaunt and haggard expression on his face, as he breaths a big sigh of relief at this unexpected bit of good luck or Godsend, with this close of an encounter with the authorities he'll take either one.

Sitting across from him, Tony says, "I feel in my heart that I did what I did because the Lord instructed me to do it."

"Whoever instructed you, I would like to thank them. You just saved my life, and for that I will never forget you."

Smiling Tony replies, "Just make sure you keep your promise."

Looking at him oddly, "What promise, I made no promise to you," retorts Jason.

Tony gives a quick glance at the heavens, "Not to me my son, but you made a promise to the Lord did you not?"

Not liking this kind of talk, Jason answers, "How did you know that I made a promise to God?"

"I have been in a great many dangerous and trying situations, it is common for a man to make such a promise when he believes that the situation he is in looks hopeless. As a last desperate act he makes promises he hopes will get him out of the trouble he's in. Asking the Lord for help and repaying that help a person almost always promises to start going to church, so you see I'm not a mind reader, but I know men's hearts."

Feeling humble, Jason bows his head, he knows by just going to church that it cannot pay back what this preacher has done for him.

The two sit in silence, as an eerie calm comes over the woods. The preacher, his eyes closed seems to be muttering. Jason can only guess that Tony is trying to explain to the Lord what he has just done. Looking up at the night sky, Jason begins to see the stars as never before. They seem brighter and almost seem to move about. Staring into the dark void, he wonders what is really out there, is God looking down on him right now.

Shaking off this weird sensation, he says, "You know I have to leave."

Opening his eyes, Tony smiles, "I know,—I know."

"You should also leave," states Jason. "The police will soon find out that you lied to them about me and they will come to arrest you."

"I will be just fine young man, now you go."

The two look at one another, a feeling of respect and mutual understanding is felt by both.

Shaking Tony's hand, Jason says, "I hope we meet again someday, but under better circumstances."

Giving his usual smile, "I would like that Jason, I would like that very much."

Opening his hand, Jason sees a cell phone, he gives a quick look at Tony.

"I thought this may come in handy, seeing how you have trouble finding your way around."

Again Jason is at a loss for words, holding back his emotions he can only smile and nod his head.

Turning around quickly a very thankful and indebted Jason disappears into the dark woods.

His thoughts are about if the police will charge Tony with any crimes. If they do that is out of his hands, he must now concentrate on reaching the city limits.

Remembering that Tony said the edge of the woods was only another twenty minute walk, he heads in that direction. It isn't long and he steps out of the trees and in the distance can see the lights of a city. He debates if he should continue walking or if that will be too dangerous.

Holding up his cell phone, he isn't sure it will work this far from the city, and with a press of a few button, he can hear his old friend Crow on the other end.

"Where have you been," Crow exclaims. "We thought that the police captured you."

"I'm fine, but I need a ride, are you busy?"

"That's funny," answers Crow. "Just tell me your location."

"I really don't know for sure where I'm at."

"Describe what you are looking at, maybe a landmark or a bridge, something that will point me in the right direction."

With it still dark he can't make out any objects, just the street lights in the far distance. "I'll try getting closer, maybe I'll see a street sign, I'll call you back in 30 minutes."

"Okay, I'll be waiting for your call, out."

Jason now follows a gently sloping hill that leads down to a set of railroad tracks. He'll follow these until he can sneak in behind a few houses and get close enough to the street to read a sign.

With the night air still and hardly any noise the scene is very peaceful, except the occasional dog barking.

This tells him he is not in Landore, crime in that city does not rest just because of darkness. If anything the criminals prefer to do their dirty work at night.

Still too early in the morning for most people to be up and about, it is the perfect time for him to find something to get his whereabouts.

He very cautiously leaves the safety of the railroad tracks and ducks in-between two houses. He can see the street sign but is too far away to read what it says.

Taking a last quick look around making sure that there is no one on the street he darts towards the street sign. Once there he looks up at it and immediately begins to curse. The sign has been damaged to the point where it is unreadable. With no choice but to hurry back to his cover, from here he can see that several blocks ahead are the head lights of cars as they cross the rail road tracks.

This crossing he knows for sure will have a sign, but getting close enough to read it without being spotted will be difficult.

Walking close to these houses until he is just inside the shadow of the street lights, he can see a street sign but can't read what it says. He must wait until there are no cars before leaving the concealment of the shadows. Finally in what seemed an hour, it appears there is a low in the traffic, this is his opportunity and he races to the sign and after quickly reading it he disappears back into the darkness.

Back on the cell phone he gives Crow the names of the streets and with his knowledge of the surrounding cities Crow is confident he knows the location. Jason waits patiently, if this is not enough information for Crow than he'll need to find a bridge or a building with a name on it.

But luck is with him this night and within 45 minutes the familiar taxi pulls up and the two quickly exit the area.

Back at the apartment he is warmly greeted by his two elderly friends.

"Crow had informed us that he had received word from you shortly after you contacted him," says Doc. "So we have been waiting patiently for you to walk through that door." With said he gives his young apprentice a bear hug.

Feeling like he is among old trusted friends again Jason is so relieved to be back in this apartment that he puts his hands together and says, "Thank you Lord."

His two friends smile at hearing this, and they hope this is a sign that Jason has begun thinking about God as the both of them are very religious.

"We had heard rumors that the police had captured you," inquires Edward. "But as time went by there was no news flash that the Vigilante Assassin had been apprehended."

"We thought that maybe you had a shootout with them and you died trying get away," says a very concerned Doc, his face showing how stressed he was while waiting this whole time.

Sitting back in his chair, a rather ragged and exhausted Jason replies, "There was a few moments when I was nearly captured, but I think someone upstairs was watching over me."

"You gave us quite a scare young man," says Edward as he pats Jason on the back. "Now get some sleep, you can tell us the details in the morning."

Doc nods his head in agreement, "We aren't as young as we used to be. Why in my younger days I could stay up for days at a time."

Cutting in Edwards declares, "Those days are long gone, so just go to bed."

Giving his old friend a sneer, Doc pats Jason on the shoulder as he walks by him.

Jason can now sleep, confident that no bear or police will disturb his slumber.

CHAPTER 13

The Mayor is overjoyed that there has been a break in the case. He is on his way down to the police station to congratulate the detectives and to question the witness himself.

Lt. Wilson is smiling, believing that the evidence and the witness will finally put an end to the reign of the Vigilante Assassin.

A detective stands in his doorway, with a disappointing look on his face. "Sir," he says hesitantly, "I have some bad news."

Abruptly getting up from his chair, "Don't come in here and tell me that, this is going to be the greatest day in department history," a clearly agitated Lt. Wilson barks out.

Slightly nervous with what he is about to say, "Sir, It seems earlier today one of our officers had the vigilante cornered just a few miles from where El Diablo was Killed."

Clapping his hands together, Lt. Wilson says, "Praise the lord, we finally got that bastard."

Sighing, the detective continues, "The police officer was working alone, he had set a trap for the Vigilante Assassin and did not tell any of us."

"That moron, I'll have his badge for this. But at least we got our man, that's the most important thing."

"That's what I'm trying to tell you sir, we don't have the Vigilante Assassin, he somehow outsmarted the officer. We found him lying on the ground handcuffed."

"Of all the idiotic things, to have this man that is our most wanted fugitive and then to let him get the jump on you because you didn't want to call in backup," states a perturbed Lt. Wilson.

"It appears that way sir, but the Vigilante Assassin stole the officer's car and several squad cars gave pursuit."

"Well then tell me, you put up road blocks didn't you?"

"Yes we did, and we had a bridge he was headed towards completely sealed, there was no way he was getting through."

"Now tell me that you then arrested him and he is now on his way down here to the police station."

"Not exactly sir, the Vigilante Assassin drove the police car off the bridge and into the river."

"Since he's not a fish, and if the initial crash didn't kill him he had to come to the surface and attempt to swim to shore. I'm hoping you will now tell me that at that point you arrested him, am 'I right?"

No sir, the car floated down the river, and we gave pursuit but we were unable to keep up. Every police officer on that bride emptied his service revolver into the car that the Vigilante was driving so it is most likely that he is dead at the bottom of the river."

"I don't believe that for one second," declares Lt. Wilson. "My hunch is that he is still alive."

"The woods in that area are very thick," continues the officer. "Very few roads go along the river. We have men stationed at the next bridge, but that one is more than 15 miles downriver."

Picking up the phone, "I want a chopper in the air right now," barks out a very upset Lt. Wilson. "I also want men in speed boats out on that river within the hour."

Looking at his detective, "Call in everyman this station has, I want men with dogs combing both sides of that river, now move!"

Now clearly agitated as he dreads the call he must make to the Mayor.

CHAPTER 14

The next day is spent filling in the details of his exploits, and the two old men can only shake their heads at how their young apprentice manages to get out of so many jams.

It is a joyous day as the three congratulate each other on eliminating their most hated enemy.

Disappointed that such a magnificent rifle was lost, however Edwards promises that they will get another to replace it.

This happy occasion is short lived when they receive an email from Sparrow. He informs them "Evidence has been gathered at the crime scene where El Diablo was killed. They have finger prints, and worst of all they have a witness."

The two old men give Jason a concerned look, as this might put a stop to their mission. With the police about to I.D. the Vigilante Assassin it won't take them long to track him to their apartment. Jason bows his head, looking mystified he says, "I saw no one when I was there, just the two men I killed. It must have been someone inside the house that by sheer coincidence had looked out the window at the precise time that I walked by."

Throwing his hands into the air, "That's it," says Doc. "Our mission and the crusade is over, your cover has been blown."

"Just a second," states Jason. "The police have been unable to find me up to this point, what makes you think just because they know who I'm that they will suddenly know where to look for me,"

Still shaking his head, "Doesn't matter," replies Doc. "The fact is that the situation is much too dangerous for you to continue with this vigilante mission you are on."

Looking at Edward, "Can you explain to Doc that nothing has changed, we can still continue as before."

Puckering his lips, Edwards hesitates for a moment,

I think Jason is right," he tells Doc. "Knowing the identity of the Vigilante Assassin still will put the police no closer to him than they were before."

"But they now know what Jason looks like," Doc replies angrily. "If he is spotted anywhere the police will be there in minutes. As much as I would like to continue this mission, it is just too risky."

Now changing his attitude, as perhaps with Jason's picture soon to be plastered on every post office wall and fliers nailed to every telephone pole in the city, this may indeed be the time to stop all operations.

"I think we need to have a conference call with the other members," says Edward, "and get their opinions. Then we will vote on whether to continue ridding the city of its evil, or we cease all operations and shut everything down."

Not liking this, but understanding the need to discuss this matter with the other members, Doc reluctantly agrees.

However having all the members of F.L.O.C.K. on the internet at the same time, has many of the members concerned. They know that the police are monitoring the internet closely, and some members fear that a breach in their security may occur by having all member logged in at once.

Urged on by Doc and Edward, who are hoping that a vote against continuing this crusade will be enough to convince Jason to put down his rifle and that it is truly time to stop the killing.

The members are not happy with this arrangement, but they realize that there is no other way, this discussion must happen as soon as possible. By contacting each member separately it will take too long, this problem needs resolving now.

A time is set and Doc and Edward ask Jason if he wouldn't mind leaving the apartment while they discuss this matter with the other members. Understanding this, Jason goes downstairs and out the back door. Sitting in the alley behind several bags of garbage, he needs this time to think. Feeling that what he has been through, along with the deaths of his friends on his hands, he cannot stop the job he started.

After his last narrow escape from the jaws of the authorities he believes more than ever before that he has a guardian angel watching over him, protecting him from harm and guiding him when he is lost. God was surely on his side, how else can he explain his remarkable ability to prevail time and time again after what seemed the end of his run.

First being cornered in that shack, getting the jump on that police officer and managing to get away, or being shot at by dozens of guns as he drove towards the bridge. Bullets had blown out all the windows as they whizzed by his head, and yet he was not hit, not a single scratch.

His plunge off the bridge and into the river, that alone should have killed him. This was followed by more divine intervention, being able to hide under that large tree that just happens to be floating by. Then there is the bear, it could have come up that tree after him but it didn't, he was unarmed, despite being completely defenseless. Next is meeting that preacher and why the man would help a wanted man, this is all too good to be by accident and chance.

Looking up Jason whispers, "I know you are protecting me, and I will not let you down. I will continue my crusade, regardless of how the others vote."

As the hours pass Jason gets up from his hiding place and goes back to the apartment.

He can see Doc sitting at the kitchen table, both hands are clichéd tightly together.

Edward approaches Jason and says, "The members voted to continue our mission, Doc pleaded his case against continuing, but in the end he was out numbered."

Now sitting across from Doc, Jason says, "I promise to be extra careful, I'll double check every alley before stepping into it. I'll only go on missions that you and Edward approve, no more rouge missions.

This job I'm doing I feel is right and justified, the dangers are great, but the end result will also justify this risk."

Looking up the old man seems sad, as if he has just lost a close friend.

"You will promise me," he says, looking into Jason's eyes, "that once we decide that there has been enough killing that you will lay down your gun and put all this behind you, can you promise me this?"

"I can give you my word, that when you two say enough is enough, than that will be the end of the Vigilante Assassin."

Nodding his head, Doc gives his apprentice a smile.

Looking over his next endeavor, Jason decides that he needs to maximize his efforts. Taking out one or two criminals at a time is not very efficient. Even killing all those bikers was a rare feat. The street gangs seem to fill the void every time he kills one of them, he believes it is a losing battle. Besides he must wait for another rifle to be delivered before he can continue his nightly assassinations.

He scans the internet in search of a way to eliminate a great many undesirables with one fell swoop. Shooting proved effective, but it is time consuming and he is always at great risk.

Ideas of making a bomb and blowing up a drug house are quickly put to the side as innocent bystanders may be killed. Poisoning the gangs may work, but getting close enough to them will be a problem. Going into one of these drug invested buildings with guns blazing is also a possibility. But he knows his chances of coming out alive are slim to none, and if he is killed who will carry on the crusade.

No, there must be a better way, one that affords him the opportunity to escape after his mission is completed.

Looking at the help wanted section, his eyes light up, he believes he has just found what he has been searching for. The ad is seeking a part time cook at the state prison in a city just 75 miles away.

This has possibilities; and Jason Karsten, vigilante, ponders this brainstorm for most of the night.

He goes over dozens of ways to inflict the most damage on these prisoners that the state has deemed too violent to release. Several methods and ideas are examined, and he crosses off each one as he finds a weakness in its design. Finally he is looking at the perfect plan, it is going to be daring, and there is a possibility that he may get caught.

A terrible thought runs through his head, that if he is ever caught they will incarcerate him inside one of these prisons. The prisoners will quickly find out who he is and his life will be a living hell. In the heel of his shoe is hid a cyanide capsule. He will take his own life first before ever being captured.

He will first need fake documents showing that he does have experience as a cook. Thanks to Edward's contacts, this will be no problem.

Confiding in his two mentors this new plan, they at first seem against it. Their point is that it could cause the death of a lot of innocent people, this alone would be enough for them to reject Jason's plan. But for Jason to walk into a state prison in broad daylight, knowing that the authorities have the I.D. of the Vigilante Assassin is asking to be caught.

His nightly missions to kill only one or two criminals with his rifle assured them that innocent people would not get killed.

This plan that Jason has is reckless and foolish and his two mentors strongly advise him against it.

Much arguing is done by Jason and Doc and at times Edward has to stand in-between the two before fists started flying.

Doc is adamant with his views about this crusade, that no chance should be taken if innocent people may die as a result of it.

Edward backs up his friend, as the two have nearly the same philosophy on taking a human life. Deeply religious they have both struggled at times with this crusade that has tested their faith and their sense of right and wrong.

Jason on the other hand is very determined to carry out this new mission, regardless if it may cost some innocent lives.

"We all knew that before this crusade is finally over," states Jason, "that innocent people would be caught in the middle. We weighted the pros and cons, looked at the end result and we all determined that it was worth the risk. Each member of F.L.O.C.K. signed off on this historic endeavor, we were united then and we should be united now."

The two old men are taken aback by these words, yes, they had agreed to this crusade and they were instrumental in its concept and they also knew the risks. To stop now before their mission is complete would mean everything that the organization had done to clean up this city up to this point would be wasted.

The two old men now ponder this next phase of their operation, fearing on one hand that it has reached its zenith and now the taking of innocent lives is being ignored. But on the other hand, too much time and effort has been put into it to stop operations at this critical moment.

Not personally knowing the other members of F.L.O.C.K. it is difficult to understand and judge their true feelings and how deeply they are committed to this crusade of cleaning up Landore.

Will these other nameless individuals continue this operation no matter how high the death toll goes, and as that death toll climbs so will the number of innocent people caught in the middle.

Doc and Edward state their case to these other members that a great many criminals have been killed and the crime rate is beginning to come down, they ask if maybe this is the time to cease operations.

The response they get is swift and firm, "The Vigilante Assassin will resume his mission as before, and all members will continue to give him their full support."

Not liking this at all the two men are bound by their loyalty to the group, despite their objections they will for the time being give Jason any assistance he needs.

With that issue behind them the three spend hours going over details and what methods to use for this daring mission. Edward in a short time receives the fake documents, and after filling in the blanks on the job application they are quickly sent out.

After submitting his application, he and his mentors assesses his plan over the next two weeks. They try to think of every possible thing that could go wrong, and then they work out a solution for it.

Contacting sparrow who works at the court house, they receive the blue prints for the layout of the prison. The three study it carefully, locating all the entrance and exit doors. They are given the procedures for entering and exiting the prison, and the types of searches on individuals that come and go.

They learn vital information as to what time the shift change is for the guards and meal times for the prisoners. They receive names of prison personnel and their job descriptions, nothing is left to chance.

Being inside this state prison will be nerve racking and Jason must remember his teachings from Falcon, to remain calm and relaxed. To feel as if nothing can prevent you from completing your task, focus your thoughts on what is around you. Hoping he has learned what is necessary, Jason now must wait.

Having curtailed his nightly forays to only every other night it has given him a chance to rest and to concentrate on his upcoming venture.

Finally after two weeks a letter arrives from the department of corrections, it says for Jason to meet at the prison Monday morning at 5:00 A.M.

Now he has two days to gather the supplies he needs, and with help from Hawk, who has a degree in chemistry, he concocts a formula that will work nicely. Putting cyanide crystals and rat poison into a pop bottle, Hawk assures Jason that death from this mixture will come quickly.

Doc's attitude has changed completely and he seems almost giddy about this venture, he's as excited as a kid on Christmas day. Pacing the floor and mumbling about biblical prophecy, Doc believes that this coming adventure was foretold in the scriptures. His religious beliefs border on the absurd, and he tells Jason, "God will put an invisible cloak around you to protect you from harm."

Thankfully Edward does not share these views and he has told Jason to ignore Doc when he gets like this. His hunch is that Doc may be suffering from the early stages of dementia, and his mood and actions can be unpredictable.

Knowing that there is no cure from this terrible affliction, Jason appeases his mentor by agreeing with him. Jason remembers how Floyd and Harriet acted and he has been noticing this same behavior in Doc.

Dementia aside, Jason sometimes has to question Doc's sanity; he is a devious man when he wants to be. As many people that he himself has killed, Jason often stops to question his own sanity, is he doing the right thing?

He has a great deal of blood on his hands, yes it is those of criminals, yet it is still a human life. The bible teaches that life is sacred, and killing is considered an evil act that will send a person to hell.

He believes that when he finishes ridding the city of all this evil, that the end will justify the means. He will be judged before God and not of men, and his acts of vigilante justice will either be looked at as a noble and righteous act or a horrific and immoral crime against humanity.

The citizens of Landore will be safer because of his daring acts, they will be glad that someone had the courage to take this type of action. The people will not hold him in content of the law, as the end will justify the means.

At least he's hoping that people look at it that way. Perhaps when he is finished, he should remain nameless, just an urban folklore.

The law will never stop searching for the Vigilante Assassin, he will be a wanted man the rest of his life. With the authorities having finger prints of the Vigilante Assassin, it gives them an edge in catching their most wanted fugitive.

Although Jason is sure his finger prints are not on any police file as he has never been arrested, he knows that one minor run in with the law will be his undoing. The computers will match his finger prints to the Vigilante Assassin's within seconds, his days of freedom fighting will be over.

With his acceptance papers in hand Jason and his mentors now go over the final preparations for this daring and dangerous mission.

The plan is for Jason to be in and out of the prison in just a few hours. The name on his fake I.D. card reads, "Jonathan McDaniel's."

It sounds legit to Jason, and he hopes once inside the prison that he doesn't see anyone he knows, as this could blow his cover. Edward is a master of disguises, and after he finishes with Jason, his own mother wouldn't recognize him.

They all know that the authorities do have a description of the Vigilante Assassin, so Jason must be prepared to make a quick getaway if necessary.

Getting up early Monday morning, he carefully puts the chemical concoction into an empty pop bottle. This will sit in his lunch pail, hoping that no one at the prison does such a thorough search of his stuff that they actually open the bottle to test what is inside.

Knowing that they will be searching for contraband such as drugs and weapons, his poison should go undetected.

Sitting at the kitchen table as usual, Doc and Edward share breakfast with their young fearless crusader.

"Remember," says Edward, "At the first sign that something isn't right, you get the hell out of there any way you can."

With a half-smile, "Things will go just like we planned," replies Jason.

Shoving his plate away, Doc says, "There will be no one to assist you should something go wrong, you will be at the mercy of the guards and prisoners."

Finishing his meal very quickly, "This mission will be our greatest triumph against crime," retorts Jason. "It will be so grand that people will be talking about it twenty years from now."

Edward can only shake his head, the thought that perhaps 30 to 40 inmates will die today is weighing heavy on his conscious.

Perhaps he now believes society will look at the Vigilante Assassin differently after today, to take the lives of so many in such a short period of time may frighten the people. What if they turn against this unknown crusader and look at him as a monster.

The whole operation could be jeopardized and many of its secret contacts may also believe that the group has gone too far in their methods to reduce the crime rate.

Without these contacts on the streets and also those in key positions throughout the city the group would have to shut down operations in order to protect its members.

Edward hopes it doesn't come to that, this secret group calling themselves the F.L.O.C.K. has been instrumental in eliminating the hardcore criminals from the streets, it would be a tragedy that only a few could comprehend.

Saying his usual, "See ya later," Jason leaves the apartment, confident in his abilities to carry out this historic mission.

With the aid of Crow Jason arrives an hour and a half later at the prison, but they park several blocks from it. Having been taught how to hotwire a car he steals one and drives himself the rest of the way to the prison. This he and his mentors are hoping will make it difficult for the authorities to track him after he has finished his mission. Arriving at the rear of the prison, here he sees that there are another two men waiting to get in. The big burley guard standing in front of the gate says after checking Jason's papers, "We are waiting on one more before we can proceed inside."

This time standing around will give Jason an opportunity to study the other two part time cooks that he will be working alongside. One of them is an older man, he's guessing maybe forty five years old. He is perhaps 30 lbs. overweight and is hunched at the shoulders. His clothing is baggy and his socks don't match along with having not shaved for several days, this is a good indication that he's not married.

The other person is no more than a teenager, and he looks scared to death. Tall and skinny, with hair down to his shoulders, he acts jumpy at every little noise, Jason is guessing that this must be his first job.

While the three wait they small talk about sports and the weather, as this will take Jason's minds off of the work ahead.

After fifteen minutes the guard in front of the gate announces, "We can't wait any long, you three follow me." Turning around and motioning with his hand the three quickly form a line behind him.

They pass through three sets of gates, each one electronically controlled by the men up in the watch tower.

As each gate opens and they step forward and the gate behind them slams shut, this gives everyone an ominous feeling.

After passing through the last gate, Jason is surprised that their lunch pails have not been searched. Also they have not been patted down, this is another indication that the prison lacks major security procedures. After going down a long hall the three are led inside the kitchen area of the prison, and here they are told to wait for another guard that will brief them.

Jason can see the prisoners looking through the glass at them, and he figures that they must be thinking, "Another group of dead beats that couldn't find a better job any place else."

This is probably true as who would want to work in this type of place where at any moment you could be stabbed or killed.

A very big guard walks in, with a crew cut and holding a baton, he is very intimidating. The heel of his boots snaps the floor as he walks back and forth all the while smashing the baton into the palm of his hand. In a firm and rough voice, one that suggests he likes authority, he tells the three new cooks, "Sit and shut up."

Quickly doing as they are told the three sit silently, their eyes focused on this man.

He goes over where they can and cannot go, and who they can and cannot talk to.

"Do not give the prisoners anything," he states firmly, "and do not accept anything from the prisoners."

With a quick swing of his baton it cracks against the glass window causing several prisoners who had been closely watching the new cooks to jump back.

Now facing the three he states, "These prisoners are the worst of the worst, you have to constantly let them know who is in charge." The guard continues, "The most dangerous criminals you'll probably ever see in your life are here. Most are serving multiple life sentences, so if they catch you with your guard down, they won't hesitate to cut your throat."

Hearing this renewed Jason's reasons for being here, these criminals have no right to live. They should not have been sentenced to life in prison instead they should have gotten the death penalty.

This man in charge takes a cautious glance around making sure no other guards can hear him, leaning forward he says, "If it thought I could get away with it I would shoot every dam inmate in this prison."

Having just met this guard, Jason likes him already. His attitude would make him a good candidate to join the organization, this he will pass on to Doc and Edward.

The three are now led into the kitchen, a guard points at a sack of potatoes and then at Jason, "You can start peeling those," he says with a half grin.

The other two men are also given tasks, and as he peels, Jason has an opportunity to survey the area.

He can see the guards just outside the doors as they walk back and forth, occasionally they stop to look over the room. The outside windows must be twenty feet from the floor and are covered with steel mesh. All the tables and chairs are bolted to the floor, and most of the cabinet doors have a heavy padlock on them.

At that moment two inmates are brought in, and they are put to work washing dishes. They are to Jason's right and when he looks at them they stare back with cold hard eyes. These inmates don't blink their eyes or show any emotions. Heavily tattooed, the men snarl their faces at Jason and the other two cooks.

This causes the hair on the back of his neck to stand up, he can feel their evil. These men are your typical career criminals, all they know is how to steal, rob or murder to get what they want.

Again Jason is surprised that by this time that he and the other two cooks are not searched for contraband. Security in this state prison has always been subject to rumors that the guards are being paid not to search incoming visitors or workers. This would explain the high rate of death of inmates due to an overdose of drugs. The money passed around by the drug lords it seems has corrupted these officials, and they no longer support their code of honor. With the drugs so readily available behind these prison walls it's no wonder many of the inmates quickly commit another crime once they are released.

One of the inmates now begins to look around in a cunning and sly manner. He slides his feet across the floor inching his way closer to Jason. Jason swallows hard, fearing that this inmate may try to cut his throat.

Looking out the window he sees no guards walking back and forth, now his anxiety is rising. "Why have the guards left their posts?"

"They should be here protecting him and the other cooks from these dangerous inmates."

With no weapons and nowhere to run Jason braces himself, ready to fight off an attack if necessary.

In a rough voice the inmate whispers, "Did you bring any drugs in with you?"

Caught off guard by this, Jason shakes his head no.

Looking past Jason he asks, "What about one of them, do they have any drugs?"

"I don't know, you'll have to ask them."

With his face distorted in anger and getting right up into Jason's face the inmate whispers, "If you're lying, I'll cut you real bad."

Jason steps away, hoping that a guard will come in very soon. He again shakes his head, "No, I'm not lying, honest."

With a sneer still on his face, the inmate now gradually makes his way over to the other two cooks. Jason can hear talking between them but he can't make out what they're saying.

The teenager cups his hand together and moves it towards the inmate. In an instant the inmate puts something into his mouth and he moves quickly back over by the other inmate.

It is very obvious to Jason that the teenager just gave the inmate some drugs.

"This is crazy," a very perturbed Jason mutters.

The two inmates keep to themselves, and at times laughing out loud.

Jason had thought if one of the cooks was a drug carrier he would have guessed the older one. Who he believes may still have smuggled some kind of illegal substance in with him, he just hasn't transferred it to an inmate yet.

As Jason is going over in his head the plan that he and his mentors have devised that is when one of these inmates begins acting strange.

Clawing at the walls he screams out loud that huge bugs are eating his flesh. Several guards rush in and subdue him to the floor. He is sedated and carried out on a stretcher, the guards act like this is no big deal. They calmly go about their duties as if nothing has happened.

Another inmate in brought in to take his place, he looks as dangerous and spaced out as the one taken out on the stretcher.

Jason knows not to turn his back on them, he now must be careful around the other two cooks. Believing that if one of these other cooks was crazy enough to smuggle drugs into a prison than he is a dangerous individual.

After several hours of preparing the food the three are ready to prepare lunch for nearly three hundred inmates. The guard allows them to take a short break before the inmates will file into the dining area.

Jason sits just outside the kitchen doors with the other two cooks. Beginning to get a little nervous as the hours pass and the moment of action gets closer. Opening his lunch pail, he picks up a bagel, and slowly bites into it.

The teenager sees Jason's bottle of pop and as he's reaching for it asks, "Mind if I have a drink."

Nearly choking, Jason swiftly pushes his hand away.

Holding the bottle tightly to his chest, "I have a fear of germs," Jason tells him, "I get sick very easily."

Nodding his head as he giggles the teenager accepts his answer.

"Didn't mean to freak you out man,"

Jason moves a little farther away, acting scared he wipes down his arms several times.

When the break is over the three go back inside and resume preparing the meal. With a guard standing directly behind him Jason turns and asks, "Do the guards and staff eat the same food as the prisoners?"

Laughing out loud, he replies, "Hell no we don't eat that slop, are you kidding."

Smiling back, Jason shakes his shoulders and replies, "Sorry, I didn't know."

The guard makes a grunt noise and moves out into the hallway.

He had been hoping and praying that the guards didn't share the same meal as the inmates, his contacts on the internet were not sure either. If this had been the case a new plan would have been used.

With the other two cooks busy this is Jason's opportunity, and pulling the pop bottle from under his shirt he pours its entire contents into a large bowl of beans.

He now touches a button on his cell phone, and this sends a signal to Edward. Within minutes and before the inmates are allowed to begin eating, Jason is called to the main office. Acting surprised, "What is wrong, what happened?"

Waving his hand, the guard says, "Just calm down, we just received a call that your wife has just gone into labor."

Putting his hands over his mouth Jason paces back and forth, doing his best acting at being nervous and excited.

"Oh my god, I can't believe it's time."

Laughing the guard says, "Well don't just stand there, get out of here and to the hospital you dummy."

Jason breaths as fast as he can, constantly repeating, "I'm going to be a dad."

Not bothering to pick up his lunch pail, he heads directly to the rear of the building. Having already been informed the guards in the towers let him quickly pass through all three gates and soon he's driving away.

The plan worked better than he and Doc had hoped, and Jason parks the car back near where he had stolen it. Waiting there is Crow, and with just a nod the two begin the long drive back to the apartment. Jason is congratulated by Doc and Edward upon meeting them.

The rest of the day there is a constant stream of police cars and ambulances going to and from the prison. Special news broadcasts interrupts the regular T.V. shows with updates on the ongoing tragedy there. Little by little the media is told that a number of inmates have died. As the day goes on, that number increases substantially.

The authorities will not give out the cause of death of these inmates, but they have ruled their deaths a homicide.

By the next morning the number of inmates confirmed dead has reached one hundred and eighty three.

The news reports that no suspects are in custody at this time, but the police are working on several leads.

In one fell swoop, Jason had rid society of a very large number of individuals that are deemed unfit to ever walk the streets again.

Doc and Edward are appalled at this news, they were expecting perhaps 20 to 30 maybe at the most 40 inmates would be killed, that to them was acceptable. Now with the number approaching 200 the two are very disturbed, Doc prays for forgiveness. Edward is so emotionally upset that he has to take several pills to calm down.

"You have gone too far," states an upset Edward. Now pacing the floor, with his head constantly shaking back and forth, and his hands waving in the air, he mumbles to himself.

Doc continues to pray, asking the Lord to forgive him.

Jason is confused at this reaction. Why are his two mentors acting this way, isn't this what they wanted?

"I have done exactly what we planned, nothing more," states a confused Jason.

He is hoping that these two will explain their sudden disappointment in him.

"This is way beyond what is necessary," states Edward still visibly upset. "We have killed too many too quickly, this will turn the public against us, not to mention our contacts."

"I too am surprised by the number of deaths," replies Jason. "It is more than six times the number we had figured would be killed. Perhaps the poison was a lot stronger that Hawk had calculated. "

Doc now approaches the two and says, "The Lord is not happy with this, he will punish us for this sin." Going back over to a small statue of Jesus Doc continues to pray.

Grabbing Jason by the shoulders Edward leads him into another room, "I now believe we were wrong in the taking of so many lives, this unfortunately is something that was out of our control. It could have been worse if any of the guards or staff had been killed I'm sure that the F.L.O.C.K. would have shut us down immediately. This tragedy has a silver lining, we eliminated a great many people that deserved to die. But in the future we must be more careful, the next time innocent people could be killed."

Jason is happy that at least Edward is looking at this in a positive way, Doc on the other hand with brew and stew for a while but Jason is sure he will come around.

Killing so many at once is at first a little troubling for Jason after Doc and Edward's initial reaction. He begins to question this method of execution, this mass elimination of people. For several nights he lay awake, second guessing what he has done. Killing one or two criminals at a time seemed right, he would first stalk and then shoot them.

However this new method seems to bother Jason, and he needs to do a great deal of soul searching.

If only there were others like himself, that went into the night and took out one or two criminals.

But he is alone in this business, and killing one or two people a night did not make a difference. It seems that the low life's are repopulating as fast as he can take them out. So perhaps this more efficient way of eliminating large numbers of law breakers is right. If someday we are ever going to take back the streets, than this new method is justified.

It is quickly learned from the finger prints on the lunch pail left at the prison and from the stolen car that it was the Vigilante Assassin that is responsible for the mass killings at the state prison.

The days pass as the media is all about the killings at the state prison, the newspapers headlines read, "Prison mass killing attributed to the Vigilante Assassin."

It was a mistake leaving his lunch pail at the prison, and Jason berates himself for being so foolish and careless.

"You have committed a grave error," cautions Edward. "Let's hope it doesn't come back to haunt you."

The three discuss the repercussions of this mistake and the possible consequences it may cause.

In the end they conclude that it will not alter their mission, as the authorities already had the finger prints of the Vigilante Assassin, another set of prints will do them no good. They still do not know the name of this Vigilante, or where he lives therefore the authorities are no closer at apprehending him then they were before.

CHAPTER 15

Doc and Edward are informed that a store just up the street is being used by federal agents for surveillance operations.

The D.E.A. has also set up in several other stores to do surveillance on the drug gangs in the area. They are hoping to learn the pattern of the Vigilante Assassin, to track his every move and then capture or kill him.

With the mass killing at the state prison, a special branch of the F.B.I. has gotten involved. These agents are sharp shooters and masters of camouflage. They will hide in key locations around the city, hoping and waiting for a chance to kill the Vigilante Assassin.

CHAPTER 16

Doc and Edward worry about Jason, he now seems withdrawn, preferring to keep to himself.

The three had thought the deaths at the prison were at first a great victory, tragic in the number of lives it took but still it accomplished what they set out to do. But this mass killing soon began to weigh on their conscious.

The newspapers had declared this single act of mass murder identical to how the Nazis killed the Jews during World War Two. The authorities labeled those responsible for the killings nothing short of terrorists.

The U.S. government now sent a special task force to help capture those responsible. The group consisted of agents from the C.I.A., homeland security, F.B.I., and the secret service. The group is given free access to all information available. The President of the United States personally briefed the group, telling them, "The perpetrators of this hideous and revolting act must be stopped. You have authority to use every means necessary to execute your mission and bring this case to a close."

Doc and Edward could tell from their contacts on the internet that the authorities were putting the pressure on everyone. Houses all over the city are being searched, people by the dozens are being brought to the police station for questioning.

The two now seriously think that this might be a good time to cease all operations, to shut down for an extended period of time until this show of force by the authorities subsides.

Jason on the other hand, totally refused.

"I cannot stop what I started, not for a month, or a week not even for a single day."

"You are not looking at this in a reasonable manner," argues Edward. "There is just too much law enforcement out on the streets to chance continuing."

Stepping beside his old friend, Doc says, "He's right, we can't risk all that we have accomplished up to this point. We can pick up where we left off in a month or two."

Taking in several deep breaths Jason replies, "You are asking me to do the impossible, my heart and soul tells me to continue. God has also given me signs that I need to continue with this crusade."

The two old men look at each other, this is what they had feared, that Jason would be unable to stop the killing. They can see in his eyes a different person than the young man that they nursed back from the brink of death. That man was responsible, caring and most of all he listened to his elders. He obeyed their orders and rarely questions their reasons and methods. But slowly by slowly the good has been pulled from him and he is turning more towards the dark side.

Now delusional and moving into the realm of fantasy he has begun thinking that he has divine powers and is the right hand of God.

It almost brings tears to their eyes, to watch this tragedy unfold before them.

They realize that it is their fault, that they are responsible for turning this mild mannered person into the killing machine standing in front of them.

"You know that they have your description and your finger prints," states an angry Edward. "That it is only a matter of time until you are caught if you continue, you must know this."

Taking several deep breaths as he composes himself, Edward continues, "But yet you cannot comprehend the seriousness of the situation and use common sense to refrain yourself. We have no other choice but to order you to cease any and all operations until further notice, it is for your own good."

Standing in defiance and breathing in short breaths Jason throws his jacket to the floor.

"It would be turning my back on God if I stopped doing his work."

Pointing his finger, "This is no longer God's work, this enjoyment you get from killing. No, you have turned to the dark side, you are headed for a cruel end to your life."

Waving his hands back and forth, "I'll not stop and neither you nor Doc can do anything about it. This time in our history has been foretold in the bible, that good will conquer evil."

Edward can see that Jason is not listening, and believes that his young apprentice is lost.

Biting his lip, and beside himself with remorse Doc nods his head and he and Edward go into the kitchen.

The two have a serious dilemma on their hands, just how are they going to stop Jason. Neither one can bear the image of ending this young man's life. To strike down someone they considered a son, it tares at their hearts. But they have discussed this very scenario before, and both know that Jason must be stopped regardless of their feelings for him.

Too upset to continue this discussion they decide to put it to the side for now, hoping and praying that Jason will change his mind and stop the killing on his own.

For the next several days the apartment is quiet and tranquil with very few words being spoken between the three.

It is on this third day of calm when Jason receives a tip, an unknown source has let him know that a major drug transaction is going to be taking place in an abandoned warehouse next to the docks on the east side of the river.

Reading the message alongside his young apprentice, "This sounds like a trap," cautions Doc. "You know there is a high price on your head."

"I cannot think about whether someone is setting a trap for me, I must investigate this. To stop this drug transaction and keep the drugs off the street is more important."

Now walking into the room, "You may need back up," suggests Edward. "Let us call in someone to assist you."

Nodding his head, "You know I only work alone, and we both know that there is no one else that you can call."

Hoping to persuade his young apprentice, Edward insists, "You should let this job go by, there will be others. I too feel that this could be a trap, so let's be cautious and restrained."

Grabbing his backpack, Jason replies, "Sorry to disappoint the two of you, but I'm going to go to this warehouse and see if there really is going to be a drug transaction. If I feel our informant was telling the truth then I'll do what is necessary."

Lowering their heads the two elderly men seem frustrated, Jason continues to go against their advice. They know that one day soon that this bullheaded young man will meet his end. His belief that he is some sort of avenging angel sent from heaven and that nothing can stop him will be his undoing.

Again the two talk secretly about how and when they will stop Jason. They continue to put off what both believe must be done, the death of the Vigilante Assassin.

With heavy hearts they watch their young apprentice as he rambles on about the different ways he plans on killing those at the warehouse.

The two fear that if Jason ever gets the slightest hint of what they are planning they are sure he will kill them without hesitating. They agonize and struggle over these thoughts, in their hearts they know that he has gone so far to the left and that he will never be able to return.

They have discussed poisoning him, but that would be difficult as they all eat the same foods. Another idea was to tip off the police of his whereabouts, let them kill him. But again the thought of them being the ones behind his death is too much.

The two old men now sit in silence, realizing that they have broken the number one cardinal rule, do not get too emotionally close to those you work with. Now as they look upon him as a son, they cannot execute what both know has to be done.

As odd as it sounds they secretly hope that Jason is killed during one of his missions. In the months that the Vigilante Assassin has been operating, the number of dead has risen to more than 290.

The mass killing at the prison was supposed to be the end, he was to lay his gun down and walk away, but again he refused. The killing continued as Jason repeatedly said that the city has not been purged yet, more needs to be done.

During the last meeting of the members of F.L.O.C.K. all had unanimously agreed that there has been enough killing, that a great many criminals have been eliminated from our society, and they feel that they have accomplished what they set out to do. Doc and Edward suspect that it was the mass killing at the prison that forced these members to come to that decision.

Despite being told about this decision, Jason ignored them, he stated that he will decide when it is time to stop. That he knows better than them when the time will be right to stop.

His conviction that a holy spirit is protecting him from harm drives him on. This, the two elders know is a false belief, one born from taking the law into his own hands and at first having their blessings. They are responsible, they are at fault, they should not have let this get so far out of hand. The burden of stopping this killing machine falls on their shoulders, and they are not sure if they have what it takes to stop him.

Jason has only one day to set a trap for those drug dealers going to this warehouse, he emails Hawk for some advice. With several P.H.Ds to his credit Hawk is an intelligent person and has been vital to their operation. After he is given a rough estimate of the size of this meeting place Hawk quickly has a tactic for killing those that will be inside and relays this to Jason.

Keeping this info from Edward and Doc Jason quietly gathers the things he will need and puts them into his backpack.

Checking his list, rope, two full one gallon glass jugs, steel pins and a hammer along with his usual gadgets all compile the vital things he will need.

Jason waits until two A.M. before going to the warehouse, as there will be less people on the street. Slipping out without waking Edward or Doc, Jason goes down the trusted dark alleys he has grown so accustomed to. The night air is still, dark clouds overhead indicate that rain is on the way.

It takes Jason nearly two hours to make the trek over to the docks and to locate the precise warehouse.

He first checks the side doors, finding them all locked he cautiously makes his way around to the front. Finding this door unlocked he goes inside, walking astutely as these places are often used by the homeless, or worse, drug users.

Shining his small flashlight around, he is relieved to find the place is empty. In the middle of the room is a wooden table, surrounded by several chairs. This is where drug transactions take place, this is their meeting place.

This warehouse seems secure and out of the way, a perfect place to exchange money for drugs.

Looking 20 feet directly above the table he spies a pipe that runs the length of the room.

Pulling out his rope Jason throws one end up and over this pipe, next he attaches the two one gallon glass jugs to it. Inside one jug is vinegar and in the other is bleach. According to Hawk when these two chemicals are mixed together they release toxic chlorine gas. This chlorine gas is a pulmonary irritant with intermediate water solubility that causes acute damage in the upper and lower respiratory tract. When chlorine gas comes into contact with moist tissues such as the eyes, throat, and lungs, an acid is produced that can damage these tissues. If not immediately removed from the source death can result in as little as a few minutes.

He takes the other end of the rope over to a small window, opening it he pushes the rest of the rope through. After this task he now goes around to every one of the side doors and using a hammer he pounds in steel wedges along the frame of these doors. This will prevent these doors from being opened, no matter how hard the men pull on them thus trapping those inside. Going outside and around to the back of the building, he grabs the rope and begins pulling it, watching as the two jugs gently rise off the floor. Continuing this steady pull until the jugs containing the deadly mixture is resting against the pipe on the ceiling. He now ties the rope securely around the handle of a dumpster.

His trap is set, and baring no unforeseen complications Jason expects this to be another triumph in this long crusade against evil. He is sure that the members of F.L.O.C.K. will bestow their warmest congratulations on him. Someday he envisions that they will make him a member of this secretive and highly exclusive club.

After all he believes he is the chosen one, and he has done all the dirty work. There would be no reason that he shouldn't rise quickly in their ranks.

Going back to the apartment, he informs Doc and Edward, "Everything is set, there will be no escape for those drug dealing bastards."

The two watch Jason closely, they are sad, they see him slowly drifting away from them. His actions and words are changing, his body language is that of a man possessed.

Jason sits on the couch, he now must wait, this is the hardest part of this job, this duty that he put on himself.

Tapping his feet on the floor and constantly looking at the clock, he shows a great deal of impatience.

"You need to relax," states Doc. "You act like this is your first mission."

Giving the old man a quick stare, Jason answers, "I don't want to fail. I can't let a single criminal go unpunished."

"You are being too hard on yourself," replies Doc. "No one man can possibly eliminate all the crime by himself. There will be failures and disappointments in this dangerous game that you play, you are only human, and being human entitles you to make mistakes."

Gritting his teeth as if he has just been insulted, "I will not fail, I will not give up and most important I will not be stopped."

Now turning he glares at his old mentor.

Doc swallows hard, he can sense a change in Jason and it causes him to move out of the room swiftly.

Sitting in the far corner of the kitchen again the two discuss how to stop Jason, as the situation seems to be spiraling out of control.

Late the next night Jason ventures back out into the darkness and moves swiftly along the river until he reaches the warehouse. Hiding behind the remains of a demolished building he has a good view of the warehouse.

It isn't long and several cars pull up and stop outside the front doors, he sees six men enter the building, the way they are dressed tells him that they are high members of a drug gang.

With the drug lords inside the building he next needs to block the front doors preventing anyone from escaping.

Cursing he can see two of the drug lords henchmen are sitting in a car in front of the building, they are the lookouts. These two hired guns will stop anyone from getting near this building. Jason has to get them out of the way first or his plan won't work. Sitting back down in his concealed spot he glances to the heavens, "If you have any ideas this would be the time to send me a sign on what I should do."

Several minutes pass and he seems disappointed that the heavens did not open up and an angel did not fly down with a message from God. Wondering if his two mentors may have been right about him thinking that he was the chosen one, perhaps he has gone a little far with his beliefs that God is directing his every move.

Debating if he should abort this mission, as at the moment he has no clue how to remove these men from the front of this building without causing a lot of commotion, thus warning those inside.

Bowing his head, Jason cracks a smile, "I was really starting to think I was God's right hand man, and that no one could harm me." Realizing how foolish he had been and the crazy thoughts that went through his head, he takes a last look around before exiting the area.

Moving among the rubble he spots a cat choking on a hair ball, and instantly he pumps his fist in the air.

Looking up he whispers, "Thank you."

Coming up with a fast and crazy idea, one he positively attributes to a higher power, he staggers from the rubble hunched over towards the two men in the car. As he continues towards the building, he knows this will get their attention. Both men quickly jump out of their car and point their guns at him. Jason now pretends to have a seizure by putting several elka seltzer tablets into his mouth. He falls to the ground and rolls his eyes back as far as he can. The two henchmen slowly kneel down next to Jason and roll him over. When they see the white foam coming out of his mouth they both put their weapons into their pockets.

Jason then quickly pulls out his little twenty five auto pistol and puts two shots into each of their chests before they can react.

Yes it is a small gun, but at this range it did the job quite nicely and it made very little noise. He drags the two bodies around to the side of the building and out of sight. He now proceeds to park their car right up against the front doors of the warehouse. After shutting off the car and setting the emergency brake he runs to the back of the warehouse, along the way he tosses the car keys into a garbage can.

Peering throw a window he is delighted to see at least two dozen men have gathered around the table. These drug dealers and weapons merchants had not noticed the glass jugs twenty feet above their heads. Wasting no time Jason quickly cuts the rope and he moves away from the warehouse. He can hear the glass breaking and this is followed by yelling and cursing. The trapped men begin pounding on the doors and several gun shots ring out. Within minutes it is all silent, there is no more screaming or gun shots. He wants to get a look for himself, to make sure that these men are truly dead. However, it is too risky, sure that his job has been accomplished, he must leave at once. Slipping past the other warehouses he manages to avoid detection from any of the night watchmen. Elated and feeling as if the Holy Spirit is surrounding him, Jason now more than ever is sure he is doing God's work. There can be no other explanation to his uncanny ability to get out of every situation, even ones that seem hopeless and impossible. Add to this that he never gets caught or seriously injured only strengthens his belief of a divine intervention guiding and protecting him at all times.

With the last perilous accomplishment behind him, he travels back along the river until he reaches the apartment.

The next day's newspaper tells him everything he needs to know. The headlines read, "Vigilante Assassin Strikes Again." It seems that more than twenty men in that building died that night. With the most notorious being El Diablo's brother Razar, this is an added bonus that Jason especially takes pride in.

The police again promised the citizens of the city that they will catch this vigilante.

"We will not rest until this self-appointed judge, jury and executioner is arrested and behind bars," the police captain is quoted as saying.

Jason is again congratulated by his two friends, they are glad that he is safe.

Listening to the news Jason doesn't understand why the city is making it a priority to capture him, after all he is ridding the city of violent criminals.

Only those that commit violent acts, or sell their poison on the streets have anything to fear.

He does not consider himself a criminal, he is merely doing what the police legally cannot do.

Doc and Edward praise Jason for a job well done, and for his puzzling ways of solving seemingly difficult and challenging problems that he encounters.

"You have once more made the streets a little safer," Edward says. "The papers all say how the crime rate has been steadily falling and it is at a reasonable and safe level now."

Giving this information a moment to sink in, "Now that it appears there are no more major drug traffickers in the city," a hesitant Edwards says, "This would be a good time to cease operations, don't you think so Doc?"

Looking up from his paper, "Yes, this was our final mission, the need to continue this crusade would be senseless."

With a smirk on his face, Jason angrily replies, "We have much more work to do, we are nowhere near completely this mission."

Taking in a deep breath, Doc stands and waving his finger declares, "You cannot keep on killing, and you cannot continue to disobey us and the other members of F.L.O.C.K.

We all agreed that when the time came to end this crusade that the organization would cease all operations. You cannot do this job by yourself, you will get no help from the members if you continue. What you have become is evil, the same evil that you go out after each night. You have turned to the dark side, no longer do you kill for justice and righteousness but now you kill for the joy of it. Your soul will be damned to hell, you are not a martyr do you understand?"

Not happy with being told he will be on his own he fires back, "How dare you judge me, how dare you tell me what I'm doing is evil. I wouldn't be doing this dirty work if it weren't for you two. You have no right to condemn me, to denounce what I'm doing. The burden of this whole mess falls on both your shoulders, remember I'm the student and you are the teachers."

"We had an agreement," Edward yells back. "You were to stop the killing when we deemed that enough has been done to cause the crime rate to drop. We feel it has and with the massacre at the prison, the authorities are determined to arrest everyone assisting the Vigilante Assassin."

He continues after recomposing himself, "Our contacts inform us that several key members have already been taken down to the police station for questioning. What they have told the authorities we don't know yet, and because we only contact each other over the internet, they have no way of identifying any of us. However, these contacts do know our code words and cryptograms and at what time of the day we correspond with each other. Enough bits and pieces of information could be pried from these individuals to seriously compromise our safety.

There is a lot of risk involved by ignoring these warnings. We feel that to continue this crusade will be jeopardizing our safety and security, therefore with no other option we must cease all operations before the authorities get too close."

With a stern look on his face Jason begins to understand their point, maybe it is time to cease operations, but just temporarily.

"I will make you a promise," says Jason. "I will temporarily put down my rifle, but not now. I have several more missions to carry out, these should only take a few days."

The two old men give each other a cautious look, they know each time Jason goes out, the police gather a little more evidence and they are one step closer to arresting all of them. Conceding this time, "You have three days," Doc says in a firm voice, "Then we stop all contact with the other members. If after that time you still choose to go out and kill again, you will be on your own, you will get no help from anyone."

Nodding his head in agreement, Jason replies, "I have some loose ends to take care of, I'll be back in a few hours."

With that said he grabs his back pack and without saying goodbye he exits the apartment.

The two old men now sit down to discuss this matter.

With a wary look, Doc says, "We both know he will not stop in three days, he has lost his mind."

"Just keep on praying that he will see the light and come around to our way of thinking," says a disappointed Edward.

The two have begun plans to leave their apartment, with Jason out of control it is only a matter of time before the police will come knocking on their door. At their age they cannot fathom the possibility of spending the rest of their lives behind bars.

Unable to stop the monster that they have created, their only alternative is to flee the apartment. Having made prearrangements to live far from this city, they wait the three days that they have given Jason, if after that time he refuses to stop the killing than they will leave while he is out on a mission.

CHAPTER 17

At this time the Mexican Mafia has tolerated the Vigilante Assassin long enough. He has disrupted their drug distribution network, stolen their money, and killed many of their operatives working in the United States.

They have placed a one million dollar bounty on the head of the Vigilante Assassin, this they believe will test the loyalty of his closest allies.

They have also sent an assassin of their own to track down and kill the Vigilante Assassin. He goes by the name of the Dark Knight, and he is ruthless and merciless.

With connections inside several Mexican prisons, the top drug lord in Mexico has this man released from prison. They order the Dark Knight to seek out this Vigilante Assassin and kill him.

Shortly after Jason has left the apartment, Doc and Edward are alerted to this news, but they again have no way of contacting Jason to warn him. Doc and Edward have heard of this Dark Knight, he has a reputation for killing everyone that he has targeted. Some rumors even hint that this deranged man eats part of his victims. The two know that facing an adversary of this temperament and genre will be Jason's toughest foe.

They hope that Jason is on heightened alert, and that he is not too distracted by their conversation earlier.

Heading for the abandoned railway station, Jason wants to rid that area of any gangs or drug pushers. This is a part of the city that he hasn't spent enough time in, but he made himself a promise long ago to revisit this area.

Unknown to Jason a sinister figure has arrived here several hours earlier, and only one thing is on this man's thoughts.

At six feet eight inches tall and over three hundred pounds the Dark Knight is an intimidating figure. Crouching down on one knee the Dark Knight hides in the shadows waiting for his pray. He had earlier forced one of Jason's contacts to give him information about what alleys the Vigilante Assassin takes, once given this vital information he quickly killed the contact.

Still perturbed, a troubled Jason is walking with his head down. He has forgotten the lessons that Falcon taught him. Not to forget where you are at all times, to listen for the slightest sound and watch for the smallest movement that may indicate that danger is near. His mind clouded with a tough decision, to stop the crusade or risk going on alone.

As Jason continues to walk down the deserted alley, his sixth sense suddenly puts him on guard. He reaches into his pocket, grabbing a slender steel rod pointed sharply at one end that he often carries with him. But it is too late, five shots ring out before he can react. The bullets rip into his chest tarring away his jacket. Shocked and surprised at the suddenness of this attack Jason falls face down onto the brick surface, his arms extended from his sides, he lay motionless, not moving.

The Dark Knight waits several minutes before venturing out from his hiding place, his heavy boots clang against the bricks echoing in both direction of the vacant alley.

Standing over his victim, he pauses before turning Jason over. He can clearly see the bullet holes in Jason's shirt, a wicked smile crosses his face. Not content with the million dollar reward, he reaches down and begins going through Jason's pant pockets.

Gripping the steel rod in his left hand, Jason thrusts it up with all his strength. The pointed end of the rod catching the Dark knight in his lower jaw and it penetrates through his bottom jaw and into the roof of his mouth. Reeling back, shocked and in severe pain as he holds both hands against his face, the Dark Knight curses out loud.

After a moment and screaming in pain, he falls to his knees, the blood running down his shirt and onto the brick surface of the alley.

Jason rolls to his left, hoping to catch this man with a blow to his head, and he swings his foot at him. But the Dark Knight blocks the kick and delivers a crushing blow of his own just above Jason's left ankle.

Now in pain himself, Jason manages to scoot backwards as this man in front of him continues to swing wildly.

In the dim light he has his first look at this person that dares to take on the Vigilante Assassin.

The man's face has a dozen piercings, along with tattoos of swastikas on his fore head.

As this mad man struggles to remove the steel object sticking out of his chin he continues to move towards Jason. A scour on his face and evil in his eyes it is a sight that Jason won't soon forget.

Now on his feet, Jason steps back and as he is raising up his revolver the Dark Knight swings a long slender object knocking the revolver from his hand.

Now bearing down on Jason this maniac seems to pay little attention to the steel rod protruding from his jaw.

The blood is flowing freely from his face and he barks out words in Mexican that Jason doesn't understand.

Feeling that he is in control the Dark Knight stops and stares at his latest victim, his hands now reach up and grabbing tightly onto the steel rod he pulls it from his jaws.

This has Jason spooked, never has he seen anything like this, and the man seems to totally ignore the pain.

Holding up and glaring at the bloody steel rod the Dark Knight says, "Is this the best the great Vigilante Assassin can do," followed by laughter.

Jason stands in a defensive posture, still shaken by the sight of this man.

"It is time for you to die," utters the Dark Knight. He now swivels his head back and forth in an odd way.

Pulling the large knife from his boot Jason moves quickly and delivers several vicious cuts on the torso of this man. To Jason's surprise this crazy man laughs as more blood begins to run down his shirt.

Looking at his victim the man smiles, "You will die this night."

"Not if I can help it," Jason shouts back.

Moving in again he is able to dodge the big man's grasps and drives the knife deep into his side.

Standing back fully expecting this hired assassin to succumb to his injuries he is shocked that the man seems to ignore his injuries and now walks towards Jason, all the while smiling.

The Dark Knight reaches into his pocket and as he is pulling of a gun Jason throws the knife with such force that it actually goes through the Dark Knights hand and into his thigh.

As the big man struggles to free his hand he begins screaming.

The sound causes Jason to shutter, it unnerves him like nothing he has ever heard before.

As this menacing figure steps closer Jason reaches around and pulls a revolver from his belt,

and fires a single bullet into the Dark Knights left temple.

Stopping and putting a hand where the bullet hit him the Dark Knight seems surprised. Removing his hand his eyes stare straight ahead, a moment later the big man crumbles to the ground, his lifeless body and baggy clothing resembles a large heap of garbage.

Thankful that his bullet proof vest did its job, he needs a moment to calm down.

Jason walks away as another hired assassin lay dead, and he wonders how many more the drug cartels will send after him.

This was a close call, too close. After returning to the apartment and telling his two mentors what had happened, they insist that he leave now.

"The drug lords and cartels will keep sending these assassins after you until they finally succeed," says Doc sternly.

"He's right," adds Edward, "you must relocate to a city far away. We will keep in contact over the internet."

Still showing the signs of his near death experience, a pale faced Jason answers, "This time I must agree with you. It may be the right time to get away for a while."

The two old men breathe a big sigh of relief that their young apprentice has finally seen the light. They no longer have to toil over something they were regretting doing, to stop Jason themselves would have been the most agonizing decision that they have ever had to make.

Doc presses his hands together and lowering his head he begins to recite several prayers. Edward to is also very grateful for this remarkable turn of events, and with his hand on Doc's shoulder he can only nod in agreement with what Doc is saying.

CHAPTER 18

The three now must decide on a new location for Jason, somewhere far away where he won't be recognized. With so many law enforcement agencies pursuing the Vigilante Assassin they know that this new location will have to be very far away and preferably in a small isolated town. The two old men suggest Jason go high up into the mountains of Colorado or Washington.

Their idea is that in one of these small isolated towns the news about the Vigilante Assassin over the last year has drawn little attention. After all they assume, the vigilante has only operated in one city, none of the nearby cities seemed to worry a great deal about this serial killer coming to their city, with the one exception being the state prison.

There is a good chance that a small out of the way town across the country may not of even heard of this Vigilante Assassin.

Jason doesn't like this, and he has another idea that he discusses with Doc and Edward.

"You realize," he starts out, "that killing gang members and an occasional gang leader did not stop or even slow down the narcotics coming into the city. We must get at the root of this scourge, this rampant epidemic that is destroying our social wellbeing."

Now sitting the two old men ask that he continue, as this sounds very interesting.

"Almost all narcotics come from South America," Jason says, "and with the dense jungles concealing their operations and corrupt officials affording the dealers protection from the law this is where I must go. The vast rain forests of South America is the perfect place to produce the drugs that they ship north to the states. These drugs are shipped first through Mexico before reaching the United States. Our border guards seem to be unable to stem this tide, despite their sophisticated tracking devices."

Wiping his face a concerned Doc says, "What you are suggesting is very very dangerous, you will be out of this country and on foreign soil. Americans are not looked upon very favorably there, you will be alone with no back up and no means of escaping, do you understand?"

"I do, and I believe in my heart it is the best decision. Staying in the United States will also be risky, a great many bounty hunters will be constantly looking for me, even in the smallest towns. At least in South America no one will have even heard of the Vigilante Assassin, so this will by itself should take some worry off my shoulders."

"Okay okay," says Edward. "Let's say you decide to venture that far south, what is your plans once there?"

Beginning to get the feeling that his two mentors are starting to see things his way he continues, "As in all deadly creatures, it is best to render the head useless first. By taking out the head or main source of the drug manufacturing it will stop this poison from reaching the United States. If the head of the beast is in one of these Latin American countries, then that is where I must go."

Looking at each other the two old men smile, this plan has some danger involved, but at least Jason will be far away from this city.

They both nod their heads in approval, "This is a good plan," states Doc, "we will begin getting things ready."

With the authorities getting closer to him each day, he knows he must leave. Feeling satisfied at what he has accomplished so far, he has reduced the crime somewhat. Still he wishes he did not have to go, but for the safety of his two old companions and the others that have helped him, he must leave for their sake.

For the next month he studies maps of the places in South America that he suspects the biggest cartels operate. Locating a major drug network is fairly simple, he just finds the cities where the most police officers have been killed.

He decides on Columbia, situated between Brazil, Venezuela and Ecuador. This country is at the hub of all drug operations. With dense forest, secret runways and a government that is rumored to be on a few drug payrolls, makes this an ideal spot.

Numerous anti-government militias also operate in this area, along with roving gangs of thugs makes this is a very dangerous place to be.

He knows that these men working for the cartels in these lawless countries are much more dangerous than those he has encountered on the streets of Landore. Many of these men are trained killers, they live for the thrill of the violence they cause. Human life means absolutely nothing to them. It is learned that the cartel recruits these men from the prisons that house the worst criminals.

Stories on the internet tell of brother killing brother or young teens killing their parents over a bad drug deal. Jason will have to be very cautious as any foreigner will draw suspicion.

Doc and Edward are sad to see their young apprentice leave, but they also know that it is best this way.

Turning around in his chair, Doc says, "Your documents and passport will be ready in a few hours, you should have no problem going through security at the airport."

Putting his few belongings into his backpack, Jason replies, "I will miss you two, so take care while I'm gone."

With a smile, "You just keep your wits about you," counters Edward, "and keep away from the women, they're nothing but trouble."

The three laugh, as they know that despite the humor that it may be the last time they see each other. The room grows quiet, and putting his hand on Jason's shoulder Doc says, "I'm going to miss you young man."

Looking up at his old mentor, "You two can always accompany me," states Jason. "Why not leave before the authorities break this case and arrest you."

"No," answers Doc, "We are too old to be traveling so far. We would only slow you down and hinder your mission. No, our days of covert operations are in the past. You go there and complete this mission, this crusade that we started. The world will someday understand that all of this was worth it, that the killings are justified in the eyes of our God. You are a righteous, honorable and decent man, don't you ever forget that."

Wiping his eyes, as he is having trouble controlling his emotions the old man walks back over to his chair and begins reading his paper. Jason can see the sadness in both their faces, usually very talkative, they now sit in silence.

Trying his best not to get emotional, Jason stands and begins walking towards the door. He wants this to be a quick goodbye, no need to get all emotional.

He is sure that Doc and Edward will find a safe place to live out their remaining years, as it is unlikely that he will ever return to the United States.

He knows there can be no correspondence between them, not a letter or phone call, not even a quick email message.

It is the only way that will safeguard them from being connected to the Vigilante Assassin.

With so many law enforcement agencies working on this case he knows that they will break the code that the F.L.O.C.K. uses to communicate with its members.

When this code is broken those men whose identities have remained a secret with be exposed.

Jason is sure that it will be an eye opener as some of the members he is sure hold high positions in this city.

How many people will fall when the dust settles Jason can't even guess.

He knows these members are very smart so it is also likely that when he leaves the country that they will shut down all operations. There is no one to take his place, so these members will go back to playing their virtual reality game just like they did before he came along.

    Meeting him at the door Doc and Edward shake his hand firmly, they struggle to hold back their heartache.
    With his voice cracking, "We will never forget you," says Doc. "You are our hero and savior, and may God bless and protect you always."
    Edward can't speak, with his hand over his mouth, he can only nod his head.
    Standing tall and feeling that his life has changed for the better since meeting these two, "You two have been like a father to me, without your help I would have died long ago. It is you two that are my hero's and saviors. I will keep your memory in my heart forever."
    Stuttering his words, "Just don't forget us," says Edward as he needs a handkerchief to wipe his eyes.
    With a big smile, "How could I ever forget you two, what a silly thing to say?"
    A moment passes as the three stands in silence, and their sighs indicate a sad departing.

    After a brief hug by both, Jason turns and exits the room quickly.
    He glances at the stairs and the walls as he descends to the ground floor. He didn't realize until that moment just how much he will miss this place. It felt like home, it felt like he belonged here. But he knows leaving this place is best for all involved.
    He is sure that his two mentors can take of themselves; after all that they have been through in their life, he is positive they can handle anything that comes up.

    Stepping out the back door for the last time his old reliable friend Crow is waiting as usual in the alley to take him on another mission. But Jason has told no one else of his plans to leave the country, this secrecy he is hoping will prevent the police from following him. He knows that he may never return to the states, his thoughts are with

Edward and Doc. Hoping that they leave that apartment very soon, he would be crushed if they were arrested and sent to prison.

Needing to do one last job before leaving the country he tells Crow, "Take me to a spot several blocks from the courthouse."

"What is there," he asks.

Jason tosses a newspaper onto the front seat, Crow picks it up and reads a section that is underlined with a black marker. "Known child molester set free."

Speaking up Jason says, "This man has openly admitted to several hideous and repulsive crimes against children, but the authorities are setting him free over a little technicality."

Giving a lance in the rearview mirror, "It is daylight, you cannot shoot this man in broad daylight, you'll be caught."

"I know I'm taking a great risk but this has to be done, are you with me?"

Without hesitating Crow replies, "From day one I have always been there when you needed me and I'll always be there now."

Smiling Jason knew his old friend would not let him down, Crow is the most trusted of all his contacts.

Parking in an alley just blocks from the court house, "This man will be leaving the courthouse in half an hour," says Jason. "Be ready to drive like hell when I get back."

"I will be here my friend, you can count on that."

Now climbing up the fire escape he enters an open window on the back side of a church. The room looks like no one has be in it for some time, he figures it is just a storage room. Cautiously opening the door there is no one in sight and he quickly ascends the steps that lead up to the tallest part of this church. Opening a small door just above his head he crawls into the bell tower. From this vantage point he has a good view of the court house and wastes no time in assembling his rifle.

With the wind blowing at about 15 M.P.H. Jason must add this into the distance of his target and hopes that his calculations are accurate.

He has an excellent view of the front of the court house and the surrounding area and wonders why he never used this perch in the past. With several minutes until his intended target will appear he removes the gun clip from the rifle. In his vest pocket he pulls out a single bullet, this one he had earlier drilled out the tip and inserted a small amount of botulinum.

This deadly poison attacks the nervous system quickly shutting it down and the person dies in excruciating pain in a matter of minutes. Jason believes it is a fitting end for such a despicable man.

This is another means of killing given to him by an unknown but very disturbed individual that works for the organization.

Jason knows from this distance that the bullet he fires may not kill this child molester, the range is just too great, but he is sure that this deadly poison will finish the job.

Sighting in his rifle he soon spots the man as he calmly almost arrogantly talks to the reporters that have gathered on the court house steps.

Pulling the trigger it is a moment before the man falls, those around him run in all directions.

Climbing down quickly and running to the taxi Jason orders Crow, "To the airport if you don't mind."

As the taxi makes its way down the narrow alley Crow asks, "Why the airport, you taking a vacation?"

"Don't I wish, No, I'm meeting a contact here that will give me information about a drug transaction taking place in a few days."

As the taxi pulls up in front of the terminal, Crow asks, "Are you going to need a ride home?"

Shaking his head, Jason replies, "I don't know how long this will take, so no use in waiting around, if I need you I'll call."

"One more thing," says Jason. "Where I'm going I can't take my rifle, would you keep it in a safe place for me?"

Crow gives his young friend a smile, "I have been around for a long time," he says, "By doing this I know it means you will not be coming back here again, am 'I right?"

Hesitant, Jason gives his old friend a pat on the shoulder, "You take care, you here."

With a nod of his head Crow understands, and after Jason steps out and closes the door he drives away.

Feeling sad about leaving these people that have helped him, he had looked upon them like family. But he knows it is for the better, too many lives are at stake for him to stay any longer.

Walking through the airport his fake Id gets him through airport security without any problems. After going to his boarding gate his attention is drawn to two security officials that are looking at him, in their hands is a piece of paper that they are pointing at.

Jason does know that the police were able to recover a set of finger prints from the lunch pail left at the state prison. The computers can quickly match the prints with a name and description.

Now hoping that yet another of Edwards disguises will fool the authorities and that he is not recognized.

With no place to run he must sit and patiently wait to board the plane. At this time the two security officials approach Jason and ask, "Can we see your passport sir?"

Pulling out the documents from his pocket, "Here they are, is anything wrong?"

As the two examine the documents one of them asks, "What is your reason for going to Venezuela?"

"I'm on a research project from the University of Miami to study the rain forest."

The two officials scrutinize his documents very closely as they occasionally glace at him.

Jason remembers his teachings from Falcon, and he relaxes his muscles, his body language is as calm as an innocent man's.

After several minutes they give him back his papers and continue walking without saying a word.

Calm on the outside, his insides are turning over, but he is happy that his fake documents worked.

His flight out of Miami takes him directly to Caracas Venezuela. From here he will decide which direction he will go. With his passport saying he's traveling to South America to study the rain forest, he should at least dress like a college student.

After purchasing the necessary clothing that resembles everyone else, this cover should keep the locals satisfied and not draw undo attention onto him.

Like in all lawless cities, you can buy anything, as long as you have the money. His first need is to purchase weapons and supplies.

But seeking out these weapons dealers is a tricky matter, as the cartel's leaders are always on the lookout for American D.E.A. agents. They know that the United States will try an infiltrate their organization, so they have people watching the streets very carefully.

Finding a hotel room was not difficult, as he has noticed that most of the people around here are too poor to pay for a room. Horse stalls and vacant buildings house these unfortunate individuals.

With his room being on the third floor it affords him a good view of the streets, he can monitor everything that is happening without leaving his room.

Over the next several days he stops shaving to let his beard grow, hoping this with add to his disguise. He buys some grubby clothes and a wide brimmed hat as to blend in as best he can. However, we Americans look very different than our South American neighbors. We are much paler, we walk more upright and as he learned very quickly very few people indigenous to south America can grow facial hair. Watching and observing the locals he imitates them, how they move their feet to the way they gesture with their hands. His only Achilles heel is his inability to speak the language.

Knowing only a few words he points at objects and nods with his head when he wants something, this seems to be working for the time being. However he realizes that this limited vocabulary will catch up to him at some point.

He does manage to purchase several guns and other necessities from the locals that are hauling these drugs in and out of town. It seems that the military is so corrupted that they are known to sell weapons to the highest bidder which most of the time is the cartels.

These weapons he acquired from these locals are old and outdated but they will do for now until he can purchase the special rifle he will need later.

He will keep his recon activities to the night time hours, trying to keep as low of a profile as possible.

He frequents several canteens in this small town, trying to strike up a conversation with some of the locals. It seems his cover isn't working very well, he sticks out like a sore thumb. The locals seem to know that he is American and they avoid him.

Jason quickly learns that in this poor country, the drug cartels are by many looked upon as saviors. The money that comes from the selling of drugs fuels the local economy. The people in these impoverished regions only exist because the cartel brings in the goods that they need. In return these simple people grow, harvest and transport the drugs out of the jungles and into the hands of the buyers.

It is a dangerous and unpredictable life, with hundreds of people being killed every year. The drug cartels fight each other as well as the government troops. The numerous militia groups that call the rain forest home have been known to raid the local drug operation camps and steal money and supplies.

With the police looking the other way, a great deal of these narcotics can be seen being moved right in broad daylight. Oxen pulling carts piled high with marijuana come and go down the dirt streets with no one paying it any attention. The local police are rarely seen, and when they are in the area they are either drunk or hauling these drugs themselves.

Jason grows angry at the pitiful law enforcement here, and his hand grips his revolver tightly. He would so much like to continue his work here as he did in Landore, but he must first shut down the cartels.

After the source of all this misery is eliminated than he can begin to target the individual criminals that roam these cities with near immunity.

These are innocent and decent people who are caught in this never ending cycle of death and despair. They seek only a peaceful way of life, it is the outsiders that have come into their country and corrupted the elected officials. These dealers of poison bring with them guns, violence, and disease which has disrupted a tranquil existence here.

Jason can see by the way the general population moves about that they are not a war like people, soft spoken and kind hearted it is sad to see them in these cruel circumstances.

Jason must get to know the customs, the way people live here if he's going to blend in.

At two in the morning he closes down a small canteen, again unsuccessful at finding someone that could help him.

He desperately needs a guide so that he doesn't become lost in this endless expanse of jungle.

This someone must have connections to weapons and also the whereabouts of the nearest cartel.

It may be like finding a needle in a hay stack, but against these odds Jason feels that with a guardian angel guiding him he's sure that he will find this person.

He only drinks a small amount of alcohol at these canteens that he frequents, as he must always be on high alert for any sudden danger that may arise quickly. Frustrated after not being able to make friends with anyone he leaves the canteen and heads for his hotel which is just a few blocks away. This late at night the streets are deserted, except for a few stray dogs that seem to bark at nothing. This town does not have street lights, and the only light to see by is from the moon.

Staying close to the buildings Jason has only gone two blocks when he sees three men dragging a man down the street. He can hear this man's feeble attempts at calling out for help. Jason had promised himself that he would not get involved at trying to bring law and order to this or any other town, not just yet anyways.

Taking a deep breath, as this act is very difficult for him to walk away from, he turns his back and continues up the street. Having only taken a few steps this is when he hears these chilling words.

"For refusing to help the cartel, we are going to cut you into a dozen pieces."

He stops dead in his tracks, the word cartel has made him change his mind. Looking back over his shoulder, he can see that these butchers that obviously work for the cartel are going to cut this man right here on the street.

Jason swallows hard, and takes a deep breath, and he prays that he isn't about to make a big mistake.

Stepping out from the building he waves his arms in the air, calling out, "Hey you, get away from that man."

He is hoping that the three men will realize that they have been spotted and run away. But he is wrong, and instead they turn and look at him with a fierce stare.

He can see that they are all armed, and by their posture they have no fear that anyone has seem them. They do seem a bit surprised that someone actually is trying to help this man.

"You must be loco in the head," one calls out, "do you know who we are?"

Jason is fully armed, with two pistols in his belt and a large knife in his boot he prepares to act if necessary.

He stays on the opposite side of the street, studying each man carefully. Two of these men are drunk, but the third is not. This third man stands tall and his right hand is inside his jacket indicating that he has a gun. The other two that are drunk stagger down the street in Jason's direction while the third man stays back and keeps the poor helpless man pinned to the ground.

"You better run away as fast as you can," they call out, "or else we'll cut off your ears."

This has both men laughing, but Jason stands his ground. Moving back a little he is now partly hidden by the shadow of a building, and he now eases out one of his revolvers.

The two men stop, confused that this man that dares stand up to them has not run away. They turn around and look at the other, who yells, "What are you two waiting on, go kill that bastard."

Jason has slipped into the darkness by the time the two men have turn back in his direction. Startled they call out, "Where the hell are you."

Jason doesn't answer, he moves silently around to the back of the building moving along until he comes in from behind the third man. This man has his foot on the throat of the poor man on the ground, who is gasping for air. The gunman is looking across the street as his two friends search for the one they say is loco in the head.

Picking up a lead pipe Jason steps close to him, and from behind he whispers, "Hello buddy."

Before the man can turn around Jason levels the pipe against his head, it is a loud thud and the man falls to the ground, where he lays motionless.

Reaching down, Jason grabs the frightened man that had been the focus of these men by his arm and helps him to his feet. With his eyes are as big as ever, shaking he steps away from Jason and in a terrified voice says, "That man you just hit works for the cartel, you should not have helped me, now they will kill you."

Looking in both directions, "We'll see about that," Jason replies, "first let's get you out of here."

The man grabs onto Jason's arm and points out into the street. There the other two men have seen what has just happened and they are walking straight towards Jason. Reaching around Jason grabs a percussion grenade from his belt and toss's it towards the two men.

As the grenade stops by their feet they begin to laugh. Pointing at it they call out, "What kind of a joke is this?"

At that same instant the grenade explodes sending both men back and onto the ground holding their faces.

Jason continues helping this man as they both move quickly down the street.

After a short distance Jason asks him, "What's your name?"

Still shaken by these series of events he replies, "Pablo, my name is Pablo."

"Okay Pablo, I think we need to leave this area now."

Moving between the buildings Jason decides it is safer to take the back way to the hotel.

Getting over his initial shock, Pablo walks on his own. He constantly stares at Jason as they walk, trying to figure out who he is.

Moving swiftly up the back steps, and once inside the room, Jason can see that this man is not injured, he is just shook up.

With a quiver in his voice he asks, "Why did you help me, I don't know you?"

Sitting in the chair looking out the window, Jason glances at him and says, "I thought it was the right thing to do at the time."

Shaking his head, "Senor, those men will find you, if you want to live, you must get away from here quickly."

Scratching his chin, "I can't do that, I have a job to complete."

"This job must be very important."

"Why were those men going to kill you Pablo?"

"I would not help them deliver their drugs," he answers, as his face tightens up, "I would rather die first."

Jason can see by Pablo's emotions that there is no love lost between him and the cartel.

"They come into town and take whatever they want, they brain wash our young into thinking that by working for them that they will make lots of money. But this is not true, the cartel pays very little, just enough to survive. The drugs they give my people make them dependent on more, turning them into virtual zombies. When someone wants to leave this business, they are killed. The cartel will not let anyone testify against them, they keep a strangle hold on this whole area."

By his eyes Jason can tell that this hurts Pablo deep down inside. To see ones family and friends pulled into this nightmare of a life is tragic.

"I believe we can work together Pablo, to rid this area of the cartel."

"That will not happen my friend, the cartel is too strong, they are viscous monsters and they won't let anyone stop them."

"We will see about that my Friend, but first you need to tell me everything about this cartel. From their meeting places to their growing fields to their transportation routes, will you help me?"

"I owe you my life, if not for you they would have killed me. From this day forward I will always be indebted to you, ask me anything."

Happy that that he has made a friend of a local, Jason's job just got a little easier. The two talk the rest of the night, and in the morning Jason now has the information that will be invaluable to his cause.

The first thing the two have to do is leave this area as Pablo has told Jason that the cartel will be here shortly and they will search every hotel and building in this whole town for the ones that killed one of their members.

"People will be dragged from their homes and tortured," says Pablo. "The cartel does not fear the police, in fact it is the other way around."

"Then we must leave as soon as possible, do you have transportation?"

Nodding his head, Pablo gestures with his hands, "I have just what we need, it is the fastest way of getting around these parts."

Hoping that the vehicle that his new friend brings will be fast enough to outrun the men from the cartel, Jason feels confident in escaping this city.

Pablo leaves for a few minutes and when he returns he is guiding a horse and wagon down the street. Pulling up in front of the hotel he signals for Jason to come down.

Taken aback by this, Jason can only smile. He now feels foolish to have thought that a village out here in the middle of nowhere would have a high performance car.

Not at all what he was hoping for, nonetheless he quickly jumps in beside Pablo and the two head out of town.

They watch the people run back and forth as if a tornado was coming.

"They have received word that the cartel will be here soon," says Pablo, "they will try and hide hoping to avoid being tortured."

Jason can see the fear in their eyes and the panic on their faces. These simple people are scarred for their lives, but they have really no place to hide.

The two continue out of town, they take several roads that are in need of repairs. Soon the road turns from gravel to all dirt and it is down to a single lane.

"The cartel will not take these roads," says Pablo, "we should be safe."

Satisfied that his new friend knows his way around, Jason sits back and takes in the scenery.

The view has gone from the old structures that made up that town to a green lush landscape. The jungle has come alive will the sounds of the many animals that call it home. The thick and tangled under growth is like a finely woven tapestry. So thick in places that it conceals anything that may be right behind it watching the two as they pass by.

Jason watches with amazement as several species of monkey jump from tree to tree, they seem to be following the two.

"They are looking for a handout," says Pablo. "But do not give them anything, if you do they will not leave us alone. They will continue to follow and the noise they make will draw attention to this area."

Putting away a small sack of bread, Jason focuses on a flock of birds with such colored feathers that leaves him speechless the likes he has never seen before,.

"Do not be fooled by the beauty of this place," warns Pablo, "there are many dangers just out of sight."

Jason knows a great deal about the rain forest from studying about it on the internet prior to coming here. He smiles at his friend, "I will watch where I step."

At that instant Pablo pulls back hard on the horse's reins. Stopping the wagon this abruptly Jason is mystified by this. He pulls out his revolver expecting bandits or the cartel to jump out of the jungle at them.

Pointing to a spot only 20 yards ahead of them, Pablo says with a whisper, "We must wait until that beast is out of our way."

Looking in that direction, Jason is dumbfounded by what he sees. Slithering across the road is the biggest snake he has ever seen. Estimating its length to be at least 35 feet long, it is a troubling sight.

"We call this beast, Sucuriju gigante, The eater of men," says Pablo as his voice is quiet and shallow. "It is the most feared creature in the entire amazon. It can strike without warning and once it has a man in its grip, there is no escaping."

The two can only wait while the huge beast takes its time crossing the road.

The two remain perfectly still, and it is several minutes before this slithering giant is finally across the road and out of sight. Holding his revolver tightly, Jason scans the area ahead.

Laughing, Pablo says, "My friend that little gun would not stop that beast, it would only cause it to eat you quicker."

"Then we better get some bigger guns," replies Jason.

Sure that they are safe they continue their trek into the heart of the jungle.

Several hours later as evening is approaching they spot a settlement in the distance.

"We will be welcomed here," says Pablo now smiling for the first time on this trip.

As they get closer Jason can see that a single two story house is surrounded by a high wall reaching nearly 15 feet. Going through a set of huge double doors and into this compound several people come out to greet them.

It appears Pablo knows them very well and they hug him tightly.

He introduces Jason to them and they are ushered into the house where it seems they have arrived at supper time.

Jason is treated like a member of their family, even though he is a stranger and doesn't completely know their language.

After the meal they go outside to talk with some of the others and learn if the cartel has been in this area.

Pablo corresponds with them in his native tongue.

It seems several of these people can actually speak English and they tell Jason about the need for such a fortified compound.

"At first," states one of them, "These walls were meant to keep out the large cats and snakes that prowl this area. But now they help protect us from bandits and the men that work for the cartels. We are attacked at least twice a month, they were here two weeks ago and three of my friends were killed."

"Why do they attack you," asks an inquisitive Jason.

"We plant our crops on very fertile soil, the cartel wants us out of here so they can plant coca here. It is where there drugs come from, but we refuse to let them run us off. We have been fighting them for years and as our numbers get smaller theirs get bigger, we are waging a losing battle and some day we will be forced to leave."

Jason can see that these are good hard working people that just want to farm their simple crops, they want nothing to do with harvesting drugs. He walks around inspecting this fortified compound, noticing a small catwalk about two foot wide and several feet from the top of the wall, but still at least eight feet above the ground, it runs completely around the compound. Although only two feet wide, he watches as a man marches along this catwalk very easily, his eyes stare out in the distance. His job is to alert the others when danger is approaching.

The sound of the huge double doors closing causes him to turn quickly. There is a set of these doors at both ends of the compound.

The 15 or so people that live here seem to relax now, feeling secured inside these walls.

A tap on the shoulder from Pablo and he points to the house.

"We will sleep inside tonight, my friends have prepared our beds."

Smiling at their hospitality, Jason feels a close connection with them already, these people live a simple and uncomplicated existence. Despite not having the internet, computers or even a cell phone these people are happy with their lives.

"A man from the big city once lived here," says Pablo. "This was his house and we worked for him. But several years ago he got sick and died and we have stayed and farmed this land."

Jason examines the inside of this house closely and by the paintings on the walls and the type of furniture he figures that this man had great wealth.

Going into another room Jason is startled to see a collection of guns in several cabinets. These he can tell are very expensive weapons as many of them have intricate carvings in the wooden stocks.

"These belong to Senor Bataan," says Pablo. "He was a great hunter and no one has touched them sense he died."

Jason quickly spots a rifle that immediately draws him closer to it. Opening the case he pulls out a chrome plated sniper rifle with a large scope mounted on top.

At that moment several of the people in the room become agitated and they ask him to please put the rifle back.

Understanding by their actions to him touching this rifle that they must of had a great deal of respect for this man called Bataan. Putting it back into its cabinet, Jason apologizes if he has offended anyone.

Leaving this room Jason secretly plans on coming back here and stealing this beautiful rifle before leaving this place.

He does not feel bad about this decision, after all these people have not used it and it would be a shame to let this rifle just sit inside this case. This rifle will replace the one he gave to Crow, and he is hoping it will be just as accurate and reliable.

The next morning the two are feed breakfast and soon Pablo is showing Jason the surrounding jungle.

To the front of the compound it is barren, nothing but rock and clay, he is told that it is the aftermath of a failed mining operation years ago. The people living inside the compound have cut the jungle back away from the other sides, to a distance of 50 feet. This space makes it easier to spot anything or anyone approaching.

Going into the jungle Jason sees where the people harvest their different crops, many he has never heard of.

He is told by Pablo, "A few miles away is a small river, it is where they catch fish, a type called, Pacu. But we must always be on the alert for the Vampire fish. These are very dangerous fish, and they have been known to kill people with their large teeth. Another fish to stay away from is the piranhas, I'm sure you Americans have heard of these devils."

"Oh yes, we certainly have heard of piranhas," replies Jason. "I will keep an eye out for them, you can bet on that."

The farmers take Jason deep inside the jungle, he is shown plant species he has never seen before.

Holding up a rather odd looking bluish colored plant, they say, "This plant will stop your stomach from hurting."

Holding up another strange looking plant, this one with yellow and red leaves, they say, "we call this gruhen, if you eat its leaves it will stop the blood from leaving your body."

This is remarkable to Jason, here are plants that have remarkable medical purposes that the scientific community knows nothing about.

The village shaman now approaches Jason, in his hand is a brown powder.

"This will stop a snake's poison from killing you, keep it with you always."

Thanking the shaman, Jason puts the brown powder into a small container. The shaman refuses to divulge what plant he produced this brown powder from, he tells Jason, "Only a few know the secret."

Not wanting to break any tribal rules, Jason does not press the issue of what it's made from.

The rest of the day is spent in this new and amazing place. His memories of life in the big city have faded far into the recesses of his mind.

Arriving back at the compound late in the afternoon, Jason talks to Pablo about how to make this place more secure for the people that live here.

"We will first need better weapons," states Jason. "The guns these farmers have must be 50 years old."

'I agree my friend," answers Pablo. "But these are poor people, they have very little money."

"But there are very nice guns inside the house," says Jason. "Why don't these people use them?"

"These people are very superstitious," replies Pablo. "These guns belonged to Senor Bataan, and they fear if anyone touches them that his spirit will come after them."

Wanting to make a comment about this Jason decides to keep his opinions to himself, but this still has not changed his mind about stealing that rifle.

Jason is determined to help these people stand up against the bandits and drug cartels that threaten their way of life.

CHAPTER 19

At that instant a young boy comes running into the compound, out of breath and obviously very shaken. The people gather around him and after he has calmed down he says, "I saw the ground moving, it is coming after me."

Those standing around laugh and remark that the boy is imagining things.

"You should not make up stories," Pablo tells the young lad.

Waving his arms he defiantly repeats, "I 'am not lying I swear, I saw the black ground moving."

Jason begins to have an odd feeling that he can't explain, an ominous premonition that something terrible is about to happen.

He climbs up and unto the catwalk and looks out as far as he can see. It all looks normal, he sees no dust clouds on the road indicating that we have unwelcomed guests arriving.

Putting off as a child's imagination, the others simply go about their business.

His inquisitiveness urging him to investigate this further, Jason has a sixth sense that there is danger approaching.

Jason locates this boy and asks him, "Can you take me to where you saw the ground move?"

Still shaking, the small boy huddles in the corner. Refusing to come out, however he does point Jason in the direction that he had just come from.

His curiosity is now getting the better of him, he just has to have a look for himself. He leaves Pablo in charge, telling him, "Lock the gates behind me, I don't want to take any chances."

"It is simply a young boy being scared of his own shadow," replies Pablo.

"We'll see," and Jason rides off in the direction the boy had pointed.

He covers maybe five miles when his horse begins to get spooked. It rears up and stomps the ground, he can feel how nervous it is. His first thought is that a leopard is nearby and so he pulls out his rifle. Scanning the area while trying to control his mount, he spots something in the distance. Dismounting Jason walks over to a small ridge, looking over the top, he sees a sight that takes his breath away. For miles in all directions a black solid mass covers the land.

Dumbfounded at first, this is something he has never seen or even heard about.

At first it appears that oil is gushing up from a well and is spreading in all directions.

Suddenly he begins to get bit in several places at once. Quickly wiping at the source, he can see it is ants. Then it hits him, the black mass is billions of army ants and they are heading this way. Quickly mounting his horse he rides back to the compound as fast as possible.

Approaching the compound he signals for the men to open the gates. Once through he jumps off his horse before it has stopped, he tells the people that have gathered around, "We must all leave at once, there is a mass of army ants heading this way."

Instantly the people began to panic, they are familiar with what their ancestors called the, "Black Death."

Some of these people are in near hysterics, he can see the fear that is in their eyes. Jason soon learns how devastating these army ants can be.

"I was told as a child," Pablo says, "that when the great mass of these ants decide to leave the ground and hunt for food, there is nothing that can stop them."

He can see the terror and utter disbelief in the people's actions, this he had never noticed before. These people fear these ants more than they do the bandits and cartel.

"We will need to leave at once," Pablo insists.

"Maybe they will stop before they get this far," Jason questions, "we should send someone out to keep a watch on what direction they are going."

Shaking his head, "No one will volunteer for that job, I can assure you,"

Seeing everyone packing up their belongings, he has no other choice but to leave with them.

There are maybe twenty five people crowded onto two trucks and three cars. The group sets out in the direction of the nearest town, from there they can pick up more supplies before moving farther away.

Pablo informs Jason, "This town we are going to is only fifteen miles away."

"We can warn them about this menace once we get there," says Jason. His eyes now looking closely at the ground, hoping he never sees a sight like he had earlier.

"I'm sure they have heard about the Black Death heading in their direction," replies Pablo. "This type of news travels quickly."

This odd collection of vehicles with its occupants crammed tightly inside continues to rumble down the bumpy dirt road. Jason is in the front seat with three others, and he can feel them shaking, their eyes are wide open as if they had seen a ghost.

He wonders why they are still so afraid, after all we have left the compound and are heading in a safe direction. He knows that these army ants don't move faster than they can drive so the people should be relaxed, yet they are still very terrified.

However, after only half an hour, they spot a car racing in their direction.

As this approaching car slows down a man sticks his head out the window and yells, "You cannot go that way, the town is overrun with ants." Pulling in his head he quickly speeds away.

"Then we'll take another road," suggests Jason.

"That is not possible," replies Pablo, "this is the only road, we must go back."

"Can we walk to another town," suggests Jason. Still believing that to go back is a bad decision.

"This town that we were headed towards had the only bridge," a concerned Pablo answers. "The rivers that we must cross are too fast and deep, we would drown trying to cross them."

After hearing what this man said the cries of the people grow loader, many begin to pray.

"We have no choice but to go back," says Pablo.

Agreeing with Pablo about trying to cross the river as many of these people are too old and they would easily drown. Jason has the people get back into the vehicles; a heart broken look is on their faces.

Giving his friend a serious stare, "These army ants are very smart," says Pablo, "they purposely cutoff any exists, forming a ring around this whole area and now everything inside their ring will die."

Jason is bothered by these comments, still hoping to figure a way out of this situation, and the more Pablo talks, the dire the situation seems to get.

The vehicles turn around and are soon back inside the compound.

The people stand mute, holding each other, they have the look of that of a condemned man.

Jason realizes that if they can't escape, then they will have to fight.

Taking charge he stands on an oil drum, from here Jason tells everyone, "Listen to me, we may be trapped but that is not a death sentence. We can defend ourselves here, we can hold back the army ants."

A man yells, "Just how can we stop all those ants, we have nothing?"

"That's right," calls out another, "nothing can kill that many ants, they will come over the walls and eat us alive."

Hearing this causes many of them to break down and falling to their knees they begin to cry, others look to the sky and pray.

Never one to give up no matter had bad things looked, "We can stop them," barks Jason, "we will surround this compound with a ring of fire."

After hearing this the people move closer to this one man that has given them a sliver of hope.

"We must all work together, and we must start right now."

The people smile, now believing that they have a chance and that death is not certain.

"I estimated that we have about twelve hours before the ants reach us," declares Jason. "There is no time to waste."

With these encouraging words the people now seem eager to help, and they line up waiting for his orders.

Jason demands that everything be brought out of the house that is flammable. Tables, chairs, beds, window curtains and every stitch of clothing is removed. All of this is put on the outside at the base of the 15 foot high wall that surrounds the compound. They ring the entire perimeter with the material they have gathered.

Walking around the perimeter Jason makes sure there are no gaps in his defense. Next he has them empty the hundred or so plastic water jugs that are stored in a small shed. These jugs were used to hold the seeds for the coming planting season. He next drains the gasoline and oil from all the vehicles. Jason figures they wouldn't get very far in them anyways before the ants managed to find a way into the cab and over power the driver.

Like a general directing his troops, "We will stand our ground and fight," Jason tells the frightened people. He has groups of men go into the jungle and any wood that they can carry is brought back, and over the hours it begins stacking up very high in the center of the compound. Jason keeps the men busy brining in anything they can find, right up until the very last minute.

Jason and a few men go out about fifty yards from the compound to where he believes the first wave of ants will appear. He has them put ten poles that are about seven feet tall into the ground. Next a board is put across the top of each pole, and they resemble a hangman's tree. These poles are spread out from each other by roughly twenty feet, and he attaches a container of gasoline to the top boards. Lying on the ground directly below these jugs he puts a piece of metal. They have nothing to use but the doors and hoods off the vehicles, when that isn't enough he gathers up an arm load of pots and pans from the house and places them on the ground directly below the gasoline filled jugs.

"But Senor, I don't understand," utters Pablo, as he scratches his head.
"Oh you will just trust me."
"Very well, you seem to know what you are doing."
While Pablo is busy building this, Jason goes back and walks the perimeter of the compound, again checking for any gaps. He knows how important it is to not let the ants get in. If these demons can get in it will break the moral of these simple people causing chaos and mass panic.
Next they scatter bales of hay across the landscape, separated again by twenty feet, connecting these bales of hay he places a line of oily rags.
They go so far as to drain the brake, power steering and even the transmission fluid from the vehicles, these are all flammable liquids and they will be desperately needed as their wood and other combustible material begins to dwindle.
Jason's first priority is to not let the fire ring burn down, it is the only thing that can keep the ants at bay.
Even their precious homemade whiskey hidden in the basement is sacrificed to keep the fires burning if necessary.
East of the compound he again has a dozen structures erected, these resemble crosses. On each end he hangs a gallon of paint. His trusted side kick is confused by these things but Jason assures him that they are necessary.

With all of their defenses in place, the lookout can now see the first wave of this Black Death coming over a slight ridge. This mass moves like a well-orchestrated army, as they fan out in all directions. When this first wave of ants appears Jason recalls everyone back inside the compound and the front gates are closed and securely latched.

He is constantly climbing up onto the catwalk making sure there are no holes in their defenses.

The lookout begins ringing a bell, signaling that the ants are coming.

Standing up on the catwalk Jason watches as the ants are covering about ten feet a minute.

"It looks like there main attack is coming from the south," he calls down to Pablo.

Guessing right, this is where he has placed his best deterrents.

Calling Pablo over, "I need you to go into the house and bring me out the rifle I had looked at earlier."

But Senor," replies Pablo, "The people are afraid that Senor Bataan's spirit will be angry."

Grabbing him by the shoulder and in a stern voice, "Forget about that damn spirit nonsense I need a rifle to shoot these targets that are set up, I can't hit them with a pistol, now go!"

Hesitant at first but believing his friend knows what he's doing Pablo quickly retrieves the rifle and brings it up onto the catwalk.

Jason checks the clip, happy that it is full. It is an older rifle but it has been very well maintained. The caliber is something the size of a 30-06, plenty of firepower and range for what he needs.

He waits until the ants have completely covered the traps he has set, and then he fires his rifle at the first jug on the far right. It swings back and forth as the gasoline is pouring down in all directions, next he shoots the car door lying on the ground directing below it. The bullet striking the metal causes a spark which ignites the gas.

Jason proceeds down the line shooting every jug until there is a wall of fire. This has slowed the ants but it does not stop them nor does it deflect them from the path they are on. Bypassing this temporary roadblock the ants move closer and soon they cover the bales of hale like syrup on pancakes. Jason now gives the order to light the first bale. One man throws out a flare and it quickly ignites the hay. The fire follows the oily rags to the next bale of hay and this continues until a vast area in front of them is a sea of flames.

Everyone is pleased so far, but Jason reminds, "We have a long ways to go before we can declare victory."

The ants have begun to bypass these fires also and now they begin to close in on the compound from the west and east. This is when Jason gives the order to light the perimeter fire. Soon they are standing in a ring of fire that resembles something from a medieval painting.

With the flames reaching ten feet into the air it seems to be keeping the ants at bay.

Jason is happy that his plan seems to be working, and he is positive that the hordes of ants attacking the compound will exhaust themselves long before the material is all used up.

Everyone is kept busy, either bringing up wood to the cat walk where it is tossed onto the ring of fire or removing even more things from the house that is burnable.

Just as Jason is feeling confident in these simple peasants, he sees the gates at the opposite end open and a truck drives out. The gates are then quickly closed.

Running across the catwalk until he is standing directly above the gates, he yells, "Where the hell are they going?"

"They are afraid, they think they have a better chance this way," a man calls up.

"Those idiots, don't they know we drained the gas and oil from that vehicle?"

Others have climbed up to the catwalk and standing beside Jason they watch as the vehicle speeds away. In less than a half mile from the compound the truck sputters before coming to a halt. The brake light is on, and Jason is hopping to see the men jump out any second.

He orders Pablo, "We need to get ready to attempt to rescue those men when they begin running back this way."

Pablo and two other men gather several containers of oil, when given the signal from Jason they will pour half of the oil on themselves, keeping the other half for the men running from the truck. They are hoping that the oil will provide temporary protection from the biting ants.

Watching from his perch up on the catwalk, Jason nervously waits for the men to exit the vehicle.

But to his dismay there is no movement from the vehicle, all he sees is the endless horde of ants consuming the truck. These mindless masses look like a black tarp, and only parts of the truck are visible. To the dismay of everyone they stare in disbelief when a moment later the brake light goes out on the truck.

Lowering his head, clearly disappointed, he calls down to Pablo, "Forget a rescue attempt, it's too late."

The people are upset over this, much screaming and crying now echoes about the compound.

Beginning to feel boxed in, Jason desperately searches his bag of tricks for a way out of this terrible situation.

Scanning his surroundings, he realizes that getting out of here alive will be his greatest escape. The ants have effectively blocked all escape routes, and they cover the ground for miles around. There is no possible way of going through this mass in an attempt to reach safety. He is trapped inside this cauldron with the others, and it is going to be a fight to the death stance.

All he can do for the moment is watch as the ants continue their suicide attempt to cross the ring of fire. The smell of the burning ants is horrendous, and he is forced to cover his mouth and nose.

Jason patrols up on the catwalk relentlessly, constantly circling the compound. His mind franticly trying to come up with yet another way to stop these ants, however, he keeps drawing a blank. Hour after hour the assault continues unabated on the fire ring. The sound these ants make is like someone stepping on egg shells. It is constant, and it radiates towards the compound from all directions.

This crunching sound is beginning to bother him, and he can see that it is also affecting the others. This incisive noise is endless, nerve racking and it never lets up. It is all around them and at times he thinks it will shatter the walls. Some of the people stuff cotton into their ears, while others wrapped strips of cloth around their heads.

It's worse than the sound a horde of locust makes, and it reminds him of someone crunching a cracker next to his ear.

The image of these parasites crawling on his body causes him to constantly wipe down his arms and legs. Jason begins to think they are in his pockets, his shoes and even his hair.

Realizing that if he panics so will the others so he must control his emotions, he must look strong and courageous. The others will follow his lead, and up to this point they have followed his orders faithfully, so despite his fears he cannot for a second let anyone see that he too is afraid.

This new threat is like nothing he has ever encountered before, a single bulled or poison will not stop these hoards of ants.

Inside this fortress of death, even the bravest man will eventually break down. With seemingly no way out, and death inevitable, it isn't long and the strain on these simple farmers begins to show.

Jason constantly goes around to each one and tries his best at boosting their morel. He promises that they will make it through this crises, but they must remain brave and steadfast, there can be no letup in their defense.

Calling out from the catwalk he yells, "Keep the fire ring burning, it is stopping the ants, keep up the great job."

Going among the people Jason pats them on the back, urging them to be vigilant and alert. Seeing the pile of material in the middle of the compound stating to get smaller he enters the house and begins removing any wood that he can pry from the walls.

When this is done the house resembles the drug houses that he remembers back in Landore, it is nothing but a shell. Everything possible has been stripped bare, there is nothing more that can be salvaged. Knowing that what is piled up in the center of the compound is all the material that they have left, Jason prays that the hoard of ants will stop their advance before it is all used up.

Looking to the west of the compound he watches as a woman screams in pain. Ants are pouring through a small hole at the base of the wall. He grabs a jug of gasoline and hurries up the ladder, racing across the catwalk, looking over the wall and down he can see a small break in the fire line. Here the ants have sacrificed themselves and died by the thousands causing this narrow path through the fire ring and into the compound. He pours the gas onto this gap quickly eliminating this threat, Pablo is quickly beside him with an arm load of wood and the gap in the fire ring is repaired. Looking back into the compound and despite everyone's efforts the woman that was attacked by these ants dies.

Jason knows these types of ants aren't poisonous so he surmises that the woman probably died of a heart attack.

The remaining ants that are inside the compound are either burned or stomped on until they are all dead. He knows they avoided a potentially drastic situation, had the ants not been stopped as quickly as they were the people would have been overwhelmed.

Barking out commands he tells the people, "We must be vigilant, we cannot let down our guard, not for a second. You each must take turns watching the fire ring, let someone know if you see the fire getting low."

The people are shaken by this latest incident but they do as they are told.

Jason now focuses his rifle on the paint cans, after putting several holes in each he watches as the paint oozes out and saturates and incapacitates a large number of ants. It has slowed their advance in this area, but the horde does not stop.

These defenses and deterrents that he has put in place have eliminated a great many of these ravenous creatures, it has caused them to alter their advance which has gained those inside the compound precious time.

Despite the burning gasoline and large area of hay on fire these ants have managed to zig zag around these obstacles. Their main goal it seems is to overrun the compound, and they refuse to bypass this insignificant obstacle. Jason is mystified by this behavior, as there is nothing inside the compound that would draw these creatures to die in mass just to get inside.

Why, he wonders, do these mindless insects continue to attack his fire ring? It is suicide, they are dying by the thousands, but they are hell bent on conquering this structure that is standing in their way.

One man is unable to control his paranoia, he sits on the ground waving his arms in the air. "We are all going to die," he screams.
Before anyone can act, he puts a revolver to his head and pulls the trigger.

There is no time to mourn, and no time to bury this man. Jason quickly drags the body out of sight; he must keep the others busy.
"Everyone must man the defenses and be watchful for any emergency that arises," Jason calls out. He is hoping that others don't follow this man's paranoia, as he needs everyone.
The noise suddenly subsides, and an eerie silence causes everyone to freeze where they are.
Frozen with fear, not knowing the meaning of this abrupt end to the incessant noise, the people are very worried.
They stop what they are doing and now stand mute looking at each other. A look of utter surprise is on their weary faces. The air becomes still and the sun begins to peek out through the clouds. Just as quickly as the noise stopped the people start to smile. A feeling of jubilation fills their hearts. Some drop to their knees raising their arms skyward. They praise the Lord for rescuing them from certain death.
Others hug and embrace whoever is near as they dance about. Laughter and yelling echoes inside the compound that they all believed would be their graves. Their moods have changed from a feeling of doom to one of open jubilation. Many now cry openly, believing that their prayers have been answered.

Climbing up the ladder and looking over the wall, Jason can see the black mass of ants still have them surrounded. They still cover the ground for as far as he can see, but they have stopped advancing.

Not liking this at all he calls to Pablo, "Why did they stop, what's going on?"

Shrugging his shoulders, he throws his hands in the air, "Sorry, I have never heard of them acting this way."

At this time Jason's attention is drawn out to a spot some twenty yards in front of him. The ants begin acting strange here and they start circling around a depression in the ground. Suddenly after a few minutes the ground opens up and out climbs a huge red colored ant. He can see that it must be thirty times bigger than the others. Jason knows instantly that it is the queen ant herself. This is very rare as the queen never comes to the surface. The queen ant guides her army from a safe distance deep underground.

Not wanting to waste time speculating about this odd occurrence, he does what comes naturally. He quickly shoulders his rifle, placing the cross hairs of the sight midway on her body. Hoping that by killing their queen the masses will then retreat back to the hollows of the Earth from where they came from. Pulling the trigger the queen ant shatters into a dozen pieces. This bitch, this mother of billions will never spawn another murderous clan again.

The ants seem to react to their queen dying in a way that he didn't think possible. They gather up her remains and carry them back into the ground that she had come from. Several other ants now appear, they too are different than the hordes trying to overrun the compound.

They are long and thin, their antenna's seemed to be actually pointing in the direction of the compound. During the killing of the queen, all the ants had stopped moving about. It's as if they were mourning her death.

Jason still hoped that these ants, now without their queen to guide them would give up the fight and return to the ground from where they came from.

But he is wrong, now seemingly instructed by these new leaders the hordes of ants turn their fury and rage once again on the compound. The noise of billions of ants quickly grows to a pitch louder than before. On the march again, wave after black wave burn themselves to death trying to cross the ring of fire in their attempt to get into the compound. Despite their futile suicide attempts and the mounting pile of their dead they still march forward. Climbing over this burnt mass, they seem totally indifferent and unconcerned.

It seems there is no end to their numbers. The noxious stench from this burning mass is now causing the people to cover their mouths. The gray and black colored smoke is now billowing up in great waves and at times the wind blows it down into the compound. The smoke, at times being so thick, that many of the people are forced to crawl about on their hands and knees to keep from wondering around in circles.

Trying his best at keeping the others from panicking, Jason has an idea that may bolster their confidence. He and Pablo remove the fencing from around the chicken coop and quickly dragging it across the ground he brings it to a spot in the center of the compound. Setting it up by using several poles driven into the ground it forms a 15 foot circle. Next, he hooks up jump cables from the generator and attaches them to this fence.

After the firewall burns out this will be where he and the others will make their last stand. He is hoping that the voltage from the generator electrifying the fence will be strong enough to withstand the avalanche of ants attacking it. It is crude and unsophisticated, but he has run out of ideas.

Taking an assessment of the supply of material left to fuel the fire ring and the mass of ants outside he knows that it is only a matter of hours until these creatures begin to climb the walls.

Guessing that the ants, once they are inside the compound, will simply continue their march to the East? How many of his fellow prisoners here will survive, he knows not many. Some will run through the gates, hoping to get through the carpet of ants.

It is impossible to believe that any of them attempting this will survive. The mass of ants cover so many square miles of land that even the best fit athlete does not stand a chance.

This horde of black-death will simply over power and mass itself onto its victim until they cannot carry the weight any longer. Once on the ground death will be cruel and painful. When the ants are done there will be nothing left of the body, not even the bones will be spared.

Now as the day progresses, the more Jason thinks about this last stand enclosure, the more he begins to doubt that it will work.

These army ants have shown a remarkable sense in how to adapt and exploit a weakness it finds. With the ferocity and rage that they have shown sense he dispatched their queen, he now believes that his small electrified enclose will not stop these ants.

Jason will have to think of a better way out of this impossible nightmare.

Growing frustrated that their supply of burning material is nearly exhausted, it has kept the ants at bay for nearly 18 hours and yet the ants still keep coming. He cannot even phantom the number of ants that lay piled up just outside these walls, and yet their numbers seem inexhaustible.

Getting desperate, the people throw theirs shoes onto the ring of fire to keep it burning. The men even remove their shirts and toss them over the wall. Heavy on their minds is that this ring of fire, this barrier from certain death must not be broken. With no escape beyond these walls it is imperative that the fires are kept burning, their very lives depends on it.

As the fires continue to get smaller, panic is clearly seen on everyone's face. It is a look of knowing that you have very little time left on this earth.

Jason sits dejected on the catwalk, head down, he is thinking, "This is a sad way to die, no glory or splendor. When the ants finish with him there will be nothing left to bury, it just isn't right."

He is helpless to do any more, he has done everything possible to stop these ants. Shaking his head, he had thought that long ago the hordes of ants would have run out. He was so sure that all his preparations would have been adequate enough to withstand their onslaught.

However, there seems to be no end to the Black Death coming over the ridge. The charred and burnt remains of tens of millions of ants fills the air, their stench irritates the nose and lungs.

Contemplating whether he should have kept one vehicle intact, for a last effort to escape if the fire ring didn't hold. Frustrated with himself, it is too late now, he must concentrate on keeping the fire ring burning at all costs.

Having removed everything possible from inside the compound that they could burn, it is now evident that soon the fire ring will burn out. The people also realize this and they run about screaming, terrified at what lays just outside these walls. Some have decided to cover themselves with oil and when the ants come over the wall they will open the gates and make a run for it.

Jason takes one last look while up on the catwalk. Scanning all around, the Earth is still covered with a blanket of these crawling black masses. He knows the people that will try to run through this black mass have no chance. Death is all around, and the noose is getting tighter and tighter.

Still believing that there has to be a way out of this seemingly impossible situation, Jason glances back at the compound. Hoping and praying that he will spot his salvation, another miracle to get him out of this death trap.

Lowering his head, he is exhausted, feeling like a boxer in the last rounds of a fight. Knowing you have lost, yet you get back up when the bell rings.

Climbing down the ladder, the people rush over and beg him to save them.

There is nothing he can say or do, the battle is lost, the victors wait for their opportunity to storm the walls.

Their supply of oil and gas has all been used up, the large pile of wood is nothing more than twigs and bark. The people coward to the center of the compound, they cry, they pray, they hold onto each other tightly.

As the ring of fire begins to burn out in a few places, it is here that the ants begin climbing the walls. Wave after wave of this black moving mass begins covering everything. The people now run in panic. Some open the gates and start running, they scatter in all directions.

Jason and Pablo and two other men run for the house, here they will make their last stand.

Two other men have decided to stay inside the electrified fence enclosure as they must have figured this is better than the house.

Seeing this, Jason hollers, "You won't last very long in there, it won't work, you need to follow us!"

To his disappointment the men simply wave him on, it is their choice and he wishes them well.

He and Pablo and the two other men race into the house and up the stairs. Going out the second floor window, they climb out onto the porch roof. As Jason is turning to climb higher Pablo grabs him by the arm. Looking at him Jason can see the fear in his face and eyes. He doesn't say a word, but nods his head to the left. Looking in that direction Jason can see that the ants have surrounded the two men inside the electrified fence.

The electrified fence seems to be working, and the ants are dying in mass. Gritting his teeth, Jason feels now that he may have made a grave mistake in not staying inside that electrified fence. There is no time to second guess his decision and once he and the others reach the top of the house, there is nowhere else to run. He curses at how he had made a too quick of a decision, and now these three men that followed him are now doomed.

They have a brief respite from the ants, they don't swarm over the house as he had expected, and instead the ants have concentrated all their efforts on the two men inside the electric fence.

As the number of dead ants begin to pile up new ants take their place, they are sacrificing themselves on purpose. Soon the mound of dead ants reaches the top of the fence and the small generator by this time is struggling to keep running. The ants quickly climb inside the fence and they begin attacking the two men trapped there. It is a horrible sight, one Jason will never forget. Unable to escape yet it is suicide to stay where they are, the men face a gruesome death. Jason and the others cover their ears at the screams of agony and suffering by these men echo above the constant crunching sound made by the relentless ants. The ants have conquered yet another obstacle and now they turn and advance towards the house.

Jason helps each man unto the roof, and then he lights three flares throwing them through the window. He is going to burn down the house along with them. He has his revolver and looking into the faces of these men, he knows what they are thinking. As no man wants to end his own life, it is against the preaching of the bible.

Without them saying a word, Jason shakes his head, "Don't worry, I'll do all of us before I let those dam ants get here."

With a sad expression, they turn and continue up to the highest point on the roof. As Jason reaches the old brick chimney, smoke is by now beginning to come out of the windows. With the house being very old, he knows the fire will spread quickly.

He can hear a sizzling sound as tens of thousands of ants are being burned as they ascend up the steps and walls. Their unrelenting and overpowering urge to get at these men is truly remarkable. He wonders if it has something to do with him killing their queen. Are they seeking revenge, he never knew wild creatures could feel such emotions and dedication to their leader.

The ants have managed to find a path through the fire and are now on the porch roof. It looks like the end is near, Jason never would have guessed that he would die this way.

As the four of them stand together on the very peek of the roof, Jason pulls out his revolver.

He had no problem ending the lives of criminals, but these men are good people, they don't deserve to die this way.

The thick black smoke is rising up obscuring their view, coughing, they pull out bandannas to cover their mouths to filter the air. Jason will wait until the very last second before shooting his friends. As the first ants begin to crawl up and onto the edge of the roof, there is a sudden strong downward blowing of wind. This causes the two men to lose their footing and they are blown off the roof. They are lost in the thick black smoke, and their cries for help are short.

Jason at first thinks that this wind blowing down is a sign from heaven.

But he stops, reminding himself of the hundreds of lives that he has taken.

Confused, "If this is not a sign from heaven," he yells to Pablo, "then just what is going on?"

Turning around, he sees a rope ladder dangle several feet in front of him, looking up he sees a helicopter. Without hesitating Jason begins climbing up but stops when he sees Pablo holding tightly to the chimney.

"Follow me Pablo, we are being rescued,"

Nervously shaking his head, "I'm too scared I'm afraid of heights."

"If you don't come right now you will die."

The first ants have started climbing onto the roof.

Frustrated, Jason shakes his head, it is too late to go back and help his friend, and he continues climbing up the ladder. Suddenly he feels the ladder become tight. Stopping and looking down, he sees Pablo holding onto the ladder.

Glad that his friend is safe he waves for him to continue climbing.

Once both are safe inside the helicopter, Pablo falls to his knees and begins praying.

Jason reaches up to the pilot and pats him on the shoulder. Sitting back he stares out the window, below what was once a jungle is now a wasteland.

He is shocked by the magnitude of the devastation, as these ants have stripped the land bare.

They have destroyed everything, there are no plants or animals left in sight. Even the trees are stripped of their bark and leaves. It is a barren and desolate landscape, and Jason is in awe that these tiny ants could cause so much destruction.

The helicopter takes them to a city forty miles away where a makeshift tent city has been set up for all the people made homeless.

Once on the ground the two are taken to the first aid tent, and they see the lucky ones that managed to escape.

Jason learns that this type of massing by ants is something that happens about every three to four hundred years. There is nothing the people can do to stop the ants but get out of their way.

Sitting in a corner by himself, he feels grateful to be alive. Wondering if this miracle rescue was a sign from God, he presses his hands together. Is this God's way of saying that there has been enough bloodshed, enough killing. That Jason should change his ways, to put the guns and knives down, to start leading a better life.

Closing his eyes, Jason must answer these questions, and it will take a lot of soul searching to find the answer.

Exhausted and worn-out, he lays down on a small blanket, feeling safe for the first time in days, he quickly falls asleep.

Waking up to the sound of gun fire, he jumps to his feet and looks out the small opening in the tent.

He can see men with guns, and they have several of the aid workers herded tightly together.

He assumes that these men must be from the cartel and they are here to rob and kill. Gritting his teeth he can feel the rage building up inside, here are the men he has come so far to find. Having dropped his pistol while climbing up to the helicopter he is unarmed, but far from helpless, he will do what comes naturally.

Crawling out the back of the tent, Jason quietly makes his way around several other tents until he is directly behind one of these armed men.

Reaching out he puts his arm around the man's neck, holding him tightly he grabs the rifle the man is carrying. Pushing this man out into the center he yells, "Release these people or this man will die."

All the gunmen immediately point their weapons at Jason, and they move until they have formed a circle around him.

A man pushes his way through this group of armed men and calmly walks up to Jason and in broken English says, "Who the hell are you?"

Still holding his prisoner tightly, "It doesn't matter who I'm," he replies, "You dirty drug smugglers are not going to hurt these innocent people."

With a surprised look, and cocking his head to the side the man answers, "Who are you calling drug smugglers, don't you know who we are?"

"If you are not drug smugglers than you must be bandits."

As this man, who seems to be their leader walks back and forth, he gives Jason a long look.

"We are not bandits either," he says, "we are called the Patriots."

Concentrating on this man Jason does not see the man sneaking up behind him. In a quick move he is hit in the head which causes him to drop his rifle. He is shoved out and onto the ground.

As the men rush to him, their guns only inches from his face, Jason gets to his feet and stands defiantly.

Now the leader of these men walks up to Jason and says," You are not like the others, you choose to confront us and not coward down, where are you from?'

Looking at this group of men he can see they are a tough bunch, heavily armed and wearing military fatigues, he at first thought they were drug traffickers but now he's not so sure. They don't appear to be hurting anyone and they didn't kill him right away.

"I'm from the United States," he replies.

"I'm the leader of the patriots," the man says. "I'm called Batman."

On the inside Jason finds this man's name comical, but with several rifles pointed at him he dare not laugh.

Motioning for Jason to follow him, Batman goes inside one of the tents. With no other option Jason follows this stranger into what he hopes isn't some type of torture chamber.

Sitting at a small table Batman asks, "Why on earth would you come here, there is nothing here but poverty and sickness?"

"I came to stop the cartels from sending their drugs into my country."

The men inside the tent laugh out loud at hearing this. Batman leans forward and says, "You are by yourself, yes?'

"I 'am."

Sitting back with a big smile, Batman says, "So one man thinks he can take on the cartels by himself. You are either the bravest man alive or you are nuts in the head."

Again the men standing around laugh at this.

"I have a mission to complete, and that calls for the elimination of these cartels that harvest and transport their drugs north."

"We have similar goals," says Batman. "I to would like to see the cartels removed from my country. My men and I have been trying to do this for years, but our success has been insubstantial. We are not strong enough to confront the cartels, so we must use hit and run tactics."

"So why have you come into this relief camp brandishing your weapons?"

"We need supplies, so we are forced to get them anyway we can. We will not hurt anyone, everyone will be set free once we leave."

Jason is now beginning to understand that these men are not drug traffickers but men with views similar to his own.

Batman informs Jason that they are also antigovernment, as they believe that the officials are corrupt with many on the cartels payroll.

"Our group of anti-government and anti-cartel fighters has been getting smaller, and we are running low on supplies. We do not get the recruits like we did in the old days, our numbers have dwindled to the point where it is suicide to attack military convoys or large groups working for the cartels."

Seeing a great opportunity, as now he doesn't have to fight the cartels by himself, "I believe we can work together," states Jason.

Batman looks over his new recruit, a smile crosses his face.

"Yes, I believe we can do much damage to these cartels," insists Batman. "You seem like a man with no fears."

At that moment the sound of vehicles can be heard approaching.

Jumping from his chair Batman rushes to the tent opening, he can see the dust in the air as a great many trucks are headed in his direction.

"It is the military," says Batman. "We must make a hasty retreat."

Circling his hand in the air, all the armed men gather together around Batman.

"We leave at once," he calls out. "Pick up the supplies."

As these armed men begin to disappear into the thick brush, Batman turns and asks, "If you are joining us, I suggest you move a little more quickly."

With nothing to lose by following these men, Jason hurries across the small camp and is soon gone from sight. He had stopped for a moment to look for Pablo but he was nowhere to be found, guessing that he ran into the jungle as these men were entering. He hopes that his good friend is safe and that they will meet again in the future.

Jason struggles to keep up with these freedom fighters as he has labeled them. He is surprised that they are able to move so quickly through the dense jungle, even the ones carrying the heavy backpacks seem to glide across the ground.

Over the next two years Jason allies himself closely with this group. With his expertise in the art of killing as well as his knowledge of fighting tactics that he learned from his two mentors he is soon treated like a brother. He passes this knowledge and training on to these freedom fighters. Together over the years they make many hit and run raids on the cartels drug operations. However because of their small numbers they were never able to inflict a crippling blow to them.

The thick jungle has afforded these rebels an escape route that proved impossible for anyone to catch them.

As good as a safe haven that the jungle is it also contained great dangers. Malaria, parasites and skin disorders constantly plague these freedom fighters. Add to this is poison snakes and jaguars, and with no medical doctor to treat the infected men they die a slow agonizing death.

Accidents and skirmishes with the cartel and government troops further reduce the numbers of these freedom fighters.

Jason himself suffered from the bite of a poisonous snake and was on the verge of dying when his comrades kidnapped a doctor and forced him to treat Jason until he was fully recovered.

He has endured gunshot wounds, broken bones and malaria but his determination to stop the cartels at all costs has made him a hero and an inspiration for the men that now follow him.

The deadly piranha's that are native to South America caused the most single day death toll among the rebels.

Striking like lightening hundreds of these killer fish swarmed around the men as they were crossing a river. It happened so quickly and with such ferocity that the men were stunned and completely caught off guard. The slaughter was over in a matter of minutes and 7 of the men were unable to escape. These deaths cause the rebels to be always undermanned and out gunned, and their attacks on drug supply convoys cause little more than a nuisance to the drug traffickers.

Jason soon learned what native tribes were friendly to outsiders as there were times when they found themselves low on food. These friendly tribes literally saved the rebels from starving on several occasions. He also has been taught which tribes to stay clear of. Despite what the officials say, there are still several tribes that are cannibalistic, we call them head hunters. These tribes still practice the ancient art of head shrinking and they do not discriminate between rebels and cartel members. Jason is told stories of their encounters with these blood thirsty natives and how it takes several bullets to stop just one of them.

The deep and dark interior of this immense rain forest holds many secrets, some lifesaving others very lethal. Jason is astounded by the people that call this place home. Life is hard here with living conditions substandard, and the weather can be unpredictable and severe.

There is always a dozen militia groups at any one time threatening to over throw the government. Work in the cities is scarce, healthcare inadequate. Drug use is rampant, and many of the young flee this impoverished life and hope to make it to the United States.

These young people are tricked into working for the cartels that promise's them that after a few weeks of work they will be given visa's allowing them into the United States.

But these young people are worked 18 hours a day and given very little to eat. They are beaten when they want to leave. Bound by a rope around their necks they are virtual slaves, and are at the mercy of the cartels.

Quickly hooked on mind altering drugs these poor souls resemble zombies, they walk around in a dazed and confused state of mind. Malnourished, brain washed, drug dependent and abused they last only a short time in this state. When they can no longer perform the tasks assigned to them they are deemed dead weight, by the cartel leaders, at which time they are murdered or left where they fell.

During one of these hit and run raids Jason and his rebels did rescue a few of these individuals, however with their brains fried from drug overdoses, and their bodies covered with multiple open sores there is very little hope of them ever resuming a normal life again.

Jason and the rebels have made a valiant and courageous effort to shut down these drug cartels, but despite all their efforts, all their blood, sweat and tears they have failed.

Now tired, his ego deflated and feeling old, Jason decides to chance a contact with his two mentors. He believes that after all this time and with no more vigilante killings having taken place In Landore that the pressure to apprehend him should have lessened by now. Hoping that the memory of the Vigilante Assassin has begun to fade from the people's thoughts, and now he is only an urban legend.

CHAPTER 20

Before leaving for South America Jason had agreed with Doc and Edward that there would never be any contact between them. The risk of the authorities intercepting a message could prove the deciding clue that would bring the whole organization down.

Knowing that their last goodbye would be the last time the three would see each other was very emotional. Jason understood the need for this silence, he knew that the police were waiting patiently for just such an exchange of greetings, and he agonized over this for several weeks.

Finally he decided to risk just one brief message to his two old friends, he needed to know if they were well. Had they moved to a safer location, further removing themselves from the prying eyes of the law?"

His worst thoughts were that it was not the police that caught up to Doc and Edward but El Diablo's henchmen. He lowers his head at this terrible thought, to think that his two mentors were tortured and killed is almost more than he can stand.

He must find out if they are alive, to do this he will chance a contact with them.

After informing his comrades of his intentions, they have agreed at taking a risk to get him close to a city. The rebels now under Jason's guidance have moved through the jungle until they are very close to a small city.

Here they wait and observe the inhabitants, looking for any signs that government soldiers or drug traffickers are in the area.

After two days Jason is given the green light to go into this city and contact his friends.

He soon learns that this small town has only one computer with access to the internet. So he must sign a long list with perhaps twenty five names on it before it will be his turn to use the computer.

Sometimes it can take two weeks before your turn comes up. Waiting that long is out of the question, so he is forced to bribe his way to the front of the line.

As he is sitting in the thatched hut, a man signals to Jason, "You have five minutes."

Stepping in the booth, he closes the curtain behind him. Hunched over so that no prying eyes will see his password, he quickly types in the information. Keeping his questions short and to the point, he nervously taps the floor in anticipation of the reply.

This is an old model, and it takes nearly two minutes before his email reply comes up. He's over joyed at first seeing an email message from doc. However the short message is not good. "Do not return, F.B.I. knows who you are. I and Edward are in hiding."

It is short and to the point, Jason hesitates for a second, asking himself, "Should I reply?"

No, he decides, it is better this way, as long as he knows that his two mentors are still alive he is content. He deletes all information from the computer.

Rejoining his comrades they retreat a safe distance from the city, here Jason must decide what he will do with the rest of his life.

Going back to the states at any time would be foolish, with the authorities having his name and his description. He had managed to elude them up to this point, going back he knows he would be apprehended very quickly. But he has a nagging feeling that his two old friends are in trouble, and that they need his help.

He owes his life to them, and to turn away when they may need him is an agonizing dilemma.

These freedom fighters that now surround him also have come to rely on his courage and instincts. He has learned their language and they have even given him a name, "Cardinal."

He wishes that he could tell Doc and Edward this, how they would find it funny that finally their young apprentice has a nickname and it's of a bird, just like all the rest of the members of F.L.O.C.K.

Jason has not told this new family anything about his past, how he is the most wanted man in the United States. How his old name The Vigilante Assassin would send chills up the spines of the criminals in Landore. No, that information is best left in the past, with going home now out of the question he gathers up his few belongings and along with his comrades he disappears into the thick and endless expanse of the amazon jungle.

PREVIOUS BOOKS WRITTEN BY MARK A. WILSON =

The Amazing Gift From The Woods
The Legend Of Crawley Creek
Curse Of The Lost journal
The Secret Of Gray View Manor
The Old Man's Secret Friend
The Demons Within
Sasquatch—Legend In The Shadows
Final Destination—Earth

Would you like to see your manuscript become a book?

If you are interested in becoming a PublishAmerica author, please submit your manuscript for possible publication to us at:

acquisitions@publishamerica.com

You may also mail in your manuscript to:

**PublishAmerica
PO Box 151
Frederick, MD 21705**

We also offer free graphics for Children's Picture Books!

---

www.publishamerica.com